Avoiding Responsibility

A novel by

K.A. Linde

Copyright © 2012 K.A. Linde

All rights reserved.

ISBN: 1481060953
ISBN-13: 978-1481060950

February 13th

1

PRESENT

A sing-song tune echoed from a distant location far removed from the king-sized bed where Lexi Walsh lay curled up amongst the sheets. The muffled chorus of a popular radio song hit her ears causing her to roll over and bury herself farther into the depths of the bed. An arm wrapped around her waist and the warmth of a body pressed against her skin. The man trailed his fingers gently across her stomach, down the curves of her side, and over her toned thighs. She giggled as his touch turned more insistent, rocking her body back and forth.

"Mmm," she groaned her eyes fluttering open. "It's too early."

"I know," he agreed moving his hands back to her flat tanned stomach. "Too early for your phone to be going off," he whispered into her ear.

Lexi sighed and nuzzled into his chest. "Agreed," she mumbled lacing their fingers together

"Are you going to answer that?" he questioned, his breath hot against her earlobe.

Lexi lazily shook her head and shifted, ever so slightly imploring his lips to her ear. "Mmm, no," she said breathily.

"You sure?" he asked further succumbing to her wishes.

She angled her body, allowing herself a look into his hazel eyes, and smiled. "Do I look like I want to get out of bed?"

A confident smirk crossed his face. "Not in the slightest."

"There's your answer then," she muttered yanking the sheet up around her bare shoulders and relaxing into him.

He responded by holding her tight against him as his other hand swooped up and ran through the long thick strands of chocolate brown hair. He splayed the curls out across the creamy white pillow and brushed her bangs off her forehead. He leaned forward in bed and planted a light kiss on her forehead careful not to adjust her easy slumber.

"That feels nice," she murmured into him.

"I thought you'd fallen back asleep already."

Lexi kissed his chest and held onto him a little tighter. "Not quite."

"So who could be calling you so early in the morning?" he implored her.

Instantly, Lexi's heart sped up. She knew the reaction was entirely irrational. The last time she had been awoken at such an early hour on a Saturday morning, Jack had called her. That fateful conversation nearly a year earlier had led to an outrageous week where she had not only traveled to Atlanta to see Jack and his new girlfriend, Bekah, but had been suckered into attempting to convince said girlfriend that Jack was ready for marriage. What a sham that had been!

She had been set-up by Bekah and, inevitably, after a few rather inappropriate experiences with Jack, had convinced him that he was, in fact, ready to marry Bekah. After six years of trying to work things out between her and Jack, he had proposed to another woman with a duplicate of the ring he had promised only belonged to Lexi. She had walked away with some semblance of the closure she had desired, but returned to New York with a whole new world of heartache she hadn't been prepared for.

But Jack hadn't called her since she had left him standing alone at the airport in Atlanta, and she knew he wouldn't be calling her now.

That didn't lessen the thumping of her heart though.

"I…I dunno," she told him turning back to face the open loft so that he couldn't see the dejected look on her face.

She didn't care who was calling. She didn't want to be forced from her tranquil environment to face the realities of the real world. And if she was honest with herself, a part of her was afraid that one day Jack would come crashing back into her existence. Didn't he always?

Jack. The man who had taken her from a brilliant, confident, controlled woman to a love sick, uncontrollable girl at the first glance from his blue eyes. Together they had ruined relationships, friendships, and families with their heated desire and relentless passion. But those days were over.

The familiar lyrics began playing again, and this time Lexi could pinpoint the location of her purse amongst his impeccably clean décor. She sighed wishing the noise would stop allowing her the peace and quiet she desired.

"Perhaps you should attend to that," he muttered into her ear, "while I go fix you some breakfast."

Lexi groaned as he shifted next to her, hauling his tight ass across the bed and over to his closet stocked with expensive suits. He threw on a pair of black boxer-briefs and took the stairs two at a time down to the landing. He returned a second later with her purse in hand and placed it gently on the bed. She smiled up in his angular face and was rewarded with a kiss on the lips full of promises.

"Answer that," he commanded pointing at the phone that was still lit up from the previous phone call. "Come down when you're finished."

She watched his backside retreat down the stairs and out of sight before picking up her purse and fishing out her new cell phone. Up until a couple months ago, she had had the same old, dinged-up, flip phone since college. The thing had lasted nearly seven years, much longer than modern technology. They had had their rough spots along the way, like when she had lost all the numbers after dropping it in the toilet once, but it had been good to her nonetheless. Chyna, her best friend, had finally gifted her something a bit flashier. She claimed it was a graduation present since Lexi absolutely abhorred the thought of mooching off of her best friend's exorbitant wealth.

Her new touch screen came to life at the tips of her fingers as she grumbled at the early hour. Her night had been pretty insane, and the last thing Lexi wanted to do was be awake at that moment. She groggily clicked on the message that claimed she had two missed calls.

Lexi cursed under her breath as the name filled the screen: Ramsey Bridges.

She could think of a million and a half reasons for him to be calling her. None of which she wanted to deal with at this moment in time.

Lexi threw her head back roughly against the incredibly soft down pillow and bit the inside of her lip to keep from cursing aloud. Just as she was about to swing her legs over the side of the bed and trek downstairs, the phone lit up one more time. This time the ding alerting her of a text message filled the empty bedroom.

Reluctantly, Lexi clicked on the message and read it to herself. "Sorry it's early and for everything else. Call me. Please. I miss you."

Lexi banged her head back and against the pillow case several more times in frustration. This could not be happening to her right now. She knew that she should wait to make the phone call. She had an incredibly attractive man making her breakfast downstairs and the last person, well second to last person, she needed to talk to was Ramsey.

But she couldn't just ignore him. Something was up or else he wouldn't be calling her. And despite her better judgment, she phoned him.

"Lexi," he breathed into the other line.

His voice sent chills up her spine, and the intense way he said her name only made it worse…or better depending on how you looked at it. A wave of peppermint seemed to overtake her at the sound of his voice. She couldn't believe that the taste of him could be so alive in her mind when he was thousands of miles away in Atlanta. She shook her head clearing her mind of her vivid imagination and answered him, "That's right."

"Hey," he muttered, surprisingly at a loss of words.

"Hey," she said back.

"Uh, how have you been?" he asked, fishing for information.

"I've been great, Ramsey. Did you need something?" she asked cutting the conversation as short as she could.

"Yeah, we have a lot to talk about."

Lexi shook her head. No. She could not do this right now. "I don't think we do."

"Come on. You know we do," he told her.

"Now isn't a great time," she said glancing around the loft.

"Oh, yeah, it's early. Sorry about that," he said. She could almost feel him scratching his head at that statement.

"It's fine. Did you need something or were you just calling this early to chat?" she asked being as rude as she had ever been with Ramsey. Depending on the day, he could bring that side her of out better than anyone else she had ever met.

"No, I have something to ask you," he stated hesitantly.

"Ok?" she asked curiously. She knew that it would be better if she got off the line with him. She was at some other guy's house, and it was too early in the morning for this kind of conversation. The last thing she wanted to do was be reminded of her past right now.

"Look, I don't really know how to ask this of you so I guess I'll just spit it out. Will you go to my sister's wedding with me?" Ramsey asked in a rush.

Lexi sat there in silence unable to believe what she had heard. She couldn't honestly believe that Ramsey would be asking her to go to the wedding. She had been doing everything she could *not* to have any knowledge of the wedding *at all*. And it hadn't exactly been easy to keep her head down and out of the news. She hadn't received an invitation, which hadn't really surprised her. On one level, she had been surprised Bekah's vindictive side hadn't surfaced and invited her out of spite. Another part of her was even more surprised that Jack hadn't been begging her to come back again. After all, another year had rolled around and it was about time for him to try to ruin her life.

She hated having to think about Jack that way. Even though she had let him go back in the Atlanta airport, she couldn't help but reminisce back to the good times of their so-called relationship. Apparently, he hadn't been thinking about that or else her comments when leaving him behind would have struck home.

But now she had no idea of the date, time, or place of the wedding. She told herself this was more for her sanity's sake, but she wasn't sure if that was the only reason. She didn't trust herself enough to not go, and she knew that she would only make a fool of herself if she made the mistake of attending.

That brought her back to reality. Ramsey had just asked her to attend the wedding she had been pointedly avoiding at all costs for the past year. He wanted her to go with him to see Jack and Bekah say their vows and become legally tied to each other. He wanted her to go to a wedding that *he* didn't even want to attend.

There was only one explanation. Ramsey had lost his mind. There was no other way to describe it. He had to know, if anyone knew, that there was no way she was going to be in attendance.

"Lexi, are you still there?" Ramsey questioned anxiously into the phone.

She snapped out of her trance. "Yes."

"Yeah?" he asked, excitement evident in his voice.

"Yes, I'm still here," she mumbled.

"Oh," he said sullenly, "I thought you meant yes you would go with me."

"Oh, no," she replied shaking her head side to side even though he couldn't see her.

"Lexi, please."

"Ramsey, are you out of your mind?" she asked running her fingers through her long brown hair as she tried to keep her voice level and under control. How dare he ask her such a ridiculous request!

"Probably a little bit," he admitted his voice wavering.

"You'd have to be crazy to think that I would go with you," she said pinching herself to keep from yelling at him over the phone.

"Is this about me or Jack?"

Lexi huffed out an angry breath. "Do you *really* have to ask that?" she grumbled.

"You're right. You're right," he quickly amended. "Sorry for asking."

"Whatever. Ramsey, I'm not going to that wedding with you or with anyone," she told him firmly.

"Lexi, what happened a couple weeks ago..."

"Please don't," she whispered into the phone, laying her forehead into her hand, and wishing she had gone with her first instinct and ignored the call.

"I am sorry about...everything," he murmured his voice filled with emotion.

"I know. You said that."

"I just...I don't want to go with anyone else," he told her.

Lexi could feel the tears beginning to well in her eyes at the admission. She really did not need this right now. She quickly swiped at her eyes hoping the effect of his words wouldn't show through.

Stepping off of the bed and wandering towards the closet, Lexi stood before the full-length mirror and took a good long look at herself. Her eyes were rimmed pink, but as long as she held it together, the coloring would go away quick enough. Her cheeks were flushed, but it was a nice look with her tanned skin. She hadn't let one tear trickle down her face. She was getting better at controlling her emotions.

"You can't ask that of me Ramsey. You know it isn't fair," she finally responded.

"Can I just give you the date, and you let me know if you're available?" he pleaded.

"What?" she shrieked. "No, don't give me the date." Pulling the phone promptly from her ear, Lexi glanced around the room and over the balcony to see if she had caused a disturbance. She hadn't intended on losing control, but the thought that after all her hard work Ramsey was going to spoil everything made her impulsive. After reassuring herself that her explosion hadn't drawn any unnecessary attention, Lexi placed the phone back to her ear.

"Lexi? Hello, are you there?" Ramsey asked concerned.

"Yes, I'm here. Sorry, I didn't mean to yell," she said tucking a lock of hair behind her ear out of habit.

"It's fine. Look, I won't tell you the date, if you don't want to know, but will you at least think on it? I really don't want to be there without you."

"Did you ever think that maybe I don't want to be there at all?" she whispered into the phone and ducking into the bathroom.

"I know you don't want to be there, but I have to be. It's my sister's wedding and since I have to go, I'd prefer to be with you. I always prefer to be with you," he told her using his easy charm. The words fell husky and persuasive off of his tongue.

She sighed quietly and closed her eyes as her mind traveled to a year ago. She had told herself she would contact Ramsey when she could hold her head up high. So much had changed and evolved, and it was harder now to resist him. He had always had an influence over her, drawing out emotions in her that she hadn't realized she could even feel. Even in the beginning, his all-encompassing personality made her rude and took her out of her element. Those emotions had only intensified with time.

But she couldn't let another man have control over her decisions. She was not, under any circumstances, going to see her sorta-non-ex-boyfriend get married, to anyone. She couldn't do it and nothing *he* said was going to make a difference.

"Ramsey, I can't," she mumbled. "You have to understand. I just...can't."

"Please think about it," he begged.

"I have to go. I'll—I'll talk to you later," she said hanging up the phone without giving him a chance to respond.

She clicked off the line and hung her head in front of the sink. How did these things keep happening to her? Here she was attempting to enjoy herself, to forget him, and he managed to bring up the one thing that would ruin it all—that damn wedding.

All Lexi needed was a fresh start. She thought she had been getting that with Ramsey, but with the way things had ended up, she knew that had been a mistake. Everything she had done—at least romantically—was a mistake.

It didn't matter how he made her feel. She should have known better than to let her emotions get in the way of her judgment. Now she just needed to get over it. Let. It. Go.

She wasn't going to that wedding.

Lexi grabbed a long-sleeve, white button-up from a hanger on the back of the door and slung it on over her head. She scrunched the too-long sleeves up to her elbows and watched as they instantly fell back to her wrists. The shirt hit the top of her thighs barely covering her butt from view. After approving her appearance, Lexi trotted down the stairs and into the chic kitchen. She ran her fingertips across the black marbled countertop and approached the stove. She circled around the island in the center of the room and moved to wrap her arms around the man in front of her.

He jumped slightly, then bent down and kissed her on the forehead. "You surprised me."

Lexi grabbed his left arm and pulled it around her body as he flipped a pancake over with the other hand. "That smells amazing," she murmured reaching up on her tiptoes and kissing his cheek.

"Thank you. This is my mom's recipe. Have a seat." He gestured for her to sit on a low-backed bar stool tucked under the counter. When she did, he placed a pile of pancakes covered in strawberries and syrup with bacon and orange juice in front of her. He turned off the stove, filled his own plate and moved to eat beside her.

"Oh my God," Lexi groaned. "This is incredible." She shoveled the pancakes into her mouth not even caring that she probably looked ridiculous.

He chuckled softly to himself. "I like a woman with a healthy appetite."

Lexi choked on the food she had put in her mouth, chewed a few more times, then swallowed. "Well, when you put it that way," she said putting her fork down and turning to face him. She pulled one leg up and tucked it underneath herself.

"It was a compliment," he reassured her setting his own fork down to stare back at her. He reached up drawing her face towards him and kissing her lips affectionately.

Lexi's mind was still on the conversation she just had and she knew that she wasn't putting as much emotion into the kiss as she had the previous night. He smiled at her when he pulled away and went back to his breakfast. She was grateful that if he had noticed, he didn't say anything. She dug back into her food.

"So, was your conversation important?" he asked.

Lexi nearly dropped her fork onto the plate at the question. She shouldn't have been surprised that he would ask about the call since it had woken them both up much too early. However, she wasn't prepared with a response. How could you tell someone that a guy you dated wanted you to go to a wedding with him for a guy that you had been sleeping with on and off for the past six years? Yeah, that wouldn't exactly go over well.

"Uh, yeah, I suppose it was," she mumbled incoherently.

"Ahhh," he said raising his eyebrows slightly, "you don't want to talk about it."

"It's really not worth discussing," she told him taking a big swig of the orange juice in front of her.

"Alright," he said doing the same. "What are your plans for the day?"

"I'm meeting Chyna to go shopping," Lexi said, a smile creeping up onto her face at the question. She was happy to know that the sex hadn't changed what was going on between them. He still wanted to see her. Butterflies crept up into her stomach at the knowledge that this could actually go somewhere—this could be something, if that's what she wanted.

"Let's do dinner then," he suggested a confident air taking over his cool demeanor.

"Tonight?" she asked lifting her eyes to meet his.

"Yes. We're always so low key. I want to take you somewhere nice," he told her pulling her off of the bar stool and wrapping his arms around her waist.

"We're not low key," she said giggling as he covered her mouth with his own.

"We're low key compared to where I want to take you," he said pulling her back towards the bedroom.

"I'll think on it," she said following him upstairs.

"Don't make me wait too long," he said watching her strip out of his shirt.

"Never," she told him. His pupils dilated and he began to walk towards her. "Hey now. I really do have to meet Chyna," she said holding up her hand to his chest as his slid down her sides.

"She can wait," he breathed against her neck.

"It'll be another hour before I'm out of here."

"You make that seem like a bad thing," he said nibbling across her collarbone and up her neck. "Stay."

"I can't."

"Please," he pleaded gripping her hips.

"As much as I want to."

"Then stay," he groaned against her lips.

"Another time," she said extracting herself from his grasp. "Next time," she repeated. She pulled her tight black dress from the previous night back over her head and slid into her heels.

Snatching her purse up off the bed, Lexi kissed him one more time. "When is next time?" he demanded prolonging the kiss.

"I'll call you," she breathed, reluctantly removing herself from his eager arms, and exiting the apartment.

Lexi ran her fingers through her tangled hair and twisted it up into a tight ponytail at the back of her head. A few loose locks fell out of the holder and swept down across her forehead. She swatted in vain at the bangs willing them to stay in place as she hailed a passing cab. The yellow car slowed to a stop and she fell into the backseat.

As she was whisked across town, Lexi tried not to think about her conversation with Ramsey. She had an entire list of things she needed to accomplish—mostly related to pampering herself post-Bar madness.

She had sent out her resume to over a dozen law firms in the past two weeks, and was waiting patiently for offers pending passage of the Bar exam. She wasn't too worried about either scenario though. The bar had been grueling, time consuming, and painfully nerve-racking, but it was over. All in all, she figured she had passed and that was all that mattered. The job offers would present themselves in good time. She had been fortunate enough to have intern positions for the past two summers, and due to that good fortune, Lexi was even less concerned with finding a job. Thus, relaxation was in order.

Now Ramsey was calling her trying to take away her last few weeks of bliss before entering the "real" world. She needed some serious downtime to forget about that conversation. Luckily, she was supposed to be going out with Chyna all day, which always helped.

"Mr. B," Lexi said nodding her head to Bernard, the doorman, as she stepped out of the taxi and approached the entrance to Chyna's Upper East Side apartment.

"Miss Lexi, it is always a pleasure," he said with a giant smile across his face. He pulled the door open wide for her.

"Always a pleasure to see you as well," Lexi complimented him stepping up to the threshold. He tipped his hat in thanks letting her pass through the frame. The elevator stopped on the top floor where Chyna's penthouse was located, and Lexi breezed down the hallway to her destination. Fishing through her tiny clutch, she realized with despair that she had left her keys behind somewhere. She cursed under her breath and stomped her foot wondering how she could be so stupid. She knew that she had a spare keychain made for these such circumstances, but it didn't make it any better knowing her keys were out there for someone to take.

After another brief dig through her purse, though there wasn't much space to begin with inside the tiny thing, she banged on Chyna's door hoping she was both alone and awake. She had forgotten, in her clouded thoughts, to ask Bernard if Chyna had arrived home alone last night. Just as Lexi was about to dial Chyna's number, she heard the sound of the bolt sliding out of place. The door creaked open about an inch and one of Chyna's emerald green eyes was visible.

"Yes?" Chyna asked eyeing her up and down.

Lexi smiled at her best friend. "Hey, C. Let me in."

Chyna slammed the door closed, fiddled with the lock, and then reopened the door. "Are you in walk-of-shame attire?" Chyna asked trying for condescending. She flipped her long black hair over to one shoulder and pulled the door all the way to the wall.

"Good to see you too," Lexi mumbled sarcastically rolling her eyes. She stepped through the entranceway in her four inch, peep toe heels from the previous night and across the white marbled foyer.

"Oh yes. It's always good to see you, chica," Chyna said slamming the door shut and following her to the living room, which was currently in shambles. Lexi scooted away from a disturbing looking plaster and over to the covered black leather sofas. She took a seat and sighed resting her head back against the plastic covering.

"At least I'll only have to endure this the first time."

"Oh, so you think this will continue?" Chyna questioned lying back against a cream psychiatrist's chair that Lexi had never seen before.

Lexi realized her mistake and attempted to pivot the conversation. This wasn't what she was here to talk about with Chyna, and she didn't particularly want to discuss her love life. "Has Frederick approved these changes?" Lexi asked glancing at the half-upturned carpet, strings of bamboo blinds, and other, more exaggerated, environmental pieces.

Chyna upturned her nose at the comment, swinging her legs back off the chair, and onto the floor. "Frederick," she said as if the name alone caused her physical discomfort. "Frederick does not matter."

Lexi laughed out loud at her best friend. She always did have a flare for the dramatic and a not so secret crush on her rather gay designer. "Frederick would murder you if he saw this room."

"Precisely," Chyna said her eyes glimmering with thoughts of indiscretion. "But enough about me. Tell me about your walk-of-shame."

"Chyna, I told you, it's not a walk-of-shame."

"I know. I know," she said cutting Lexi off and stepping around her living room as deftly as possible to take a seat next to her friend. "So, is it serious?" she questioned arching an eyebrow.

"We'll see," Lexi said shrugging her thin shoulders. "I think he wants it to be."

Chyna puckered lips together and blew herself a kiss in the adjacent mirror resting against the wall. When she glanced back at Lexi, she had a devious look in her eyes. "Of course he does, darling."

Lexi pushed a loose strand of hair behind her ear. "It doesn't matter."

"Because you spoke to Ramsey this morning?" Chyna asked batting her eyelashes and tearing her gaze from her reflection to flick a glance in Lexi's direction.

"Wha...?" Lexi asked returning the gaze her mouth popping open in surprise. "How did you know that?"

"You have that look on your face," she said as a matter of fact.

"And what look is that?" Lexi asked mystified by her friend's observation skills. She would have never guessed

"Like this," Chyna said looking doe-eyed, her mouth turning up into a half-smile as if she were keeping a secret from the rest of the world, her head tilting slightly upwards, and a small sigh escaped her lips.

"I do *not* look like that," Lexi cried pushing Chyna away.

"You had that exact look when you walked through my door. I'd know it anywhere. You have looks when you're thinking about someone. I know you too well not to notice."

"Oh yeah? Who else do I have one for then?"

Chyna's eyes slanted seductively sideways, licked her pouted lips, let a smirk cross her face, and breathed out heavily a few times. Lexi stared at her in awe wondering what this was all about. After a second, Chyna returned to her typical look and said, "That was when you think about Jack."

Lexi colored slightly at the reenactment. "Whatever," she said huskily wishing she could cover her embarrassment. They didn't typically talk about Jack, because it tended to bring up memories Lexi didn't like to dwell on.

"Anyway," Chyna said clearing her throat, "what did Ramsey call to talk to you about? He did call right?" Lexi nodded slowly and pushed her fingers through her hair as she yanked the ponytail holder out of place. She stood up from the plastic covered furniture and made a slow circle around the part of the room that wasn't a disaster. "This can't be good," Chyna ventured.

"No, it's fine. I'm just letting it get to me," Lexi told her.

"Well don't, whatever it is, don't let it get to you. You know you need to work on not letting these boys control your emotions, chica."

"I know, C. Don't remind me. That's all I've been thinking about since he called. I need to control myself. But it's not that simple," she cried throwing her arms down and staring helplessly at her friend.

"Girl, I know better than anyone. I've been here through it all for you," she said reassuringly. Chyna stood and moved next to her. "So what's up with him? Something different?"

"He..." Lexi sighed hating that she had to say this out loud, "he invited me to the wedding."

"What?" Chyna asked taking a step back. "As in *Jack's* wedding?" Chyna's eyes had expanded to record proportions, eyebrows raised, and mouth forming an "o" in disbelief.

"Yeah, as in Jack's wedding," Lexi confirmed.

"Is he out of his fucking mind?" Chyna cried.

"I asked him if he was," Lexi said chuckling quietly.

"You can't go!"

"You think I don't know that?" Lexi asked pulling away from Chyna and looking out across the living room. "He wanted to go with me—to be there with him."

"I know how hard it must be, but you can't let him do this to you," Chyna told her trying to be the voice of reason. "It doesn't change what happened. I know it doesn't make things better. But at least you know now."

"I know," Lexi said nodding. "He's just, you know...Ramsey."

"I know," Chyna agreed sympathetically, "but you can't go to that wedding. Did he tell you the date?"

Pop music sounded in the living room causing both girls to jump. Lexi walked around the side of the couch and scooped up her purse. "No. Thank God," Lexi told Chyna reaching into her bag. "I almost had a heart attack right there when he tried to tell me the date."

"I'm not surprised."

"Hold on," Lexi said clicking the green button and answering the call. "Hello?"

"Lexi," Ramsey's voice filled her ears.

"Uh..." Lexi stammered glancing anxiously at Chyna and mouthing who the caller was. Chyna shook her head vehemently and held her hand out for the phone as if she were ready to dismiss the call at any moment. "Hey," Lexi said waving Chyna away.

"Hey. I know I called earlier, but you said you would talk to me later and I thought now is...well...later. You know? I didn't really get to talk to you this morning, and I need to talk you," he said babbling nervously.

This made Lexi smile despite herself. He was always so cute when he babbled on about things. Chyna glowered at Lexi's reaction and poked her in the side to remind her to stay on track. "Yeah, well this morning really wasn't a great time, but the answer is still no, Ramsey." Lexi wandered down the hallway and into an empty guestroom to continue her conversation in peace.

"I know. I mean, I knew all along you were going to say no," he said dejected.

"Then why even bother asking me?" she couldn't help asking.

"I was hoping you might change your mind," he said hopefully, "if you knew everything."

"I'm pretty sure I *know* everything," she grumbled.

"Parker is going to be there."

Lexi cringed to keep from saying anything stupid. She really did not want to be having this conversation. When she had left things with Jack, she had promised that she would never again let anything like that happen…not even close. She needed control. She needed to be in control. Ramsey swayed her emotions in a completely different way than Jack, and she was alright with that. It was just when the lack of control started creeping in that she couldn't handle it.

The way Ramsey just brought Parker up like this hoping to influence her decision made things even worse. She and Ramsey weren't together. It shouldn't matter to her whether Parker was going to be there or not.

But it did.

Of course it mattered to her, which is exactly the reason why he brought it up. And it was exactly why she couldn't let it get to her or else he would have her hook, line, and sinker.

"Great," Lexi stated as fake cheerful as she could get.

"Look, I want you to be there if Parker is going," he told her, willing her to finally agree to come with him to this wedding.

"You want me to be there *because* Parker is going to be there?" Lexi asked incredulously. "That doesn't make any sense."

"I'd feel more comfortable knowing you're around," he told her pleading with every word.

She really hated hearing him beg her. If things had been different and they hadn't gone through so much together, then maybe she would have changed her mind, but probably not. She had to keep reminding herself what he was asking her to do. She could not go to Jack's wedding under any circumstance.

"So you can control what's going on?" she asked dryly, a sting of venom in the comment.

He sighed heavily once more. "No, that's not it at all. Parker is just…you know, and I want you to be there too."

"Ramsey, as much as I'd love to be around you and Parker at the same time," Lexi told him sarcastically. "I cannot…no, I will *not* go to that wedding. Can you not understand? This is Jack we're talking about marrying *your* sister. I cannot fathom a reason good enough to go."

"To visit me?" he asked hopefully.

"If I wanted to visit you Ramsey, I would fly to Atlanta. I wouldn't have to go to that miserable wedding to see you," she muttered angrily. "So please, don't ask me again."

Lexi could hear the defeat in the next breath he took. He was weighing whether or not to push her on the subject. It wouldn't be smart on his part. She wasn't wavering on this one.

"Alright, Lexi. I won't ask again. Sorry for bothering you. Will I see you again?" he asked sounding even more disheartened than when she had first told him that she wasn't going to be in attendance.

She didn't know how to answer him either. She strode across the bedroom to stand in front of the large vanity mirror on the hard oak dresser . Her mind was telling her that she should tell him no, but she couldn't help that her heart was telling her otherwise.

She hadn't seen him in the nearly three weeks since she had left him all alone in Atlanta. A wave of déjà vu passed over her in the aftermath of her reminiscence. She had now left two men behind in Atlanta.

Jack—it was difficult to even think about him—was a necessary loss. They were self-destructive when in each other's company. Their emotions were too strong, too heated. Their senses heightened and imaginations set free. They left a path of pain for whoever ventured near, and Jack and Lexi weren't immune to the catastrophes they created. There was a reason the sin of lust was whirled around for eternity in Dante's *Inferno*. No matter where they went, they couldn't help but ceaselessly be in a whirlwind, always crossing that fine line between love and lust.

But did Ramsey have to be a necessary loss as well?

"I…I don't know Ramsey," she mumbled finally giving him the best answer she could muster.

"Well, that's better than no," he said always the optimist.

"Yeah, I guess so."

"Please let me see you. I promise I won't bring up the wedding again. I just…I miss you. I'm so sorry about everything. I'll understand if you're mad at me and don't want to see me, but I really, really miss you. I've never met anyone like you, Lexi, and I don't want to waste anymore time letting you slip through my fingers," he announced.

"I don't know," she murmured not wanting to let him know that his words were affecting her.

"I wish I was there to kiss you," he whispered huskily into the phone.

"Ramsey," she said warningly, but her voice had lowered impishly with the comment.

"Tell me you'll see me again," he commanded, but the words were gentle.

"I..." she trailed off. "Are you planning on being in New York?" She assumed he didn't have plans to be up here, not that money was an issue. But if he didn't already have plans, then she could stall just a little bit longer. If he crashed back into her life so soon, she wasn't sure she'd have the will to walk out again.

"Actually, I am," he told her cheerfully knowing, somehow, that he had her in a corner.

"Oh," she blurted out in surprise. She hadn't been expecting that. Maybe he was bluffing. "What are you doing up here?"

"I have...business to attend to," he muttered vaguely.

Lexi's eyes darkened. She did not want to have anything to do with his business matters. "Well count me out," she told him fiercely.

"Something for good ole Daddy, Lexi," he mumbled obviously perturbed about the whole situation.

"Oh," she said again. That changed things. His father, the owner of Bridges Enterprise, a multi-million dollar conglomerate, frequently had Ramsey attend to business matters when he was traveling. Ramsey, who hated working for his father for so many reasons, usually did them more for Bekah than anyone else. They had a strange bond as brother and sister. A bond Lexi didn't much like since Bekah was the scum of the universe.

"So, what do you say?" he asked hopefully.

"Uh, alright then," she agreed listening to the devil on her shoulder, "you can visit, but Ramsey..."

"Yes?" he asked practically giddy with excitement.

"Don't you dare bring up that wedding," she warned him.

2

SEPTEMBER ELEVEN MONTHS EARLIER

Using her excess student loan money, Lexi signed up for Pilates classes upon returning to New York. She just wanted to forget everything that had happened in Atlanta. She was still in shape from her semi-regular jogs around the city, but it wasn't enough. No matter what she did, law school managed to add a few extra pounds when she wasn't looking. Not to mention after two years without gymnastics, her flexibility was basically shot. She could barely fall into a regular split, and to any prior gymnast, it was an embarrassment.

Lexi rolled over on her purple mat as the teacher instructed her into a plank position. Her core muscles hardened underneath her as she struggled through the push-up like pose. She could feel her body begin to shake from the effort, but she held her head high and kept a smile on her face to loosen her features. Just when she thought she would collapse, the teacher instructed them to release. Lexi pushed over her toes, laying her legs flat against the mat, and arching her back. Her abdominal muscles expanded, and she let her head drop backwards.

Rolling back over her toes, Lexi shot her butt up into the air in a downwards dog position giving her calves and shoulders a thorough working. She alternated feet, pressing each heel into the ground, and holding the move.

The tiny Pilates instructor came up behind her and flattened out her back, adjusting the position to extract the maximum potential out of the movement. "Very good," she complimented. She flung her waist length braid over her shoulder as she stood and moved to another student.

Lexi breathed into the position letting all the built up energy of the past month release from her body. Her course work was rigorous for her final year of law school, but the anticipation of graduation looming over everything relaxed students and faculty alike. Relaxed was a relative term, of course, since she still had reading for obscure law courses in statutory interpretation and other such material that was supposed to prepare her for the Bar and the "real" world.

Just as the instructor began working them through the next series of movements, a loud jingle began playing from one of the bags stuffed against the adjacent wall. Lexi's face colored as she realized that was her ring tone. Cell phones were strictly forbidden unless turned off. Lexi hadn't even realized that her phone had been on until that second.

Jumping up from her seated position, Lexi scrambled to the other side of the room and switched it off. The teacher gave her a disapproving look, and then went back to her work. A few other faces still glared at her as she flipped open the phone and glanced down. Chyna's name appeared across the front and a text filled the screen.

"911! Get your ass over here."

Lexi groaned inwardly at the abrupt change of course her afternoon was taking. She stuffed her cell phone back into her purse and threw it into the pile with her other stuff. She wanted to kick herself for giving into Chyna's hysterical whims, but her friend was important to her. And if Chyna said there was an emergency, Lexi came running. Chyna had always been there for her when she needed her most.

With that in mind, Lexi rushed back to her mat and began rolling it up. She slipped the cover over the squishy material and slung it over her shoulder. "Kathy, I have to run," she said approaching the woman and smiling apologetically.

"Come back and make it up later in the week," Kathy said, her smile warm and understanding. The woman was a god send, honestly.

After signing up for a make-up session with the receptionist, Lexi rushed out on the busy Manhattan street and pulled her phone back out. *"What's the 911, chica?"* she punched into the system and hit send.

She pushed a loose wisp of hair behind her ear and continued down the street dodging pedestrians. Almost instantly she had a return message, *"Tell you when you get here. Hurry!"*

Lexi sighed and broke into a light jog. She wasn't certain if it was necessary for her to be rushing to Chyna's apartment, but she didn't want to take the chance. Chyna was prone to dramatic flairs, but it wasn't typically a 911 situation. Running out of breath and energy, Lexi briskly walked the next few blocks, resting momentarily as she reached the door front to

Chyna's apartment. Her lime green messenger bag smacked one last time against her back as she reached forward to hold onto a pole for support.

"Miss Lexi, are you alright?" a concerned Bernard asked her.

"Fine, just ran across town. Chyna said it was 911," she managed to get out through gasping breathes. "You know anything about this, Mr. B?"

Bernard averted his eyes to the ground and gulped. "I can't really say," he mumbled.

The two years Lexi had known Chyna, Bernard had always given her a straight answer. Yes, he sometimes answered her in a goofy, even sarcastic, manner, but he still answered her. She had never been blown off by him. He had never had a reason to. His reaction pumped a fresh wave of adrenaline into her system, and she bolted through the open door. The elevator took a century to reach the top floor of the building. The classical music was more grating than normal. Lexi could feel her heart beating in her ears as the elevator stopped and deposited her on the floor. She pushed hard against the opening door forcing it to move just a fraction of an inch faster.

Hopping onto the cream carpet, Lexi bolted down the hallway. She fumbled with her key too anxious to get the thing out of her bag properly. The keychain slipped out of her hand and onto the floor. She cursed under her breath as she reached down to pick up the thing. Inserting the gold key into the lock, she twisted the handle and burst through the open door.

"Chyna?" she called racing into the immaculately decorated living room.

Lexi skidded to a halt at the end of foyer, her blood turning to ice at the scene before her. Chyna was seated on her leather sofa, legs crossed, in a demure, black, pant suit. Lexi wasn't certain Chyna even owned clothes in this fashion. Her beautiful Italian skin was sheet white with the lightest twinge of green coloring her face. Her green eyes were glassy and near to tears, but her head was held strong. She was stubborn and refused to let the hardness leave her features for fear of breaking down. Lexi had never seen her friend look quite so distraught over anything, but she could understand why.

Standing directly in front of Chyna in a very expensive, black suit was a man who was everything Lexi imagined him to be. She had only seen him in photographs, never in person. She gulped hard feeling a knot form in her stomach and making it hard for her to swallow.

He turned at Lexi's approach and made her body quiver even more at the incredibly threatening and overpowering aura that radiated from his very being. He was well over six feet tall with sharp, all-knowing brown eyes and cropped brown hair. With just one look, it was obvious he commanded attention, not unlike the woman sitting before him.

"Hello, Mr. Van Der Wal," Lexi stammered standing uncomfortably before Chyna's father.

His eyes traveled the length of her body taking in every detail while at the same time remaining strictly professional. He was observing her as if she were cattle ready for slaughter. No emotion marred his face as he continued his inspection.

Lexi was distinctly aware, in that moment, of her tight, black Yoga pants that hugged every inch of her lower half and the flimsy white tank damp with sweat from her class. Her hair was in a messy bun stuffed haphazardly onto the top of her head. Wisps were loose from her brisk jog to the apartment and the back of her neck was still slick. She shifted awkwardly onto one hip and waited for him to finish staring at her and actually say something.

"She'll do," he commented indifferently as he glanced back at Chyna. Lexi had no idea what that meant, but she was sure that she didn't want to find out.

"Are you sure?" Chyna asked, the sarcasm dripping from her voice as she cocked one perfectly waxed eyebrow to the ceiling.

"Don't get smart with me, young lady," he snapped, his face hardening into a look that could make anyone shake in their boots.

Lexi was proud of Chyna for not flinching under such scrutiny. Instead she swept her long black hair over to one shoulder and smiled as sweetly as she could. A little bit of color crept back into her cheeks when his attention had been briefly diverted and given her the courage to speak up.

"Never, Daddy," she purred lowering her long black lashes.

He growled something incoherent and tore his eyes from Chyna. "Just do what you're told," he grumbled before brushing past Lexi and exiting the apartment.

The wave of relief that followed his exit crashed into the room. Chyna slumped back against the sofa and heaved her chest up and down. She placed her hands over her eyes to keep the tears back. Lexi instantly went to her side and wrapped a comforting arm around Chyna's petite shoulders. It didn't matter what had just happened. All that mattered was that she was here now to comfort her.

"Are you okay?" Lexi asked pulling Chyna close. She knew it was a stupid question. Obviously, Chyna was not alright in that moment, but what else was there to ask.

Chyna pushed her hands up through her silky hair and took a deep breath in an attempt to calm herself. "I'll be fine," she mumbled.

"I know you will eventually, but what the hell was all that about?" Lexi couldn't help asking. "When I walked in, you looked like a ghost. What is your dad even doing here? I thought you two had nothing to do with each other."

"We don't," Chyna said standing from her spot and pacing the living room. "That's the way we like to keep it. Didn't you hear what he said?"

"About what?" Lexi asked confused.

"He told me not to act like my fucking whore of a mother," she cried slapping her hands down against her thighs angrily.

Lexi's mouth dropped open. She knew the history between Chyna and her parents. They had divorced when Chyna was in high school because they were both sleeping around. Then after giving her the apartment Chyna was now living in, they had equally decided they wanted nothing to do with her. Chyna was too much like her father in personality and her mother in appearance for either of them to be able to handle their daughter.

"I can't believe that," Lexi mumbled in shock.

"He can't even look at me without thinking of her. I can't believe he had the gall to come here and speak to me like that in my own home. I don't give a fuck if he paid for the place tenfold. He has no right to barge in on me and boss me around. Then he springs a fucking bomb on me."

"What happened?" Lexi asked her curiosity getting the best of her.

Chyna turned around and faced her best friend. The color was draining out of her cheeks again at the realization that she was going to have to talk about what occurred. "My dad is getting remarried," she finally sputtered out.

"What?" Lexi balked her eyes bulging out. "Since when?"

"Since four months ago when he proposed to her," Chyna muttered dejectedly.

"Four months? Oh C, I'm so sorry," Lexi said hopping up out of her seat and standing in front of her friend.

"I've never even met her," she blubbered falling into Lexi's open arms.

"The bastard," Lexi cried encouragingly.

"I know," Chyna said pulling back and swiping at her eyes. "I'm sorry that I'm all…" she trailed off waving her hands in front of her face.

"Oh, you don't have to worry about that. How many times have you seen me in a fit?" Lexi asked knowing the answer. Lexi had her fair share of moments over the past two years. Chyna was certainly due tears if she wanted to cry.

"I know, but this is dumb."

"What?" Lexi asked astonished. "You think it's smarter for me to cry over *Jack*, then for you to cry about your parents?"

Chyna chuckled once and let a small smile tease the corners of her mouth. "Well, when you put it *that* way."

"See, I'm much more dysfunctional than you. You have every right to be upset."

"There's more," Chyna mumbled letting her green eyes rest back on her friend. Lexi didn't like the way she said that. What more could her father want from her? After barely speaking to Chyna for two years and dumping that tidbit of information on her, it was an asinine move to then continue the conversation.

"What else could he possibly have to say to you after that?"

Chyna took a deep breath and crossed her arms over her chest. "He needs me to be at the engagement party this weekend."

"He cannot expect you to show up to that."

"He didn't ask me to. He told me to," she said tilting her chin up.

"You don't have to go."

"No, I do. You don't know what he's like. If I'm not there, it will be the end of the world. Even though I'm twenty-one, he still has direct access to my trust, and he's the owner of this apartment. He could kick me out on the streets," she murmured helplessly. "If he wanted to."

Lexi gasped. "He wouldn't dare!"

"Wouldn't he?" she screeched. "Did you see the look on his face when you got here? He was murderous. If I'd disobeyed him, I wouldn't have put it past him to ruin my life."

"But you're his daughter," Lexi cried unable to believe what she was hearing. How could anyone be so cruel?

"The daughter who is a constant reminder of his past life, of the life he was trying to get rid of. The daughter he was so eager to get rid of."

"Chyna, I…I don't know what to say," Lexi muttered sympathizing with her friend's pain as best she could.

"Just say you'll come with me."

"Oh," Lexi stammered surprised by this response. "Yeah, I guess I could. Wouldn't that be awkward?"

"My dad is a big dick, but he insisted that I be there and come with, as he put it," Chyna gulped, "a *boyfriend*."

"He wants you to come with a boyfriend? But you don't have a boyfriend," Lexi said unable to keep from stating the obvious.

"I know," she stated barely above a whisper. Her voice was getting raspier the longer they had this conversation and Lexi could tell she was trying to keep the tears from unleashing on the world again. "You should have heard the way he was talking to me before you got here. He said I better not bring one of the guys I'm normally with. What is he trying to say that I run an escort service? That all the guys I date are man whores? That they can't conduct themselves in proper society?"

Lexi didn't know how to respond to that. Honestly, a good number of the guys Chyna hooked up with were those kind of men. They were relatively well-off, but still they were hardly up to her standard. It hadn't mattered up until now, because she never wanted a boyfriend. She was never interested enough in any one man to want to be around him for multiple occasions. Now her father, the judgmental asshole, wanted her to pretend to have a steady boyfriend, because the cheating bastard didn't approve of his daughter's way of life.

It was one of the most hypocritical statements Lexi had ever heard. If anything, the circumstances surrounding her parents' divorce had only further pushed Chyna the direction she was already heading with regards to relationships.

"So what are you going to do?"

"Find a boyfriend I guess," she sighed unhappily. "I have no idea."

"Is that why your dad gave me that creepy once over? Because he wants me to go with you too?" Lexi asked putting the pieces together.

Chyna groaned. "Oh God, I am so sorry for his ridiculous behavior. But yeah that's why and he needs you to bring a boyfriend too," she muttered.

"That's going to be an issue," Lexi said falling backwards on to the plush leather sofa.

"I know," Chyna grumbled sitting down next to her. "I'm so sorry that I dragged you into this." The tears were beginning to well in her eyes, and Lexi could see her breaking point was drawing near. Her bottom lip quavered in an adorable fashion if she didn't look so utterly miserable. "I can't believe he's doing this."

"Don't cry. It'll be okay," Lexi said comforting her. "We'll figure it out. Let's go out tonight and look for guys. We'll figure it out."

"The last thing that I wanna do is party," Chyna huffed crossing her arms back over her chest.

"Now that's something I never thought I'd hear come out of your mouth," Lexi said giggling despite the dour mood.

Soon enough, Chyna had joined in as well and both girls were laughing out their issues rather than crying. It felt good to release the tension that was so strained from her father's entrance back into Chyna's life. The girls knew that they had a tough night ahead of them. Neither of them could think of anyone they would want to pretend to be their boyfriend's for the afternoon, and the last thing they wanted to do was search for that man.

Regardless, they didn't feel as if they had much choice in the matter. Keeping Chyna's dad happy was of the essence since he all but owned Chyna. With that in mind, the two girls dressed extra careful for the evening out hoping to find a man that they found suitable for a second date.

That's how they ended up having martinis at a Manhattan bar scoping out the men in attendance. The atmosphere was a bit more conducive to casual conversation than the normal, pulsing, hip-hop beats that broke through the speakers at the destinations they typically frequented.

The girls had dressed the part for sure. Chyna's black mini dress skirted her ass and gripped her body tightly in a silky, flimsy material. Her black heels shimmered in the mood lighting that emanated from every hidden light bulb in the place. Her long black hair was swept up onto the top of her head into a sexy concoction. Her long lean features were accented while keeping the focus on her well-sculpted body.

Lexi wore super low-rise, black, skinny jeans with hot red pumps. She paired that with a sheer red tank that buttoned up the front. She let her dark brown locks flow down her back with thick, chunky bangs covering her forehead. Her eyes were smoky and seductive while her bright red lips were both pouty and inviting. Together they were a dynamic duo, the Sirens of the New York City nightlife. It was unlikely that anyone who fell into their trap was going to escape their clutches.

Chyna smiled at a sleazy looking man who had been eye-fucking the shit out of her for the past ten minutes across the bar. He took that as an invitation and sidled up to her side. She downed the remnants of her drink and took his hand as he escorted her out on the dance floor. Lexi's eyes followed them into the dark center of the room, and an uneasy feeling hit the pit of her stomach.

He wasn't the type of person Chyna normally surrounded herself with, and something about him seemed off. His features were too angular, too sneaky. His height and bulk were threatening rather than enticing. Lexi wasn't sure why, but the way he had grabbed her hand even seemed forceful. From her view, albeit a shadowed view of the couple, Lexi could even tell he was handsy. That was really saying something for a person dancing with Chyna.

Lexi sighed heavily and tried to clear her mind. There was no need to overreact. They were just out for a good time.

She took another deep breath and let her own eyes roam the crowded room once more. A number of drunken girls were singing and dancing in a corner to cluster of admiring onlookers. Lexi had a strange reminiscence of doing that with her own friends in bars during college. The alcohol was beginning to set in and the different groups of people were beginning to blend together. She wasn't sure why her buzz was so strong already, but she kind of liked it. She would start coming here more frequently if they poured drinks this well.

After another martini, a complete haze took over her mind. A part of her wished that she had stopped at one because she didn't want her judgment impaired without Chyna at her side. But she couldn't take back the decision now.

Pressing the palm of her hand to her forehead, she attempted to keep the spinning from gripping her conscious. After counting to ten, Lexi seemed to feel a bit better and slowly angled her body back towards the bar. She didn't need a drink, but she did need someone to sweat out this alcohol with. The dance floor was calling her name.

One of the guys she had been eyeing earlier seemed to notice that she was without a drink and approached her. "Hey," he slurred smiling drunkenly at her. His eyes darted to her chest and then back up to her face. "I've never seen you here before."

Lexi wanted to retort some snide remark about how completely original he was, but he was kind of cute so she refrained. Instead she smiled at him in an all-knowing way that would make his addled mind kick into over drive. "You're right. I've never been here," she murmured.

"What?" he cried trying to hear her over the music that had increased in proportion to the length of time she had spent in the establishment.

Lexi leaned forward resting her hand on his chest. She rose up onto her tiptoes until her mouth was next to his ear and said, "I've never been here. Perhaps you could show me around."

The guy's eyes nearly popped out of their sockets at her comment. He turned back to his friends and made some kind of fist pump. They all cheered him on as if she wasn't standing there. Lexi felt a little sick to her stomach at how dumb he was already turning out to be, but she couldn't exactly turn back now. She at least owed him one dance after her forwardness.

His hands gripped her hips forcefully as he corralled her out onto the dance floor. Even as drunk as she was, she knew that he had no rhythm. And when she said no rhythm, she really meant *no* rhythm. If the guy had two left feet, he would be able to dance better than he was at that moment. She knew that alcohol made you more willing to dance, but this was embarrassing. She almost felt like someone was playing a practical joke on her.

But she couldn't figure a way out of this situation. His hands were like a vice lock on her hips as he sway backed and forth uncoordinatedly. Every time she attempted to slip away, he would grab her even harder and she was starting to wonder if she was going to be bruised in the morning.

Finally, she reached in for her last ditch effort and leaned back to speak into his ear again, "Can we get out of here?" she asked hoping he would take the bait.

He managed one last horrible dance move before grabbing a hold of her wrist, and veering her towards the front door. She stood in place for a second as he attempted to yank her around. "Hey, don't move. I have to use the ladies room and I'll be right back," she said watching recognition reach his brain. He let go of her wrist and leaned back against the wall to wait for her…indefinitely.

Lexi made a beeline for the ladies room to check out the damage from dancing with that idiot. She knew it had been a mistake to come out to a place like this in hopes of finding someone who would be boyfriend material. The last thing she wanted in her life was some loser pretending to be her boyfriend. She couldn't do that for anyone. She didn't even care if Chyna's father assaulted her with his menacing eyes one more time. A cold chill rushed down her back at the thought and she tried to push it aside.

After elbowing her way through the line at the bathroom and reassuring about a dozen girls that she wasn't cutting, she eventually made it in front of a mirror. She adjusted her top and peered at herself through the dim lighting. Perhaps she had been overreacting when she had been out dancing. The skin wasn't sensitive to the touch and all in all she still looked stellar. Her hair was wild, but it worked for her. She liked how her flushed appearance only added to her sensual appeal.

Several girls began shoving Lexi out of the way to wash their hands so she quickly exited the bathroom. Surveying the surrounding area to make sure that guy hadn't followed her, Lexi wandered back towards the bar in search of Chyna. She just needed to get out of there.

As she approached the bar, Lexi noticed the crowd clearing from the direction of the dance floor. Curious, Lexi moved forward to find out what was going on. Her heart began pounding furiously in her ears. She sobered up quick as adrenaline pumped through her system at record speeds. She darted forward into the open space her breathing accelerating with fear.

"What happened to her?" Lexi asked reaching her hand and placing it on Chyna's forehead. A man was holding her limp in his arms. "Is she okay?" She knew her voice was hysterical, but she couldn't control it.

Lexi didn't even care who the guy was that was carrying her. She was so terrified that she was losing her best friend. How could she let one more terrible thing happen in her life? Hadn't she suffered enough?

"Do you know this woman?" the man asked his voice deep and husky.

"Of course I know her. She's my best friend. What's wrong with her?"

"Let's get out of here," he said nodding his head toward the exit.

Lexi didn't even think twice. She bolted towards the door. All she could think about was Chyna's safety. A wave of guilt washed over her as she thought about how she had let her wander off. Had she allowed this to happen? Somehow she couldn't help thinking that this was partly her fault. What type of person let this happen?

As they reached the door, she felt a hand reach out and grip her wrist. "There you are." Lexi recognized the man who she had been avoiding and nearly cursed a loud.

"Get your hands off me," she cried unable to deal with him while she had Chyna to worry about.

"Oh come on, baby. Let's go back to my place," he moaned groping her body. She smacked his arm with her free hand, but he was too drunk to even notice.

"Stay the hell away from me, you sick, twisted fuck," she yelled rearing back and kicking him full on in the shin with her high heel.

The guy stumbled backwards a few steps directly into a large bouncer dressed head to toe in black. "You stupid bitch," the guy yelled pulling his leg up and hobbling on one foot.

"Sir, I'm going to have to ask you to leave," the bouncer commanded gripping the obnoxiously drunk man by the shoulder and shoving him out the front door.

Lexi couldn't even take time to consider what had happened because she was too worried about Chyna. She followed the man who was carrying Chyna out the front door of the bar. "Sorry about that. What's going on?" Lexi asked concerned.

"Honestly, I think she's been drugged. She's still conscious. I think she needs some looking after and will be better in the morning," he said setting Chyna uneasily back on her feet. She took one step forward giving Lexi the faintest burst of energy and then slumped back into the man's arms.

"Oh my God! She's been drugged. Like roofied?" Lexi asked hysterical. "How could this happen?"

"Can we get her somewhere safe first?" he asked worrying about her safety first and foremost.

"Oh, you're right. Hold on," Lexi cried punching a number on her cell phone. Less than a minute later, Chyna's town car was pulling around the corner. Her driver parked and hopped out anxious to see that his beautiful celebutante was all but dead. The two laid her down carefully in the backseat before diving in after her.

"I'm Adam. Sorry about your friend," he said consolingly slumping back against the leather interior.

"Lexi," she managed a half-smile in his direction as an introduction. "What happened?" Lexi asked brushing hair out of Chyna's face and staring at her with a worried look on her face.

"I don't know everything really. She was dancing with some guy. When I finally noticed something was off, he was dragging her out the backdoor. She wasn't quite this bad then, but she was a mess for sure. I politely told him to back the fuck off or I'd deck him. He didn't listen," he explained calmly, "So I decked him."

"Wow!" she said assessing him more closely. "How did you know she was drugged?" Lexi asked her eyes wide with admiration for Chyna's savior.

"My girlfriend...uh ex-girlfriend," he said sighing heavily, "it happened to her a couple months ago. Same signs." He shrugged it off as if it meant nothing, but Lexi could see the hurt take over his features. She knew that feeling and could empathize with his pain even if she didn't know the whole situation.

"Wha...what happened with your girlfriend?" Lexi asked cautiously.

"She was fine. The next morning she had a killer headache, but other than that she was fine," he said.

"Oh, well that's reassuring," Lexi said letting them fall into silence as the town car took them through the city traffic. Lexi gripped Chyna's unresponsive hand in her own and prayed that Adam was right. Her friend would be alright by the morning and things would be back to the way they were supposed to be.

"Hey," Adam said reaching out cautiously and touching her knee. "Try not to blame yourself."

"Blame myself?" Lexi squeaked out.

"I did. It doesn't help. It was just a mistake, alright? Nothing you could have done," he said sitting back once more and staring forward.

Lexi nodded knowing he was right. There was no way to know that sleaze ball was going to drug her friend. They had been out together a million and a half times and nothing like this had ever happened. What were the chances that tonight of all nights it would happen? That it would ever happen?

When they stopped in front of Chyna's building, Bernard rushed forward to help them, but Adam insisted that he could handle it. Bernard looked at Lexi skeptically, wondering if it was appropriate to be leaving her with a perfect stranger. Under different circumstances it would have made Lexi laugh that Bernard was concerned about something like that since Chyna brought a whole lot of strangers back here. Tonight was not under different circumstances though.

Adam carried her up to her room and deposited her on the bed. He left the room allowing Lexi to change Chyna into more comfortable clothes. She then tucked her under the covers and left her there to sleep off whatever was in her system.

"Are you sure we shouldn't take her to the hospital?" Lexi asked anxiously.

"I think she'll be fine. If I was worried, then I would have already taken her there. I think she just needs to sleep it off," Adam told her standing in the middle of the living room rather comfortably.

Lexi was a bit surprised about this since most people who saw Chyna's extravagance were either amazed or incredibly uncomfortable. "Is there any way we can repay you for what you did?" Lexi asked knowing for some reason that he would never take money even though he could tell Chyna had plenty of it.

"Absolutely not. I would have done the same for anyone," he reassured her.

"Are you sure?"

"Look if you want to do something for me, then take my number and let me know how she's doing in the morning. I'd feel like a real dick if she was really hurt and I didn't do anything about it," he said running his hand through his cropped brown hair.

Lexi smiled for the first time since she had found Chyna in the condition she was in. They exchanged numbers and Lexi showed him out the door. "Thanks again," she said before closing the door behind him.

She couldn't believe the night that she was having, but it really put things in perspective. What if something had happened to her or what if their relationship faltered because of it? Isn't that what Adam had alluded to in the car? He and his girlfriend had suffered because of this. It wasn't worth it to wait around and hope that everything was going to be better when so much could come crashing down unexpectedly. She needed to take action.

Falling backwards onto the leather sofa, Lexi kicked her heels off and then dug around in her purse for her cell phone. Finding the number she was looking for, she punched the dial button and waited. She didn't care that it was almost three o'clock in the morning.

"Lexi?" Ramsey's voice answered clearly surprised to hear from her. She wasn't sure where he was, but wherever it was had a lot of background noise.

"What are you doing on Saturday?" she asked louder than she wanted to speak, but she wanted to make sure he heard her.

"Hold on one second." After a minute, Lexi heard the noise die down and his voice come back through the line. "What did you say?"

"What are you doing on Saturday?" she repeated her question unable to believe she was doing this.

"Um…working probably. Why? What's up?" he asked, his voice tentative but curious.

"I have to go to an engagement party, because Chyna's dad is getting remarried. It's a long story, but I'm supposed to bring a boyfriend, and…I don't have one." She heard his breath of relief through the line, which spurred her forward. "Will you go with me?" she asked. Her stomach had started knotting all over again at the fact that she was actually asking him to do this for her.

"You want me be your boyfriend?" he asked skeptically. She was pretty sure he had never been asked that before.

"I want you to…go to the party as my boyfriend," she amended.

"Just to the party?" he asked egging her on.

"You don't have to. I just…uh…it's for Chyna. She's really beat up and she got roofied tonight."

"What? Is she okay?" he asked flipping out.

"Yeah. She's crashing right now, but I need to make this right for her."

"I'll get out of work and be at JFK as soon as I can Saturday," he said immediately.

"Oh! Thank you," she said honestly grateful that she wouldn't have to search for another guy to go with her.
"Hey Lexi…"
"Yeah?"
"It's really good to hear from you."
Lexi smiled to herself. "It's good to hear from you too."
"Even if you don't have everything together, I'm really glad you called."
Lexi couldn't help but think how glad she was too.

3

PRESENT

"You know I like Ramsey, right?" Chyna asked, sighing as she fell backwards onto her plush, king-sized bed. The comforter had recently been changed into a maroon and gold ensembles, with massive quantities of matching throw pillows of every size and shape imaginable covering the pillow top.

Lexi looked up from where she had been digging through her backpack and smiled. She knew exactly how Chyna felt about Ramsey. He was one of the few guys who had ever bypassed her appearance for her personality. Chyna found that type of behavior extremely appealing. If he made it a point not to be interested in her, then she could respect his devotion to Lexi. Chyna always had a weak spot for loyalty.

"Yeah, I know," Lexi told her reaching back into her bag and pulling out her laptop and power cord.

"Then you also know that I think you're an idiot," Chyna remarked staring up at her ceiling. Lexi could hear her sigh which only broadened her smile.

"Yeah, I know," she repeated popping the top on her laptop, pressing the power button, and waiting for the system to warm up.

Chyna shot up from her place on the bed and stared down at Lexi. A broad smile had formed on her face. Lexi knew that look meant only one thing. Chyna was up to something devious. Lexi tucked a strand of hair behind her ear and waited for Chyna to let loose her revelation.

"You know what?" Chyna asked.

"Nope."

"You could always just...*not* go."

"Wow, what a revelation," Lexi muttered sarcastically.

"Oh, come on," Chyna cried throwing herself back on the bed. "This is not good for you. I thought after everything that happened you wouldn't put yourself through this all over again."

"This isn't like Jack," Lexi said defensively.

No, this wasn't like Jack at all. Jack had taken over her world, and she had forced herself to push him out bit by bit. Ramsey had forced himself in her world bit by bit and filled a void she hadn't known existed. And she knew all too well what it felt like being with and without Jack. Ramsey was something altogether different. The emotions he elicited from her were foreign, and thus, incredibly vivid because they had never been tamed, harnessed, or numbed over years of self-torture.

So no, this was nothing like Jack.

"This is exactly like Jack," Chyna muttered under her breath.

Lexi closed her eyes. She didn't want to have this argument right now. Ramsey would be picking her up shortly and she didn't need those thoughts swirling around in her mind. By allowing him to visit, she was taking a huge leap of faith, one that she wasn't entirely comfortable with.

"Can we talk about something else?" Lexi pleaded, opening her eyes and fixing them on the computer screen in front of her. She pulled up a blank webpage and directed it to her inbox. A confirmation email was highlighted at the top of the screen with information about Ramsey's flight into JFK airport. If everything went alright, he would be landing in only twenty minutes giving her just enough time to mentally and physically prepare herself for their evening together.

"Sure," Chyna replied, her tone snarky. "How about the fact that you still haven't given me Mystery Man's name yet?"

Lexi gulped hard, a tentative smile spreading across her face as she looked up at Chyna. "Why are you so desperate to know?"

"Oh, I don't know. Maybe because you never hide anything from me. Maybe because I've never met him. Maybe because I have to wrestle information out of you. Do you want me to keep going?" Chyna asked arching an eyebrow. She flipped her feet to the other side of the bed, rested her elbows on the comforter, and leaned over to get a better look at Lexi's reaction.

"Well it's nothing, that's why it doesn't matter," Lexi stammered out under the intense scrutiny of Chyna's stare.

"Or maybe it's because it's a huge fucking deal and that's why you keep it a secret," she hypothesized, her green eyes taking in every movement that might tip her off to what was going on.

"It's not such a big deal," Lexi huffed returning her eyes to her computer to escape Chyna's fierce looks. She wasn't ready to tell anyone about what was going on with her Mystery Man yet. They had gone out a couple times before and, now, after the night they sex, but she refused to tell Chyna about it. She wasn't ready...not with Ramsey flying in to see her any minute.

"You're such a terrible liar."

"No, I'm not," she cried knowing that was a lie too. Chyna knew her too well though. She knew when something was up with her.

"Yeah, you really are. So who is he? Are you going out with him again? Has he called?" Chyna blabbered on asking questions Lexi had no intention of answering.

"I don't want to talk about him, alright?" Lexi asked shutting her computer with a bit more force than she anticipated.

"Ohhh," Chyna cooed, "someone is defensive."

Lexi took another deep breath. "Please stop. I really do not want to think about anything while I have this...thing with Ramsey tonight."

"Date is the opportune word, chica. Don't think you'll be getting away with not talking about this forever. After your...thing," she said mimicking Lexi's tone of voice, "I want details on Mystery Man. Please, please, please just give me a name," she begged.

"No can do," Lexi told her hopping up off the floor and wandering into Chyna's massive closet.

"You're so incorrigible," Chyna cried following behind her.

"Big words," Lexi said sarcastically her eyes widening and mouth opening in surprise.

"Don't be such a shit," she said smacking Lexi on her arm. "Just because I didn't go to college doesn't mean I wasn't smart enough to go."

"You don't have to tell me twice," Lexi said knowing full well that Chyna was brilliant and succeeded at anything she applied herself to. The only problem was getting her to apply herself. She preferred to live a luxurious life of leisure rather than work. Not that she blamed her.

"What's the latest endeavor?" Lexi asked, hoping to distract Chyna. She needed to keep the focus away from her life at the moment. She seemed to endlessly be discussing the different men in her life.

As Lexi perused Chyna's closet for something to wear that evening, Lexi's mind drifted over the experiences in the past seven years. Her memory landed on a green tourist bench. She could feel her face flushing at the image of her first time with Jack at the beach house. She licked her lips as her hand trailed over a tiny pair of skinny jeans. She knew she shouldn't risk letting her mind travel down memory lane, but sometimes it was so difficult.

Her memory was so vivid that sometimes it was as if she were reliving her past. The feel of his skin hot against her own, breathing in the salty air with rapid inhalations, his intense blue stare reflecting the ocean. She could feel him almost as if she were in the moment.

She shook her head and tried to focus on Chyna talking about the new thing that she was interested in at the moment. Her mind couldn't focus however, and suddenly she was swept back to a time when she was cuddled up in a familiar navy blue comforter. She could hear him whisper his affection for her and pull her closer.

She cleared her mind and blue eyes were replaced with green ones staring intently into hers on a balcony overlooking the Turner Field baseball stadium. The way he seemed to wash away the knowledge of what was going on that night. Her hair pulled high on her head and the light breeze on the back of her neck gave her goosebumps, or was it the way he was looking at her. Her breath hitched as his head tilted to meet her waiting lips.

She forcefully closed her eyes and willed her mind to stop picturing her past. Tonight was about new futures…another new future.

"Are you even listening?" Chyna whined pushing Lexi out of the way so she could get a closer look at her closet.

"Nope," Lexi said giggling and falling back into a plush cream chair.

"Hopeless," Chyna muttered flipping through her closet.

Just as Lexi was about to retort, Chyna's hand brushed against an article of clothing Lexi had never seen. "What was that?" she blubbered, shooting out of the chair, and reaching forward to latch on before the item disappeared into the depths of Chyna's closet.

Lexi unhooked the hanger from the metal rod it had been resting on. Her hand rubbed gently against the silky plum material. She smiled softly to herself and wondered how she had never seen Chyna wear this before. When she flipped the dress around to closer examine the front, Lexi got her answer. A black rectangular price tag still hung from the dress. Lexi gaped at the price. She didn't think she would ever get used to seeing price tags in the three, four, or even five digit range for one garment…especially not something to throw in the closet and never wear.

"You've never worn this?" Lexi asked her voice unable to believe it.

A sly smile crept up on her face at Lexi's reaction. "Do you like it?"

"Like it?" Lexi groaned. "I love it. How could you never wear this?"

"Because it doesn't belong to me," she said airily.

"Then what's it doing in your closet?" Lexi eyed her suspiciously.

"It belongs to you," Chyna told her, immediately putting her hands behind her back to keep Lexi from giving it back to her.

"Really?" Lexi asked pressing the material to her chest and looking at herself in the full-length mirror. Nearly dropping the dress, Lexi rushed forward and crushed Chyna with surprising force. "You're the best."

"You're not going to fight me on this?" Chyna asked skeptically.

"I can't believe you left the price tag on," Lexi scolded her, "but no, I'm going to keep it."

"Finally, you've come to your senses," Chyna teased.

A short while later Lexi was all zipped into the strapless dress. The deep plum color focused attention on the curves of her breasts and hips. Her brown hair had been tamed for the night into neat loose curls down her lower back. Her side-swept bangs fell into her eyes whenever she made too sudden of a movement, but the overall effect was seductive. Light makeup completed the look with a dark shimmer gloss coating her full lips.

The time and effort put in paid off when Ramsey's eyes lit up at the sight of her. Lexi knew him well enough to know that she could have showed up in a black trash bag, and he would have thought her beautiful. However, the shock and awe that followed her entrance proved that he fully approved of what he saw.

With a long hug, Ramsey escorted her to a waiting cab. They were dropped off at a restaurant that they had been to before and, as Lexi crossed the threshold she got a sick feeling of déjà vu. Her heart pumped wildly as they were seated at the same table, in the same place and probably ordered the same food. She wasn't sure what about the experience was making her body kick into over drive. Something had overtaken her body and paralyzed her in place. She realized that she had been staring forward into Ramsey's concerned face for a full minute without speaking…or really seeing.

"Are you alright?" he asked reaching across the small table and taking one of her clenched fists.

"Oh," she gasped taking in a huge gulp of fresh air. "I'm sorry. I spaced out."

He smiled knowing that she was lying. He could always tell. "Should we have gone somewhere else?" he asked intuitively.

"No, I love this place," she said visibly relaxing to his words. He hadn't done this on purpose. He wasn't trying to put her on edge. If anything, he had probably brought her here to make her comfortable, to keep her around the familiar. She was making something out of nothing.

Ramsey leaned forward his voice lowering compassionately. "You look like your dog just died," he said a smile spreading across his face.

Lexi giggled despite the depressing image that filled her mind. "I do not!"

"There that's better," he said congratulating himself as he leaned his back against the chair once more. "Your smile lights up the room."

Lexi smiled even bigger at the compliment. She had forgotten how much she had missed his presence in her life. A month's time wasn't all that long to be away from each other, but she had been attempting to block him from her life. Now, when she looked at him, everything came rushing back to her. Every second they had spent together, every laugh and smile, every tear and moment of pain. She coughed uncomfortably at the wave of emotions. She reached for the glass of wine placed before her and took a large gulp.

Yeah, alcohol was exactly what she needed.

"Woah there," he said seeing her discomfort, but knowing alcohol really wasn't the answer. "We haven't even gotten our food yet."

She took one last swallow and placed the glass back on the table giving him a falsely apologetic smile. She had taken too many trips down memory lane today leaving her heart exposed. It wasn't a feeling that she liked to accustom herself.

"I'm really glad you called. I wanted to so many times, but I knew you needed your time. I felt that if I stepped in too soon you'd just hate me even more. I'd understand if you did hate me more. I kind of hate me," he blabbered on.

Lexi smiled at his adorable habit of rambling whenever he was nervous. It was completely out of step with everything else in his personality, and thus, Lexi loved it even more. His apologies were long winded and sometimes completely incoherent. That was the way she knew that they were genuine.

"Can we not?" she asked quietly, hating reliving anymore of her past. Seeing him was enough self-induced pain that thinking about the other stuff was threatening to make her nauseous.

He looked up from his wine and into her wide-eyed expression. "Of course," he said, his eyes taking in her appearance. "There is something I wanted to talk to you about," he murmured.

She watched him divert his eyes from her face, and she looked at him suspiciously. She wasn't sure what this was about, but by the look on his face she was pretty sure she didn't want to know. "What about?" she asked cautiously, her curiosity getting the better of her.

"I…" he began.

"Oh *my* God, Ramsey Bridges," a girl squealed rushing up to their table completely uninvited.

Lexi looked the girl up and down and groaned in protest. She was gorgeous—tall but still rail thin with long flowing blonde hair and perfectly flawless skin. She could have been on a runway. Lexi tore her eyes from the girl and moved to Ramsey face. His cheeks flushed a light pink, and she could tell in his eyes that he wasn't happy about the interruption.

"Ashley," he acknowledged her standing to give her a hug. "What a pleasant surprise."

He said the words, but his mouth was strained around the edges. His body wasn't comfortable with the touch of another woman. Lexi knew he wanted to be far, far away from this moment in time. Though she was curious who this woman was, she was more satisfied with his discomfort.

She wasn't sure how he always found himself in this situation….oh wait, yes, she did.

"Holy cow, what are you doing in New York City?" she crowed, her Southern accent coming out thick with his recognition of her. Lexi figured she had to go through a lot of work to get rid of that.

"I'm actually here with my girlf…uh…," he stammered, breaking off his statement and glancing at Lexi. He cleared his throat awkwardly. "I'm visiting my friend, Lexi," he corrected gesturing in her direction.

Lexi smiled sweetly and extended her hand politely. "Ashley Turner," the girl replied shaking her hand meekly. "Pleasure to meet you."

"Likewise," Lexi said hoping she sounded sincere.

"Ashley went to private school with me," Ramsey informed Lexi filling in the gaps. Lexi raised her eyebrows once. She had bad luck with people that Ramsey had known for long periods of times. Hopefully, the girl would just disappear, but she wasn't that lucky.

"Mind if I interrupt your friendly dinner," Ashley asked snapping her fingers at a passing waiter and commanding him to bring her a chair. "My hubby can wait." She wagged her fingers at a handsome gentleman across the room who barely noticed her disappearance.

Lexi looked around at the restaurant and wondered how many people came here when they weren't on dates. The tension between her and Ramsey was palpable, and this girl needed to get a clue.

"Uh…actually, Ashley," Ramsey said scratching the back of his head awkwardly.

"Oh come on. I'll only be a minute. I haven't seen you in forever," she practically pleaded.

Ramsey looked at Lexi anxiously who stared back. They hadn't seen each other in almost a month and after everything they had gone through, they both knew that this interruption wasn't a good idea.

"Geez, I've never felt so unwelcome by a Bridges family member before. Aren't you supposed to bridge all my troubles or whatever?" Ashley asked expertly arching an eyebrow.

"By all means," Ramsey murmured, gesturing for her to take the seat that was offered to her. Lexi clenched her hands together under the table.

"So, tell me what's going on with Bekah?" Ashley gushed. Lexi involuntarily gagged at the mention of her name. She sputtered a bit and made it seem like a cough, but the look on Ramsey's face showed that she wasn't playing it off very well. "Oh dear, are you alright?" Ashley asked reaching out and touching Lexi's arm.

She cleared her throat once and tried to force a smile. "I'm *just* fine," she said shooting Ramsey a look that clearly stated—*change the subject.*

"She's doing fine," he murmured.

"Isn't she, like, getting married?" Ashley asked wide-eyed.

Lexi nearly lost it. She quickly stood from her seat scraping the chair back against the floor. "I...uh...need to use the restroom. Excuse me," she said throwing the napkin on the table and stalking out of the room.

Lexi wandered into the bathroom and waited for her anger to subside. She knew that she shouldn't have reacted so viscerally towards the subject, but she couldn't help it. She wasn't sure she would have been able to control herself if she had sat there any longer.

After a few minutes, she figured it would begin to look suspicious if she stayed away for much longer. Lexi peered around the bathroom door towards her table and pleasantly saw Ashley standing up and walking back towards her own table.

Lexi sighed and made her way across the room to Ramsey. Their eyes locked together as she sat down. She wasn't going to apologize for leaving, and he knew that she had every right to want to leave. Luckily, their food arrived, and they didn't have to fill the uncomfortable silence with anything but the scraping of silverware against glass.

Dinner ended without any additional complications. After an evening on Broadway, Lexi and Ramsey headed back to her apartment. She knew he had a hotel in the city somewhere, most likely the Plaza, but she was more comfortable with the idea of him coming to her place...at least for a little while.

Fumbling with the lock, Lexi finally pushed open the door to her apartment. Ramsey's arms were around her instantly holding her flush against him. He kicked the door closed with his foot and his mouth came down upon hers. He kissed her feverishly, hungrily as if the last month had been years. It had certainly felt like it. His hand crawled up silky material of her dress to cup her breast. He groaned into her mouth at the feel of her.

They heard someone clearing their throat behind them, and Lexi quickly backed away. She quickly adjusted her dress and ran her fingers across her wet lips. "Ray," Lexi murmured staring between Ramsey and her roommate. "I didn't know you were back in town."

Rachelle had been interning much of the summer at a Boston law firm. Lexi hadn't seen her since she had gotten back into town. "Ramsey," she said nodding her head in his direction but glaring nonetheless.

"Rachelle," he said smiling guiltily.

"Claire and Elizabeth are in town so we were all going to meet up," Rachelle told her. "I thought you'd be home and would want to come out with us."

"You're going out?" Lexi gaped at her anti-social, study-aholic, recluse of a roommate. They had lived together for three years, and Lexi could count the number of times they had all gone out on two hands. She was actually a little disappointed that she was going to miss it.

"Yeah, but I guess you're busy," she said eyeing Ramsey again. "I was heading out now anyway." Lexi watched Rachelle scamper out of the apartment as fast as she could get away.

Letting out the breath she was holding, Lexi wandered over to her couch and plopped down. All the interruptions were really starting to get old, first Ashley and then Ray. Would she ever be able to enjoy herself with Ramsey or would everything else always be looming over them?

That thought hurt her and all she wanted to do was push it away. She knew she was over analyzing. It was a common thing for her to do, but sometimes she couldn't keep her mind quiet. She threaded a piece of hair behind her ear several times before glancing up at Ramsey. "Well, are you going to sit down?"

He smiled and walked over to meet her. He grabbed her around the waist and pulled her into his lap. "You look tense," he murmured reaching up and tilting her head to meet his gaze.

"You know why," she said looking into the depths of his green eyes. They were a rich emerald green with gold specks shooting out from the center and a deep brown rim circling the iris.

"I know," he said his hand beginning to massage the back of her neck. "I want to make it better."

"I know, Ramsey," she said her eyes closing of their own accord as his expert hands moved from her neck to the knots in her shoulders and upper back. Her hand reached out and gripped his upper thigh as he worked out a particularly troublesome spot. She could feel him tense under her at the abrupt movement, but she didn't change her position.

His hands were so large when laid out flat against her back they covered the entire width of her body. Reacting to her touch, his hands moved from the massage and came around to the front of her body, rubbing her stomach. When they reached the curve of her breasts, Lexi's head dipped back on his shoulder. He took that as encouragement and moved to cover her once more. She tilted her head to the side and kissed his neck. A smile crossed her face as she felt his black pants tighten underneath her.

She groaned as his hands moved from her breasts to the hem of her dress and began working the muscles in her inner thighs. A pulsing began in her lower half, and the heat coming off her body only increased his growing desire for her.

Unable to continue, he effortlessly picked her up in his arms causing her to latch onto him. Carrying her into her room, he laid her down on the bed. He quickly untucked his white button up, and threw his black slacks to the ground—where they belonged. In only his black boxer briefs and half-unbuttoned white shirt, he continued his work on her thighs. As his hands dipped closer and closer to the most sensitive part of her body, her back arched with desire. His fingers brushed as lightly as he could allow against her thin black underwear causing her to buck against him.

He smiled knowingly and moved to her other leg. "Ramsey," she murmured opening her eyes and begging him with them to continue.

"Yes?" he questioned, acting all too oblivious.

She wouldn't say anymore. If he wanted to pleasure her into submission, she was perfectly okay with that for the time being. His head dipped down and kissed a trail up her leg across her now wet underwear and back up the other thigh. Her body was already very ready for him, and he knew her body all too well.

Her dress slipped up over her butt and revealed all of her tiny black thong. His hands moved up to her hips and pulled her farther down on the bed wanting to get a closer look. He pushed his body firmly against her, pressing all of his manhood, covered only by a thin layer of cotton, against her. She moaned loudly at the pressure of his dick against her and began to grind in circles. She could feel how ready he was for her, and it was almost unbearable to have the barriers of clothing between them.

His lips came down on top of her, and he passionately kissed the breath out of her. Her hands shot up and grabbed onto his short blonde hair, forcing them even closer together.

When they were together like this, she wasn't able to think properly. Even though she knew that she should be mad at him, and stay mad at him, her brain just wasn't putting two and two together. Her body was *very* happy to see him.

His hand moved between their bodies and began massaging her clit through the soft material, pushing her closer to the edge. She broke apart from his lips gasping for air. Biting down on her bottom lip, she lustfully looked up into his eyes giving him all the information he needed. He hopped off the bed and began swiftly unbuttoning the remaining buttons on his shirt. Lexi sat up and tried to find the stupid zipper on the side of her dress. She fumbled with the hook and eye on the top, but the zipper worked just fine.

As they were all but nude, the ring tone from a cell phone ripped through the apartment. Ramsey cursed and then looked up at Lexi apologetically. "Sorry, give me a second," he said looking for the source of the noise. He grabbed his pants that he had hastily tossed on the floor and dug out his cell phone.

Lexi's mouth opened in surprise that he would stop their exchange to *answer a cell phone*. Really? She couldn't believe this. It really *must* be important or she was seriously going to have a fit.

"Hello?" Ramsey asked after checking the caller ID.

"What?" he asked cursing under his breath at whatever he was hearing on the other line. "No. No, don't leave. Fuck. No. I'll take care of it."

There was a pause while someone on the other line spoke. Ramsey looked pissed—really pissed. His eyes were fiery. His fist clenched to his side as he listened to someone ramble on. "I said I'd fucking take care of it. Jesus Christ, just hold tight. I'll be there as soon as I can."

Ramsey hung up the phone and threw it down on the bedside table. He closed his eyes and his breathing was deep and heavy. Lexi couldn't believe he looked so utterly furious.

"Uh…what's up?" she asked cautiously.

"I have to…take care of some business," he muttered through clenched teeth.

"Right now?" she asked refastening the hook and eye in her and dress and closing the zipper.

"Unfortunately, yes," he said buttoning his shirt up and throwing his pants back on.

"You're serious?" she asked standing.

Ramsey stopped what he was doing and moved towards her. His hand came up and cupped her cheek. "If there was any way I could get out of it, I would."

"Well, where are you going?"

Ramsey sighed and looked back up at her. "I just have to take care of something."

"Is this about work?" she whispered into the silence that had followed his comment.

"No," he said shaking his head. "I wish."

"Can I come with you then?"

He was shaking his head before he even answered. "You're not going to want to do that."

"Why do you always have to be so fucking secretive? We were just about to fuck and now you're running off to somewhere you won't even tell me. Stop doing that," she yelled at him.

"Fine, come with me then," he growled stuffing his phone back in his pocket. "But we have to go now."

Ramsey flagged down a cab as soon as he reached the street and gave the guy an address. Lexi leaned back against the scratchy cab cushion and wondered where in the world he was taking her. The cab drove them clear across town and as the lights started fading into darkness. one sign in particular caught her eye. A bright, neon yellow sign above all others read— Erotica: Live Girls XXX.

Lexi's stomach dropped. "What the fuck are we doing?" she cried looking over at Ramsey in surprise mingled with anger. "I thought you said…"

"I said I had to take care of something. You insisted on going with me. I'm sorry, but this is where we're going," he murmured unhappy about the situation as well.

Lexi huffed noisily, crossing her arms over her chest. "I can't believe we stopped having sex for *this*." The look on Ramsey's face promised that it was only going to get worse before it got better.

The cab dropped them off in front of the entrance to the strip club. A burly man dressed in all black checked their identification before allowing them inside. A petite buxom blonde took Ramsey's card to pay for the cover, but after taking a look at the name handed it back to him and told him it was on the house.

"Go figure," Lexi murmured walking past the blonde who had sidled up to Ramsey.

"Excuse me," he told the woman pushing her arms back at her sides and rushing after Lexi.

"So what's the big emergency?" she asked, her eyes sweeping the dimly lit club filled with girls clad solely in g-strings or getting close to that point of nudity.

"Uh..." Ramsey began but was cut off by Lexi's squeal.

Lexi was lifted off her feet from behind and spun around in a circle twice. When she was set back down, she swiveled around quickly ready to assault whoever had hoisted her off the ground. "What the...?" she cried, her hand coming back. As her eyes began to adjust to the lighting, the face before her registered in her mind and her mouth dropped open in surprise. "Seth?" she questioned, wondering if perhaps she was seeing things.

"Lexi, baby," he crowed reaching forward and running his hands up down her sides of her body. She would have normally slapped him away, but she was in such a state of shock that she didn't even know what to do. She could tell he was severely intoxicated, and from the rush of women surrounding his approach of her, he had obviously wasted a good deal of money.

"Are you the present?" he slurred keeping his hands pressed to her hips.

"Am I what?" she asked her brows furrowing together.

"That's enough, Seth," Ramsey cut in knocking his hands off of Lexi.

As soon as she was free from Seth's grip, her eyes moved to the people standing behind him. "Hunter, Luke," she murmured barely loud enough for them to hear. She felt as if she were taking a trip back in time. When she had been in college, she had done everything with these guys and now they were here...in New York City...at a strip club.

Her eyes doubled in size as everything started to come together. "No," she muttered her vision losing focus.

She didn't deserve this.

This could *not* be happening to her.

Someone was speaking to her, but the words weren't processing correctly in her brain. Her stomach turned, and she thought she might be sick at any moment. Her hand reflexively came up to twine around a loose strand of hair and she pushed it behind her ear. Of all the things for her to insist on being in attendance, she never in a million years would have guessed that *this* would be the place she would end up.

"Lexi, are you alright?" Ramsey asked putting a comforting hand on her shoulder.

"Don't touch me," she spat venomously, shrugging his hand off her shoulder. She didn't care if this wasn't his fault. She needed someone else to blame other than herself for this, and he was the easiest target.

"Come on, don't be like that," he pleaded.

"You brought me *here*!" she cried louder than she had intended. Seth, Luke and Hunter, despite their inebriation turned to look at her along with a few additional patrons and rather unhappy strippers. "So take care of the big emergency!"

"Lexi, you're gonna need to chill out," Seth said motioning drunkenly around him. "We're celebrating. Let's do a shot, honey."

"Do I look like I want to celebrate, Seth?" she growled.

"You look fucking hot."

Lexi rolled her eyes. She should have known better than to think she'd get a straight answer from Seth. He had always been the one to goof off. Ever since she had known him he had been the one who made everything a joke. Nothing should change now…seven years later.

"Come on, Lexi," Hunter pleaded his eyes glazed over. "You've gotta celebrate with us."

"Yeah," Luke agreed.

"I think not."

"But it's Jack's bachelor party," Seth told her smiling as if he'd just told her the best news of her life…instead of the worst.

4

SEPTEMBER ELEVEN MONTHS EARLIER

The accumulated wealth in the sea of people surrounding Lexi was astounding. Expensive tuxedos, silk formal dresses, and hundreds of thousands of dollars worth of diamonds were twirling around the magnificent domed ballroom.

She should have expected something like this. In fact, Chyna had warned Lexi that her father took extravagance to a new level. She had even warned her that it might be worse than normal, because it was such a huge event for her father.

Lexi was dressed the part in a floor-length navy dress with tiny spaghetti straps that flowed out behind her as she walked. Her back was almost completely exposed and her long, dark hair fell down in ringlets to meet the material. Even in a pair of Chyna's Manolo heels, she was a head shorter than the majority of people in attendance. This was due in large part to the number of fashion models circulating the premises.

"You look nervous," someone said coming up behind her and placing a comforting hand on her shoulder.

Lexi twirled around, a little jumpier than she had thought she was, and stared up into the handsome face. "Adam!" she cried surprising him by throwing an arm around his neck and pulling him into a hug.

"Hey, woah, calm down," he said extracting her arms from around him and taking a step back. "I can't play a convincing boyfriend, if you've got your hands all over me."

A blush crept up on her cheeks, but she got over her embarrassment at the easy smile on his face. "Sorry to pull you into this whole thing," she told him.

"Hey, glad I could help," he said sliding one hand into the front pocket of his tux.

Chyna sure did get lucky with her savior that night. When he had first helped her out, Lexi hadn't even noticed how attractive he was. Now that he was standing in front of her all cleaned up, it was hard to ignore the way his dark brown eyes seemed to light up and his dark brown hair curled lightly at the edges. He was really tall, but then again everyone was tall in relation to Lexi.

Most of all she liked how put together he appeared. He had the same air that he had while being in Chyna's apartment – cool and confident. Lexi could admit that it was endearing.

"You're more than helping," she finally muttered looking out across the ballroom. "And anyway, do I really look nervous?"

He laughed at the nervous face she flashed his way and nodded. "Just calm down," he said offering her his arm. She placed her hand gingerly on his black suit and allowed him to escort her to the refreshments table.

"Why are you so calm? Did you see who walked by?" she asked trying to keep from staring at the platinum blonde celebrity who had passed them.

He handed her a glass of red wine as he took his own glass of scotch on the rocks. "They're just people. You can't forget that fact. As soon as you do, you get that look on your face," he said pointing at Lexi's star struck expression. He took a swig of his drink and smiled as she immediately closed her mouth.

"They're just people. Right," she muttered following his lead and indulging in the alcohol presented to her. She needed to loosen up a bit.

Lexi still couldn't believe Adam had agreed to play Chyna's boyfriend. They had known each other less than a week and had only hung out twice, outside of the unusual circumstances that surrounded her drugging. After Chyna had found out what he had done for her, she had insisted on doing anything she could to thank him. Just like that night, he had refused any payment whatsoever for his help. He swore that he would have done it for anyone if they had been in that situation.

Chyna hadn't been able to let it go though. She had coaxed him into going out to dinner with her, and they had seemed to hit it off really well. She had then invited him to come to her father's engagement party. Chyna had neglected to inform him that he was doing her a huge favor, and Lexi accidentally spilled the beans by asking him how he felt about being a fake boyfriend for the night. He had come around to their side, but now they owed him double.

"Where's your faux boyfriend anyway?" Adam asked scanning the room.

Lexi sighed, wondering that same thing. After her call of desperation, Lexi had spoken to Ramsey relatively frequently. She had admitted to him that she was terrified of relationships after having such a rocky past, and they had agreed on some boundaries before his arrival. She wanted to make sure that she knew what she was getting herself into before he showed up and, no doubt, swept her off her feet.

This arrangement had somehow ended up with him meeting her at the party. Now she was just anxious to see him in person. It had been so long since she had left him all alone on the tarmac with just enough hope to keep him interested. She hadn't been sure that she would ever call him. Even though she did have some measured interest in him, he wasn't Jack.

The past month without him had been difficult. Before she had always wondered if he was going to show up in her life again, but now she knew that he wasn't going to be around. He wasn't going to find her. She felt like a huge hole was left in the center of her chest that he used to occupy. Sure, she had been strong when dismissing him, but the reality of letting him go was a much different story.

"I'm actually not certain where he is," Lexi said pulling her phone out from the tiny black clutch she was carrying with her. "Have you seen your faux girlfriend yet?"

"Yeah, she found me right when I got here. She said she needed to take care of some things," Adam said vaguely, "but that she'd find me later."

"Well, this is going to be a fun night," she murmured flipping open her phone and seeing no new calls or texts. She knew his flight had been delayed in Atlanta due to weather conditions, but she hadn't heard from him since then and had assumed everything was alright. She figured she would have at least heard from him by now.

"Looks like it's just me and you," Lexi said downing the rest of her wine in one big gulp.

"Where's your date?" Adam asked concerned.

"His flight was delayed so I'm guessing he's stuck somewhere," she told him trying to keep the disappointment out of her voice.

"He'll turn up," Adam said placing his hand reassuringly on her shoulder. Lexi smiled up into his comforting brown eyes.

"Well isn't this sweet," Chyna cooed coming up from behind them. Adam immediately dropped his hand to his side glancing away from Lexi.

"There you are," he said a genuine smile crossing his face. "Get everything taken care of?"

"As much as could be done about the situation," Chyna announced slurring her words slightly. She took a step forward to steady herself but managed to almost fall into Adam. He caught her easily and steadied her against him.

"Are you drunk?" Lexi asked glancing around to make sure no one was paying them any attention.

"I just had a bottle of wine. It's no big deal," Chyna said falling into a fit of giggles.

"Fuck," Lexi cursed under her breath, wondering how they were going to be able to handle this catastrophe when Chyna could barely even stand up straight.

"I'll take this," Adam said snatching the glass of wine out of her hand and handing it off to a passing waiter. Chyna stuck her bottom lip out and leaned her head back against his shoulder.

"Oh stop pouting," Lexi grumbled.

"I'm not that drunk," Chyna said standing tall and smiling brightly. If Lexi didn't know her so well, she wouldn't have thought her drunk. But knowing the kind of impression she needed to make tonight made Lexi nervous. Chyna's eyes were glassy and she was a bit wobbly on her feet.

"Let's just hope your dad doesn't notice."

"Oh, fuck him," she muttered, "him and his new trophy wife."

"Chyna, shut up," Lexi hissed latching onto her arm and pulling her and Adam away from any potential eavesdroppers. "You know what's on the line. Pull it together!" Lexi snapped at her.

She needed to show the world that Chyna Van der Wal held her head high under all circumstances…even when she was breaking inside.

"You're right. Sorry," Chyna mumbled covering her eyes with one hand. She inhaled deeply shaking her head side to side. "It's just so hard."

"I know, but it's one night," Lexi reminded her.

Chyna eyes were rimmed with unshed tears when they next glanced into Lexi's. "No, I'm sure I'll be forced into similar situations for the rest of eternity." Chyna's features hardened at the admission, and she raised her chin. "Well, I don't need him. Let's get this over with."

At that moment, a bell dinged somewhere in the ballroom. The guests took that as their cue and began shuffling to their assigned seats. Lexi followed Chyna and Adam to their table close to the center of the room. She stared wistfully at the empty seat next to her before sitting and checking her phone one more time to see if there was any update, but without any luck.

Another bell dinged and the room began to fall silent. Lexi looked at Chyna in disbelief. Chyna just rolled her eyes in response.

As dramatic as Lexi could have imagined, Chyna's father walked into the room through the grand double doors with his future bride at his side. Lexi had to admit the woman was beautiful. She was only a few inches shorter than Richard with long, flowing, blonde hair that could have been in commercials. The princess cut dress showed off her large chest and teeny tiny waistline. The massive diamond twinkling on her left hand was evident all the way across the room.

The woman was about as far from Chyna and her mother as anyone in this world could get. Where Chyna was dark, tanned, and exotic this woman was light, pale, and comely.

Likely the most disturbing part about the entire situation was her utter youth. She couldn't have been a day over thirty, and that was really hitting high. She had a perfectly flawless appearance and not from botox and countless hours of plastic surgery, but from the fact that she was young enough to be her sister.

Richard made a quick speech thanking everyone in attendance for coming out to his "little" get together to celebrate his beautiful bride-to-be. Lexi about gagged through half of the speech as he made a ridiculous spectacle of cooing at his fiancé repeatedly. Lexi had no idea how Chyna was able to sit through this, but she managed. The couple took their seats at the center of the room, and as another bell sounded, waiters appeared from all sides of the room with dinner for the evening.

"That was interesting," Lexi murmured to Chyna.

"I don't want to talk about it," Chyna said requesting another glass of wine from a passing server.

"Is that really smart?" Lexi asked concerned.

"I don't give a fuck. Why did he have to put me through this?"

"I don't know," Lexi said shrugging uncomfortably. "I just want you to make it through. He doesn't matter. Can we do this together?"

"Fine," Chyna said crossing her arms and waiting for their food to arrive. She tapped her toe anxiously under the table, but a smile broke out across her face as she glanced across the room. "Hey, stop checking your phone," Chyna commanded. Lexi's head snapped up. "Look straight ahead."

Lexi mouth curved up in a smile as Ramsey strode confidently across the ballroom floor. Eyes followed him as he made his way towards Lexi, but he didn't seem to notice any of them as his green eyes found her brown ones in the crowd. She licked her lips and butterflies took over her stomach. She hadn't seen him in a month, and damn did he look good. She had forgotten how strong and classically handsome his features were. The Armani suit that adorned his body had obviously been tailored specially for him, and Lexi could surely admit that it was worth every penny. His body looked incredible.

When he finally reached her, he bent down and lightly kissed the top of her head. A wave of peppermint filled her nostrils, and she shivered at the memories that scent filled her mind with. "Sorry I'm late," he said not taking his eyes from her face. He yanked the chair out from the table and sat down hardly acknowledging the rest of the room. His hand reflexively came out and fingered a strand of her loose, even curls. "It's shorter."

Lexi bit her lip to keep from pushing a chunk of it behind her ear. "Yeah. Uh, I just trimmed it," she was surprised he noticed. She had only cut off the dead ends.

"Well either way, you look gorgeous," he said reaching forward and capturing her lips in a soft kiss.

Lexi was surprised by his boldness. After turning him down and then not seeing or speaking to him in a month, he was rather forward with his affections. "Thank you," she muttered pulling back her voice breathy. She wasn't certain why she was so nervous. She had never been nervous around him before. In fact, she typically was pretty forward and rude in his presence. She didn't give into his easy charm and he had seemed to like her more for that. Perhaps, since it had been under different circumstances and her mind had been so focused elsewhere, she hadn't even realized what she felt for Ramsey. She still wasn't sure and that made her more nervous than she would have been.

"Am I playing the boyfriend role well enough?" he asked still staring longingly into her eyes.

Her heart stopped and then sank. He was acting. Of course that would make sense. She had put him up to this role. She had set up the boundaries. "Uh...yeah," she said turning from his powerful gaze. "Where were you?"

"I told you my flight was delayed."

"That was hours ago. Why didn't you call or text?" Lexi asked hating that she sounded like the overbearing girlfriend, but she really had been worried. At least if they were acting, everyone would believe her role.

Ramsey dug into his pocket and pulled out a black iPhone. "The damn thing died mid-flight and we were circling JFK for about an hour. I had no way to get a hold of you. I'm sorry," he said reaching out and grabbing her hand under the table. "I got here as soon as I could."

"I'm glad you made it safe," she said forgiving his lateness easily. She was still too concerned about his acting abilities to care.

Suddenly Ramsey seemed to notice that everyone had been watching them and turned to face the table. "How's it going?" he asked smiling like the confident heir to an empire that he was. "Pleasure to meet you all. I'm Ramsey Bridges."

Everyone shared their name with him, but one particular couple seemed fascinated by his name and began speaking in hushed whispers. Lexi could only imagine what they were saying.

"Hey man, I'm Adam," he said shaking hands with Ramsey across the table.

"Nice to meet you," Ramsey reciprocated squeezing a bit harder. "How do you know this bunch?"

"I'm here with Chyna," he said placing his arm across the back of Chyna's chair.

"Nice," Ramsey said with an easy-going smile.

Chyna dug into the salad that had been placed before her. She looked around the table, noticed everyone else's food, and nearly dropped her fork. "What are you eating?"

Lexi glanced down at her plate which was filled with a zesty, grilled, lemon-pepper chicken breast with garlic asparagus and a tiny helping of mashed potatoes. "Chicken?" she muttered, confused by the question.

"Right. It looks incredible. Why the fuck do I have a salad?" she asked seeing that everyone else around them had either chicken or steak placed before them.

"Uh...it was probably a mistake," Lexi reasoned. This didn't look good.

"A mistake?" Chyna asked looking around at the rest of the ballroom. "Is *anyone* else eating a salad?"

Lexi bit her lip as her eyes shifted around the rest of the room and realized, in fact, that no one else had a salad placed before them. "Uh..."

"Is he trying to say I'm fat?" Chyna squeaked out in horror.

"He's trying to get a rise out of you," Ramsey informed her. "If you give into him, then he's won."

"And how would you know?" Chyna spat out. She was too angry to care who she was speaking to and in what tone of voice.

"Let's just say I have a lot of experience dealing with father figures who want to control everything and everyone. The first tactic employed is degradation," he said taking a sip of the water in front of him. "If he can make you feel like you are less than you are, he thinks he can have more power, more control over you."

Chyna huffed not wanting to give into his good reason. Lexi could tell she was fuming, but she was trying to hold it in. Ramsey's advice was sound, and she wanted to take it, but that didn't make it any easier. Chyna murmured something incoherent into her salad, but finished the rest of the meal without complaint.

Dinner ended without another hitch. As plates were cleared away, music filled the ballroom and dancing ensued. Chyna looked as if she might combust with the anticipation of meeting her soon-to-be step-mom. A line had formed before them as hundreds of introductions were made.

"Perhaps we should wait," Ramsey suggested standing, and holding his hand out. "May I have this dance?" he requested formally.

Lexi placed her hand in his and let him escort her onto the floor. Chyna and Adam followed them and they twirled around in circles to the jazz music playing through the speakers. Soon enough they were surrounded by other couples happily dancing to the music.

Lexi rested her head against Ramsey chest letting her eyes close as they swayed back and forth as a slow song came on. "I really am sorry that I was late," he whispered stroking her lower back. "I wouldn't have missed this for anything."

"It's fine. It wasn't your fault," she reassured him breathing in his minty freshness.

Ramsey's hand came up and tilted her chin up to look into his eyes. "Thank you."

Lexi raised her eyebrows in confusion. "For what?"

"Letting me be here," he said capturing another gentle kiss from her.

Lexi had to do everything in her strength not to pull his face back down towards her and cover his mouth with her own. Her body was being very needy in that moment. All she wanted to do was ditch this place and go back to her apartment.

But she knew that she couldn't do that...even if she wanted to.

She had to give herself time. She knew Ramsey could be so much more if she let herself feel again. That's why they had set up boundaries. So that he knew before hand that she wanted to take things slow, because she wasn't usually all that clear when overcome with sexual desire.

"I have to go meet her," Chyna said breaking up their intense moment and sidling up next to Lexi. Adam was at her side and seemed to look between Ramsey and Lexi with idle curiosity.

"We'll go with you," Lexi said using this as an excuse to step out of the physical tension that had formed between her and Ramsey. Ramsey licked his lips before finally breaking his gaze from Lexi's face and following the rest of them towards Chyna's father.

"Chyna," Richard acknowledged his daughter. His eyes traveled from her to the rest of the group, resting on Ramsey for a second longer than the rest, and then returned to Chyna.

"Dad," she muttered. "You remember my friend, Alexa?"

"Of course," he said smiling as if he hadn't ogled her like a prized stallion and insulted her without another word last she had seen him.

"This is my boyfriend," Chyna almost choked on the word, "Adam Preston and Alexa's boyfriend, Ramsey Bridges."

Richard sidestepped Adam completely and turned to face Ramsey. "Bridges, you say?"

"Yes, sir," Ramsey told him shaking his hand firmly.

"I thought I recognized you. Great man, your father. You're the spitting image of him too. Great things come from your family," he told him. Chyna could see the look in her father's eye. He didn't even have to say anything to her, but she could tell he was wondering why she hadn't come with a man like Ramsey Bridges.

"Thank you, sir," he said through gritted teeth. Lexi would have laughed in any other scenario knowing how Ramsey acted towards his father and how he felt about the business.

"Next time you see him, let him know Richard Van der Wal says hello."

"Of course, sir. I'll make sure to do that," Ramsey said stepping back to open the conversation up to the rest of the group.

Richard smiled, pleased with at least some of the choices of the group. Lexi guessed that he had been expecting some nobodies to give him more leverage. Adam didn't exactly carry the prestige that the Bridges name carried but he was a nice guy. Lexi didn't actually know what he did or if he had any money.

"I'm sure you're all very anxious to meet my darling," Richard said turning around to smile at his fiancé. "Victoria, this is my daughter, Chyna."

The two came face to face, dark meeting light for the first time. Chyna swallowed a lump in her throat. "So nice to meet you," Chyna whispered as she pulled back slightly.

Victoria smiled slyly. "You too. I'm sure. You look different than Richard described you though dear," she said eyeing Chyna up and down. "Wasn't your mother a model?" she asked arching an eyebrow up.

Chyna's mouth dropped open slightly at the insult. Her eyes widened ever so slightly. She glanced at the people surrounding her. "She *is* a model, actually."

"Really? At her age?" Victoria asked astounded.

Chyna forced a fake smile. "She's actually in Milan right now prepping for a show."

"Well, isn't that wonderful. Does she have the same problem with alcohol giving her dark circles under her eyes?"

"You don't have circles under your eyes," Chyna said in confusion.

"No, but you do," Victoria said smiling sweetly. She turned to face Richard who was talking to a French couple about their American tour. "Richard, dear," Victoria called not giving Chyna time to respond.

"Yes, my love?" he asked, excusing himself from the couple and coming to snuggle up against Victoria's neck.

"Can we go dance? I've been standing here far too long," she pouted.

"Of course," he said escorting her onto the floor as he brushed past his daughter without another word.

Chyna twirled around and stared at them in complete shock and awe. "What a vile creature!" she cried her mouth still hanging open from her encounter.

"Yeah, she's a real bitch," Adam agreed.

"I thought you handled that well though," Ramsey acknowledged Chyna.

"I can't believe she said those things, and right in front of your dad," Lexi said.

"He doesn't care. Let's get the fuck out of here," Chyna said making a beeline for the exit. Lexi, Ramsey, and Adam trailed behind her. Lexi was amazed that Chyna didn't even look back. Maybe she was just too drunk. They descended the final flight of stairs that led to the city street, and Chyna's driver pulled up in front of the building almost instantly. "You guys need a ride?" Chyna asked reaching out for Adam.

Lexi glanced up at Ramsey. He smiled and answered, "No, we'll take a cab."

"Let me know if you need me," Lexi said hugging Chyna good bye. "I'm sorry about everything that happened."

"Don't worry about it. Not your fault. My dad is stupid for thinking that twit wants him for anything more than his money," Chyna told her.

"I know, but still—let me know," Lexi told her. Chyna nodded and then dove into the car. Adam shook Ramsey's hand one more time, smiled at Lexi, and then followed Chyna.

"So," Lexi began staring up into Ramsey handsome face. "My place?"

They hailed a cab to Lexi's apartment, and soon were both comfortably relaxing in her bed. Lexi smiled up in Ramsey's handsome face feeling incredibly content with the way things were going. They had put on a movie for background noise as they talked about inconsequential aspects of each other's lives. Lexi informed him that she was a gymnast while he confessed he had played soccer and football in high school, but when he had gone off to college he'd really gotten into lacrosse. They discussed their love for the ocean and Ramsey promised to take her sailing. The stories were endless and as Lexi was beginning to fall asleep wrapped in his arms, he brought up one more topic.

"So, what ever happened with you in Atlanta?" he whispered into the silence.

Lexi scrunched her feet up underneath her and wrapped her arms around her knees effectively cutting him off from her. She closed her eyes and tried not to think about Jack. Her breathing hitched and she bit down on her lip hard enough to keep her mind occupied with the pain. "Uh…I just had to get away," she finally muttered.

He scooted closer to her on the bed and wrapped an arm around her shoulders. "Hey, I'm not trying to pry. I'm just curious."

"Well, can we not talk about this?" she asked looking up at him with a fearful expression across her face. She had no idea what would happen if she started talking about Jack at that moment. She might end up blurting out what had actually happened, and with everything in such a delicate position in her life—both Ramsey and her emotional state of being—she wasn't sure she could handle it. He might turn and run in the opposite direction if he knew. That would be the logical thing to do.

"Yeah, sure, if that's what you want," he agreed. "I don't want to see you hurt like that ever again."

"Maybe another time," she told him relaxing some into his body. She was so afraid to talk to Ramsey about relationships in the event that he would in turn ask her similar questions. But she was so curious about his past. Even though she had just refused to talk to him about what had happened in Atlanta, she couldn't keep herself from asking, "Have you ever been in love?"

Ramsey stiffened at the question his entire body going rigid. Lexi glanced up into his eyes which had hardened. His jaw was set tight; his breathing controlled and even, as if he was thinking about each inhalation. Lexi had no idea that simple question would have elicited such a reaction, but she immediately regretted the decision to ask.

"Uh, sorry," Lexi said trying to do damage control. "I guess it's a sore subject."

He breathed out heavily and turned to face her. His features had returned to their normal softness. "No, I'm sorry. I didn't mean to flip out. You just caught me off guard."

"Oh. Sorry. Really, I didn't mean to pry."

"No need to apologize," he said waving off her apology. "I should have just told you—I've never been in love."

Lexi's eyes widened in surprise. That certainly was not what she had expected. "What? Really? Haven't you ever had a girlfriend?"

"Not in the real sense of the word."

"*Never?*" she asked in disbelief.

"I've...dated," he said that word carefully, "a lot. I've just never had anyone hold my interest."

How could someone have gone through their entire life without a girlfriend...without ever being in love? She wasn't exactly good with relationships, well she was terrible, but she had been in love. Tragically in love, but still there was always that cliché statement—to love and lost is better than to never have loved at all.

She was reminded of Bekah's comment to her about Ramsey being a player. She didn't know how to take that now that she knew what kind of person Bekah really was. On the other hand, hadn't he just confirmed his player status?

And if nothing ever held his attention, why was he still after her? Was it because she denied him what he wanted?

"Wow," she managed. "That's...seriously depressing."

Ramsey laughed aloud. "It's been kind of lonely if that's what you mean," he said pulling her into him.

"But you're so attractive."

He laughed again heartier this time. "Thank you. I feel as if that is a contributing factor in why I have never found someone to hold my interest. I've heard," he told her sliding his hand into her hair and beginning to massage her head and down to her neck, "that most women are interested in my appearance. This makes it rather difficult to find anyone who wants more than that, or if they do, they want my money."

"Uh huh," Lexi said closing her eyes as his worked his way down to her shoulder blades.

"You never seemed interested in either."

"I'm interested in your looks," she murmured cracking a smile.

"Oh really?" he asked kneading the knots out of her back.

"God, that feels good," Lexi huskily said pushing her body back against his. She was trying to suppress her physical desire for him, but the way his hands were moving made that more and more difficult.

Ramsey groaned at the feel of her. "Yes, yes it does."

"Oh," Lexi said realizing that she had effectively pressed herself flush against him and that a simple massage was beginning to turn into much more if she didn't stop herself.

Ramsey turned her body around and stared into her big brown eyes. His eyes drifted lower landing on her lips. He smiled as she did the same thing. Coming forward his lips pressed firmly against hers. His tongue darted out opening her mouth and massaging her tongue with his. She groaned from deep in her throat. Her hands came up and pushed up into his blonde hair egging him on. His arms wrapped around her waist pulling her closer.

Just as Lexi was about to scramble to strip his clothes off, he pulled back from her. "As much as I want to continue," he said his eyes smoldering with desire. "I know we should take this slow."

Lexi's bottom lip came out to pout involuntarily. Even though she knew that this was a bad idea that didn't mean she wanted to stop. He came forward and kissed her bottom lip. "We'll have plenty of time for the other stuff if I have anything to say about it," he said encouragingly.

After everything he had just told her about himself, could she really believe that he would stick this out? She presumed that as long as he didn't get what he wanted, then he would be around. But then she didn't understand why he would wait it out. Perhaps, there was more to him than she even knew. She really wanted to figure out the mystery behind Ramsey…but she wanted to do that without revealing her jaded love story.

She sighed and lay back against the bed. He wrapped his arms around her holding her close. At least in this moment, they could be content together with their secrets.

5

PRESENT

"I think I gathered that. Thanks, Seth," Lexi said rolling her eyes at the proclamation that this was Jack's bachelor party.

She felt like a complete idiot. She knew she should have listened to Ramsey when he said that she didn't want to be involved. She hadn't been able to stop herself though.

After such an abrupt interruption, she just needed to know what was going on. She didn't want any more secrets. Granted, he should have told her what was going on. It wasn't fair to spring Jack's bachelor party on her.

What was Jack doing in New York anyway?

Of all the places to have a bachelor party! Honestly!

She had heard the stories of Seth's big weekend in Las Vegas, and heard things that no girl should ever hear. And now Jack had brought his bachelor party here, to her front door. It didn't make any sense.

He had lived here awhile himself, so there was really no point in seeing the sights. He'd already done all of that. He had some friends left in the city besides Lexi, but as far as she knew his old roommate, Stella, at least, had left. That, thankfully, ruled out that possibility.

Lexi's vision was swimming as these thoughts filled her head. She didn't know why Jack had decided to come to New York. After their history, this city had to hold too many memories for him. He had been with Lexi here. He had screwed up everything with Lexi here, in this city. He had to know Lexi was in New York. And with his rapidly approaching marriage, she wouldn't think he would want to be reminded of all these emotions. Lexi had always been the masochist of the relationship, not Jack.

"So, are you going to celebrate with us?" Seth asked, swinging his arm across Lexi's shoulders, inexplicitly keeping her from falling backwards into a rather inviting black chair. She just wanted to sleep away the rest of the evening. Her stomach was in knots and she didn't know which way to move to clear away the mist that fell over her mind at the knowledge that Jack was here in this city…in this establishment.

"No, we're not here for that," Ramsey said glaring at Seth's hand making its way towards Lexi's breast. "Tell me the whole story this time. I need to know who I need to talk to."

Lexi snapped out of her trance as Seth's hand completely cupped her breast. She smacked his hand and he released her. His drunken brain must have processed that she wasn't a stripper…or it was just Seth.

"Yeah, Seth, what the fuck is going on?" Lexi asked shrugging his arm off her shoulder and taking a step away. She didn't want him to think about touching her like that again. She didn't care how drunk he was. "Why did you drag us out here?"

"Well, I didn't know you were going to be with her or I would have called sooner," he told Ramsey as he turned to face Lexi. He moved closer placing his hands on her hips. He began to sway them from side to side like a middle school couple at their first dance.

"Cut it out," Lexi said smacking his hands away as they came dangerously close to crossing the line. Seth dropped his hands and stumbled backwards a step.

"Yeah, you said Jack's missing and everything was stolen?" Ramsey prompted leaning towards Seth. He towered over Seth as he demanded answers to his questions.

"Hunter. Luke," Seth called turning from Ramsey's determined gaze. "Did I tell him Jack was missing?"

Ramsey stepped forward, grabbed a fistful of Seth's shirt in each hand, and yanked him towards him. "Give me a straight answer. Now," he growled. His demeanor had completely shifted. The anger that was radiating from his body was almost palpable. His blind rage at the situation was taking over his body, and it was pretty obvious that if Seth stepped over the line Ramsey would *not* be happy. Eyes found them from around the room as it dawned on everyone that a fight was about to break out.

Lexi noticed the bouncer's general shift of attention towards their group. A few even began taking a few steps towards them. She could tell they were still deciding if something was going to go down or not. Neither of the guys were touching the women, but still Ramsey and Seth were both big guys. She was sure the bouncers didn't want to have to deal with unruly clients especially not ones who had been funneling money into the place all night.

"Ramsey," Lexi murmured placing her hand lightly on his bulging bicep, "people are staring at us. You need to be careful."

"I don't need to be careful here," Ramsey said never taking his eyes from Seth.

"I know, but really, just back off. He's drunk and an idiot," she said trying to calm him down. The last thing she wanted was trouble.

"Don't make me ask you again," Ramsey told Seth ignoring Lexi's comments. His eyes narrowed at Seth who had finally given his full attention to the gravity of the situation. "If Jack is missing, I have to *deal* with it. I can't stand around and let you drunk frat boys continue to drink yourselves silly when something serious happened. So, answer my damn questions."

"We were never in a frat," Seth managed his voice shaky as his brain tried to catch up with what was happening. Lexi could see a glimmer of laughter in his eyes, and wasn't sure she liked that look.

"Seth," she murmured softly at his ridiculous response.

"Just back off man and I'll tell you," he said shifting his eyes from Lexi back to Ramsey. With that look she saw that he had finally caught up to what was going on. Ramsey was threatening him.

She could tell that at that realization Seth was kind of scared of Ramsey. She would have never guessed that someone as cool and collected as Seth was scared of anyone. She was so accustomed to his flirtatious, overly-confident outwards appearance that the look of terror in his eyes really threw her off.

She knew Ramsey was a tall and really, *really* well built. Then again she also knew that deep down that bulk didn't characterize him. His personality never fit him being this kind of guy. She always found it strange when he played the tough guy. Even that night nearly a year ago when he had walked into Jack's apartment and threatened his life, she had never thought of him as scary...as if he might actually follow through with it.

He was, as a general rule, naturally calm and laid back. When he was with her, he always tried to be the most comforting person possible. He was cute, funny, and charming. He could string words together like a poet one minute and ramble like a nervous fool the next. She knew he wasn't this guy that he was putting on the act to be. Thus, it was too strange to see the fear reflected in Seth's eyes. Ramsey would never hurt him, right?

"Don't play games with me," Ramsey said releasing his shirt and pushing him backwards.

Seth smoothed out the wrinkles in his black button-up. "Chill out. Geez."

"I'll chill out when I get a straight answer from you. You called me in a panic, made me leave everything I was doing." His eyes shot to Lexi's for a brief moment. "I want to know what is going on now, Seth."

"Wait, what was that look?" he asked pointing between Lexi and Ramsey. A slow smile crept up onto his face and instantly turned into Seth's characteristic smirk. "Was something going on between you two? *Is* something going on between you two?"

Lexi's face instantly turned beet red. She couldn't help herself. She hadn't intended to go that far with Ramsey, not that it should matter to Seth one way or the other, but she still felt kind of silly. After all, they had been about to have sex when they were interrupted with Seth's stupid phone call. She could feel the warmth of her skin heating her face and her heart raced at the thought of having sex with Ramsey. She knew her mind shouldn't wander there while she was standing before Seth, but she couldn't help it. And she was very thankful that the room was dark, and Seth couldn't tell how bad she was blushing. She would have certainly given herself away.

"Stop changing the subject," Ramsey said pointedly changing the subject.

"I'm not," Seth interjected smoothly. "I just know that look. I know it so well that I could have picked it out anywhere."

"What does it matter, Seth?" Lexi squeaked out.

"I can tell what's been going on. You guys were together all night when you were supposed to be here with the guys, right?"

"Seth, it doesn't matter. God," Lexi muttered, shoving a piece of hair behind her ear. She didn't know what Seth was getting at, and it was really annoying to have him badger them about their relationship. She didn't want to have this conversation at all, let alone with a drunk Seth. He was one of the most vulgar people she knew, and if he got talking about sex, if he thought for one moment that they had been about to have sex, the conversation would be endless.

"Oh, but it does matter," he said contrarily.

"It really doesn't matter," Ramsey agreed with Lexi. "Just tell me what happened here," he said exasperated and clearly ready to get the hell out of the strip club.

"But don't you know?" Seth asked his eyes shifting to Lexi's. He winked at her causing her blush to deepen.

She really had no idea what he was getting at now. What didn't Ramsey know that Seth thought he could tell him? He had to know that they had been together. He was, after all, Jack's best friend. He was the person he had been friends with the longest. And if she had to guess, he was probably the best man at his wedding. Jack had been his best man. They had a bond unlike any other. And if Jack knew that she had been with Ramsey, then Seth did too, which brought her back to having no clue where Seth was going with all this.

"Know what? I don't have time for these games," Ramsey growled.

"She's Jack's girl."

Lexi's mouth dropped open at his words. Her ears were ringing and all else was blocked out. It was as if the strip club had instantly gone silent. The pain of those words shot through her like a knife through her heart. The nonchalance of the statement hit her to the core. She didn't even have words. She couldn't even correct him.

She had worked a year to get him out of her life as much as she possibly could. But Seth's easy placement of her belonging to Jack catapulted her to a different place in her life. And she had to forcefully remind herself to be angry that he had placed her with Jack. After all, it was pretty fucked up that he would say that about someone who was about to be married. Let alone to the man she had been dating.

As the proper emotion filtered into her system, anger bubbled up from the pit of her stomach. She wanted to smack him across the face for ever uttering something that had always been such a complete and total lie. She wasn't Jack's girl. She had *never* been Jack's girl. Jack only cared about himself. He was happy to leave her behind while he married someone else.

"Jack is marrying my sister," Ramsey stated each word carefully. Lexi saw the same raw anger reflected in Ramsey's eyes. "Perhaps you should think about that before you speak again."

Seth's easy smile was something Lexi was extremely accustomed too. He was in his element. For some reason, even drunk, he was having fun with this. "He might be marrying her, but it's not like he's going to get rid of Lexi. I mean, have you seen her?" he asked gesturing towards Lexi who was still in her sexy plum dress from their night out. His eyes crawled over her body hungrily, the alcohol getting rid of the last bit of inhibition that he had. Not that he had much to begin with. "She's fire hot! And anyway, they've been together forever."

"You are talking about people I care about, Seth. You should watch what you're saying," Ramsey tried to remind him. Seth talked about Lexi and Jack as if them being together was inevitable, as if she had no choice in the matter. "You are telling me that Jack is going to cheat on *my* sister with the woman standing before you just because they have a history?" Ramsey asked.

"If he hasn't already," Seth said scoffing. He was so certain of his deduction of the situation; he couldn't even see the effect he was having on the both of them. Or if he did, he didn't realize the significance of what he was ensuing.

Lexi, however, saw what was coming before it happened. Ramsey couldn't let his comment stand. The same thought had crossed his mind too many times, and she knew that he couldn't stand hearing it from one more person.

Ramsey cleared the distance between them in a split second, hoisting Seth up by his shirt one more time. "Do not ever imply again that Lexi is a whore or that Jack would be stupid enough to hurt either one of them. He knows what I would do to him if that day came," he snarled.

"Ramsey, put him down," Lexi cried, guilt washing over her at the fact that Seth was right. Jack had already cheated on Bekah with her. They had kissed several times, and then that dreadful decision to sleep with him on his birthday. She had let those things happen. But she was bound and determined not to get in the way again. "People are coming over here," she said nodding her head towards the approaching bouncer.

"Alright man, sorry. It's the alcohol talking," Seth muttered running his hand through his hair when Ramsey finally put him down.

"Is there a problem here?" a bouncer asked getting in Ramsey's face.

"No," Ramsey said flashing his pearly white teeth. "In fact, we're perfect. We'll be leaving shortly."

"Make it sooner rather than later," the man said menacingly before turning, walking a safe distance away, and staring at the group.

"Charming individual," Ramsey mumbled before turning his attention back to Seth. "Now stop changing the subject and tell me why you called me. Where is Jack?"

"So, yeah about that," Seth said scratching the back of his head. "He's probably just in one of the back rooms where we sent him off about thirty minutes ago."

"You are saying...that Jack...is here? That Jack...is fine?" he asked through gritted teeth.

"Yeah," Seth mumbled looking away from Ramsey's angry gaze. "We just wanted you out with us. We know you said you had business to take care of, but we thought you'd be back out here with us having a good time already."

"Seth, I could kill you," Lexi said smacking him on the shoulder. This was completely typical of something he would do. He was only thinking of himself.

"Oh, do it again," he moaned commenting on her less than playful smack. His arms came up to circle her waist again, but the look on Ramsey's face made him halt his efforts.

"Let's get out of here," Ramsey said latching onto Lexi's elbow and ushering her towards the exit. She stumbled under the weight of his grasp, but he held her up as she scurried helplessly, attempting to keep up.

"Come on, man, don't be like that," Seth said rushing behind them. Hunter and Luke were close on his tail.

"Yeah, Ramsey, you can't leave now. You just got here," Hunter called after him.

"Don't you want to be involved in Jack's bachelor party?" Luke asked.

"This is ridiculous," Ramsey said stopping to face them.

"It's not *that* ridiculous. We skipped out on Vegas for you. We only came to New York on your request. Then you don't even come out with us," Seth complained. "That's pretty fucked up."

Lexi's eyes shot to Ramsey. Coming to New York had been his request? This had nothing to do with Jack. If Jack had it his way, he would be in Las Vegas right now partying it up like the guys in the movie *The Hangover*. He probably hadn't even considered Lexi in this decision.

"You wanted to come to New York?" she breathed. A part of her was relieved that this had nothing to do with Jack. She couldn't handle him right now. Her heart had been through the shredder too many times to count, and she still had a small bit of hope left in her that she didn't like to admit. She certainly didn't like to think about it.

"Yeah, Lex," Seth began. Lexi cringed at the pet name. She still couldn't hear it from anyone without feeling slightly sick. "Can you believe we did all this for him, and he didn't even come out with us?" Seth asked.

"Yes, actually I can," she murmured just loud enough to be heard over the music playing through the hidden speakers. She certainly believed that Ramsey would reroute their rendezvous to come to New York City.

"So, we just wanted to get you out here," Seth told him gesturing around to the naked women and hundreds of bottles of booze that lined the bar. His meaning was clear—*why wouldn't you want to be here?*

"I feel as if I've been to one of these before. It's not the highlight of my evening." Seth's eyes widened at his response. "I had better things to do until you called and told me that things had gone south. So, please, don't tell me that you interrupted my evening for absolutely no reason."

"I mean, we had a reason," Seth said stretching the truth only slightly. "We wanted you out with us. You're a fun guy," he told Ramsey clapping him on the back. Lexi was surprised Seth could be that affectionate or even that forgiving after Ramsey had hoisted him up off of his feet by the collar of his shirt. She was pretty sure if it had been anyone else, a fight would have broken out.

"And everything is alright with Jack? Someone didn't steal all of your money?" Ramsey asked fire in his voice.

Seth smiled impishly. "Nah, Jack is *perfectly* content, if you know what I mean," Seth said with a wink for emphasis.

Lexi's stomach rolled at the comment. Of course Jack would be in a back room with a stripper for his bachelor party. It only made sense. And really, she didn't care that it *was* happening. It was more the fact that this rite of passage solidified in her mind that he was going to go through with this; he was really going to marry Bekah.

"Yes, I know what you mean," Ramsey said his eyes on Lexi.

Lexi's skin suddenly pricked up and all the hair on the back of her neck stood on end. She knew someone was watching her. She could feel the eyes from across the room. As her gaze found who was blatantly staring at her, her heart melted. "Jack," she murmured barely audible to the outside world.

Even from across the room, she knew that he wanted her. It was such an intense emotion, one that she was so accustomed to, that she could tell instantly where his mind was. She didn't think it helped that he was both drunk and likely incredibly horny from the stripper's antics.

The rest of the group caught on as Jack made his way across the room. "Hey man, how was it?" Luke asked as Jack passed him.

"Do you need more cash?" Hunter questioned him, digging around in his pockets for some to give him if necessary.

Jack stopped in front of Lexi without acknowledging the rest of the group. Lexi could feel Ramsey tensing next to her, but she couldn't look away. It was like they were on the beach again when she had expected to see him. He was a vision that day drenched in sunlight and full of energy. He was looking at her the same way as if she weren't real, as if he had conjured her up out of thin air.

"Lex," he huskily muttered.

"Jack," she acknowledged, not tearing her eyes from his crystal clear blue gaze filled with desire. She wanted to hold onto the disdain she felt for him that afternoon when she found out he was engaged. She wanted to feel the chains being broken and her release from his enslavement. She tried to hold onto that, but his blue eyes were calling out to her.

She took a deep breath and moved to take a step backwards, a step out of his reach. Just as she moved, he stepped right into her personal zone and circled his arm around her. She gasped at the sudden movement and the feel of his arms around her.

Jack picked Lexi up off her feet as he straightened. Grappling for support, she reached up and wrapped her arms around his neck. As this happened, her head dropped down to the crook between his shoulder and his neck and she breathed in sharply. His familiar scent filled her nostrils and she reflexively sighed out pleasurably. He smelled exactly the same. It was the exact scent of sex mixed with the most delicious cologne in the world. She hadn't realized, but when she thought about sex this was the smell that came to mind.

For just a brief moment, that scent carried her back in time. She was where she was supposed to be. Jack was pressed against her, his lips pressed to her neck as he nuzzled close to her. His fingers grasped her thin waist digging into the silky red material. She could close her eyes and remember a simpler time when this had been her world, her source of happiness.

Even though it had been a year, she couldn't keep her instincts in check, not with his body pressed so tightly against her. Her body knew what Jack was capable of doing to her and, out of basic desire, it wanted that. With him so close to her, she couldn't imagine another time before this moment. Her world was right side up again and all the difficulties she had struggled with for a year were stripped away.

Her heart was racing, and if she pulled away just fractionally, she knew his lips would be on hers. The alcohol coming out of his pores was too strong and his inhibitions were thrown out the window. Her brain, thick with the memories of past desires, didn't want to think of a reason to pull away.

Then, suddenly, all the sights and sounds of where she was and what she was doing came crashing down on her. The music seemed too loud and her ears popped as they adjusted to her brain waking up from its daze. The beer and whiskey clearly potent mingled in with the stale smell of the strip club. She gasped into his shoulder as the smell of sex, which had been so enticing just a moment ago, completely overwhelmed her. She needed to get away from him. Her mind had finally caught up with what she was allowing to happen, and she forcefully shoved him away from her.

Her breathing was coming out in rapid spurts, and she thought she might hyperventilate if she didn't calm down. She glanced at Ramsey and tried not to over-analyze the disappointed look on his face. She needed to calm herself down enough to be able to give a proper response to Jack's appearance.

Before she could come up with something, Jack spoke, "You're here to celebrate with me."

"That's what I said," Seth agreed hurrying to intervene before Ramsey got a chance to speak.

Lexi just sputtered in shock. Why would he want her to stay? This hadn't been his idea. He didn't have a clue that this was going to happen, and now he wanted her to stay? She couldn't process this right now. She was at a strip club for Jack's bachelor party with Ramsey. She couldn't think of a more uncomfortable situation. She was not prepared for this.

Suddenly a round of shots appeared before them that Luke had ordered at the bar. Lexi hadn't even noticed until a shot glass filled with clear liquid was shoved into her hand.

Seth raised his glass high. "A toast. To Jack's freedom. Soon enough, he won't have it anymore!"

The guys laughed and downed their shots. Lexi stared at the liquid that she knew would only make this night worse and debated. After a moment of hesitation, she poured the shot down her throat letting the burning sensation wash away any emotion she was presently feeling.

"Vodka," she sputtered covering her mouth and searching around for a chaser. She snatched a drink out of Hunter's hand and took a big gulp not caring what was in the glass. Not exactly a wise decision, chasing vodka with a large gulp of bourbon. She swallowed hard and tried to force back the tears that were threatening to be unleashed from the sheer toxicity of what she had just consumed.

"Are you okay?" Ramsey asked placing his hand gently on her lower back to steady her.

"Peachy keen jelly bean," she muttered indignantly.

The rest of the group had settled back into a cluster of chairs in the corner. It was pretty clear that they were all obliterated, and most of the cash they had brought with them was depleted. The bouncer, who had spoken to them earlier, appeared at Ramsey's side. "If you guys aren't going to be spending any more money, then you should probably do as you originally intended and get out of here," he said motioning towards the door.

Ramsey took the man aside and had a few words with him, but eventually agreed that perhaps it was the best time to get out of there. The guys had gotten in their good times, and had a few too many stories already about the trip. Ramsey corralled the group and forced them out the door. He stuffed the four guys in one cab and took a separate one with Lexi to their hotel.

The ride to the hotel was silent. Lexi was still pissed about the entire situation. She hated herself for her moment of weakness with Jack. She hated it even more that Ramsey had had to witness it. There was no way this was how he had intended their night to progress. When she had invited him into her place, she was sure that everything was going to work itself out. Now she didn't know where they were going from here...or even where she wanted them to go.

When they arrived at the hotel, they noticed that the guys had waited outside for them. Whether they had done that out of courtesy or because they were too intoxicated to know where their room was, Lexi wasn't certain. She followed them up to their room with every intention of wishing Ramsey a good night, and then heading home. She was both physically and mentally exhausted from the emotional night they had endured. All she wanted to do was go home and sleep off the hangover she knew would result from mixing various types of alcohol.

They stepped into the hallway and Ramsey slid the keycard into the slot allowing everyone to enter. As she was about to walk inside, Jack latched onto her arm. "Can I talk to you for a minute?" he asked resting his arm against the wall for support. He was *really* drunk, and without the support the wall provided, he would have already fallen over. This probably meant bad things for her.

But as always, she was torn. It wasn't like Jack could do much more harm to her life than he already had. And she was supremely curious about the conversation they would have if she stayed.

"Lexi, come on," Ramsey said glaring at Jack.

"Uh..." she muttered her eyeing moving between the two guys.

Ramsey's green eyes pleaded with her to just say no to him. He was begging her to follow him into the room and not care what Jack had to say. "Please," he implored.

"Uh, just give us a minute," she said taking a step away from the door.

"You're serious?" he asked.

"It'll only be a minute," she promised. "If it's much longer than that, come out here and save me." She sent him a reassuring smile, but she could tell he wasn't reassured. The last thing he wanted to do was leave her out here by herself. But being the gentleman that he was, he smiled forlornly at her, walked into the hotel room, and closed the door.

One minute.

"What do you want Jack?" she asked.

"I just..." Jack began unable to keep from slurring his words. "I'm glad...I g-g-got to s-s-see you." His eyes were half-closed and so the beautiful blue eyes underneath weren't able to focus on her. This gave her a little more confidence

"You didn't expect to see me though," she prompted hoping to catch him.

"No, but it was a g-g-great surprise," he told her.

"Yeah, at least for one of us," she muttered sarcastically.

"You didn't want to see me?" he asked his eyes popping open and looking at her like a sad puppy. She sighed and tried to remember her anger. He was gorgeous. She had always known that. But that's all he was now.

"Jack, why did you want to talk to me?" she prompted, changing the subject away from dangerous territory. She didn't realize that she was actually moving into worse grounds.

"Are you going to be at my wedding?" Jack drunkenly asked, stepping into her personal space.

Lexi's chewed on her bottom and took a stutter step back in surprise. She couldn't believe he would bring that up. What a terrible thing to do! She had loved him with everything, and now he was going to throw what she had lost in her face. She couldn't believe it. She didn't want to be hurt by his statement, but she was. "Jack, no..." she trailed off not wanting to let him see he was affecting her so strongly.

"But you're not in school."

"No," she confirmed.

"Well then, I'd like to invite you," he stammered. He took another step forward clearing the distance she had left between them. His hand left the wall which was holding him up and he reached out and grasped her hips.

Lexi bit her lip harder as his head bobbed considerably close to her mouth. She tried to fend him off but he was too drunk to really know what he was doing. She put both her hands flat on his chest to hold him backwards. "Jack, I don't think that's such a good idea. Otherwise, you would have sent me an invitation."

Jack seemed to notice her efforts to get him off her and stood a little straighter. One hand snaked up to rest on her cheek, tilting her head up to him. His blue eyes bored into her deep chocolate brown ones. "You're drunk," Lexi murmured.

"Yes, but it doesn't change what I said."

"Actually, it does," she told him.

"I want you to come to the wedding."

"Why, Jack?" she asked shaking her head. She couldn't think of a reason for her to be there. This was just torture for both of them.

"Lex, I know that you're over me," he began. Lexi tried to hide the shock from her face. "You were my best friend for a long time. You've been at every important moment of my life, and it wouldn't feel right not having you there."

"You think I'm…" she started, but was cut off by Jack leaning forward and resting his forehead gently against her own.

"I'm sorry. You know that, right?" he asked his voice full of remorse.

She breathed in the familiar scent that she associated with Jack, and tried to keep her mind clear. This was harder than she had ever imagined it would be. "I know, Jack, but like you said," she began taking a step backwards, "it doesn't change anything."

Even his drunken brain could process the fact that she had used the same words as him a year ago. He sighed heavily and nodded. "That's fair. But know that I want you there." Lexi nodded stuffing a strand of hair behind her ear anxiously. "No need to be nervous, love," Jack murmured taking her hand in his own and tucking another strand behind her ear affectionately.

The door clicked open behind them, and Ramsey cleared his throat as loud as he could. Jack gave her a despondent smile as he ran his hand through her silky hair. Lexi coughed uncomfortably, taking another step away from Jack, and out of his reach. She allowed him to walk past her into the room and the door to close before she turned to face Ramsey.

He didn't even have to say anything. The look on his face said it all. She hoped that everything would just blow over. She couldn't deal with all of this tonight.

"Can I stay with you?" Ramsey asked.

Lexi stared up at him. She wasn't sure why he was letting it go, but she was sure glad he was. She probably wouldn't have if she had walked in on that. They hadn't done anything but the emotions were strong between them. "I think you have enough on your plate as it is," she murmured, remembering how all the guys were stumbling all over each other.

"I know. I just thought it would be nice to get away," he told her taking a step closer to her.

"I wish we could pick up where we left off," she said looking up at him, her eyes hopeful. But she knew that they couldn't. Too much had happened that they had bottled up.

"Me too," he said glancing around. She could tell he wasn't sure about where to go from here. It was quite clear that he wanted to wipe away the awkwardness of the past couple hours, but that simply wasn't possible. "I know I said that I wouldn't bring up the wedding, so I'm really sorry about all this."

Lexi sighed and nodded her head at him. "Yeah, I know you didn't mean for any of this to happen. And Jack kind of just brought up the wedding to me," she admitted cringing slightly at his sudden awareness.

"He did?"

"Yeah, he invited me."

Ramsey ground his teeth together in frustration. "What an idiot. I can't believe he asked you."

"I think I'm going to go, if you still want me to go with you," she mumbled knowing that it was the wrong decision to begin with. She never thought in a million years that she would go, but she was compelled. She didn't know what it was that made her do this. She just couldn't say no to Jack—completely and totally obliterated he still managed to affect her.

"What?" he sputtered, stepping forward, closer to her. "Why would you want to do that? I was about to apologize. There's no need for you to be there. It was terrible for me to bring it up. It was terrible for Jack to mention it. You shouldn't have to go through that."

"No" she said shaking her head emphatically. "Turning you down showed me how much I need to let things go, to work things out. And I know it's probably stupid, alright? I know that. It's just, if you want me to go as your date," she took a deep breath trying not to think about all the reasons that she shouldn't be around Jack or Ramsey, for that matter, "then that's what I want to do."

"So, you'll go? As my date?" he asked his brow crinkled together in confusion.

"Yeah, I think I will."

6

NOVEMBER NINE MONTHS EARLIER

Lexi stared upwards at the colossal white structure looming over Peachtree Street in the center of downtown Atlanta. The High Museum of Art with its crisp green lawn, succeeding circular edifices, and blocky surrounding structures looked as modern art as the MET appeared to be a classical castle. Surprisingly enough downtown wasn't as crowded as Lexi had anticipated on her way in from the suburbs. With Thanksgiving only three days away, she had feared that traffic would be a nightmare. Luck had been with her. The interstate had only been congested for a brief period of time as cars merged on and off the Perimeter, and then it was smooth sailing the rest of the way.

Despite that fact, she still managed to arrive behind schedule. Rushing to button up her new, bright red pea coat, she scaled the hill in her knee-high, black boots. Lexi slid her hands in the pockets of her jacket and ducked her head against the brisk breeze blowing in. She could never figure out why Thanksgiving in Georgia was always so much colder than Christmas. Last year she had been able to wear a tank top on Christmas Day, but she had been forced into multiple layers to stay warm on Thanksgiving. It hardly made sense.

A man graciously held the door open for her as she entered the large white foyer. She thanked the man as her high heels clicked against the white marble floors. Not seeing her date, Lexi ducked into the nearest bathroom to check her appearance.

She smiled at her reflection enjoying her windblown curls. She narrowed her big brown eyes as she inspected the hint of auburn highlights now apparent in her dark chocolate locks. When she was satisfied, she dug her hand into her black leather purse and pulled out a tube of red lip gloss that she dabbed across her slightly chapped lips. Stepping back from the mirror, she turned to exit the bathroom.

As the door swung closed behind her, Lexi heard a familiar voice that made her eyes light up and a smile cross her face. She was about to jump around the corner to surprise him, when the topic of conversation piqued her interest. Against her better judgment, Lexi leaned back around the corner to hide from his view.

"Dad, I told you already, I don't want to talk about the wedding," Ramsey muttered into his iPhone. Lexi strained to hear the other end of the conversation, to no avail.

"I know what Bek wants. She always gets what she wants." Lexi rolled her eyes dramatically.

"You want to talk about who I'm bringing?" he asked in disbelief. "What does it even matter to you?" Silence ensued for another minute.

"Are you kidding? No, I am not bringing her. Absolutely not. We're nothing. Nothing. Do you understand me? Can you drop it?" His voice was venomous.

After another minute, he responded, "I know who her family is. You don't have to remind me. Honestly, why are we even still having this conversation? I know everything about her. I know how you and Mom feel about her. I know how you feel about *everything*," he spat. During the next pause, Lexi could actually hear his deep breaths. She imagined his chest was rising and falling as he brimmed with anger.

"Just stop, stop talking. This conversation is over. We can discuss it more some other time if you insist," he said.

Lexi, realizing that the discussion had come to a close, kicked the swinging bathroom door with her foot to make it sound as if she had just left the bathroom, and rounded the corner. He turned at her approach and a full smile filled his gorgeous face. "Lexi," he muttered huskily taking in every inch of her.

"Hey," she acknowledged him nodding slightly. He scooped her up into a sudden embrace, lifting her effortlessly off her feet. She giggled and wrapped her arms around his neck glad that whatever had transpired didn't affect their time together.

"It's great to see you. How was the drive in?" he asked setting her back on her feet and gesturing for her to proceed him.

She teetered briefly on the tiny heels attached to her boots before walking up to the ticket booth, all the while explaining her brief encounter with traffic. Ramsey purchased the tickets and followed Lexi into the main entrance. "At least it wasn't that bad. I would have picked you up, you know?" he said smiling down at her.

"You told me," she reminded him. "But I just borrowed my mom's car. No biggie."

Lexi desperately wanted to ask him more about the conversation she had eavesdropped on. She didn't really want to talk about the wedding. She was bound and determined to never hear about it, but she couldn't help her curiosity. Ramsey had to attend that much was clear.

But his necessary appearance at the wedding wasn't what had aroused her interest. What she really wanted to know was who this woman was his father had suggested to him. Lexi could hear Bekah's words about Ramsey being a player echo in the back of her mind. It wasn't like Bekah was the only one who had warned her off Ramsey.

She tried to shake off the feeling of discomfort that was creeping across her temples. Sure, she didn't know Ramsey all that well, but so far he had been nothing but cordial. In fact, he had been a perfect gentleman. They had gone on at least a dozen dates since she had invited him to the engagement party and thus far, all they had done was kiss. She welcomed the change though. After practically throwing herself at him that night, she had vowed to give herself the time she needed to heal. Immediately jumping into bed with another man was the worst idea she could fathom.

Though it did make her wonder sometimes if he was dating other people. She had never had it in her to ask if he was seeing other people. She couldn't imagine that he would only be dating her. They saw each other so infrequently and, sex…well, it was something she was willing to work towards.

She gulped hard at the thought of him with someone and tried to hide her discomfort. The last thing she wanted to think about was Ramsey with someone else. She knew that she had no claim to him, but they were just at the beginning of a relationship and the idea made her nervous.

"So, what does your family do for Thanksgiving?" Ramsey questioned her.

"Oh, nothing fancy," she said shoving a loose strand of hair behind her ear. "Usually it's just the three of us. My mom cooks, and we snuggle up in front of the fireplace to watch the Macy's Thanksgiving Day Parade. But this year for some reason," Lexi rolled her eyes, "my mom decided to invite everyone to our house for Thanksgiving. Both sets of grandparents are flying in tomorrow. All of my aunts and uncles and their kids are here already. It's a mad house."

"Sounds nice," he said dreamily.

"Psh, nice," she muttered sarcastically. "What do you do? It has to be better."

"When I wake up, I put on a suit to go have a formal breakfast with my father's most prestigious business associates. They talk business," he stated dryly. "I'm expected to contribute now that I am older. From there, every minute of the day is mapped out with things we're supposed to be doing to help the business. The business this and the business that," he quoted sardonically. "My grandparents are shoved in their somewhere briefly, before we finish with a more formal dinner at the Club."

"Let me guess, they discuss business?" Lexi asked only half joking.

"Ding, ding, ding," he said raising his hand in the air.

A wave of compassion flowed through Lexi's body. She knew that Ramsey wasn't exactly fond of his father or Bridges Enterprise, which his father and grandfather had built from the ground up, but she had never envisioned why. She had always assumed that he had everything, but she was starting to realize that there was much more to Ramsey than she had originally anticipated. "Ramsey I'm sor…" she began, but she was cut off.

"Please, you're the last person I want sympathy from," he said gently. "I shouldn't have even mentioned it."

"No, it's alright," Lexi said averting her eyes and staring into a large mural of the ocean.

"I'm really not trying to play the poor-little-rich-kid routine," he muttered, disgust in his voice. "I guess this time of year just grates my nerves."

"You have every right to be upset about it," she told him gingerly, dancing around the subject.

"Well, there's no point in discussing it," he said veering away from her and into the next exhibit room. "It is what it is."

"I think talking helps," she murmured almost instantly regretting that statement. He could ask her a million and a half things that she had no desire to discuss. She knew he was curious about her, but she was hesitant to share too much information about herself. What she could share—what she had shared so far—was barely scratching the surface.

He would find out eventually the kind of person she had once been. She knew it was inevitable. If Ramsey had any knowledge of what had occurred between her and Jack in her past, he didn't act like it. And for now, at least, she wanted to keep it that way.

"I think talking can be helpful," he agreed, "but not right now." He shot her a quick smirk his green eyes glowing. "For now, I'm on a date with a beautiful woman, and I should be enjoying that."

"Oh, you think we're on a date, do you?" Lexi asked playfully crossing her arms over her chest and giving him a devilish grin.

"Is this not what this is?" he questioned, taking a step towards her.

"Well, I don't know. Are you going to take me out to dinner?" she asked him following his lead and stepping into him. "Sweep me off my feet? Walk me to my doorstep and give me a lingering kiss good night?" She arched one perfectly shaped eyebrow.

Ramsey leaned into her, pulling her body close to him. He dipped his head down close enough to huskily whisper into her ear, "Can I give you a lingering kiss on *my* doorstep and convince you to make it more than linger?"

Lexi let a faint gasp pass through her lips at his words, and the gentle nip on her ear sent shivers down her entire body. She forced her body to stay in check, biting down forcefully on her lip to keep her emotions under control.

They were taking things slow.

She could take things slow. She repeated the words to herself over and over in her mind as he slowly backed away from her.

She had been impulsive in her past and look where that had gotten her. Nowhere. She certainly didn't intend to keep repeating the same mistakes all over again. Taking a deep breath, Lexi glanced up into Ramsey's glistening green eyes. He was laughing at her with those beautiful eyes. He had been teasing her with her desire. But she could tell there was more. Despite the playful look apparent in his eyes, she knew he had really only been half-joking. He wanted her to come over, and he wanted to do more than kiss her.

"Perhaps I'll grant you your wish then," she said just as playfully as he was acting, "but only if you can catch me." She tapped him on the shoulder and muttered, "You're it," then darted off through the museum.

She knew it was childish and not to mention dangerous. If she made one wrong move, she could land on a priceless piece of artwork. She hadn't been able to help herself though. It was completely irrational. He would be able to catch up to her in an instant in her boots, but she darted around the exhibits nonetheless. Ramsey followed in pursuit seemingly unaware of the older couples who were shooting them death stares.

Lexi dove behind a large statue stifling her giggles as she heard his approaching footsteps. Just as the steps came to a halt, she raced out from her hiding spot and through an open hallway filled with classic black and white photographs. She glanced over her shoulder to see him lightly jogging behind her more intent on her backside than actually catching up to her. Giggling, Lexi turned around just in time to find her face to face with an imposing older gentleman.

"Excuse me, ma'am," he said briskly sidestepping her urgent run.

"Sorry," she cried teetering on her heels as she rounded the corner, barely avoiding colliding with the man.

She heard Ramsey mutter something which sounded apologetic to the man, but she didn't slow down long enough to find out. She wasn't certain what had come over her. A part of her felt so carefree like all her worries had been wiped from her mind. The sound of her feet clicking underneath her kept time for her movements. A bright smile played across her face as she darted past a young couple. They seemed annoyed at first by the disturbance, but when they saw Ramsey in pursuit, their soft chuckles rang in her ears.

"So what do I get if I catch you?" Ramsey called teasingly down the white expansive hallway.

"Didn't you hear me the first time?" she asked between breaths.

"Oh, I heard you," Ramsey said. Lexi could hear his steps smacking the floor harder as he picked up speed. "I just want to make sure I know what I'm getting."

"Me!" she crowed making a risky pivot turn and nearly falling over as her shoes slid against the slick floorboards. She caught herself just before Ramsey reached her, taking a few hesitant stutter steps before breaking away from him and into a massive open room filled with modern art.

She raced across the room hoping to make it to the next exhibit before he got close, but there were no turns and nowhere to hide. She couldn't evade him in here. She simply had to out run him, and that wasn't going to be possible.

Lexi felt a hand graze her shoulder and she tried to duck out of the embrace, but Ramsey latched onto her. He grabbed her by the waist, turned her in a full 180, and pulled her into him. He dipped his head down to her face and captured her lips in a searing kiss. Her breath was coming out heavy, from the chase as well as his steamy kiss.

"I caught you," he murmured against her lips.

"Indeed you did," she agreed.

"Can I change the terms of our arrangement?" he questioned formally.

"You don't want me?" she asked giving him another peck on his cheek and flashing him a devious smile.

"Oh, I'm still keeping you," he said gripping her tighter around the waist. "I just have a better idea."

"And that is?"

"I want you to meet my friends," he told her smoothly.

Lexi stared at him perplexed. She had originally offered him her body, and now he wanted her to meet his friends. A pretty abrupt change, but he had won after all. "Uh, sure," she said uncertainly.

"Meet me at my house tomorrow around five. You'll have a good time," he said smiling reassuringly. "Oh and wear something warm."

"Warm?" she asked glancing down at her outfit.

He did the same, taking in her small body and the clothing that covered every curve wonderfully. After a second of thought, he added, "And practical."

*****

The next day Lexi arrived at Ramsey's apartment at five o'clock on the dot. She had dressed as practical as she could muster in a pair of worn blue jeans, red long-sleeve t-shirt covered by an old college sweatshirt, and her running sneakers. Her dark hair was pulled up into a high ponytail with her bangs pinned back from her face. She snatched a purple and white jacket from the backseat, just in case, and stuck her hands in her back pockets as she approached his apartment warily.

This was the first time that she had been in Atlanta since August, and memories of this very apartment flooded her mind. The way she had scandalously danced with Ramsey in an effort to forget Jack. Then as Jack peered through the backdoor window to the balcony as she had impulsively leaned into Ramsey's kiss, their first kiss. She had ended up staying the night, but Ramsey hadn't tried anything, even then, in her weakened position.

She had ended up here again—broken, destroyed, torn to pieces. She had been used, abused, and she was no longer the Lexi that she had once been. Her carefree side had vanished into thin air with Jack's callous behavior. Ramsey had tried to help her, but after almost giving into his desires, she had run out of his house in the middle of the night. She hadn't even been able to trust her own shadow that day. As she gazed up at his ritzy townhouse, she couldn't help but feel overwhelmed with all that had occurred.

Taking a deep breath, Lexi knocked on the door and waited for Ramsey's quick response. His smile lit up at the sight of her. "You're here," he said snatching her up into his arms, turning in place, and planting her on the floor in his apartment.

"Yep," she said unable to keep from smiling at his boyish exuberance. He looked as gorgeous as ever in a heather grey, long-sleeve, Henley shirt, dark jeans, and boots.

Ramsey's two roommates bounded down the stairs, and Lexi was momentarily frozen as she realized she didn't remember either of their names. She had met them only briefly several months ago and wasn't entirely certain whether or not she had learned names even then.

"Is she here finally?" one of them asked snottily.

Lexi smiled at his false annoyance. "Lexi, I doubt you remember my charming roommates," Ramsey stated sarcastically alleviating her brief moment of stress, "Brad and Jason."

"Sorry about your first meeting," Jason said walking forward and shaking her hand. "We're not ourselves wasted." He added a shrug for good measure.

"Speak for yourself," Brad said sending a quick jab in Jason's direction.

Ramsey shook his head at the two guys, as he yanked the door back open, and gestured for them to exit. Lexi followed them to the parking garage and once inside just stared. She knew Ramsey had his pretty little Mercedes, but there were several other cars inside as well. She wasn't even sure why they kept them all there.

"The Jeep is Brad's, which we'll be taking today," Ramsey said, instructing her towards the bright yellow vehicle. "That's Jason's little red Porsche. He thinks it helps him pick up girls."

"It does," Jason whispered to her, before sliding into the front seat of the Jeep.

"But then...is that...?" she opened the door to the Jeep, but couldn't tear her eyes from the Italian sports car she had only ever seen on the TV show, *Entourage*.

"Yeah, you like that?" Brad asked popping the key in the ignition and revving the engine.

"Uh, yeah," Ramsey said, scratching the back of his head thoughtfully. "It's a Maserati."

Lexi's mouth dropped open. She knew how much that car cost. "Hell yeah," Brad cried, "You should see the Ferrari he keeps in storage. It's a damn tragedy not to drive that beaut around the city."

Lexi swiveled instantly, catching Ramsey's eye. She could tell he was embarrassed by the display of exorbitant wealth before her. He typically tried to tone it down for her, but she knew he had money. She just didn't really *know* as much as she thought she did. She took a large gulp and slid into the back seat beside Ramsey still taking in the knowledge that he owned two cars that cost more than any house her parents had ever owned.

"Maybe if you're lucky, he'll take you out on the Ducati," Jason said turning around to look at her as Brad pulled out of the driveway.

"The what?" she asked unfamiliar with that name.

"Ducati, it's a motorcycle," Ramsey informed her.

"You have a motorcycle?" Lexi asked, a shiver of anticipation going down her back.

"Yeah, if he can ever get the damn thing working," Brad interjected. "You should just take it to a mechanic."

Ramsey shrugged the comment off as if he'd heard it time and time again. "I like to work on it myself. Makes me know that it's getting done right."

"You work on motorcycles?" she asked in disbelief. Her mind was spinning with all the new information about him. How had she ever thought he was some stereotypical Country Clubber? There was obviously much more to Ramsey that she had no idea about. He was an enigma.

She tried to force out Bekah's words, but she couldn't help hearing them over and over.

He's a player.
You don't know him.
You've only ever seen one side of him.

Ramsey had only shown her one side, but nonetheless Lexi was seeing a new side. A side she liked, though it scared the hell out of her. She hated to think Bekah had been right in anything. She hated having doubts about Ramsey.

And though she had a hard time dispelling her reservations, she needed to focus more on having fun with him then analyzing his every move. She had been hurt before, but she didn't want that to define her.

Brad kept the music blasting to old 90s rock music the entire ride, leaving very little room for conversation from that point on. That was fine with Lexi. She was still processing, and didn't really want to blabber a slew of personal questions in front of Ramsey's roommates. She could wait for later.

Brad pulled the Jeep off the road and down a winding path that had once been paved, but was now cracking and bumpy. Lexi understood why the Jeep was used instead of the other sporty cars. Wherever they were going was not meant for the lavish and luxury Lexi had witnessed in the garage. She hadn't really been an outdoorsy type. She had spent most of her time growing up on school work or locked in the gymnastics studio. However, when she was younger, she had been a girl scout, and she had always had a love of camping and bonfires.

Living in the city for nearly three years made her forget just how bright and beautiful the stars were…not to mention how *many*. Thousands upon thousands of twinkling white beams stared down at Lexi through the glass. Her eyes lit up at the spectacle, entranced by the beauty of the countryside.

A break in the tree line appeared before them and Brad began to decelerate as they approached. Lexi peered out through the front window anxious to see what lay ahead. Even in the darkness, the magnitude of the lake, majestically lit by the moon, was evident. Lexi couldn't even glimpse the opposite bank.

Brad parked the Jeep in a gravel lot beside several other SUVs. As the ignition died, only the sounds of nature filled her ears. Lexi closed her eyes taking in all the noise that wildlife produced and the smell of pine mingled with Georgia red clay. She felt Ramsey's sweet kiss on her lips and opened her eyes to smile at him.

"So, you like it?" he questioned rhetorically.

"What park is this? It doesn't look like Lake Lanier. And wouldn't we have had to pay for entrance?" Lexi mused aloud.

Lexi could hear a chorus of chuckles behind her, and turned to see a crowd of people standing under a covered patio with picnic benches. "Don't mind them," Ramsey said glaring in their direction. "My parent's actually own this land. I've been coming here since I was a kid," he told her as they veered towards a garage that she hadn't noticed in the darkness. "I think my dad was going to make it into some ritzy resort, but after a while he just forgot about it. With the economy all messed up right now, there's no chance he's going to do anything to it now," he added the last part with a sigh of relief. Ramsey flicked a switch that illuminated a key pad and punched in a seven-digit code.

"What's in there?" Lexi asked in awe as a side door clicked open.

Ramsey walked inside holding the door for Lexi to follow. "This is where my dad keeps his toys," he murmured softly, "and now mine." He flicked another switch and the garage lit up showcasing two boats, jet skis, a number of four wheelers, dirt bikes, a collection of rafts, kayaks, and canoes, along with other various outdoors equipment such as a hammock, tent, and camping gear.

"Holy shit!" Lexi couldn't help herself from exclaiming.

"Yeah," he murmured appreciatively. "Ever been on a four wheeler?" He walked over to a green bike in particular and set his hand down affectionately on the handle. Lexi shook her head unable to utter a single word. "This baby is a Raptor," he informed her, "you'll like her."

The garage door startled her by opening to the front. Brad wandered over to them and stared longingly at the four wheeler Ramsey had just shown her. "You riding the Raptor?" he asked obviously itching to get on the bike.

"Lexi's never been on one," Ramsey told him.

"Uh...you think I'm getting on that thing?" she asked apprehensively.

"I won't go that fast," he said winking at her. "Though it is one of the fastest models. I'll wait until you're more comfortable though."

As the rest of the group wandered into the garage and began claiming the various bikes and four wheelers, Lexi realized that there were less people than she had originally thought. There were two additional guys and four girls in total. They were evenly matched guys to girls, and she wondered if that had been planned.

"Alright, I'm not really going to go into the details, but since you've never been on one before I'll just forewarn you that the buzzing sound is completely normal, the ride should and will be bumpy, and you're going to have a lot of fun," Ramsey said. His smile was infectious and Lexi couldn't help but revel in his enthusiasm. Though she assumed it was also the thrill and anticipation of what she was about to do.

Lexi gingerly climbed onto the back of the bike. She wrapped her arms tightly around Ramsey torso and pressed herself against his back. Nuzzling into his shoulder, she tried to calm her heart which had kicked into overdrive. Ramsey revved the engine, kicked the clutch into gear and took off.

When Ramsey had said he was going to go slow, Lexi had thought he actually meant slow, but apparently their definitions were different. He raced ahead easily taking the lead. Strands of Lexi's hair released from her ponytail and whipped around in her face. She felt him switch gears and zoom forward into the tree line following a dirt trail that she couldn't make out. Her terror alleviated the longer Ramsey drove down the path, but her grip only barely loosened.

As they took a sharp turn, a fire burning in the distance alerted her that they weren't the only ones in the woods. The adrenaline from the ride kept her mind vigilant. As she became more comfortable on the bike, she also became more aware of her surroundings. A dirt path lay before her and she realized that it was wider than she had originally thought. The tree line had gradually begun to grow in overhead to fight for the sunlight, but the moon was still visible.

Lexi clasped her hands tighter around Ramsey's torso and nuzzled in closer to his warm body. She could feel his taut muscles underneath her grip. A smile spread across her face at the feel of him and she realized, despite her terror, that she was having a good time. She had *never* done anything like this before.

As she sank into the rhythm of the bumps and curves, Ramsey pulled into a clearing. He made a circle around a roaring bonfire, then hit the brakes and killed the engine.

"Did you like it?" Ramsey asked helping her off the bike and setting her carefully back on her wobbly feet.

"Uh…" she managed clamping and unclamping her frozen fingers. "You said you were going to go slow."

Ramsey laughed boisterously at her shocked face, before throwing an arm over her shoulders, and dragging her closer to the bonfire. "That *was* slow."

The rest of the group skidded to a halt next to Ramsey's Raptor and joined them by the fire.

"Man, that was awesome," Brad crowed, wandering up to Ramsey and clasping him on the back. "Haven't been up here since the summer."

"Yeah, I forgot how killer the ride is," Jason said sidling up to Lexi. "You like it?"

Lexi smiled noncommittally, though she had enjoyed herself once she had gotten used to it. The rest of the group seemed to all know each other. A few of the girls giggled about the ride up. One of them reached up and kissed a guy she didn't know, staking her claim. They introduced themselves but as soon as they were said, Lexi had already forgotten them save for one redhead, Jessie, who kept eyeing her warily.

After settling in around the fire, the group began to roast marshmallows for smores and talk about some event that had happened in high school. Lexi wasn't really paying attention to the conversation since she didn't follow more than half the players involved, but she did listen to the next thing that was mentioned.

"Do you remember when you guys came up here after prom and she insisted on wearing that ridiculous long dress on your tiny dirt bike, Bridges?" Jessie asked her eyes shifting from Ramsey to Lexi.

Lexi glanced up at Ramsey who was glaring in Jessie's direction. "Yes, I remember," he growled.

"That was a crazy night. I think I was dating Jeff Kensington," she said giggling. "He had such a crush on me. Would have done anything for me."

"I think he did," Brad said with a wink. The group laughed aloud at some private joke.

"Well, not compared to..." she began.

"Jess, we know the story," Ramsey snapped narrowing his eyes.

"Fine. Whatever," she snapped right back at him, reaching into a cooler, and pulling out a light beer.

Lexi's senses were piqued from the conversation, and she didn't even know what it had been about. All she knew was that he didn't want to talk about it, which was enough for her. She wanted to ask him what that was about, but she couldn't do it in front of all of his friends.

After an awkward silence, the conversation picked back up, but Lexi's mind was lost in Jessie's few sentences. Who was the girl that had come up with him after prom? She wasn't naïve enough to believe that they had driven all the way up here for no particular purpose.

A conversation came to her mind that she had with Ramsey when he had come to visit. He had claimed to have never had a girlfriend...to never have been in love. She knew there had been women in his life, but the conversation had never drifted past that point though. She was still too anxious about her own past to push him to find out about his own.

With Ramsey's help she was slowly thinking of Jack less and less, all the while eliminating the baggage that she had always carried around with her. Now that she sat down and thought about it, Lexi realized she hadn't even thought about Jack after the past two days of carefree fun with Ramsey.

Feeling Ramsey's fingers gently lace with her own brought her back to reality. She looked up at him and smiled. "What has you so entranced?" he asked her rubbing his thumb against her soft skin.

"I was just wondering," she began hoping to cover up her real thoughts, "why do you have roommates?"

"Hey," Brad said overhearing her question.

"I didn't mean it like that," she said backing up and correcting herself. "I just meant, well, I sound stupid…"

"You mean that I don't need to have roommates," he finished for her.

She nodded. He had all the money in the world. He could live wherever he wanted and do whatever he wanted. There was no need for him to live with two other guys. It didn't make any sense to her. She would have loved the freedom of living alone. Rachelle was great, but she had her habits that drove Lexi off the wall and vice versa. They did it out of necessity, not from choice. Yet, Ramsey had the choice and still he lived with two other guys.

"I don't like living alone," he stated simply. "I've always liked having people around."

"Oh, I guess that makes sense."

Ramsey looked at her for the first time since Jessie had made the comment. "Come with me," he said pulling her upright.

Lexi's eyes shifted to Jessie whose expression had changed at Ramsey's obvious affections. Her lip was upturned as she gazed upon them with distrust and disgust. Lexi's mouth popped open at the unexpected look, but before she could speak a word in questioning, Ramsey was tugging her in the opposite direction.

As she got farther from the fire, she wrapped her arms tighter around herself to keep from losing any heat. He guided her through the woods in the darkness and down a path that she hadn't noticed. She could tell Ramsey had spent a good deal of time on this land with the ease in which he navigated the terrain. "Here we are," he said showing her to a park bench.

Lexi sat willingly, unable to keep her teeth from chattering. "This place is beautiful."

"Yeah, I love it up here, but I don't get to come up very often anymore with…everything going on," he sat next to her, drawing her into his body.

"At least you can make time every now and again," she murmured snuggling close.

"Yeah, it's worth it," he agreed.

Lexi felt his hot lips press against her ear, placing soft kisses down to her earlobe. At that point, he drew the skin between his lips and sucked causing her to shiver all over, but not from the cold. His lips moved to her neck sucking and nibbling until she could feel herself getting warm to her very core.

"Ramsey," she murmured softly, causing him to pull back to look at her. When she didn't say anything further, he moved forward capturing her lips in a sensual kiss. He parted her lips with his tongue and began to explore the feel of her. She loved the familiar taste of peppermint that always seemed to permeate from him. A moan escaped her lips and her hands reached out to slide into his jacket. Her nails dug through the shirt and he took the opportunity to pull her into his lap.

As she came up for breath, his hands wandered up her shirt cupping her breast in his hand. He massaged it through the thin bra she had on under her layers of clothing causing her head to fall back in ecstasy. She found herself grinding against him as he continued to work his magic. He hardened underneath her tempting body. His body reacted easily to her even though she knew they were supposed to be taking it slow.

Lexi felt him beneath her jeans wanting nothing more than to continue where this was headed. However, the thought of stripping down was horrifying in the freezing temperatures. Already her exposed torso was bitterly cold. Despite everything she wanted to do, Lexi pulled back Ramsey's hand and slid her shirt back in place. She moved forward pressing her torso against his chest to gain back some warmth.

"Sooooo…cold," she chattered into his ear.

He chuckled wrapping his arms around her tightly. "I guess forty degree weather isn't the best time to try and seduce you."

"It was your choice to come up here. You set your own terms," Lexi reminded him. Lexi nibbled his ear and swayed her hips back and forth, showing him how much she wanted to continue, as well as how much he was missing.

"Now, that isn't nice." He gripped her hips tightly between his capable hands causing her to stop her movement.

"Ramsey," she murmured softly.

"Yes?"

"What was Jessie talking about?" she couldn't help but ask. She wanted to kick herself for being nosey. It was none of her business. His past was his past. It certainly didn't change how she would view him. Whatever Jessie was talking about was something Ramsey hadn't wanted to discuss. She hated that she had been a fool enough to bring it up especially after he had just admitted to attempting to seduce her. However, she couldn't keep herself from wondering. She couldn't keep herself from asking him either.

"Oh," he mumbled obviously uncomfortable. Lexi waited for him to decide what to do. If he wanted to continue, she would let him take his time. If not, then she would revel in his warmth in silence. After a minute, Lexi was certain that he wasn't going to say anything, but he sighed and began speaking, "I dated this girl in high school who I took to prom."

"But you said you didn't have any girlfriends," she reminded him. He knew how she felt about lying. It wouldn't look good for him if that was the case.

Ramsey sighed again. "She wasn't my girlfriend. We just went to a lot of stuff together and so I took her to prom. Jessie was going to tell a story about how we all came up here after prom. She stayed in her big red dress, on the four wheeler, and then played Never Have I Ever with the rest of the group. We all learned a lot about each other, and it eventually turned into more and..."

"You don't have to tell me the rest," Lexi said her curiosity not sated, but she hated making him sound so forlorn. It was like he was in his own personal hell talking about it. As if he was ashamed of every word.

"Nah," he muttered moving her back to his side, "it's just, I ended up fuck...sleeping with her next to the fire in front of pretty much everyone, because she dared me I wouldn't. Everyone thought it was hilarious, and they never let me live it down when we're up here."

"Oh!" Lexi cried unable to keep the surprise from her face. She didn't care that he had slept with some random girl after prom, but the scenario was still shocking.

"I wouldn't have brought you up here if I'd thought they were going to bring that up," he told her his green eyes glancing hesitantly into Lexi's.

Lexi shook her head. "It's not your fault. You can't change your past."

Ramsey shrugged. "Still, didn't really mean for you to hear about me like that."

"As long as there aren't similar surprises continuing to await me, then I think we'll be just fine," she told him nuzzling closer again. She felt Ramsey sigh in relief. "And if you'd brought me anywhere else, you might be getting some play right now," she told him cocking an eyebrow.

"Oh yeah?" he asked, his body coming alive underneath her at the implications.

"I do want you, Ramsey Bridges," she told him as a matter-of-fact.

"And you shall have me whenever you like."

"Whenever?" she asked smirking.

"Well, as often as possible with you in New York."

"So, Ramsey, does this make me just another of your girls? Am I just someone you'd take in front of a bonfire with prying eyes watching?" she asked, joking more than anything.

"Oh Lexi, *my* Alexa," he said her name possessively, "you could never be just one of those girls."

"So...what does that make me?" she asked knowing that she was pushing her luck. She wasn't really looking for any kind of commitment from him, but she couldn't keep herself from asking nonetheless. She did want some kind of definition to their relationship, whatever that meant.

Ramsey turned to her, capturing her lips in another searing kiss. When he pulled back his look was intense. "I haven't felt like this before, Lexi."

Lexi's heart fluttered rapidly in her chest. She could feel her palms beginning to sweat. Her stomach was turning knots in anticipation. Her pulse was working on overdrive. She could feel her throat beginning to dry up as if she had swallowed cotton balls. She didn't know what was coming over her and why she was getting so nervous about one simple question and one simple comment. *He hadn't felt this way before.*

"Lexi, this might be bold," he began taking her hands in his own, "but I think the casual dating isn't working for me."

Her stomach dropped out from under her. Was he saying that he didn't want to see her anymore? Had she misinterpreted his statement? It hardly made sense with him bringing her up here to meet his friends. That wasn't something you did when you decided you didn't want to date them anymore.

"I mean this back and forth isn't working for me. I don't like how this is all working out. It's too sporadic and hard to keep up with," he stammered out, babbling on like the first time she had officially met him. It was always one of the cutest things about him.

"So, what do you want?" she asked her voice desperate.

"I want us to be exclusive," he told her confidently. "I don't want to think that you're seeing anyone else. I want to see you as often as I can. I think about you all the time. I couldn't stand to be with anyone else with you on my mind, and I can't imagine you doing that. If I'm wrong, by all means, stop me from continuing, but if not, then please tell me."

"Oh, Ramsey," she murmured breathily scooting forward ever so slightly and putting her lips to his once more, "I'm not with anyone else."

"Not entertaining the idea?" he asked cautiously.

"No."

"Then you're mine?"

She simply nodded basking in his gorgeous smile. The realization that she was in a relationship with someone, officially, for the first time since she had broken up with Clark during college hit her fresh. She was taking a leap of faith in Ramsey. As he melted her insides with adoring kisses, her mind filled with the joy of newfound happy memories.

And she didn't have one thought of Jack. Okay, just one—he had never given her this.

7

PRESENT

"I promise," Lexi whined sliding out of Chyna's embrace.
"You promise, promise?" Chyna asked sticking her with a fierce look.
"Yes. Don't worry about me," she groaned.
"Last time you said that, you went off the deep end," Chyna chastised her smiling all the while.
"Yes, well, I was a year younger. So blame it on my innocence and naivety."
Chyna scoffed at her response. "Were you ever innocent and naïve?"
"More than you'll ever know," Lexi told her becoming serious as she leaned forward and kissed her best friend's cheek.
"Now, remember what I told you. If anything starts to look like drama, high tail it out of there. Call me, but please just try and get through this without murdering anyone," Chyna said shaking her head. Lexi could see the look of disapproval across her face, but she couldn't change anything now. Jack's wedding was exactly one week away, and she was about to board the plane that flew her directly to it.
When Lexi had sobered up the morning after Jack's bachelor party and remembered all that occurred, she had nearly died of humiliation. Of all the things she could have done, agreeing to go to Jack's wedding was one of the lowest on the list of smart moves.
And as dense as she was, she had flat out told Ramsey, after agreeing to go to Jack's stupid wedding with him that it was because of Jack! She had

smashed her face into the pillow and screamed until her lungs hurt that morning. It hadn't helped anything except to increase her killer headache.

Still now that she knew that the wedding was only a week away, she was drawn to it like a moth to a flame. She had known all along that if she had found out about the wedding, she wouldn't have been able to stay away. And here she was about to board that damn plane. Real smart, Lexi, real smart.

"I'll call you."

"Lexi, please," Chyna cried throwing her arms around her again, "don't get sucked into his trap again. I know how you are with Jack."

"Chyna, I'm not going to," she said weakly.

"Ramsey too! Watch out for him."

"Stop mothering me," Lexi said taking a step backwards. "I'm going to be fine. I can handle Jack and Ramsey all by myself. Jack doesn't even matter. I'm not there for him. I'm there to support Ramsey because he needs me. Despite what happened, I think we may still have a shot." Chyna rolled her eyes. "I might be going crazy, and I know you think I deserve better, but let's give him a chance."

"Another chance," Chyna mumbled.

"Yes, another chance, and if this week doesn't work out, then I'm done," Lexi told her more confident than she actually felt.

"For real done?"

"Yes, for real done."

"Then you can move onto your Mystery Man?" Chyna asked conspiratorially.

Lexi blushed trying not to smile too wide. Her hand itched to open her phone and scroll through the text messages from the night before. "We're not discussing him. It's not like I'm dating him or anything."

"What?" Chyna burst. "Come on! You were all bubbly after your rendezvous with your stranger, and now you're not even going to *consider* dating him? Insufferable!"

"I have too much to deal with," she said evading the question. If Chyna only knew how close they had come to dating before her meet up with Ramsey…no, she couldn't even think about that in front of Chyna. She knew her too well.

"Fine. I'm going to find out who he is eventually, you know?" Chyna forewarned her.

"I'm sure, C. Until then, wish me luck."

"You're going to need it."

Lexi laughed at her friend, but didn't disagree with her. She was going to need a lot more than luck to get through this week sane.

Ramsey picked her up when she landed safely in the Atlanta airport. It was refreshing to walk out of the doors and see his slick black Mercedes idling in traffic. She hadn't wanted to admit it, but she had missed him.

It had only been two days since her run in with the bachelor party, which hadn't really given her much time to digest what she was doing. She wondered if Ramsey had planned it this way. He had waited until the wedding was a week away before bringing up the subject they had avoided for an entire year. That way she wasn't allowed time to brood about her decision.

Now, she had made her decision and needed to stick with it...come what may.

"Hey, Lexi," Ramsey said as he opened the car door. Lexi's breath caught at the sight of him. He had obviously come straight from brunch at the Country Club, which she had thankfully missed this time around. His black suit was crisp and tailored to his build. The light blue button-up with a black and silver striped tie completed the outfit. She couldn't tear her eyes away from him.

It was like the first time they had met, when she had been caught checking out his ass after walking out of the bathroom at the Club. There really was just something about Ramsey. He was so extremely tall and with that beautiful golden blonde hair and green eyes, he made her melt. Then he smiled, and she could remember a dozen other times when that smile had been the cause of her own smile.

She sighed at the handsome man before her and made her way in his direction. Before she had a chance to put her luggage in the trunk, he was there. She dropped her bags as his arms came around her waist. She was hoisted off of her feet as he held her against him. "I missed you," he breathed into her ear.

A smile returned to her face. She closed her eyes and breathed in his peppermint scent. When she didn't say anything in return, he gently placed her back on her feet. She could tell he was hesitant about how to react to her after everything that had happened between them. She wanted to tell him that she missed him, but Ramsey wasn't the only one that was hesitant.

She was here for him. He needed her and refused to take anyone else. Perhaps she was a masochist, but that didn't mean they could just pick up as if nothing had ever happened. A lot had changed in the month that they were apart, and she was the first that knew that they needed to work on their issues before anything could be settled.

Ramsey lifted her luggage and stowed it into the trunk before settling back into the driver's seat and merging into traffic. "I uh..." he began uncertain of how to begin, "I well, I wasn't sure...we hadn't discussed..."

Lexi could tell how nervous he was, and in the back of her mind she was kind of glad. "We haven't discussed what?" she asked tentatively.

"Where you're staying," he said glancing in her direction.

"Oh," she murmured realizing that they had both overlooked this small fact. She had assumed she would be staying at his place, but at the mention of where she was staying, she realized that maybe that wasn't the best idea.

"I can get you a hotel if you want," he offered though she could tell that was the last thing on his mind. "Is that what you want?"

Lexi wished that she could answer that question without any complications. "I'm not sure," she mumbled, glancing out the window.

"I'd rather you stay at my place. It's going to be a busy week, and it would be easier if you were with me," he said rationalizing the situation.

She knew that was logical. It would be much more convenient than having him pick her up before they went anywhere. But that wasn't really the issue. "Is it going to be like before?" she asked hesitantly.

He glanced over into her face judging her question before responding. "Lexi, I'm not going to lie and tell you that I don't want to be with you." She could tell that as he spoke, he was gaining the confidence that she so loved about him. "I'm not going to push it though. I know that we have things to work through, but we're not going to solve everything in a week…especially not this week. And since you're only here for a week," he spoke the words forlornly, "I suggest you have a good time. You're going to be miserable if you dwell on everything, and the last thing I want is for you to be miserable.

"So just stay with me. I know a month isn't enough time to forgive me." He reached over and gently held her hand. She closed off the part of her mind that reminded her of all the time she had spent with another man in the past month. "I know that, ok? But I'm working on it. I promise you that I am."

Lexi wanted to ask him how. She wanted to know how exactly he was working to make everything better. She knew he likely wouldn't answer though. So it was useless to even try to argue. He was right. She needed to relax and enjoy her time in Atlanta, even if that time happened to be at Jack Howard's wedding.

"You're right."

"I know," he said smiling when she scoffed at his statement and tried to yank her hand away from him. He held on tightly, and she had no chance of escaping. Drawing it up to his lips, he placed a light kiss at the center of her hand before releasing it.

"So," she began, trying to keep the tingling feeling of his lips on her skin from overtaking her senses.

"So?" he asked as they approached his apartment.

"What does the brother of the," Lexi gulped hard the next word tasting like vinegar when she said it, "bride have to do this week?"

Ramsey smirked playfully knowing how difficult it was for her to discuss this with him. "Not as much as a groomsman."

"Wait, are you a groomsman?" Lexi asked astonished.

"Uh yeah, did I not mention that?"

"No."

"Why did you think I was at the bachelor party?" he asked incredulously.

"I don't know. I didn't really think about it. I just assumed it was because of Bekah."

"Well, it *was* because of Bekah," he told her. "She added a bridesmaid and forced me upon Jack."

"So, you ended up planning the bachelor party from there?" she asked arching an eyebrow.

"I do have the most experience with that kind of stuff, Lexi. You know that."

"Oh, I know," she grumbled. "How long have you been a groomsman?"

"Since about November, I guess."

"November?!?" she cried. "As in last November? As in almost a year ago November? You've known as long as we were together?"

"Lexi, you didn't want to talk about it, and I certainly wasn't going to bring it up," he said defending himself.

"Yeah, but Ramsey, November?" she groaned.

"You didn't want to have anything to do with the wedding plans. But I couldn't escape them. I kept you hidden from what was going on, because that's what you wanted."

"I just didn't want to know the date or talk about Jack and Bekah. Something like you being a groomsman I would have been interested to know," she said, amazed at how much he had been able to keep from her.

Ramsey scoffed at her proclamation. "You would *not* have been interested in that information. It would have been another reminder of what you weren't looking for, and I didn't want to be that reminder to you. I wanted to be the...the future," he murmured the last word softly.

Lexi knew that she had been insufferable for the past year about anything to do with the wedding. He was probably right that she hadn't wanted any clues about what was going on, but his ability to hide things from her was not her favorite characteristic about him...especially not right now.

"Okay," she finally breathed tucking a lock behind her ear, "what does a groomsman have to do?"

"Are you sure you want me to continue?" he asked hesitantly.

"Go on."

"Lexi?"

"Ramsey, go on," she demanded.

He sighed, but continued, "Much the same as usual, I suppose—the bachelor party, dinner this week, and a fitting before we jump right into the wedding plans," he proceeded cautiously. "Rehearsal, rehearsal dinner, pictures, wedding, reception."

"Right, of course." Lexi turned her gaze out the window and watched the passing buildings. Her head was dizzy from all the wedding talk, but she was trying her best to hide it. The fact that Jack would be married in less than a week still hadn't hit her yet. But it was getting awfully close.

"We don't have to talk about it…"

"I'm going to the wedding, Ramsey. We're going to have to be able to talk about it," she spoke strongly, taking a deep breath, and turning back towards him. He nodded. "So, what are you wearing?"

"I can't spoil the fun. I want your mouth to drop when you see me."

"It already does," she murmured.

"Good to know," he said smirking.

"Don't get cocky," she told him smacking his arm. The smile that broke out on his face told her that he was about to make a response about just how cocky he was. "And don't think about responding to that."

He laughed his eyes shining. "I have no idea what you're referring to."

"Sure. Sure."

Lexi was pleased that at least for now they were acting normal. She knew it wouldn't always be this way, but things were looking up. She had discussed the wedding without physically gagging, and Ramsey was being himself again. It was a relief that he didn't feel that he had to walk on eggs shells around her. They weren't exactly on solid footing, but she could handle this.

Ramsey maneuvered the car onto his street slowing down as they approached the apartment. Lexi's eyes darted to the driveway where a very pretty, very new, black BMW sat. She admired the car from afar picking out the blue and white logo easily on the back of the vehicle. She couldn't tell what the model was but it was polished and sporty. "Who got a new car?" she asked eyeing the missing license plate.

Ramsey sighed as he looked upon the car sitting in his driveway. "No one."

Lexi looked at him questioningly. "Well then…"

"It's Jack."

Lexi's mouth went dry and her stomach did a flip-flop at the statement—at the thought of seeing him. She could feel her brain kick into overdrive. One part of her desperately wanted to see him. She wanted to run into his arms and feel his body against her own. She wanted to forget everything that had happened. She wanted her world to be tipped off its axis and bask in the goodness of his love. This was the part that she so readily repressed. The other part wanted to spit on him in disgust at his very being. She wanted to find the highest building in the city and push him off of it. She wanted to destroy his life and everything in it. She realized that she repressed that side in his presence as well. The worst thing she could do is be completely indifferent.

Yet her heart skipped a beat as Ramsey's Mercedes slid into the spot next to Jack. "What's he doing here?" she managed to get out.

"We're about to find out, aren't we?" he asking opening his door and exiting the car.

Lexi followed popping the passenger door open. As she stood tall, she came face to face with Jack. Her heart wrenched as she took in the sight of him. His hair was too long and unseemly disheveled. He must have a hair appointment in the near future to look presentable for the big day. His clothes weren't the country clubbing, business executive look he had been accustomed to sporting ever since signing on at Bridges Enterprise. He looked more like *her* Jack in loose fitting denim, a grey t-shirt, and navy blue Converse.

He swished his head to the side, brushing the hair out of his eyes, and when Lexi glanced up, they were set intently on her. She locked eyes with the cerulean orbs in front of her falling into the endless depths of ocean blue. And for a split second, she was lost. Those eyes had suckered her in countless times previously. She took a deep breath and reminded herself why she was here.

"Jack," she murmured, the name coming out throaty as she controlled all the emotions currently running through her.

"Lex," he said nodding his head at her. She shuddered at the sound of him saying her pet name. "I didn't know you here going to be here." He tore his eyes from her and looked at Ramsey expectantly.

Ramsey just shrugged. "Can I help you?"

Lexi edged around the car careful not to make contact with Jack as she passed. "Why didn't you tell me Lexi was going to be here?" he asked, his voice turning possessive.

Ramsey looked at him pointedly. "Probably because you already knew."

"No, I didn't know."

"You invited her Friday, and look, voila, she's here," he muttered, waving his hand in the air. He was obviously still pissed about the fact that she had agreed to come to Atlanta after Jack had cornered her in the hotel hallway. Lexi wished she could take it all back. She was such an idiot when she was drunk.

"I…wait…what?" he asked glancing between Ramsey and Lexi.

"Regardless," Ramsey said cutting him off, "what are you doing here?"

Jack glanced at Lexi nervously. And for a brief moment, before he returned his attention to Ramsey, Lexi noticed something else in his look. She could have picked it out anywhere. He had looked at her with hunger, with desire in his eyes. His pupils had dilated at the sight of her barely-there tank top and short khaki shorts. Some things never changed.

"Can I talk to you?" he asked Ramsey focusing his eyes anywhere but on Lexi.

Ramsey opened the trunk, pulled out Lexi's luggage, and began hauling it up to the apartment. "Talk," he grunted moving up the stairs. Jack clambered after him with Lexi following distantly behind. Ramsey fished out his keys and let them all into his apartment. Dropping Lexi's suitcase to the floor, he set his eyes on Jack expectantly. "What is it, Howard?"

Jack's eyes shifted anxiously between Ramsey and Lexi. "Could I speak to you alone, actually?"

Lexi reached for her luggage. "Oh, there's something you can't tell me. Shocker!" she said sarcastically.

"Hey," Ramsey spoke sharply, reaching out, and gripping the luggage with his hand, "I've got this." Lexi looked into his bright green eyes and released her hold. "Just give me a minute," he told Jack before hauling her suitcase upstairs.

Lexi followed behind, angrier than she had originally thought. She knew that she had reason to continue to be angry at Jack. She still hadn't told anyone exactly what had gone down that fateful night last August more out of shame than anything. Jack had hurt her, but just as bad, she had let him. After seeing everything crumble before her eyes, she had been forced to keep a wall up against those feelings at all times. Even a minor crack in that wall had made her snap at him.

Taking a right into the guest bedroom, Ramsey set her suitcase down next to the dresser before turning to face her. "What was that about?" he asked her keeping his voice level.

Lexi shook her head back and forth debating whether or not it was even worth it to bring up. "Nothing."

"I know that you're not happy about all this, and that there are a lot of issues. But you asked what I had to do as a groomsman. Well, this is one of the things that I have to do as a groomsman," he said rolling his eyes. "It's not like I want to talk to him about whatever he needs, but Bekah needs to me to do this. She's my sister."

"I know, Ramsey. Alright?" she asked throwing her hands up in defeat.

"I'm not trying to make you feel bad," he said reaching forward and pulling her into his arms. "I just have to deal with him. You snapping won't help the situation. You're still going to have to deal with him either way too."

Lexi sighed knowing he was right, but hating admitting it. "You're right."

He planted a kiss on her forehead before releasing her. "Get comfortable. You know where everything is. Hopefully this won't take long."

As soon as Ramsey closed the door, Lexi kicked her luggage with such force she had to hop around on one foot due to the pain. She crumpled to the ground to examine the damage which had only furthered her anger and frustration. Her toes were red, but she hadn't broken the skin. They just felt cramped as she tried to wiggle them. After lying on the floor for another minute, she stood back up and began to pace the room.

How much longer could he really take? She desperately wanted to know what they were talking about and why it was taking so long. She assumed it had something to do with the preparations for this weekend, which made her skin crawl.

She was going to be at his damn wedding and suffer through the lies that they were going to tell each other. She was going to laugh during their vows and smile devilishly when he put a real ring next to the fake one Bekah was already wearing like a trophy. These were the things that she wanted to do, but not the thing that she wanted to do the most.

She wanted to ruin Bekah. She wanted to object in front of everyone that these two individuals were fit for marriage. When asked on what grounds, she couldn't decide which answer to give—infidelity, lust, greed, manipulation, lies. The list was endless. It would be a triumphant, beautiful moment for Lexi.

Chyna hadn't thought so. She had completely disagreed with the idea. She might be destroying Bekah and Jack, but to what end? Did it make her any better than Bekah to destroy something like this? Lexi had tried to block out those questions. She had never stooped to Bekah's level once. Not once.

There had been plenty of opportunities for sabotage. She could have ruined everything long ago, and yet she had refrained. If she hadn't been capable of doing it then, what made Lexi think she could do it at the wedding? But it was her last chance. After they married, she would no longer have a chance.

Still, she kept asking herself what she was going to have a chance for. She wasn't going to magically win Jack back after all of this. There was no potential left with Jack. Just a long lost love of someone who could never fully reciprocate those affections. It pained her through and through to know that Jack would never again be hers. He had been such a large part of her past that her future felt incomplete without him around. There were always those times when something happened, and her heart would ache for him. A hole was left in his absence and gradually it shrank, but it never completely disappeared.

A beep from her phone pulled her out of her sinking mood. She fished the phone out of her purse and clicked the button to pull up the text message. *"Hey, I tried calling earlier. Can you talk?"*

Lexi glanced up at the door, tentative about someone coming into the room. If Ramsey showed up, she knew this would be the last thing she wanted to deal with. *"I want to, but I'm kind of busy."*

"Later?"

"I'll try and find some time."

"I wish you weren't so far away. I've been thinking about you all morning."

Lexi smiled at the words pushing the dose of guilt away. *"I've been thinking about you too."*

"I really wanted to hear your voice."

"I wish I had more time to talk."

"Me too, babe."

Her heart fluttered. She could almost hear the way he said that last line and it made her tingle to her toes. *"Stupid wedding."*

"Skip the wedding and come back to me."

She shook her head with a big goofy grin on her face. *"You make it sound so tempting."*

"I can think of even more tempting things."

"I'm sure you can, but it's an old friend's wedding. I have to be here. It's complicated."

"Don't let it be."

The door jiggled as if someone was about to walk into the room so she quickly shot back a response. *"Sorry, I have to go. Talk to you later."*

She threw her phone into her purse just as Ramsey walked through the door. She tried to act nonchalant as if she hadn't really been doing anything while he had been downstairs. Her heart was racing though. Ramsey didn't know that anything had happened when they had been apart, and she wasn't planning on telling him.

She wasn't sure how Ramsey would react to news like that, but she didn't want to find out. If the time ever came up in which she would need to tell him what had happened while they had been a part, then she would think about it. Until then, her lips were sealed, and she had always been good at keeping secrets.

Ramsey saw straight through her when he entered the room. "What's going on?" she finally asked her voice staying level. His eyes darted from her face to her purse and back. She watched them flicker to her hands lightly clenching onto her khaki shorts to keep from moving. When they returned to her face, she could see that they were set and suspicious, but he wasn't going to ask.

"Nothing," he said a bit too quickly.

Lexi arched an eyebrow. She had been too focused on trying to keep from giving away what she had been doing to even really notice Ramsey. His shoulders were tensed and his face looked weary. His own hands were clenched more forcefully at his side. She had no idea what this was about. "What? What happened?"

"Nothing, Lexi," he repeated.

"Don't lie to me. Look at yourself, you're tensed for battle. What was he doing here?" she asked exasperated.

"Lexi, please don't make me say anything. He asked me not to." She could see that he was visibly fighting with himself about what to do. "I wanted to let you know that he was gone so maybe we could get some lunch," he suggested, nodding his head towards the stairs. She followed him out of the room, but was unable to get the thoughts of Jack out of her mind.

"Can I have a hint?" she asked as she trudged down the stairs after him.

"No."

"Ramsey, come on. He came here for some reason, right?"

"Yes, Lexi, but he wanted to speak to me alone for that same reason," he said, never turning around to directly address her.

"It can't be that important. He only has a week to the wedding, what could be so secretive?"

"Lexi, I'm begging you to drop this. Just let it go. I don't even want to talk about it," he said shaking his head again.

She followed him to the kitchen and watched as he prepared lunch for them. It was nothing too fancy, but she had never liked him for his extravagance. Her mind was elsewhere anyways. All she wanted to know was what had happened between him and Jack. She could see the weight of Jack's words weighing down on Ramsey. Whatever the conversation had been about had been important. It hadn't been some random discussion about what tie to wear or some last minute demand made from the groom. This was something serious.

And however she tried, she couldn't just drop the subject. It was there in the back of her mind throughout lunch. He talked pleasantries about the weather and insignificant things that had occurred over the past month. It might as well have been falling on deaf ears as much as she paid attention. She did her fair share of participating, but her mind was elsewhere and he knew it.

"I think that's the third time you've agreed with me on something that you hate," he said sitting back in his chair and taking a swig of his beer.

Lexi blushed slightly at the statement. "Sorry, I'm just out of it."

"Psh," he muttered eyeing her cautiously. "You've been like this since Jack left. Can't you just forget about it?"

A smile touched the edges of her mouth as she shook her head no. She really couldn't forget about it now, especially after he had made such a big deal about it.

"You're incorrigible. You know that, right?" he asked taking a deep breath.

"Absolutely. So, what was he here for?" she asked leaning her elbows against the kitchen table and resting her chin in her hands.

"I really shouldn't tell you."

"Probably not," she agreed cordially a teasing smile touching her features.

"Then, why am I?"

"Because you know I'll never let it go."

He rolled his eyes at her persistence. "Damn you, woman," he said standing abruptly. "I gave him my word. If I tell you, what will it be worth?"

"Jack's is worth nothing so I've no idea why you feel the need to protect him," she shot back standing to face him.

"I'm not protecting him," he said carefully, "just the fact that I told him I wouldn't say anything should be enough. You're likely the last person I would want to tell anyway."

Lexi's eyebrows shot up at the last statement. She could tell that he wanted to take it back, but it was too late. Something had happened with Jack and not only did Jack not want anyone to know, but Ramsey had some strong inclination not to let Lexi know in particular. This completely changed things. She had been persistent before, but this was a different story. This was somehow personal.

"And why exactly would you not want *me* to know?" she asked eyeing him reproachfully.

Ramsey scratched the back of his head thoughtfully as stared forward at Lexi. "You have a long...history with Jack."

"As if that changes anything."

"But it does," he said closing the distance between them. She took a step backwards not wanting the force of his presence to sidetrack their conversation, but he followed her movements wrapping a tight arm around her waist, securing her in place.

"Personal space," she muttered causing him to smile at their remembered meeting where he hadn't been able to avoid standing so close to her.

"This is where I like to be," he said leaning down and placing a kiss on her forehead.

Her eyes fluttered closed at the contact, but immediately opened back up to stare into his sparkling green eyes. "So, are you going to tell me what he wanted?" she asked trying to stay on track.

Ramsey groaned tilting his head back to the ceiling. "He's getting cold feet," he said barely louder than a whisper.

Lexi's body froze at his words. The words hit her like a splash of ice water. She could feel everything begin to move in slow motion. Her hands which were gripping Ramsey's sides began to shake. She dropped them immediately and took a step away from him. She cleared her throat just so that she had something to do with her hands.

"See! I knew I shouldn't have said anything," he said instantly regretting his actions.

"No, no it's fine," she said color beginning to return to her cheeks.

Ramsey rolled his eyes. "If you say so."

"Did you—did you talk him back into it?" she asked hesitantly not wanting to appear too eager on either side.

"I tried not to get involved, but he wouldn't let me. I told him to weigh the options and make a decision from there. He nodded along as if he had done that already, but I don't know what he's going to do. I told him that it's only a week before the wedding and that this is a normal feeling, but I've never been…uh," he paused, "in this situation so I was just going off what people told me. I told him if he thought he had been able to go through with it up until this point, that he was probably just spooked."

"Yeah," she coughed to clear her throat again. "That's good advice."

"Please, don't think too much into this," he begged and pleaded with her, reaching out for her hand.

"Ramsey, I'm not thinking into it at all," she told him giving him a smile that they both knew was fake.

8

DECEMBER EIGHT MONTHS EARLIER

Lexi's phone buzzed noisily as soon as she exited the airplane. She rifled around in her travel purse filled to the brim with items she couldn't fit in her luggage. After locating it, she pressed the green button and said, "Chyna, perfect timing."

"Perfect timing?" Chyna asked. "I've been calling you for an hour. Where the hell have you been?"

Lexi chuckled. Leave it to Chyna to forget that her best friend was leaving the state for over a week to spend Christmas with her family. "I'm in Atlanta. I just landed at the airport. Remember? We had this discussion."

"No, we didn't," Chyna said cattily.

"Yes, we did. I told you I would be gone a week to visit my family and Ramsey," she reminded her.

"We did not have this conversation. Where were we?" she demanded.

Lexi sighed as she moved through the crowd with her carry-on bag in tow. "We were getting manicures early in the week."

"Wait, was that Wednesday?"

"Yes. See I knew you'd remember."

"Oh no, I remember the manicure," Chyna said flatly. "And I had a date that night."

"You've been having a lot of those lately," Lexi said chuckling to herself. Not that it was any different for Chyna to have a lot of dates, but normally she talked about them. She hadn't said a peep about the guys she had been seeing lately. Lexi found it refreshing not to have to listen to her talk about how good they were in bed—or how terrible.

"Not anymore than usual," she stated a bit more defensive than normal, but Lexi brushed it off assuming it was another one of Chyna's dramatic moments.

"So, what can I do for you, chica?"

"I was going to have you come over to finalize the New Year's plans, but obviously we can't do that," she said annoyed.

"Not my fault. I called to see if I needed to finalize anything, and you said I didn't," Lexi told her hopping on a train to take her from her terminal to the baggage claim.

"What? No you didn't," Chyna cried emphatically.

"What's with you forgetting things lately?" Lexi asked.

"I'm not *forgetting* things," she snapped. "We just…never had that conversation. Anyway, I suppose I'll do it all myself."

"Chyna, you can email me the plans, and I can look over them. I'm going to be at my parent's house the majority of the time. It's not as if it's inconvenient," Lexi told her rolling her eyes. Chyna had gotten it into her mind that she wanted to throw the most lavish New Year's party ever. Lexi wasn't sure why they couldn't go to a party that was already being thrown, but Chyna had insisted. And when Chyna insisted, it was really better to just acquiesce than to argue.

"Oh, I guess that'll work," she agreed finally, as Lexi stepped off the train.

"Great."

"So, what are you doing with Ramsey when you're there? You haven't been together in a couple weeks because of finals. Should be a," Chyna coughed as if she couldn't find the proper word, "relaxing week."

Lexi laughed loving her best friend in that moment. "Yes, it should be relaxing. However, I have no idea what he has planned," she admitted.

"Let me know as soon as you do. I want all the gushy details."

"Of course," Lexi said standing in front of the baggage claim.

"Oh, and I'm going to send you some stuff. If you could look at that and get back to me, that would be great," Chyna said. "Gotta go. Love ya, chica"

The phone died in her hands. Lexi sighed and threw the phone back in her purse. Typical Chyna. She had been even more flighty than normal lately, and Lexi hadn't been able to figure it out. She didn't mind that her friend had been kind of MIA, but she was curious as to the cause.

After acquiring her black suitcase, all thoughts of Chyna left her mind. She walked through the double doors of Hartsfield-Jackson International Airport and let her eyes strain for the familiar, sleek, black Mercedes. She knew there were probably a bunch of them gliding past the entrance, but she was always able to pick out Ramsey's.

Her stomach filled with butterflies as she searched for the car. She had really missed him in his absence. He had been busy with work while she was trapped in the law library nearly twenty-four hours a day. Neither of them had had the time to see each other. She was distressed with how close they had gotten and hoped the distance hadn't changed him. She knew she shouldn't think like that. They had waited so long to be involved romantically and physically that she knew that train of thought wasn't logical.

Still a part of her wondered what he did while they were apart. Yes, they were exclusive, and she had told herself that she was only going to be with him. No more lies on her end…ever again.

Just when she moved to sit on a bench to wait, a black Maserati pulled up in front of her. She gawked at the extravagant car. She never could figure out why someone would drive that beautiful car around Atlanta, where the traffic sucked and no one knew how to park.

"Lexi, let's go," she heard someone call.

Lifting her eyes to the driver's side of the Italian sports car, she found Brad staring back at her smiling and waving. Her mouth dropped as she realized that this was *Ramsey's* Maserati, and for some reason he had let Brad drive it around town.

"What are you doing here?" she couldn't help but ask as she hurried towards him with her luggage. He placed her items in the trunk before vaulting back into the driver's seat.

Lexi looked into the car hoping to see Ramsey's smiling face from the passenger's side, but he wasn't there. Her heart sank. She wanted to see him. It had been too long.

Brad raced out of the airport as soon as she had closed the door. "Sorry, Ramsey got stuck at the office."

Lexi narrowed her eyes suspiciously. She still didn't know exactly what Ramsey did. The urge to find out was eating at her. She wasn't sure why, but the topic had never come up again. "And where is that exactly?"

Brad glanced at her briefly, his eyebrows knitted together. "B.E. obviously. Where did you think?" he asked.

Lexi breathed out a sigh of relief, but also frustration. B.E. or Bridges Enterprise was the corporation Ramsey's grandfather and father had built from ground up. They were extremely proud of their accomplishments, and not too thrilled with Ramsey's rebellion against all their hard work. Yet, he had rebelled and Lexi had no idea exactly what he did for the company.

"Can you take me there?" Lexi asked.

Brad remained silent for a minute before shaking his head. "Nah. I told Ramsey I'd take you directly to our place. He'd kill me if he found out I drove the Maserati anyway."

"Well then, I'll tell him if you don't take me there," she told him easily manipulating the situation in her favor.

"Really, Lexi?" he grumbled.

"Don't make me prove it, Brad," she told him determined.

He sighed realizing he was beat and nodded. "I'll have to drop you off though. I don't want anyone seeing me in this thing."

"Now, that's not something I ever thought I'd hear you say," she said with a sly wink in his direction. He glared at her as he pulled off the interstate and veered towards the tower in the distance.

When he finally arrived at the entrance of Bridges Enterprise, Lexi leaned across her seat and kissed Brad gently on the cheek. "Thanks so much."

"Just remember…I was not in the Maserati."

"What Maserati?" she asked coyly.

"Thanks. I'll take your stuff to the apartment. See your hot ass later."

Lexi rolled her eyes and slammed the door in his face. She watched him zoom down the street and through the winding traffic. Lexi made her way across the street and into the large glass building. She took a deep breath as she crossed the threshold, memories of the last time she had entered the premises clouding her vision.

It had been nearly five months since she had found out about Jack's engagement to Bekah in this very building. Five months since she had discovered Bekah's evil plot to destroy whatever she had with Jack. In the grand scheme of things, that wasn't long enough to get over everything that had happened with Jack. It wasn't long enough to erase her aching, and it wasn't long enough to erase her anger.

As she walked into the building that had tore out her heart, stomped on it, and then placed it back in her chest, like pieces of broken shrapnel, as if nothing had happened, she put one foot in front of the other and held her head high. She could do this. She knew it. Her life had changed and now she had Ramsey, her gorgeous boyfriend, who she was here to see. She couldn't feel anymore or any less for him based on his connection to a building. The building wasn't changing and it wasn't the building that had hurt her.

Sighing despite herself, Lexi meandered through the busy foyer and walked up to the first available representative. Lexi cringed as she noticed the tiny Asian woman that was standing in front of her. She had managed to get the same woman who had been absolutely useless to her when she had been here looking for Jack.

"Hello, ma'am. How may I help you?" the woman asked politely

Deciding she might as well attempt to get some information out of the woman, even if it was going to prove to be fruitless, Lexi cleared her throat and said, "I'm here to see Mr. Bridges."

The woman nearly dropped the pen she was holding. "Excuse me?"

"I'm here to see Mr. Bridges. Can you direct me to his office?"

The woman glanced over at the man who was working at the other computer and then back to Lexi. "Mr. Bridges does not take clients, unfortunately. What concerns are you having? Perhaps I can place you with another associate."

Lexi tried to keep from rolling her eyes. "Ramsey's here. I just need to see him. So if you would be so kind to tell me where he is, that would be fantastic," she stated dryly.

"Ramsey? Oh Ramsey! Mr. Bridges," she muttered putting the pieces together. "He does not take clients either, ma'am."

"I'm not a client. I'm his girlfriend."

This seemed to send her for an even bigger loop. She sputtered clicking on her screen a few times more out of habit than anything. "I...uh...I'm not authorized..."

She was cut off mid-sentence, "Perhaps I can direct you."

Lexi swiveled around and found herself face to face with a familiar face. Though, she couldn't exactly place where she knew him from.

"Mr. Calloway..." the woman sighed breathily leaning forward against the desk.

"I can take it from here, Tiff, thanks," he said charmingly adding a wink in her direction. Lexi could tell that the woman was melting behind her. And with good reason. The man before her was handsome with classic, boy-next-door, good looks. He was nearly six feet tall with short brown hair stylishly spiked in the front and chocolate brown eyes. His teeth were perfectly straight and white, and the smile he sent her way was nothing less than friendly. He had a square jaw line with light stubble across it. He wore a crisp navy suit with charcoal pinstripes over a light grey button-up and red tie. He still managed to look devious despite his self-assured appearance. "Lexi, right?"

"Right...you said Calloway?" Lexi asked following him to the elevators surprised that he knew her name.

"You don't remember me?" he asked hurt coming into his eyes.

"Should I?"

"Brandon Calloway. We met in the elevator. I gave you my business card," he said trying to bring back the memories.

Lexi gasped and reached into her purse pulling out a wallet filled with various cards. She rifled through them until she came across what she was searching for. "Brandon Calloway," she murmured softly. "You were so helpful. Thank you. Sorry I didn't remember you."

"No problem. I mean we only met once for all of five seconds," he said smiling at her charmingly again.

"Well, I appreciate you taking me to see Ramsey," she told him stepping into the elevator.

"Why do I always seem to be taking you to see other men?" he questioned her as he leaned against the metal railing in the elevator.

Lexi blushed pushing a piece of hair behind her ear. She hated that someone else had knowledge of the last time that she was in the building, but she couldn't take it back. Holding her head high, just like she promised herself she would, she smiled back into his endearing face. "I'm a popular woman," she teased.

"As you should be," he agreed his eyes flashing from her face, to her bust, to her hips, and back. The elevator abruptly stopped and several people entered. As the doors were about to close, someone shot their hand out and stopped it.

"Calloway, you have those reports ready?" a man in his late forties asked.

"Uh yeah, they're on my desk," Brandon answered.

"Well, go get them and take them to Mr. Bridges. He needs them today—now," he added hastily.

"Fuck," he muttered angrily under his breath.

"Now, Calloway!"

"Yeah, yeah," he said reaching forward and pressing the number 24 on the elevator. "Pit stop?"

Lexi followed Brandon off of the elevator and down the hallway. She had no other tour guide, so the only thing she could do was to follow him to his office. She entered the office and couldn't help but to compare it to the only other office she had ever seen in the building. It was much smaller, but still had a series of glass panes behind the desk overlooking the city. The view wasn't quite as spectacular and the room was sparsely decorated, but Lexi kind of liked it. A medium-sized desk sat in the center of the room in front of two cushioned chairs. Lexi moved forward cautiously and took a seat as she waited for Brandon to finish what he had to get.

"So, what do you do here?" she asked surveying the artwork on the walls.

"I'm an accountant. It's all a little technical. I'll save you from the boredom, but I crunch numbers for the big guy," he muttered rummaging through a stack of papers.

"Oh, nice."

"Don't kid yourself. It's a job," he said stuffing the papers into a clear binder and clipping everything together. Lexi didn't really know what to say, so she remained silent as Brandon finished up with his paperwork. "Sorry," he finally muttered standing up straight and stuffing the binder under his arm. "Ready to go?"

"Yeah, sure," she said hopping up and smiling brightly.

"So...Ramsey Bridges?" Brandon asked knowingly.

"Uh, yeah," she murmured brushing a strand of hair behind her ear.

"How do you know all of these high ranking people within B.E.? Jack Howard. Ramsey Bridges."

"Oh well, Ramsey and I are dating," she told him as they took the elevator to the top floor.

"Why does that not surprise me?" he said with a hint of sarcasm. "How long has this been going on, if you don't mind me asking?"

"Uh...I guess officially since Thanksgiving, but we've been seeing each other since August I suppose."

"August," he gasped, surprise written all over his face. He quickly hid the look, but she had seen it and heard the disbelief in his voice.

"Uh, yeah."

"August," he said more calmly. "I didn't think he had it in him."

"What?" Lexi asked scrunching her eyebrows together at his statement.

"Nothing, sorry. I've known Ramsey for a long time, and no offense, but it just doesn't sound like him."

"What doesn't sound like him?" Lexi asked confused.

"Nothing. Forget I mentioned it."

"No really," she pestered.

"It's nothing. He doesn't date people for very long is all," Brandon said with a shrug.

"Oh," Lexi said taking in what he was saying. This guy was surprised by her existence as his girlfriend. She bit her lip deciphering the statements. Ramsey had flat out told her that he hadn't had a girlfriend, but the concept was so foreign to her. She wasn't entirely sure how to process it even now.

Yet this guy knew a side of Ramsey that she didn't, and she would be stupid not to use the assets in front of her. She didn't want to, but her curiosity got the best of her. "How long have you known Ramsey?"

"Uh...we grew up together," he told her more tentative now that he knew that she was dating someone else.

"Really?" she asked surprised that she hadn't met him yet. She had hung out with his high school friends several times since the night of the bonfire, and she had never heard a Brandon Calloway mentioned.

"Yeah. Why?"

"I've just never heard him mention you is all."

"I could say the same thing about you, honey."

Lexi cringed but pushed forward with the conversation. "Well, I'm going to be in Atlanta for the next week maybe we could all get together. I'm sure Ramsey would like that."

Brandon chuckled to himself. "Yes, I'm sure he'd just *love* that," he said sardonically. "You bring it up to him and see what he says about that."

"What? You don't think he'll want to?" she asked carefully.

"Not particularly."

"Oh," Lexi said confused.

"I'd stick to his bidding, if I were you," Brandon told her standing up straight as the elevator dinged to the top floor. "It's easier that way."

Before Lexi could say anything further, the elevator doors popped open and she found herself standing in an enormous foyer connecting several massive offices. Unlike the other floors, it appeared that the entire top floor was devoted solely to the highest management of Bridges Enterprise. There were very few offices, but each of them was ten times the size of every other office in the building.

"May I assist you?" a beautiful brunette asked walking forward on her kitten heels to greet Lexi.

"Kace," Brandon purred, falling back into his cool demeanor instantly.

"Mr. Calloway," she stated, her eyes narrowing, "what brings you to the big leagues?"

Lexi choked out a cough. "I'm here to see you, darlin', of course," he suavely stated, ignoring her jab and moving towards her.

"Then you can turn yourself right around and get back on that elevator," she told him twirling her fingers at him.

"Also, I have this," he muttered revealing the binder he had been carrying. "Which Mr. Bridges needed on his desk oh…yesterday."

"You're insufferable," Kace murmured, reaching out to snatch the papers out of his hand. He grabbed her wrist instead yanking her forward to only an inch from his face. She gasped as he tilted her off balance bringing her dangerously close to his lips. When she regained her composure, she pushed him forcefully in the chest and straightened out her pencil skirt.

"Oh, and Miss Lexi is here to see Ramsey Bridges," he muttered pointing his thumb at Lexi.

"Ramsey isn't seeing anyone today…or ever," she mumbled under her breath.

"I'm not a client," she told the woman brushing a lock behind her ear.

"That's his girlfriend."

"Girlfriend?" she asked incredulously.

Brandon let loose a loud laugh at her expression. "Exactly what I said."

Lexi couldn't figure out why everyone found it so unbelievable that she was his girlfriend. She knew they hadn't officially announced it to the universe, but geez this was completely different. "Yes, I'm his girlfriend. Can you please show me where he is?"

"Sure thing. Brandon Calloway, take those papers to him right *now*," she told him pointing her finger directly into his chest.

"Yes, ma'am. I like a forceful woman," he said smacking her on the ass with his binder as he passed.

"I'm going to file a sexual harassment suit against you, Brandon Calloway," Kace threatened.

"Then I'll have to file one against you with what you did to me in that janitor's closet the other day," he muttered.

"Brandon!" she gasped shaking her head as he darted around the corner disappearing before she could thoroughly reprimand him. "My apologies." Lexi laughed at them as she followed her to Ramsey's office. It was the very last one on the right and the only one absent a secretary. "He's not here all that often," she volunteered as to why the place looked deserted. "Good luck."

"Thanks," Lexi told Kace, not certain why she would need luck as she knocked on the door. She jiggled the knob, but it remained locked so she just waited…and waited. When no one answered, she knocked again more forcefully.

"What do you want? Christ, I'm in the office for one day and you have to bother me?" Ramsey called from inside his office. He yanked the door open and stared straight ahead in surprise. His jaw went slack and he immediately looked apologetic about his attitude. "Lexi."

"Surprise," she managed smiling brightly into his gorgeous face.

"What are you doing here?" he asked pulling the door further closed.

"I came to see my boyfriend."

"Brad dropped you off here?"

"How else would I get here?"

"Right I dunno. Can you just, uh…give me a minute?" he asked nervously scratching the back of his head.

Lexi narrowed her eyes at him. "Why? What are you doing in there? Is someone in there with you?" She took a hard look at his clothing, but didn't really see anything out of place. He was wearing charcoal dress slacks with a navy blue button-up tucked into the expensive material. The top button was undone and he was without a tie, but that was hardly surprising.

"What? No, well yes, but…"

Lexi pushed the door hard letting it swing open and peered around Ramsey's large form. There sitting in one of the plush leather chairs was a tall blonde leaning languidly over a large computer monitor. Despite her casual posture, her clothes were professional in black pants, a crisp white blouse, and black dress heels. Her eyes were intense and focused, and she didn't even look up as the door swung open.

"Who is this?" she asked glancing between Ramsey and the woman.

Ramsey cleared his throat. "Lola, I'd like you to meet someone. This is Lexi"

The woman glanced up and smiled sweetly. "Hello, darling," she drawled. She stood tall nearly six feet and made her way over to them. "What a pleasure to finally meet you."

Lexi glanced between Ramsey and this Lola woman, her mouth opened slightly in confusion. She had never heard of her before. How was it that Lola had heard about her? Lexi's mind was swimming with possibilities. Everything she had just heard from Brandon and Kace filtered through her mind. Was it impossible for her to be his girlfriend, because in fact he was with someone else? She didn't want to even fathom that.

Her heart was pounding in her chest and she tried to swallow but was unsuccessful. Her mind went to the worst possible place causing her to cough and sputter in horror. How could he do this to her? She had thought he was a nice guy and all along he had been playing her the fool. She felt like an idiot.

"Lexi, please calm down," Ramsey said sliding a hand through his hair.

"How can I calm down? Look at her," she muttered unable to control herself.

Ramsey sighed heavily. "Lola, I need to handle this. Can I meet you later to finish discussing the details?"

"Of course, darling. Anything for you, love," Lola purred before stepping over the threshold and exiting the office.

"This isn't what it looks like," Ramsey said immediately.

"No?" she asked taking a deep breath to steady herself. She owed him at least the chance to explain himself. Her past had jaded her against this very scenario. "How come I've never heard about her before? Yet, she seems to have heard about me."

"Uh…it's hard to explain," he told her scratching his head again thoughtfully.

"Well, try," she commanded plopping down into one of the chairs.

"To put it plainly, Lola is my business partner."

"Oh yes, and what type of business do you run exactly, Ramsey? You still haven't told me. We've known each other for six months, and yet, I still have yet to find out what it is exactly that you do. Where do you spend all your time? How do you have all this free time to do nothing? Are you just living off of your trust fund?" she muttered the last question in frustration and immediately regretted it. She hadn't meant to ask that, but deep down she had always wondered if it was true.

"Wow," he breathed. "I'm going to assume you're a bit distraught." Lexi lowered her eyes to the ground feeling kind of terrible that she had blurted out all those questions at once. "I do not live off of my trust fund. In fact, I've barely touched that money. Sure, for special occasions I tap into it, but I try to live on my own."

"Is your Maserati a special occasion?" she asked bitterly.

He smiled despite himself. "The Maserati was a birthday present, which is precisely why you have never seen me drive it."

"Oh," she said her mouth popping open again.

"You know what?" he asked. "I think it might be better if I just show you what I do. You might not understand if I explained it."

Lexi gulped unprepared for this. "You sure she's just your business partner?"

Ramsey's smile lit up her insides. He was so magnetic. Something about him turned her body to mush when she looked at him. Not only was he incredibly handsome, but he had a certain charm, a certain charisma that she couldn't get over. And when he looked at her then, she knew that she had acted impulsively out of fear. Too long had she become accustomed to a life of secrecy that she assumed anything suspect was just that…because it always had turned out that way in the past. When she looked at him, she knew that he was hers and no one else's.

"Alright, where are we going?" she asked a cautious smile forming on her face.

"That's more like it," he said drawing her to her feet and kissing her tender lips. She leaned into the kiss letting her hands twine through his short blond hair. His arms wrapped around her slim waist pulling her body against his own.

Someone clearing their throat in the doorway made them jump apart in surprise. "Don't let me interrupt anything," Bekah cooed leaning against the door frame. Her shoulder length hair was perfectly styled with choppy bangs covering her forehead. She wore a black skirt suit over a yellow blouse with matching black heeled boots.

"Hey, Bek, what can I do for you?" Ramsey asked pulling Lexi closer to him.

Bekah strolled in the office, putting one foot in front of the other as she walked. The smile she wore was devilish, and Lexi could see the wheels turning in her mind. She looked as if she was ready to pounce. "Well, I came over to ask you about some paperwork on my desk."

"Why would I help with that?" he asked coolly.

"I was hoping that you would reconsider your position in the company. I could always use your expertise," she said taunting him.

"Right. Well, I'm not reconsidering," he told her flatly.

"Yes, I figured as much. When I got over here, I couldn't help overhearing," she said still walking slowly towards them.

"Is there a point, Bekah?"

"Of course. I was just surprised to hear that Lexi is now your girlfriend," she said crossing her arms and stopping a few feet from Ramsey. "Why haven't I heard about this? Why haven't *any* of us heard about this?"

"Really, it's none of your business," Lexi spoke up for the first time not needing the support Ramsey was offering, though she did appreciate the gesture.

"Everything that happens here is my business."

"It's a good thing I'm not *here*, isn't it?" Ramsey told her.

Bekah smiled cheerfully. "Right, that brings me back to my other point. Thank you for reminding me. I was surprised to find out that you still hadn't told Lexi about your whores."

"Whores?" Lexi asked glancing up at Ramsey. She didn't want to be taken in my Bekah's tactics, but the look on Ramsey's face was murderous. What she had said had hit home.

"Thank you, Bekah," he said her name as if he wanted to spit. "I think you've helped enough. You can see yourself out, yes?"

"Wait, you mean she doesn't know about them?" she asked completely ignoring his request. "I mean since you spend all of your time with them, I thought that she should know. I saw Lola leaving so I figured you had to have told her."

Lexi gulped not wanting to continue this conversation with Bekah in the room, but she couldn't help herself. "What is she talking about?"

"Nothing," he grumbled, glaring at Bekah.

Bekah chuckled to herself seemingly enjoying Ramsey's discomfort. "Oh, Ramsey, why don't you just give it up?"

Lexi realized for the first time since Bekah had walked into the room that this wasn't actually an attack on her. Bekah's motivations were to hit Ramsey. She didn't know what she was saying about whores, but she wasn't going to let Bekah do this. She knew how she worked now, and she was smarter than that. She would find out eventually what Bekah was talking about, but she didn't need to know what it was about just then. She needed to be there for Ramsey, because it looked like she had been thrust into the middle of some age old sibling dispute.

"Fuck off, Bek," Ramsey cried. "Stop trying to ruin everyone's life."

"I'm not ruining anyone's life. You're doing that all on your own," Bekah said with a wink.

"Bekah, just get out," Ramsey bellowed stomping towards the door and wrenching it open.

Bekah directed her attention back towards Lexi. "Well, you'll find out all of his deep dark secrets soon enough. That will be a great day for me," she told Lexi before she began to walk out the door.

"And why is that?" Lexi snapped, immediately wishing she hadn't. Bekah fixed her ice cold stare upon Lexi.

"Then you'll be out of everyone's life." With that she turned and walked out.

Lexi stormed after her, ready to give her a piece of her mind. She wanted to tell her everything. She wanted to tell her how Jack still wanted her. How that ring on her finger was a goddamn fake. She wanted to tell her about how she had fucked her fiancé right under her nose. She wanted to tell her *everything*, but as she reached the door, Ramsey slammed it shut.

"I'm sorry," he said immediately scooping her up in his arms. "She's wrong. She's all wrong. I don't want you to leave my life."

The desperation in his voice unnerved her, and she hugged him back releasing her pent up anger for the moment. When she stepped back, she looked into his bright green eyes filled with worry. "I'm not going anywhere," she reassured him.

He blew out the breath he had been holding. "Good."

"But you have to explain what she was talking about."

"I will," he said strength and determination returning to his gaze as he realized he wasn't losing her. "Come on. I'll explain once we get there." He grabbed her hand and pulled her out of the office.

Lexi had a million questions to ask him, but she remained silent. The confrontation with Bekah had given her energy unlike anything she had felt in awhile. She could feel herself beginning to bounce off the walls, but she remained quiet. She needed Ramsey to explain everything to her, and she wouldn't accomplish that by discussing all of her fears with him. She had too many to even begin to articulate which one came first. Bekah was always somehow able to get into her subconscious and eat away at her inner most fears. She really was the devil!

Numbly, Lexi followed Ramsey back through the lobby, taking the elevator to the parking garage located below the building, and into his waiting Mercedes. Lexi tried to remain calm as they traveled through the city. Her confrontation with Bekah had her on edge. She hadn't thought she was capable of despising her more…but she was wrong.

Not only had she destroyed what Lexi had had with Jack, she was trying to ruin it for her and Ramsey as well. Bekah was never going to forgive Lexi for being ahead of her in anything, especially not with the most important men in her life. Lexi just hoped that she didn't have to continually be under crossfire.

They hadn't been driving for more than ten minutes when Ramsey pulled into a mostly deserted parking lot. There was only one car parked in the far corner facing a tall brick wall. Lexi glanced around apprehensively not liking the secluded nature of their location. Ramsey took the spot directly next to the other car and killed the engine.

"Here we are," he said smiling hesitantly.

Lexi noticed the sign posted into the ground in front of Ramsey's car that read 'reserved.' The sign didn't add any legitimacy to the parking lot that they were sitting in, and she could tell her stomach was doing back flips in anticipation. "Where is here exactly?" she managed to ask turning her head to see if perhaps she had missed something.

"Come on. I'll show you," he said opening his door.

"Is it safe?" she asked before he got out of the car. His boisterous laugh as he walked around the car was answer enough. Stepping out of the car, Ramsey took her hand for reassurance before walking to the corner of the parking lot. A large, black, metal door that she hadn't previously noticed was built into the brick wall. Ramsey pulled out a key, unlocked the deadbolt, and swung the door wide for her.

She peered anxiously into the dim light that appeared down a long hallway. He ushered her inside before closing and locking the door behind him. "This way," he told her motioning down the hallway.

"Is this where you tell me you're part of the Umbrella Corporation, and I'm a test subject?" she asked a stilted laugh following the comment.

Ramsey cocked his head to the side, the smirk on his face telling her that he was amused. "Precisely. I hope you're immune."

"My name isn't Alice."

"Alexa. Alice. Close enough," he said stopping abruptly in front of a door with a brass sign on the front that read 'Employees Only.' Passing through that door, they walked to the end of the barren hallway and into what appeared to be, at first glance, a security room for the entire building. Dozens of monitors lined the walls each showing varying angles of what appeared to be a darkened warehouse. A few showed the lighted hallways they had just entered through along with other locales that Lexi had no knowledge of.

"Okay, Ramsey, fill me in. Where the fuck are we?" she asked. Her feelings of apprehension had only heightened.

"This is where I work," he said flipping several switches on a board. Instantly hundreds of lights began to flicker on all around her. But she realized that despite the number of computer screens filtering light into the room, the majority was coming from straight ahead. Lexi's attention returned to the back of the room. She had originally thought it was just a black wall, but in fact, it was an enormous window. She stepped forward to look

Avoiding Responsibility

through the panel of glass in front of her, and saw what appeared to be an empty warehouse in the blackness, come to life.

"Is this...a bar?" she asked mystified. Black granite-topped counters lined the walls on the bottom floor with hundreds of glass bottles atop intricate shelving. High-backed black chairs were tucked into tables in one corner. A dance floor with a stage against the far wall took up nearly half of the room. Carpeted stairs led up to a more secluded area, what she would have guessed to be a VIP section, with posh leather booths and a bar stocked solely with top shelf liquor.

"Yes, well, a club." He came up beside her staring out across the establishment.

"You work at a club?" she asked confused.

"Uh no," he said scratching the back of his head.

"Do you...run security?" she questioned him, trying to put the pieces together. Why would he have waited so long to show her this? It hardly seemed like it was something to be ashamed of. Sure he could be a vice president within Bridges Enterprise, but if he liked this then she couldn't say anything about it. It sure would explain why his family utterly detested his job though.

"No, Lexi, I own the club."

"You *own* this place?" she gasped despite herself. Suddenly so many things fell into place. Memories of a distant past began to fill her mind. Lexi and Ramsey meeting at a club in New York, and him claiming to prefer to do business there. The fact that his entire apartment had been filled to the brim with people partying on a Sunday night, because they couldn't on the weekends. Employees of the various clubs he owned, which also explained the stocked bar he constantly kept on hand. A strange conversation with a bartender at the 755 Club at Turner Field about his new employment; he must have worked for Ramsey at some point. The way Ramsey had edged out of conversations about his employment, and claimed that it was his job to know people. He obviously had to know people to be successful in this town, and everyone likely wanted to know him.

"Among others," he said nodding.

"How many others?" she breathed.

"A dozen or so."

Lexi's mouth dropped open as her eyes took in the scene below her. Everything in that room he owned. The building itself was massive and must have cost a fortune. Not to mention the location directly downtown along with property taxes and a sea of other concerns. The lawyer side of her brain was taking over, and she was quickly measuring up the building from a different perspective.

"About what Bekah said," he murmured reluctantly.

Stopping her endless calculations, Lexi was transported back to reality. She had completely forgotten Bekah. Yet, there must be something else to the story. Bekah had mentioned whores, and Lexi wasn't putting two and two together. Was this how he had met women previously? Was this why everyone had been so surprised that he had a girlfriend? Was he really just a player and all his employees his whores? So many more questions floated through her subconscious as she waited for him to further explain.

"It's just...not all of them are this *type* of club," he managed to get out.

"What do you mean? What type of club are they?" she asked turning away from the window to face him.

He looked at her expectantly as if she was magically going to come up with the answer on her own. When she stared at him blankly, he reluctantly continued, "What other kind of clubs exist?"

Lexi stared at him for a minute longer before realization dawned on her. Her cheeks flared red. "Do you mean strip clubs? You own strip clubs?"

"Yeah, see this is why I never have a girlfriend," he said miserably.

After taking a second to let the concept sink in, Lexi reached out and touched his arm. "Ramsey, I don't care. I still like you. I mean, I'll be honest, I don't like that you spend your time with strippers," she said unable to keep the angst out of her voice. "Especially because I've been oblivious to the fact the whole time."

The thing she hated most about the entire situation was that he had kept it from her. He had hid a *huge* part of himself from her for nearly six months. She had no idea the entire time what he did or who he spent his time with. The fact that he worked with women who were paid to take their clothes off was pretty shitty, but she couldn't change that, and she didn't want to change him. What was infuriating was his deception. He had so easily hid something so endemic in his life from her, and apparently only her.

All of his friends knew where he worked. Bekah and the rest of his family knew where he worked. Jack even probably knew what he did for a living. After all, he had been one of the first to warn her off of Ramsey. It had to have been for good reason—or at least for *some* reason. With all this in consideration, all she could wonder about was what else he was hiding from her.

9

PRESENT

Jack had cold feet.

And as much as Lexi wanted to follow Ramsey's advice, and not think about that fact, it was damn near impossible. Why was he unsure about this wedding? He had made his choice. He had chosen Bekah. It was that simple.

But she knew it wasn't that simple. Jack was terrified of commitment. He knew what could happen to a person if the relationship didn't work, and he was rushing into this. He wouldn't have slept with Lexi the night before the proposal if he didn't have second thoughts. If he was so confident about Bekah, then why did he even jump in that cab with Lexi? Why did he have to try to make it right? Even if this had nothing to do with Lexi, which she tried to actually consider, shouldn't he have been man enough to stick by his decision?

The same thing repeated in her mind. He had made his choice. He had chosen Bekah.

Yet here he was, one week before the big day, chickening out. Sure, Ramsey somehow convinced him that it was customary jitters, but how long would that last? Jack wasn't exactly unfamiliar with rash decisions.

She couldn't even process all of this. She knew what he was capable of, but she wasn't sure he would do it. He had been with Bekah for nearly two years before proposing, and then he had managed to stick it out for an entire year engagement with the witch. Why turn back now?

It's not like he was unaccustomed to long-term relationships, but he had never been faithful to a single person in his life. Danielle. Kate. Lexi. Bekah. Bekah wasn't special in the grand scheme of things. She was just one person in a line of deception and infidelity. The fact that he managed to stay with any one person for a substantial length of time had more to do with the fact that he never got caught, rather than his utter devotion to the person. How could he be committed to anyone when he always had someone on the backburner?

Now that Lexi had removed herself from that position, she wasn't sure what would happen. She wasn't sure if he had reverted back to his old ways, or if she was even the first person he had cheated on Bekah with. He might have been diddling his secretary or the receptionist for his apartment building for all she knew.

Regardless, what she did know is that Jack was having second thoughts about Bekah. A part of her was jumping up and down with that news and not for a reason she expected. She wasn't happy for herself. She was feeling more euphoric at the possibility that Bekah might get hurt.

It was a terrible thought, but she couldn't keep it back. Bekah deserved whatever was coming to her. Considering her upbringing, she must have been acting this way her entire life. As the baby of an incredibly wealthy family it only made sense that she was spoiled. What little discipline likely resulted from that lifestyle must have been snuffed out of her when she didn't have to work for anything in her life, from her private school education paid for by Daddy, to the high end job in Bridges that she was given right after graduation.

Not that it was an excuse that her parents had created a monster. Ramsey, after all, was relatively normal. He had bucked the parental guidance though. If he had stayed the course as Bekah had, would he be just another robot?

This line of thought brought her back to Ramsey, as usual. Though things were complicated with Ramsey in ways that she didn't even like to think about, she still had very strong feelings for him. And when he said not to think too much into Jack's cold feet, she knew he meant something completely different. He meant don't think about Jack. Don't even consider Jack. Get Jack out of your mind once and for all. And most of all think about him. Think about what their future could be together and where that could lead them. Think about all the things he had given her that she had never even considered as an option with Jack.

Knowing all that should have made it easier to not concern herself with Jack's cold feet, but she would have been more secure knowing Jack's feet were perfectly warm and content. That way she wouldn't have had to think about anything other than what was going on between her and Ramsey.

With all of that running through her mind, she brushed a lock of hair behind her ear and smiled back up at Ramsey. "Don't worry. It's not as if they are going to call off the wedding," she said not even allowing herself to consider the option.

"No, I don't think so either," Ramsey said eyeing her warily.

"Then, we don't even need to have this discussion," she said, cutting off the conversation. She had more to think about than Jack's cold feet. She knew she needed to figure out what she was doing with Ramsey first. Ramsey was the priority. He was the one she had been with for the last year, and the one that she had left in Atlanta for the past month without contact. She had needed time, and now that she had taken time, she wanted to know what was really going to happen between them…or if she just needed to leave Atlanta behind for good.

"Anyway, where are Brad and Jason?" Lexi asked realizing for the first time that she hadn't heard his roommates barreling through the apartment.

"They moved out," he told her.

Her mouth dropped open. "What?"

"Yeah," he told her with a shrug. She noticed that for a split second his eyes seemed sad, but then it was gone.

"Why would they move out?"

"I just needed my space," he told her vaguely.

"But when did this happen? When did you decide?" she asked him unable to fathom the concept of him living alone. "I was here a month ago."

"The decision was made a little over a month ago. They left this week," he told her.

"So, you knew when I was here?" she asked him. "Why didn't you tell me?"

"There was a lot going on," he said looking at her pointedly. "I wanted to let you know, but then you were gone."

"So, we're alone?" she questioned him, still attempting to comprehend the fact that she was here without the ever present disturbances, interruptions, and friendly banter that his roommates typically generated.

His smile grew at her question. "We're *very* alone right now," he told her stepping closer into her personal space.

She remembered the familiar dance they played in and out of her personal bubble and couldn't keep a smile from creeping onto her face. A habitual trait that she had once so detested now made her giggle with shared memories. She hadn't actually intended for her question to come out so guttural and deeply sexual, but when his green eyes gazed into her own she couldn't help but feel desire for him creep up her body.

Her lower half warmed as his eyes raked her body. He hadn't even moved forward to touch her, but she could feel her lips parting in anticipation. She swallowed hard before releasing a quick pant at the sexual tension that was palpable between them.

When his hand reached out and gently rested on her hip bone, she shuddered at the feel of him and took an involuntary step towards him. His hand did nothing more than stroke a circle into her exposed flesh, but she could feel that he wanted more. He desperately wanted more. And he wasn't the only one.

His other hand reached out and lightly tilted her chin up to him. She instinctively licked her lips as she continued to desirously gaze into his gorgeous face. His mouth came down upon her lips gently at first, testing the waters. After a few seconds of soft, gentle lip locks, his tongue darted in between her lips and met her own. As their kiss became more feverish, the hand that had been resting on her hip, gripped her waist, and pulled her flush against his chest. Lexi's arms moved up and around his neck, holding onto him as she allowed him to kiss the breath out of her.

Warning signs should have been going off that she needed to slow down. She had just been thinking about the potential consequences of Jack's cold feet. Her mind was still addled with what she had to go through with Ramsey to determine if they could rectify their relationship. Not to mention the fact that she had been talking to her Mystery Man and wishing she was back in New York only moments before. Her life was so complicated and all she wanted to do was enjoy this moment.

It was so nice just to feel Ramsey's lips press against her own and feel his rock hard body so close. His hand moved from her face down to her hip. He trailed his thumb along the inside of her shorts, and she shivered at his encouraging touch. When he reached the button on her pants, he expertly pulled it free of its enclosure before pushing the zipper down. She gasped against his mouth when he hooked his finger under the elastic of her thong and snapped the fabric gently back against her skin.

Enjoying his teasing caresses a bit too much, she nipped at his bottom lip. Taking that as encouragement, he reached his hands back and grabbed her ass firmly in both his hands hoisting her effortlessly off the ground. She broke contact with his lips as she circled her legs around his torso for support. His eyes blazed with desire. She could feel her own passion rising at the feel of him through his pants. A blush crept onto her cheeks at the intimacy of the position and her inability to keep from panting with desire.

Her body was torn between launching herself at him further, stripping their clothes off, and staying in the rest of the night having hot, wild, passionate sex, or backing away and taking things slowly. She had never been good at taking things slow, and she wanted him. She really wanted him.

He set her down on the hard, wooden kitchen table they had been positioned in front of and smiled devilishly before recapturing her lips. She groaned as his hand reached under her thin tank top to caress her breast. His hand slipped under her cotton bra, and flicked against her pebbled nipple. He swirled around the peak before forcefully pinching it between two fingers. Her pelvis bucked against him, and he ground his hips into her. No words were necessary as their craving for each other mounted. His hands were seemingly everywhere taking in every inch of her body as if he couldn't get enough of her.

He trailed down her front leaning her backwards so she was lying flat against the table, her body exposed to him. She moaned as his lips left her mouth, traveled down her neck, and hovered hot and breathy, where his fingers left off. Pushing her tank top up, he pulled away from her breasts to kiss across her stomach to the waistline of her shorts. After trailing a series of kisses close to her thong, his hands reached down and pulled her legs up and open in front of his face. He placed light, teasing kisses across her inner thighs where he was in complete control.

She whimpered as he drew closer and closer to her core and retreated each time. She was already very ready for him, but he was being deliberately slow and drawing out her pleasure. Just when she felt she was going to have to beg him for more, he yanked off her shorts tossing them to the kitchen floor. He gently rubbed against her already wet underwear causing her back to arch off the table as she released a low moan of approval.

Pushing the thin material aside, he finally made skin to skin contact. Her body shuddered with anticipation of release. Bending down his hot breath landed against her sensitive skin, his mouth closing over her clit. His fingers spread her wide to him as he sucked and licked her into submission. As her panting became feverish and climax approached, he inserted two fingers directly into her. Just the feel of him sliding back and forth across her soft, wet skin was enough to make her whole body tighten and clench demandingly around his fingers as he pushed her over the edge. Her hands covered her face as she cried out in ecstasy, completely overwhelmed by the skill in which he brought her to orgasm.

After she was spent, he stood long enough to retrieve a towel to wipe off his hands before lifting her off the table and making his way towards the stairs.

"Ramsey," she said from where she rested in his arms.

"Yes?" he asked before covering her mouth possessively with another deep kiss.

She leaned into the kiss. "Oh nothing," she finally said, deciding not to fight what was about to happen.

When he reached the stairs, a jingling of keys was heard from the front door. Ramsey paused as the doorknob jiggled.

"Were you expecting company?" Lexi asked, wanting nothing more than company.

"Uh, no," Ramsey said confused.

"Well, then who's here?" Lexi asked, suddenly realizing that she was naked from the waist down and someone was about to walk in the door.

"No idea," he said gently placing her on her feet. She scurried across the floor and grappled for her shorts as the door swung open.

Lexi froze, embarrassment immediately reddening her face. There was nowhere to go to eliminate the possibility that whoever walked in that door was going to see her mostly naked.

Bracing herself for the worst, Lexi glanced up just as a tall beautiful blonde walked through the door and smirked. "Alexa, darling, please reconsider coming to work for me. You have such a killer body," Lola said admiring Lexi as she snatched her shorts off the floor to cover herself.

Lexi's blush deepened further. "Lola," she said breathing a sigh of relief.

"Lola, what are you doing here?" Ramsey asked, drawing her attention away from Lexi sliding her shorts back on.

"Ramsey, are you certain we can't get her into the club?" Lola asked ignoring his question.

"Absolutely not. Out of the question."

"Oh dear," Lola said still looking at Lexi, "no need to blush and cover up. It's not as if I've never seen a woman naked."

Lexi laughed uncomfortably as she did precisely that. "So much for being alone," she mumbled, yanking the zipper back into place.

"Oh, were you two alone?" Lola asked, a devious smile playing across her features. "Did I interrupt?"

"Lola, an explanation please," Ramsey asked. Lexi could see him attempting to keep his cool.

"It's Sunday. I hardly thought I needed an explanation."

"Sunday, right," he said, smacking his hand against his forehead in frustration. "Fuck, I forgot."

"You forgot?" Lola asked confusion clouding her face. "I don't understand."

"Oh God, Ramsey, were you planning to have a party, *tonight*?" Lexi asked pointedly crossing her arms.

"It wasn't a plan per say," he admitted begrudgingly.

"We set up here every Sunday. It's more of a routine," Lola reminded her. "You should know that, dear." Lexi nodded, but she wasn't happy about it. The last thing she wanted was to be surrounded by Ramsey's friends and employees from the clubs. She had been to her fair share of such events, and she was hardly in the mood for what the night typically entailed.

"Lola, we have to talk about this," Ramsey said motioning her towards the door.

"Everything's already here though," she told him standing her ground.

Ramsey's phone began to ring loudly from his pocket. "Fuck, hold on," he said digging into his coat pocket and producing the thin phone. He cursed again when he checked who was calling. "I have to take this," he said apologetically to the two women in his living room. "Lola just, I don't know, bring everything in. We'll talk about this when I'm done."

"Ramsey, are you joking me?" Lexi asked following behind him. "You're really going to have a party, *tonight?*" Of all the nights for him to choose to have a party, he picked the night she got back in town? She hadn't seen him in a month, and the last thing she wanted to do was party.

"I have to take this call. I'll talk to you about this in a minute," he said his face set and stern, while his eyes pleaded with her to let it go for now.

"Ugh," Lexi grumbled stomping across the room to watch as Ramsey's apartment was transformed before her eyes. She had forgotten how easily everything was set in motion. He threw parties more efficiently than anyone else Lexi had ever met, including Chyna, which was really a feat. By the time he would finish his phone call half of the apartment would be set up, and it would likely be irreversible.

Lexi slumped down into one of the plush couches and waited for Ramsey to finish his conversation. Lola traipsed over to Lexi's side and perched precariously on the edge of the sofa. "Sorry about all this," she said swishing her blonde hair purposefully to one side.

Lexi just shrugged. There really wasn't anything else to say. "I thought it was business as usual. You haven't been around the last couple of weeks," she threw in inconspicuously.

"Uh huh," Lexi mumbled not wanting to continue to lead the conversation where it was headed.

"About your leaving…"

"Lola, let's not," she muttered.

"Yes, well, obviously it's none of my business," she began twisting a stick-straight piece of hair around her French-manicured finger.

"Then perhaps you should drop it."

Lola rolled her eyes but persevered. She was used to working with difficult women, and she treated Lexi as if she were no exception. "I am glad you're back you know."

"Wonderful," Lexi said mocking the faux British accent she insisted on using.

"Catty today, are we?" Lola asked smirking. Lexi refrained from answering. "Anyway, about your leaving—I wouldn't think too much into it. He really is working to fix everything. I'd be patient with him. He's turning his world upside down for you."

Lexi turned her full attention to the woman sitting next to her. She hadn't expected that, not from Lola. Normally, Lola was a little catty herself and entirely too flirtatious. That had always been the main reason Lexi had never been threatened by Lola and her commanding presence. She ended up flirting more with Lexi than she had ever done with Ramsey.

"What do you mean he's turning his world upside down?" Lexi asked tentatively. She had no clue what Lola was even referring to. She hadn't seen or spoken to Ramsey in a month and after she had left Atlanta, she hadn't expected him to continue to work towards salvaging their relationship.

"I'm not going to give away all his secrets…"

"I'm not sure I'm prepared to learn anymore," Lexi said glumly.

Lola smiled coyly at her. "You should trust me."

"You've given me reason to?"

"You don't have to, but what other option do you have?" Lola asked snippily. Lexi shrugged noncommittally. "That's what I thought. You're back in Atlanta for a reason, and I'm smarter than I look, alright? I know this has to do with Ramsey and not this wedding. This wedding was a catalyst. I'd trust that things will work out."

"Easy for you to say," Lexi said, glancing away from Lola.

"Of course it is, but I spend a good deal of time with him, and I know," Lola said raising her eyebrows and widening her large blue eyes. "I know *it* when I see it, and he has it…for you."

"And…" Lexi began.

"And no one else," Lola finished for her.

"We'll see."

"No," Lola said shaking her head firmly. "You'll see."

Lexi couldn't listen to her reasoning. Well actually, there wasn't much reasoning to it. Lola thought she knew everything, and regardless of how much time she spent with Ramsey, she couldn't know whether or not they were going to work out. She could say all day that Lexi should trust her judgment, but that didn't mean she was going to. There was too much still unknown hanging in the balance for Lexi to just *trust* anyone right now.

She had been ten seconds away from having sex with Ramsey only fifteen minutes ago. Now she was sitting on his couch with the woman who had seen her nearly nude, while his apartment was transformed, and he sat on a phone call. Her life was so strange.

"Sorry about that," Ramsey said sheepishly as he entered the room.

Lexi could immediately tell something was different about him. His demeanor had shifted from when he had last been in the room.

"It's alright," Lexi stated hesitantly.

Lola took that as her cue and stood. "Well, darling, the preparations are nearly complete. You're not going to break my heart by canceling, are you?" she asked pouting her bottom lip.

"No," he stated firmly. "A party is fine."

Knowing better than to argue when his mind was set, Lexi allowed the remainder of the preparations to continue without a hitch. She wasn't too pleased with the fact that she was going to have to endure a party atmosphere her first night back in town, but there was no turning back now. All she wanted to do was corner Ramsey and find out what his phone call had been about, but so far he had successfully evaded her.

She could tell it was purposive. For some reason, he didn't want her to know about his conversation. A million different scenarios played over in her head. She kept turning back to Jack, but why would he call back? And what would be the point? Ramsey would surely have told him the same things as before. Ramsey hadn't acted this strange when Jack had been waiting for them outside of his apartment. He had been calm and resolute when they had first arrived, and only slightly hesitant afterwards. He hadn't attempted to avoid her, which just left her more confused.

The usual suspects started pouring into Ramsey's apartment as the final touches were complete. Lexi was greeted with a warm welcome from Ramsey's now former roommates. She had to fend off their advances and couldn't keep from giggling as Brad's hands traveled lower and lower in their friendly embrace. She smacked him hard on the shoulder and turned towards Jason who wasn't much help.

"So, you guys moved out?" she asked hopping out of arms reach.

"Yeah, we got a new place nearby," Jason told her.

"Bachelor pad. Nice," Lexi said smiling.

"Yeah, it's too bad you moved out right when you did," Brad began, "since Ramsey was..." Jason smacked Brad's shoulder, silencing him.

Lexi glanced between the two guys. Both looked as if they had been caught with their hands in the cookie jar. "Ramsey was doing what?"

"Nothing," they both muttered in unison.

Lexi narrowed her eyes and let them dart between Brad and Jason. "Now listen here. What are you two hiding from me?"

Brad looked at Jason at the same time as Jason looked Brad, and then they both shrugged. "Hiding?" Jason asked a smirk crossing his face.

"Are you hiding something?" Brad asked Jason.

"I'm not. Are you?"

"Nope," Brad said popping the last syllable.

"You think you're fooling me, but you're not," Lexi told them over the music.

"Lexi, Lexi, Lexi," Brad said draping an arm over her shoulders, "we would never think of trying to fool you."

"Then what was Ramsey doing?" Lexi persisted.

"I have no idea to what you are referring," Brad muttered looking for Jason for reassurance.

"Yeah, you lost me," Jason chimed in.

Lexi let out a deep breath and crossed her arms over her chest. "Are you guys honestly doing this right now?"

Jason and Brad gave each other a meaningful look before venturing forward. "Look we don't want to ruin anything between you two," Jason began.

"Too late," Lexi mumbled.

"It's not," Brad added.

"Anyway," Jason said shooting daggers at Brad, "we want you to relax and have a good time. Ramsey's changed since he's been with you, and we can all tell that it's for the better. Honestly, Lexi, whatever he had planned—whatever you may not have known about—it's only good from here on out."

"Why do people keep saying that?" Lexi grumbled. "There's no way for you to know that."

"We know Ramsey, which is good enough for us," Brad told her.

"Either way, anything you need to know, Ramsey will tell you."

"Yes, because that's worked out so well for us in the past," she stated sarcastically.

"We can't change what happened in the past, and neither can you. I'd just look to the future," Jason told her before following Brad out to the dance floor.

Lexi sighed knowing that they were right. Either way, she wanted to know what Brad had been about to tell her. Everyone kept telling her that Ramsey had changed and that the future was going to be different, but she couldn't be sure whether or not to believe them. Too much was at stake this week to not be fully aware of everything that was going on.

Keeping her thoughts set on the horizon, Lexi exited through the back door and onto the porch where she had shared her first kiss with Ramsey. Lexi breathed in the humid summer air and pushed her curls off of her forehead. The weather was as sticky as ever for a Georgia summer night, and she could feel a light beading of sweat across her hairline and the back of her neck. She missed the warmth and familiarity of the place she called home. Nostalgia washed over her as she leaned back against the wooden railing and stared up into the night sky. The stars were barely visible due to the lighted backdrop of the city, but it still comforted her to look out into space.

"There you are," Ramsey said shutting out the noise of his apartment as he drew closer to her.

"Oh, so you aren't avoiding me?" she asked the bitterness from earlier gone from her voice.

"No, I was," he admitted sheepishly. Lexi smiled at his honesty, but refrained from commenting. "Things aren't going exactly as planned."

"They never do," she muttered, her head still hanging backwards and looking up into the darkness. She felt his hands lightly grip her waist when he drew closer to her.

"Sorry about the party." Lexi shrugged. "And about avoiding you."

"Please stop apologizing," she murmured.

"I'm sorry I keep apologizing," he said causing her to finally look at him with a smirk. His green eyes softened at the sight of her.

The way he was looking at her was beginning to make her thoughts hazy. She sometimes felt as if he could erase everything from her mind when he looked at her the way he was in that moment. Blinking a few times to break the spell, Lexi returned to the thoughts that were milling around in her mind.

She wanted answers to so many questions. Everyone kept telling her that he had changed, but she had no idea how they could know that or what that even meant. She liked who he was for the most part. If he had changed, would that affect the way that she felt about him?

Deciding against asking all the other questions swirling in her mind, she settled with "Who was on the phone?" It seemed at the time the most pressing issue, or perhaps just the least complicated. Though with Lexi, it seemed, everything was complicated.

Ramsey broke eye contact with her and cleared his throat. "Just uh…"

"Please don't lie to me," she said observing him closely.

"I wasn't going to," he told her defensively. She didn't tell him that his demeanor made it clear that he had been about to lie to her. That something about the way he had reacted to the question had triggered her.

"Just…don't get worked up, okay?" Lexi nodded, anticipation blossoming in her stomach. A list of names filled her mind, and though she feared he wouldn't list anyone on the short list, deep down she knew that he would.

"Parker called."

She had been right.

Lexi swallowed hard trying not to get worked up over the answer. She knew there had been a reason for him to avoid her, but she hadn't wanted to think about why. Parker was a whole new world of complications that Lexi wished she had never had to deal with. Jack was bad enough, but to have to consider both issues in one day was almost too much for her. She knew that eventually she would have to face everything that had happened, but she didn't want that to be today.

Taking a few steadying breaths, Lexi finally felt calm enough to reply. "And what did Parker want?"

"Just to talk about the wedding," he stated. "There are a lot of details that go into it that I don't care about, and I keep getting phone calls about it."

"Right," Lexi said not wanting to feel as queasy as she did. "Parker's going to be at the wedding."

Ramsey had told her that Parker was going to be there, but she had tried not to put too much thought into it. The fact that it was Jack's wedding had been enough to think about without the idea of Parker on the backburner. So she had tried to put the unfortunate news that Parker would be somehow involved in the wedding out of her mind. She hadn't been very successful.

"So you've been spending a lot of time talking to Parker then?" Lexi asked choosing her words carefully and trying to keep the bite out of her voice.

"Lexi," Ramsey said comfortingly, "please don't let this get to you. It is one week, and that's all."

"I know. I know," Lexi muttered, though she sounded disbelieving.

"I don't have to see Parker again after this if it makes you happy. You are the only thing that is important to me," he told her staring longingly in her eyes.

Lexi wanted to believe him. After all, she had come to Atlanta in hopes of believing just that. But only time would tell if everything he was saying was true.

10

DECEMBER SIX MONTHS EARLIER

"Slow down. Slow down. Slow down," Lexi cried repeatedly as she tried to pry Ramsey's hands off of her. "Chyna is going to know if we fooled around beforehand."

"Yeah, probably," he said pushing her dress further up her legs.

"I can't go all flustered."

"Why not?" he asked smiling devilishly as he captured her lips briefly.

Lexi pulled back from his eager advances and shot him a dirty look. "This is an important occasion for Chyna. She isn't going to want me to have just had sex while she's dealing with all this bullshit."

"Are you still talking about Chyna?" he asked letting his thumb rub circles on her inner thighs.

"Ye…yes," she stammered trying not to get too distracted by the proximity of his hands.

"She's hardly going to care."

"You don't know that. This is really important to her," Lexi contradicted him.

"Really? We're talking about Chyna, the girl who gets laid practically every night. She's not going to care. In fact," he began thinking better of the subject, "she's going to be happy about it…proud even." He resumed his earlier removal of her clothing.

"Chyna is not," Lexi began before Ramsey covered her mouth with his own. "Ramsey," she all but moaned against his lips.

Briefly breaking contact, he hoisted her up from where she was sitting on the couch, carried her into her bedroom, and then tossed her effortlessly backwards on her bed. Lexi giggled taken in by his enthusiasm as he crawled onto the bed after her. "You're going to ruin your suit," was all she managed to get out as he towered over her.

He smirked at her obviously amused by the statement. "This is why I like you so much," he murmured softly.

"What? What am I doing?" she asked giggling, obviously mystified by how her reactions affected him.

"Nothing, which is exactly what makes you so damn irresistible," he told her capturing her lips in a searing kiss.

Lexi giggled again throwing her head back against the pillows to break off their kiss. "Wait, wait, what made you say that?"

"Oh Lexi, my Alexa, how can you not see yourself through my eyes?" he whispered softly laying down next to her and beginning to stroke her brown locks. Lexi just looked back up at him, waiting for him to continue. "You seem to make even the most ridiculous statements sound adorable."

"Ridiculous statements?" Lexi gasped. "Nothing I said was ridiculous."

"You're concerned about Chyna not being okay with us fooling around before a wedding she doesn't even want to attend, and my suit getting wrinkled. Those are both pretty ridiculous," he said staring at her tenderly.

Lexi sat up on her elbows to get a better look at him. "Well, for one, Chyna *might* be upset about this. And two, your suit is already wrinkled," she said pointing out where the suit had bunched up around him.

"I'm still sticking to the fact that Chyna would *never* be upset about this. Since we first met, she wanted you to go home with me. And do you think this is the only suit I have with me?" he asked raising one eyebrow and looking at her hungrily.

"That was a totally different scenario. I was drunk and we were out clubbing. I wasn't responsible for my actions," she said stubbornly. "And about that suit, as far as I'm concerned it is the only one you *own*," she told him watching his face contort incredulously and then burst into laughter.

"You really are something," he murmured as he began to kiss from her throat to her navel. A moan escaped her lips giving away just how much she *really* wanted him to stop. He paused at the hem of her dress raising his head to make eye contact with her, "And as far as you're concerned, I don't need any suits."

"Why is that?" she asked breathily, his eyes captivating her.

"Because we can just stay up here in your room until the New Year," he murmured against her stomach.

Lexi's head fell back against the pillow as Ramsey's fingers slid under her dress. She couldn't argue that point, and she didn't really want to. She would be perfectly content forgoing their plans for the remainder of the evening, and staying in her apartment the rest of the night.

But she couldn't do that to Chyna. Her father was getting married that evening, and Chyna had been corralled into assisting the beast he was calling his fiancé. She needed moral support. And beyond that, Lexi had helped plan the big New Year's party for tonight. She didn't want to miss that!

Lexi twisted sideways out of the reach of his hands as they lightly grazed her silky underwear and slid off of the bed. "No!" she exclaimed boldly. Ramsey's smirk only widened. "I know you don't hear that from me often."

"Often?" he asked chuckling to himself.

Lexi rolled her big brown eyes. "Ever," she conceded. "But we have places to be tonight. You didn't ditch work on one of the busiest nights of the year just so that we could stay in and have sex all night."

"Are you somehow proving a point? I'd ditch work for that any day."

Lexi let out a short breath and shook her head at him. She tried to keep from smiling. "On any other day then," she told him wiggling her eyebrows suggestively.

"I'm taking you up on that," he said standing and straightening out his suit. He reached out for her as she passed by him. She wrapped her arms up around his neck and let him hold her close.

"Don't get all riled up again," she warned him as she ducked under his arm and walked to her dresser.

"Pointless request when I'm around you."

Lexi smiled brightly to herself as she put the finishing touches on her already perfect makeup. She then slid on a pair of heeled, knee-high, black boots and zipped them up feeling especially like Julia Roberts in *Pretty Woman*. Ramsey snatched up her black pea coat from the hook near the door and eased her into the warm material.

To say traffic was a nightmare would have been an understatement. New York traffic was always a force to reckon with, but on New Year's Eve it was a disaster. The couple inched through the streets hoping to arrive at their destination early enough, but as time dragged on they were just hoping to make it there at all.

"Is there any way that you could drive a little faster?" Lexi politely asked the cabbie leaning forward in the yellow car.

The man didn't even have the decency to answer. He looked back at her through the rearview mirror as if she were an idiot. Obviously they were in wall to wall traffic on one of the busiest days of the year. There was literally nowhere to go to avoid the mess.

Lexi slumped back against the seats. "Great. What are we going to do? We're going to be late."

Ramsey wrapped his arm around her shoulders and squeezed gently. "Can you walk in those things?" he asked nodding at her shoes.

"Sure," she mumbled. "Just not across town."

"Right," he said nodding to himself. "Hey buddy, what are the chances you're getting us to the Plaza in the next twenty minutes?" The cabbie again looked at him as if he was not only dumb but also blind, and refrained from answering. "I know that you understand what I'm saying, so an answer would be appreciated."

The guy glared at Ramsey through the mirror and muttered, "No chance."

"How about I give you an extra hundred bucks if you get us there in twenty minutes?" Ramsey volunteered. Lexi swiveled in place staring at Ramsey. She couldn't believe that he was actually bribing this guy.

"A hundred?" the guy asked, obviously in disbelief as well.

"And I'll double it if we're there in fifteen," Ramsey reaching for his wallet to show the guy that he was serious.

"Ramsey, why are you carrying around two hundred dollars in cash?" Lexi muttered softly next to him. She could feel her jaw slack at the prospect that he would throw about two hundred dollars on a cab ride as if it were nothing. She knew he had money. Of course, she knew. His family fortune along with the clubs made him the wealthiest person she had ever met, but he was generally so reserved about it around her. Sure he had done some extravagant things, but it was never something so completely pointless. Then again, if the cab driver didn't make it to the hotel in twenty minutes, he wasn't out any money.

"It's New Years," he told her, his green eyes sparkling as if that explained everything. The mischievous look on his face also told her that he was carrying a lot more than that.

"Aren't you afraid you're going to get mugged?" she breathed.

It was Ramsey's turn to look at her like she was crazy. "Have you seen me?" he asked gesturing to himself. No one was likely to mess with him.

"Two hundred in fifteen minutes?" the driver repeated eagerly.

"You bet," Ramsey told him as if the amount were pocket change. And to someone like Ramsey Bridges, it probably was. Lexi was having a difficult time wrapping her mind around that. Even though Chyna shopped more than any other human being and spent two hundred dollars on a cotton t-shirt, Lexi still couldn't understand Ramsey's decision. She hadn't been raised poor, but two hundred dollars was not something you threw away on a taxi driver.

It did seem to make the driver more adventurous. As traffic began to pick up, he swerved and maneuvered around other cars, racing down streets, and stopping abruptly. Lexi had to close her eyes for part of the ride, because she was pretty sure that they had gone through several red lights and almost been hit half a dozen more. And still they managed to make it to the Plaza in exactly twenty minutes. Lexi hadn't thought it was possible. Ramsey, true to his word, pulled a crisp hundred dollar bill out of his wallet, and handed it to the guy.

"Perfect timing," Ramsey said grabbing Lexi's hand and pulling her towards the ballroom. Lexi cleared her mind of the horrible car ride, and rushed after him.

"Oh my God!" Chyna exclaimed rushing towards them as they approached the entrance. "Where the fuck have you been?"

"Traffic's a bitch," Lexi told her apologetically.

"I was going to slit my wrists if I had to spend one more minute with that woman. She is quite possibly the devil. I mean literally the devil," Chyna said throwing her arms in the air. "I think she gives Bridezilla a new meaning."

"Is she really that bad?" Lexi asked glancing around to see who else could be listening in on their conversation.

"That *bad*?" Chyna cried. "You have no idea. I have been asked if I've gained ten pounds fifteen times since I arrived. I was told that my face looks pudgy, my hips are getting rounder, and that there's no way my ass is going to fit into the dress she picked out. Not only that, but my complexion is all wrong, my hair color won't blend in, and my nails are overdone," she said thrusting her understated French manicure in Lexi's face. "And don't even get me started on what she says about my shoes," Chyna whined pointing at the beautiful black stilettos on her feet.

Lexi couldn't help but smile. "You look gorgeous," she told her leaning forward and kissing her cheek.

"Thank you, doll."

"Agreed," Ramsey said pinching her arm. "I'm going to get us a seat."

"Okay," Lexi said nodding at him as he walked into the ballroom.

"He's adorable," Chyna said watching his ass as he departed. "He's in way deep with you."

Lexi shrugged noncommittally. "I hope so."

"Psh, whatevs. At least you don't have to deal with this bitch," Chyna told her motioning to the back rooms.

"I can't believe you actually agreed to this," Lexi told her.

"Me either. Who would have thought I would have to go through hell and back though, right? I never thought it would be *this* much hassle."

Lexi smirked at her. "The first time you met the woman she told you that you shouldn't drink red wine anymore because you have *bags* under your eyes. How could you misinterpret her purpose in life?"

Chyna giggled at the memory. "True. At least I won't have to spend any more time with her after this goddamn wedding is over."

"Speaking of wedding, don't you have a bride to finish getting dressed?" Lexi asked dodging out of the way as Chyna motioned to punch her.

"Don't fucking remind me," Chyna grumbled. "I'll meet you inside. I clash too much with her twit friends, so I'm not going to walk in. She'd rather me just sit and then stand once everyone has come inside."

"Are you *serious*?" Lexi asked in disbelief. The dumb woman that Chyna's father was marrying was really crossing a line with that one. She had asked her to be a part of the wedding, more to keep an eye on Chyna than anything, which had become quite apparent. She had, thus far, put her in the ugliest dress and forced her hair up in an unflattering manner. Still Chyna had managed to look gorgeous. Lexi was pretty sure that had pissed the woman off even more. Then after all her efforts to keep her soon-to-be stepchild from being prettier than her, she was now not even allowing her to walk down the aisle. She couldn't bear the thought of anyone drawing the spotlight away.

"Don't even get me started," Chyna said wiggling her fingers at Lexi as she reluctantly retreated.

Lexi wandered into the massive ballroom crowded with people. She found Ramsey near the front of the room on the groom's side. As Lexi drew closer, she realized that she recognized the other man who would be seated next to her.

"Adam!" Lexi exclaimed in surprise. "What are you doing here?"

"Hey," he said smiling sweetly and accepting a small hug in greetings.

"It's so good to see you," she gushed, a genuine smile appearing on her face.

"Good to see you too. I'm here for Chyna. She asked me to come," he told her.

"Wow. I didn't know you two still talked," Lexi told him. Chyna rarely continued to talk with guys after having a fling with them. The fact that Adam had managed to make a lasting impression on Chyna was something that Lexi was really happy about. Lexi had instantly gotten along with him, and much preferred him to Chyna's other choices for dates. He was actually someone Lexi wouldn't mind going on a double date with. He was so laid back and charming in his own way, and she could never thank him enough for saving Chyna that night.

"Yeah, we do," he said smiling politely back at her. Their eyes locked for a brief second before he added, "And I see you're still with Ramsey."

"Uh, yeah," she muttered breaking eye contact and looking back at Ramsey, "we are."

Music filled the air and silence fell on the waiting audience. Lexi hadn't noticed Chyna sneak in so she assumed that had happened while she had been talking with Adam. Her friend was sitting demurely in the front row, a frilly lavender t-length dress hugging her features perfectly with a black satin sash cinching in her miniscule waist. Her long black hair had been swept up into an intricate design and pearls had been knotted into the strands.

As the procession began, Lexi realized that Victoria, the bitch fiancé, had actually been right. Chyna did not fit into this mold. Not that Chyna fit into any mold. Each girl that walked down the aisle in the same lavender dress that adorned her friend's body looked insignificant in comparison. All were pale with honey blonde hair, which truly did make Chyna stand out as she stood up next to the final woman. If the goal of a bride was to make sure the bridesmaids didn't distract from their big day, then Victoria really had her work cut out for her.

All eyes flocked to Chyna's graceful stature. She stood tall, her exotic features highlighted by the pale beauties standing next to her. Those that knew her connection to the family were quickly murmuring the latest gossip to anyone seated near them. The rest just marveled at her and wondered idly to themselves.

Richard took his stance in preparation for his bride as the Catholic priest asked everyone to rise. Lexi stood and turned with the crowd to face the back entrance of the ballroom. In a flowing mass of white lace, Victoria appeared in the entranceway. A gasp echoed throughout the room at her sheer beauty. The strapless, princess cut gown fell to her feet and a long train trailed behind her. Her father escorted her down the aisle to the traditional *Canon in D* played by a string quartet.

The ceremony went off without a hitch and within the hour Chyna had a new step mother. This time Chyna was allowed to follow the processional out since all glory was already been bestowed upon Victoria. Ramsey laced his fingers with Lexi's as she followed behind Adam to the reception hall. Since they had been near the front of the room and several hundred people had been in attendance, they were some of the last people to enter.

The wedding had been a success despite Chyna having to deal with Victoria's behavior. Yet, as Lexi stepped foot into the reception area, she instinctively knew that something was amiss. Searching around for Chyna, Lexi let her eyes roam the large room with individuals milling around conversing about the wedding.

Then she spotted the group of lavender dresses standing at a side entrance. Without a second thought, Lexi made a beeline for the group. She didn't bother turning around to find out if Ramsey and Adam were in tow, but she assumed that they would be. As she approached, her feeling of apprehension only grew. Looking at her friend standing amidst that group of women, Lexi just *knew* something was off.

"Chyna," Lexi called as she approached.

Chyna turned in place, her face showing all the anxiety of her situation along with a wave of appreciation at Lexi's presence. "Alexa, thank god!"

"Aren't you glad that's over?" Lexi asked hoping to lessen the tension.

"I would be," she said turning her back on the blonde bimbos standing around her. Lexi raised an eyebrow in question.

Before Chyna was able to answer, a woman came storming out of the entrance they were standing in front of. Lexi had never seen Chyna's mother before, but at first glance there was no denying their relation. Except for the nearly twenty year age difference, the two were identical. Her mother was taller, but it was unclear if that was due to the seven inch heels on her feet or not. Her skin was a deeper bronzed color and her eyes even more vibrantly green than her daughters. She was utterly beautiful, and was wearing a look that Lexi had seen a number of times on Chyna.

"Richard, there is no use in speaking with you further," she muttered, her foreign Italian accent still thick on her tongue after all these years.

Chyna's father appeared from the doorway looking furious at the distraction. As he entered the crowded room, his temper only continued to flare as more eyes turned his direction. "Andrea, honestly," he crowed, latching onto her thin upper arm and yanking her backwards.

Lexi's eyes opened wide in surprise as he pulled her out of the busy room. "Let go of me," she said smacking his hand. "If I bruise, they'll cancel the Brazilian shoot next week."

"They'll cover it up," he growled.

"You'd know," she spat back viciously.

"Welcome to my childhood," Chyna mumbled, sidling up to Lexi for the show.

"What's your mom doing here?" Lexi asked averting her eyes from the couple.

"That's the million dollar question, isn't it?" Chyna grumbled.

"I thought she wasn't in the country. Isn't that what you said?" Lexi waited for her to nod then continued, "When was the last you saw her, C?"

"I don't know," she shrugged. "When was my birthday?"

"June," Lexi whispered afraid of the forthcoming answer.

"Yeah, June…three years ago," Chyna answered staring forward unblinking at her mother.

Lexi tried to cover her surprise. She knew that Chyna's mom wasn't in the picture. Well, up until recently, her father hadn't been around much either. But she hadn't known that it had been quite that long since she had even *seen* her mom. Lexi couldn't imagine going that long without seeing her own parents. Not that their relationship was even comparable to what Lexi was currently witnessing.

"Mom," Chyna said her voice carefully controlled. She took a confident step forward and into the conversation that was going on in swift Italian between the couple, so as not to draw more attention to them.

Her mother stopped abruptly at Chyna's interruption and looked at her own daughter as if she were nothing more than fly she wanted to swat. "Oh...Chyna, you're here."

"Yeah," she stated awkwardly.

"Isn't this nice," Andrea commented sarcastically.

"Having all three of us in one place was never considered *nice*," Chyna replied sincerely.

Andrea huffed at the statement her green eyes calculating. "Perhaps."

"What are you doing here?" she couldn't keep from asking. "Don't you have a flight your always late to catch or a shoot you've been invited to...or something?"

"Precisely my point," Richard exclaimed.

"Still Daddy's little girl, aren't we?" Andrea said directing the comment more as an insult that anything.

"I was hardly agreeing with *him*," Chyna muttered.

"Are you still running around like your father too?" she asked looking her up and down in disgust.

"I don't even feel as if I should justify that with an answer."

"Oh come on, honey. You and I both know that he's only going to hold onto this one until the next young thing waltzes into his office," Andrea cried in frustration.

"You say these things as if you aren't with every cabana boy who appears on set," her father cried incredulously. "You are the most hypocritical person in the world. You show up on my wedding day spouting old, petty bullshit about a life that no longer matters to me. About a time that might as well not have existed for me. That's how insignificant and unimportant those years were with you. Now my personal welfare might not mean shit to you, and that's fine, but don't come in here and expect me to allow you to insult me. My new, yes young, and beautiful *wife* is waiting for me. Find your own way out."

Andrea wild green eyes stormed over. The look she shot him was of pure hatred. "Well congratulations to your new whore. May you two have a wonderful life of *fidelity* and eternal devotion to one another. If you are even capable of being devoted to anyone but yourself," she spat, turning on her heel and rushing away from the group. If she hadn't acted like a complete bitch to her best friend, Lexi would have felt bad for the woman. But under the circumstances, she was just glad to see her go.

"And you," Richard began turning on his only child. The cold calculating man Lexi had met in Chyna's apartment had returned. He wore all the anger that had boiled up with the appearance of his ex-wife, and was redirecting that fury towards the next closest victim. "What part did you play in this?"

"What?" Chyna asked surprised.

"Don't give me your innocent act."

"Did you not see how she treated me? I didn't even know where she was," Chyna said defensively.

"Bullshit, Chyna! You're out to ruin me. I get your game now. After the way you treated Victoria! I thought it was petty, and you would get over it, but this draws a line. I no longer want you in my sight."

Chyna's jaw slackened. "Let me tell you about your pretty princess, you fucking asshole. She is a bitch, a terrible excuse for a human being. You think she's a goddess, because you're getting your dick wet. But let me tell you," Chyna growled stepping forward to her father. He usually held such an upper hand that it was incredible to watch her stand up for herself. "She's nothing more than a new toy to you. I wouldn't be surprised if she's fucking someone on the side already. Just look at her, she obviously just wants your money. If you can't see that, then you really are dumber than I thought."

"You will not speak…."

"No, I will speak to you however I see fit," she said looking him up and down, her nose turned up. "You raised me to be strong willed and independent. No matter how much you want me to disappear from your life, that's not happening. I'm a part of you, and you can't act like I'm a child any longer. Grow up and deal with your mistakes."

With that she turned on her heel and followed in her mother's footsteps. Lexi, Ramsey, and Adam followed quickly behind her unsure of how to approach Chyna at this point. Lexi wanted to talk to Chyna, but she knew now wasn't the time. Chyna was angry. No, she was pissed. And when she was in this state, she was a force to be reckoned with. Nothing anyone would say was going to calm her down at that moment.

When they reached the bottom floor, they piled into Chyna's town car. Without a word, the driver zipped them across town to the party that was already in full swing for New Years. They had anticipated showing up fashionably late to the event. Chyna had originally thought they would be even later than they actually were, but they had skipped out on the reception increasing their departure by nearly an hour.

Chyna's silence made it pretty clear that she was still livid about what had unfolded between her and her parents. Not that Lexi could blame her. If her parents ever treated her or each other like that, she would have been mortified. The fact that Chyna had been able to grow up a semi-normal human being was a bit of a miracle in and of itself. With parents like that, she should have been completely fucked up.

When the car came to a standstill, the group rushed into the lobby of the building to escape the frigid night air. "Party is on the top floor," Chyna told them gesturing towards the elevators. "I'm just going to…uh…take care of a few things."

Lexi looked at her suspiciously. The last thing that Chyna needed right now was to be alone. "Do you want company?"

"No, no, don't worry about me. I'm making sure things are in order," she said vaguely. "Go on up and have a good time. I'll meet you."

Chyna began walking in the opposite direction. Lexi stood there dumbstruck for a split second before starting to chase after her. She made it three steps before a hand came down on her arm. "Hey, let me handle this," Adam requested pulling her backwards.

"Uh…wha…" Lexi asked not really formulating any clear words. She was always there for Chyna. Chyna was her best friend. She would do anything to make her feel better. Not only that, she had known her for three years, and knew what made her feel better.

Adam was a fling, a nothing. Sure, he was a nice guy who had helped them out in a pinch…twice, but that didn't mean he should go talk to Chyna when she was hurting. She needed her best friend, and Adam wouldn't cut it.

"Lexi, really, I got this. Go have fun," he said smiling sweetly.

"But she needs me."

"Nah, she'll be alright. *Really*. We'll meet you," he told her pushing her gently into Ramsey's arms.

"Yeah, come on, Lexi. Let them be," Ramsey said tugging her out of Adam's grasp.

"I mean, okay, if you really think so."

"I do," Adam reassured her.

"Call if you need anything," she called to Adam as she let Ramsey guide her away. When they reached the elevators, Lexi murmured, "That's so strange."

"What?" Ramsey asked stepping into the elevator.

"That he thinks he can take care of her. That he thinks she will let him take care of her. That he thinks he knows how to take care of someone like Chyna. I mean yeah he's nice, but Chyna doesn't go for *nice*," Lexi told him.

"Maybe she does," he said smirking.

"No," she contradicted.

"If he thinks he can handle her craziness then by all means let him. I just want to have some fun with you tonight, Lexi. And I think I can handle *your* craziness," he told her playfully.

She smiled up into his handsome face. Rising onto her toes, she reached up and touched her lips gently against his. Moving swiftly he pushed her body back against the elevator wall and began to kiss the breath out of her. By the time the door dinged open, she was so hot for him her mind had completely forgotten what had occurred downstairs.

"Are you sure you want to stay?" she asked him wiping her puffy lips.

"Oh no, you dragged me here. It's time to party," he told her pulling her into the massive room Chyna had transformed into a New Years Eve bash. Even when Lexi had gone over dozens of plans for the event, she had never anticipated what was in front of her.

The black marble flooring opened up on three sides to floor-to-ceiling glass panes with a view of the city below. Fireworks already lit up the night sky in anticipation of the huge display that would occur at midnight when the Big Apple dropped in Times Square. There were several bars overflowing with alcohol. Half-naked waiters and waitresses were wandering around the premises carrying trays of champagne. Dozens of people that Lexi had met while out with Chyna were in attendance; even more Lexi had never seen before. Some waved at her as she passed by. Lights were dimmed low, and pulsing dance music filled the room. A majority of the enormous space had been crafted into a dance floor where people were already bumping and grinding to the beat of the music. All in all, the night was already a success.

Ramsey snagged two glasses of champagne, and made a toast over the increased volume of the music. "To our first New Years together." Lexi glass clinked against his, and she went to drink her drink, but he stopped her. "I wasn't finished." She looked up at him as if to encourage him to continue. "May we have many, many more to celebrate."

Lexi beamed from ear to ear at the implications in his statement. Taking a large gulp of the champagne, she motioned for Ramsey in a come hither motion. He leaned forward and she captured his lips once more. "If you keep this up, we're not going to make it to midnight."

She winked at him, before shimmying seductively out to the dance floor. He followed her, and they spent the next couple hours lost in each other's embrace. She had completely forgotten Chyna when she caught a glimpse of her long black hair, which had been pulled out of her elegant hairstyle. She motioned to Ramsey, and he nodded saying he would follow her.

As she approached, Lexi realized that she wasn't alone, and she looked much more like herself…drunk. Just before Lexi reached her, Chyna began furiously making out with the guy who was standing in front of her. Gulping hard, Lexi realized that the person she was sucking face with was Adam. Guess he had worked things out with her after all. Lexi cleared her throat causing Chyna to break away from her make out session.

She turned around smiling brightly at Lexi. Her eyes were slightly glazed over, but she looked happy drunk, which was a step up from sober angry. "Alexa!" she cried throwing her arms sloppily around her. "Are you having fun?"

Lexi giggled into Chyna's ear as she helped her stand straight again. "Yeah, C. You feeling better?" Lexi knew it was a pointless question. Chyna was obviously already better. She had probably had enough to drink in the time that she had been gone that she couldn't feel anything. She would have to deal with everything that had happened at some point, but right now was not that moment.

"Don't even know what you mean, chica. But I'm so glad you came over here," she gushed leaning into Lexi again for support.

"Oh, yeah?" Lexi asked eyeing her apprehensively as Adam righted her again.

"Soooo, you know how I've been sketchy lately?" Chyna asked her smile widening. She looked like a little kid in a candy store when her eyes refocused on Lexi. She wasn't certain what Chyna was getting at, but she did know what she was talking about. Chyna had been doing all sorts of strange things lately. Not only was she forgetting things, but she had been skipping out on plans and calling her at random hours to find out why she hadn't made it to their meeting when nothing had been planned. It had all been a little off.

"Yeah," Lexi acknowledged.

"I actually do have a reason," she admitted. "I wanted it to be a surprise, which is the only reason I haven't told you so don't be mad."

"Why would I be mad?" Lexi asked her curiosity growing.

"I have a boyfriend!"

Lexi jaw dropped open in surprise. Of all the things Chyna could have told her that was not what she had been expecting. She had never known Chyna to have a boyfriend...ever. She would go out with dozens of guys, but none of them were ever good enough for Chyna. And now suddenly she had a boyfriend? "What? Who?" Lexi asked incredulously.

Chyna glanced over at Adam and smiled seductively up at him. "Who do you think, silly?" she asked wrapping her arm around his waist.

Lexi looked between Adam and Chyna in shock. She couldn't even formulate words. She hadn't even known that Adam and Chyna were still speaking until today, let alone that they had been dating long enough for Chyna to consider him her boyfriend. How had she missed putting those pieces of the puzzle together? Had she been so lost in her own relationship that she had missed that her best friend was now in one?

Luckily, Lexi didn't have to articulate her thoughts, because Ramsey broke in, "Congratulations. Adam told me at the wedding, but don't worry I didn't spoil the surprise for Lexi." He reached forward and wrapped Chyna in a quick hug.

"Thanks! Isn't this awesome, Alexa? Now we can double," Chyna squealed acting girlier in that moment than Lexi had ever seen her.

Lexi found her eyes drifting back over to Adam. He stared at her, his expression a mask to his true thoughts. She wondered what he was thinking about all of this.

"Alexa, snap out of it. Aren't you happy for me?" Chyna asked her voice increasing in pitch.

Lexi sputtered trying to come up with the appropriate response. "Oh my God, C! I'm so happy for you. I can't believe you have a boyfriend."

As midnight approached, the foursome distracted themselves with booze, dancing, and the pleasure of each other's company. Lexi was gradually getting over her shock, and was realizing that she actually really liked that her friend had a boyfriend, especially one that Lexi got along with. It was still surreal to her, but it did make it easier to keep up with Chyna. Usually by this time, she would be off with some stranger with no hope of Lexi finding her again until morning, but now she actually got the pleasure of enjoying her company up until the clock struck midnight.

With only fifteen minutes left on the countdown, Ramsey got a phone call that he had to take. Lexi followed him off of the floor in desperate need of a break from the dancing. Her feet were killing her from hours standing on her high heels. Ramsey angled for the outside patio despite the frigid temperatures and high altitude. She waited inside for him to finish his phone call, taking a seat to give her feet a break. She couldn't wait for him to come back inside so they could complete their evening, which had been easily the best New Year's she had ever experienced.

When Ramsey did finally walk back inside though, he wore a look of panic. "What's wrong?" she asked terrified that something had happened.

"The club is being raided," he barely muttered. She had to strain to hear what he had said, but when it sank in, she looked back at him in horror. She was glad that no one was injured or anything, but this—this could be devastating to him.

"What does that mean for you?" she asked uncertain as to what he was going to be able to do about it. He was hundreds of miles away, and no one was going to listen to the owner over the telephone.

"It means I'm out thousands of dollars, Lexi. It means I'm out. It might mean I have to close the place down," he said his tone dead.

"What are you going to do?" she asked her voice reflecting all of the panic that was on his face.

"I have to get the fuck out of here. I needed to be in Atlanta tonight. What the *fuck* was I thinking? Fuck!" he cried. "I can't believe I listened to you. I can't believe I thought everything was going to be fine. Things don't run without me. They need me there, and I wasn't there. I don't fucking know what I'm going to do, Lexi, because I'm in New York City."

Lexi stared up at him as if she had never seen him before. This was not the Ramsey that she knew. This was not the Ramsey that she cared so deeply for. He was taking out his anger on her, and she knew that. She knew, but it still hurt. She tried to keep the tears from welling in her eyes as his words sliced through her. "I...I didn't know."

"That's right you didn't know. God, how could I have been so stupid to let this happen?" he crowed. He ran his fingers roughly through his hair and turned his gaze to the ceiling.

"You had no way of knowing this was going to happen either," she muttered defensively. This was not her fault. He couldn't blame this on her, even in his anger. She knew that there was no way that he could have known that something like this was going to happen to his club. This had never happened before. Even if he wanted to claim that it was because he had always been there, she knew better. This had been chance…a fluke. It just happened that he had been out of the state, but it could have happened at any time.

"Yeah, well, it wouldn't have happened if I'd been there," he growled refusing to hear reason.

"I'm sorry, Ramsey," she said weakly unable to process anything else. There was nothing left for her to say. It wasn't her fault, but she still felt bad about what had happened to him.

"Sorry isn't going to save all of this. I just…I need to get back into town. I'm going to go catch the red eye or find a private plane," he said beginning to meander through the now crowded room as everyone prepared for the final countdown to take them into the new year.

"You're leaving *now*?" she asked flabbergasted rushing behind him.

"The sooner I get there, the sooner I can piece this all together."

"But you can't fix anything tonight," she reminded him. Her panic level was swiftly increasing the farther they traversed the room. She couldn't have him leave. There was no reason to leave yet, especially since he couldn't do anything about what had happened. By the time he caught a flight everything would be over.

"I can't wait until the morning," he grumbled pushing aside a couple that was lost in each other's eyes.

"But Ramsey, it's almost midnight," she said as they stopped in front of the elevators. She knew she sounded desperate by now. He was going to leave her before the clock struck twelve. She could feel it in her bones. She understood his urgency to get out of town, but she couldn't process him leaving with only a minute left before New Year's.

"I can't be here any longer. Just—understand," he said stooping low and kissing her cheek. The kiss was rushed. It barely brushed against her skin before he pulled back and pressed the button for the elevator.

"Just a kiss on the cheek?" she asked her face stricken with concern. She couldn't figure out how the night had changed so dramatically that he wouldn't even kiss her. The elevator door dinged open and he stuck his hand out to keep it from closing.

She stepped forward into him, not letting him leave without a proper good bye. She knew he was obviously directing more irritation at her then was necessary. Grasping her tightly, he pulled her flush against him and planted a kiss on her lips. She came up gasping, her hips already sore from his forcefulness.

"I'll call you in the morning," he told her stepping into the elevator; his eyes already distracted.

"Happy New Year," she called as the doors closed between them.

Lexi walked hopelessly back into the crowded room, listening to the chanting countdown. As the clock struck midnight, she glanced around as all the happy couples moved forward to receive their first kiss of the New Year…a kiss she never received.

Making a beeline for the bar, she downed the first drink that was put in front of her, grimacing at the taste of Jack Daniels on her tongue. Pouring the remainder of the contents down her throat, she returned the glass to the bartender and wandered over to a vacant table. Several minutes later, she felt a presence next to her. "Is this seat taken?"

Glancing up sullenly, Lexi noticed Adam. "Nope."

He sat down next to her and waited a minute before saying anything. "Where's Ramsey?"

"He left."

"Where to?" he asked glancing around the room.

"Home," she grumbled

"To your place?"

Lexi turned away from him. Her heart broke as she answered, "To Atlanta."

"Oh," he said looking down at his shoes.

"Yeah."

"I'm sorry."

"No need," she told him softly, waving away his apology.

"Lexi," he asked reaching for her hand and drawing her attention back to his face. "Are you going to be alright?"

Lexi stared down at where he was lightly holding her hand, and then out across the open expanse before her. "My boyfriend left me seconds before I got a New Year's kiss, and I don't know if we're going to stay together. How would you be?"

"Good point," he reasoned. He squeezed her hand lightly, offering her all the support he could give her. "Personally, I think you'll be fine. He'd be an idiot to leave you."

"Thanks." A small smile touched her lips. That was a nice thing to say in this situation. It's what she would have said to someone. It didn't really help though.

"And as for that New Year's kiss," he said, leaning forward towards her. "I think it's acceptable to have someone fill in, in certain circumstances."

She turned and faced him, finding that they had moved closer to each other in their chairs. Her brows furrowed together in surprise at his nearness. She didn't even remember them drawing together. "Uh, Adam?" she breathed.

"Yeah?" he asked staring deeply into her eyes.

"I don't…what about Chyna?" she asked, waiting for his response. She took a deep breath knowing that this was her moment. There was always a moment, and either you could take it or not. Her mind was whirring to life as she felt him approaching her. She turned her face just a fraction of an inch as he moved closer brushing his lips against her cheek and pulling away quickly.

She dropped his hand and hoped that her cheeks weren't as red as she thought they were. When she looked back into his handsome face, his smile was nothing but sweet and friendly. He just looked as if he really felt bad for her, and wanted her to be happy again.

She touched her fingertips to her cheek and smiled back at him. "Thanks," she said tucking a lock of hair behind her ear. "I…appreciate you trying to help."

"Of course," he glanced down at her, back out at the city beyond, and then into her face again. She gulped. He smiled knowingly. "I'm going to get back to Chyna. Are you going to be alright?" he asked.

"Yeah, I think I am."

"Hey," he muttered looking at her intently once more. "If you ever need anything, Lex, I'm here for you."

Lexi nodded not even having the energy to tell him not to call her that.

She left the party shortly afterwards, taking Chyna's town car without a second thought. She hadn't brought money for a cab, because she had been expecting to be with Ramsey. She was so lost in her thoughts that she hardly even noticed when she was dropped off at her apartment.

After walking up the stairs, she threw off all of her clothes, and burrowed under the mound of covers on her bed. Her mind was all over the charts, and she didn't know which thing to think about first. Should she be thinking about her boyfriend leaving her or the fact that another man had kissed her…even if it was just on the cheek? Adam was Chyna's boyfriend, and he was just helping her out when she was down.

And she didn't feel guilty.

She had no reason to feel guilty. It's not like Adam was Jack. He had just been helping her when her boyfriend had deserted her. Speaking of her boyfriend, she wondered where he was at that moment. Had he found an airplane that would take him home or had he bribed someone again to use their plane or take their seat? She wasn't sure what to make of him. He had been unduly cruel. This was a side of him that she had never witnessed.

Yes, he had been under a severe amount of stress and strain regarding the club, but it certainly hadn't been her fault. As much as she wanted to be angry at him, she couldn't bring herself to it. He had left her there all alone, but at least he had a reason. He hadn't just jumped ship. And she wasn't going to risk their entire relationship on one screw up on his part. She would wait to hear back from him and they could go from there. With those thoughts still filling her mind, she finally drifted off to sleep.

Hours later Lexi was awoken by a vibration emanating from her phone. She reached over to her night stand to silence the sound and plopped her head back down on the pillow. A second later the noise began again. Rubbing her tired eyes, Lexi reached forward once more and retrieved the cell phone. The bright light that flashed when she hit a button made her immediately close her eyes again to shield herself. Then as they adjusted to the brightness, she saw the two text messages.

Clicking on the first message it read, "Everything is fine here. You were right."

A smile crept onto her face. She loved those words. They were some of the best words in the English language. She knew she had been right. All along he had been freaking out for no reason. In all likelihood, everything had settled down by the time he had arrived back in Hartsfield.

Remembering that there was one more message, she pressed the next button which said, "Sorry I screwed up. I'll make it up to you. Give you that New Year's kiss for real. Forgive me?"

Lexi yawned dramatically at the early hour before typing out a response. "Yes, what's the plan?" she asked before falling back into an easy slumber.

11

PRESENT

The next morning Lexi awoke to the sun beaming in through her windows. She smiled at the interruption of her slumber. The weather had been so awful in New York for the last month, it was intoxicating seeing the sun. She slowly crawled out of the bed she had slept in…alone, and peered out the window. The view was nothing spectacular since they were in the middle of the city, but it was still green. That was another thing that Lexi had been missing a lot of since being in New York. To get to greenery, she had to visit Central Park.

She threw on a pair of sleep shorts and a loose tank top, and mechanically stumbled down the stairs. Walking to the coffee maker in the kitchen, Lexi fiddled with the device until it started brewing her life force. She stared at the machine hoping it would finish quicker, but knowing that if she watched it that it would take longer. She pulled two mugs from the cabinet as the machine finished and poured the steaming brew into each mug.

"This is the best part about you being back in the house," Ramsey murmured as he staggered bleary-eyed into the kitchen.

Lexi flushed and turned back to the coffee maker. She couldn't acknowledge that kind of comment yet between them. "Here," she said handing him his favorite mug.

"Thanks," he moaned chugging the steaming contents.

Lexi giggled a little as he sputtered from the heat of the beverage. "Why do you drink it like that every time? You don't even like black coffee."

"If you can drink it that way, I can," he said between sips.

"I'm used to it. I've been drinking it like that for years."

"So give me years," he said wrapping his arm around her waist and pulling her against him. He chuckled at her unease, and whispered, "Calm down." He nuzzled her neck as if everything were back to normal. It was a nice feeling. She missed this kind of thing. But she couldn't get caught up in it…not yet. They had too much to discuss.

"I'm calm," she said pulling away from him and taking a sip of the coffee. She was thankful for the distraction.

His smile didn't falter. He just proceeded to guzzle the remaining contents in his mug and pour himself a refill. "So, are you ready for today?" he asked eyeing her carefully.

"Yeah…" she said slowly. "We're going to your—parent's house, right?"

Lexi had never been to Ramsey parents' house. It had been a continual source of contention. She hadn't wanted to go, because she feared their judgment. And she wasn't certain that he had ever wanted to bring her with him. Not that he was ashamed of her, by any means; he just didn't want to humiliate her in front of his judgmental parents. They didn't approve of him, and any girl that he would bring home would only suffer under the same criticism, even someone who was currently studying law at a top university. The lack of family connections on Lexi's part was never brought up, but she knew it was also a problem.

He nodded seeing only slight hesitation in her demeanor. Reassured by the fact that she wasn't freaking out, he continued, "Some kind of formal luncheon. Should be mostly big investors. Nothing to worry about."

Lexi was pretty sure that Ramsey was the only person that didn't bat an eye at the prospect of being surrounded by a sea of "big investors." She wasn't exactly sure what these people would look like, but if they were anything like his father then she was already intimidated. She knew how to handle wealthy people, but she wasn't so sure that she knew how to handle *these* kind of people.

"Right. Big investors. No biggie," she said shrugging her shoulders in an attempt to mirror his indifference.

He chuckled at her obvious discomfort. "You'll be fine." Lexi poured the remaining contents of her drink down her throat to keep from responding. "Hey, are you sure you're ready for this?" he asked tentatively. She knew he wasn't talking about dealing with big investors now. He was talking about Jack and Bekah, and the thought made her skin crawl. The last thing she wanted to do was deal with them together, but she couldn't help it now.

She had woken this morning feeling refreshed and prepared for the events of the upcoming week. Yes, things hadn't exactly gone as planned since her arrival in Atlanta, but things rarely did. She knew people were hiding things from her and it drove her crazy, but wasting time wondering wasn't going to help her. Sleep had given her some perspective on the situation, and she was ready to push forward.

"I wouldn't be here if I wasn't ready," she told him before turning and walking back up the stairs to change.

*****

They arrived at his parent's house a short while later. She stared up at the giant edifice, more surprised at the enormous house than she thought she was going to be. After all she had been expecting something spectacular, and they had delivered.

"This way," Ramsey said directing her to the side of the house. "You don't want to go through the front," he warned.

"I don't?" Lexi asked raising an eye questioningly.

"Not unless you want to be bombarded with a bunch of questions or run into a sea of bridesmaids," he informed.

Lexi gritted her teeth. She really needed to use the restroom. This was so inconvenient. "Do you think I could sneak in? I have to use the restroom, but I would prefer to avoid both situations."

Ramsey's eyes flitted to the giant house and back to Lexi. "Yeah. Follow me," he said walking around the side of the house. She trailed after him, skipping down the hill that lead to the backyard. "Here," he said stopping at an obscured side entrance. He pulled the door open and glanced inside making sure the coast was clear for her. Hearing his sister's voice, he quickly shut the door and waited. "There's a bathroom at the end of the hallway on the right. Give it a minute, I think Bekah just walked by."

"Alright," she said nodding. "Are you going to wait?"

"I have to go talk to my dad," he told her. "He already knows we're here. I'll see you afterwards. We'll be in the pavilion at the bottom of the hill."

"Okay," she said taking a deep breath as he trekked down the hill away from her. Waiting another minute, she opened the door and peered around the corner. Not hearing any voices, she darted down the hallway and into the bathroom. After relieving herself, she washed her hands slowly, dawdling. As she was drying them with a white fluffy towel, her phone vibrated in her purse. She retrieved it and saw the name flash on the screen. She knew she was alone, but it still made her stomach tilt at the thought of answering this number. She hadn't spoken with him on the phone since leaving New York. They had talked on the phone almost every day before she left. It felt like such a long time ago.

"Hey," she said finally deciding to answer. She weakly pushed a strand of hair behind her ear.

"Hey, babe, I didn't hear from you last night."

"Sorry, I didn't get a chance to call you back. I really wanted to. It's good to hear your voice."

"It's good to hear from you, too. Are you free now?" he asked.

Lexi bit on her lip and wondered how long she could get away with hiding out in here. "Yeah, I should be able to talk for a bit."

"How are the wedding festivities?"

Lexi shrugged then remembered he couldn't see her. "I'm not a big fan of weddings to be honest."

"Most girls love them," he said with a chuckle.

"I'm not like most girls."

"You don't have to tell me twice. So, if you don't like weddings, why did you leave me here all alone?" he asked.

"It's one of those things I have to do, I guess," she murmured. "I would have never left otherwise."

She could almost hear him smirking. "It's okay. I'll let you make it up to me."

Lexi couldn't contain her throaty laughter at the statement. "Oh, I bet you will. How do you expect me to make it up to you?"

"Use your imagination."

"I have a vivid imagination. A rather dirty, vivid imagination," she purred into the line.

"That's what I like to hear, babe. Tell me how you're going to make it up to me."

"I can think of a few things…involving a suite at the Plaza," she began tentatively.

"I'm listening…though I was thinking about a cabin in Connecticut. No one can hear you out there."

"I'm not loud," she murmured softly.

"I'll turn you into a screamer," he responded just as soft and husky.

Lexi shifted her legs together, her lower half throbbing. Her face heated as her imagination took over and she closed her eyes. "Maybe I want them to hear me scream."

"Now you're talking. Tell me again."

Lexi paused caught up in what they were doing. She licked her lips imagining all the things he would do to her if she was back in New York. She reached forward with her free hand and pressed against her dress to the pulsing core beneath.

"Babe. Tell me again."

"I want you to make me scream."

"And I will. What else do you want?"

Lexi shuddered against her own touch. "I want you to fuck me."

"I want to give you what you want."

"Don't be as gentle as last time," she told him.

He chuckled again in her ear. "I'll never be gentle again."

"Fuck," she moaned, forcibly pulling her hand away. She couldn't do this here. She wanted to, but she couldn't. She didn't have time, and this wasn't the place. Her lower half disagreed with her. It really disagreed with her.

"Come...back to me."

Lexi leaned her head into her hand and tried to control her breathing. The door handle jiggled jolting her out of her reverie. Had she locked it? "Hey, I have to go," she told him quickly. "I'll call you later." She hung up abruptly and buried her phone back in her purse.

The door handle turned again. "Hold on," she called, clearing her voice afterwards. She glanced back up at her reflection. Her cheeks were flushed and pupils dilated. God, had she been that close to climax? Splashing some cold water on her face and the back of her neck, Lexi decided there was little else she could do. She turned the locked door and opened it to find the devil herself standing before her.

"Oh, Lexi," Bekah said smiling that ever-present, sugary sweet smile. "I didn't realize you made it."

"Yep," she said, wanting to be far, far away. "Just freshening up."

"Oh, I'm sure," she said smiling even brighter.

Lexi wanted to punch her in the face. That was rational, right? Her lips strained around the edges as she tried to hold herself together. She didn't know how long Bekah had been standing there, and she didn't want to know. She just didn't want to be near the wench. "Excuse me," she muttered, inching out of the bathroom and around Bekah.

"Who were you talking to?" she piped up, when Lexi moved past her.

Lexi stopped moving and glanced into Bekah's devious blue eyes. "What?" she asked playing dumb.

"I heard you talking to someone. I assume you weren't talking to yourself," she said fluttering her long black eyelashes. She was too damn good at this routine.

"Chyna," Lexi finally told her, letting the lie slip off of her tongue.

As she turned back towards the exit, Bekah continued, "She must really miss you."

"She does," Lexi agreed, trying not to let the queasiness of the situation wear on her face.

"Well, you should be back in New York soon. She shouldn't have to wait too long."

Lexi smiled, seeing her point to maneuver the Knight into position. "We'll see about that."

"Yes, I believe we will," she said wiggling her fingers at Lexi before disappearing into the bathroom Lexi had just occupied.

Lexi raced down the hallway and out the side entrance as soon as Bekah shut the bathroom door. She felt sort of like vomiting as she leaned back against the mansion. Had Bekah heard anything that she had said? What had she been thinking? She seriously could not get any closer to being caught.

That solidified it; she couldn't talk to him again. It was too dangerous. If someone actually heard what they had been talking about, well, she couldn't even think about that. It was one week. She had too much to think about with Ramsey as it was. She needed to deal with that situation—figure out what they actually were—before agreeing to let her Mystery Man fuck her until she screamed in a cabin in Connecticut.

Taking a deep fortifying breath, Lexi pushed off from the side of the house and trudged down the hill. The back yard was several acres at least. The perfectly cut lawn ended at a clear blue lake, and from across the great distance she could see a hole from the Club's golf course. An overgrowth of beautiful trees separated their lawn from the surrounding houses giving them the privacy that they had paid for.

As Lexi looked across the expanse, finding the pavilion Ramsey had mentioned, her gaze immediately landed on Jack. Their eyes met across the lawn, and Lexi couldn't help herself, she smiled. She could tell even from this distance that he had cleaned up. His suit was pressed, beard shaven, and hair cut short once again. He looked every bit a part of the family already.

When she had seen him the day before, he had been a mess. Disheveled, uncouth, and haphazard were the words she would have used to describe him. Yes, he had looked like her Jack. He still made her catch her breath at the sight of him, but somehow it had been different. While he looked more like the Jack she had first gotten to know in that quaint coffee shop all those years ago, something about him had just been downtrodden.

She knew now, of course, that he looked that way because he had been second guessing himself. Could the man who refused to commit, who hated the idea of marriage, actually go through with his plan? She hadn't thought it possible, and apparently he hadn't either. Lexi still had her doubts.

For one, she hadn't told Bekah about their affair in the hallway. The tattered dress, proof of their indecent night together, was stuffed in the bottom of her closet somewhere. She wasn't exactly proud of herself. After all those times she had told herself that no matter what, she was not going to give into him. Then she had let everything slip through her fingertips, everything.

Breaking eye contact with Jack, she traipsed the rest of the way down the hill. Guilt crept up into her stomach, poisoning her blood stream, and traveling through her veins as her eyes landed on Ramsey. She didn't know what they were, but she knew that even though they weren't together, she was doing him wrong. Jack still struck a match in her body, and her conversation with Mystery Man…well; she didn't even need to think about that.

She tucked a lock of hair behind her ear and walked up the pavilion steps. The smile Ramsey sent her way as she approached his side was adorable, and only made her feel worse. He knew what she was thinking…or at the very least, he could tell she was nervous. She silently praised the lord that he didn't actually know what she was thinking; otherwise he wouldn't be smiling at her.

"You remember Lexi, yes?" Ramsey asked his father when she finally reached him

Lexi smiled brightly at the imposing man standing before her. He was at least as tall as Ramsey if not an inch taller. He had a hard, grim face with deep set wrinkles as if he had been frowning his entire life. His belly had long since bulged over his waist line, and the tailored suit did nothing to hide his porpoise figure. His blonde hair was sprinkled with salt and pepper gray, and his own forced smile was anything but kind. In fact, he blatantly stared at Lexi as if he should know her from somewhere, but somehow he found her too insignificant to remember.

"Oh yes, Lexi," he drawled after a moment. He took a sip from the scotch in his hand. "Pleasure to see you again."

The statement sounded like a rehearsed line, and Lexi tried not to take offense to the fact that they had been introduced several times previously. "You too, sir," she piped up.

"Where the hell is your sister?" Ramsey's father growled his attention already lost.

"I think she went inside for some lemonade, dear. Don't you remember?" his wife asked him. Her petite stature looked almost comical next to the man. Despite her age, she was no larger than a size four, and she probably would have been offended by the statement. Her blonde hair was perfectly straight and curled under softly at the ends. Her face had seen its fair share of surgeons…and that wasn't the only thing on her body that had seen a surgeon. Lexi glanced away immediately feeling her cheeks burn at the thought.

"If I bloody remembered, would I have asked?" he bellowed down to the woman.

She waived her Bloody Mary in the air. "I'll go check on her," the woman replied unaffected by his belligerence. Lexi decided against telling them that she had seen Bekah; she didn't want to get dragged back inside.

"Tell her to hurry up. It is not every day my little girl gets married. She needs to be more attentive to these types of affairs."

"Yes, dear," she drawled, waltzing away from the group.

The awkward silence that followed was unlike anything Lexi had stood through. She wasn't sure what was worse. Ramsey's father was alternating between staring daggers at Ramsey and the back entrance to the house. It was as if he couldn't determine who to be angrier at for wasting his time…or making him stand outside in the blistering August heat in a navy suit.

Lexi felt her hands clamming up and wished she could wipe them on her sundress. The sun was making her sweat and she was concerned, with the increased tension between her current company, her body would go into overdrive. She felt a bead of sweat run down her back and she sighed in protest. Luckily, she had been smart enough to wear something cotton so that it wouldn't show.

"Ramsey," his father barked breaking everyone's attention. "Go check on your goddamn sister." Ramsey opened his mouth to object, but the look of pure venom that he shot his son was unlike anything Lexi had ever seen. Finding it a battle not worth fighting, Ramsey nodded. Lexi opened her mouth to tell him, but then closed it. If she hadn't told his mother, then it would look strange if she told him. Though, the alternative was being left with just Ramsey's father and Jack. Choices, choices.

Ramsey smiled at her, squeezing her hand before he left. She watched him walk away and didn't do a damn thing to stop him.

She sighed and made the mistake of looking into Jack's eyes. He tilted his head to the side, beckoning her towards the exit. She looked away, refusing to acknowledging him. "Will you excuse us for a moment?" Jack asked Ramsey's father.

"Just be back before the women return. I'm not going to listen to their idle chatter alone," he said clapping Jack on the back forcefully. Jack tried hard not to stumble forward a step, but he couldn't help but stutter a bit with the force of the blow.

"Lexi," Jack said, snatching her up by the elbow and directing her away from the intimidating man.

As soon as she was out of eyesight, she jerked her elbow out of Jack's grasp. "Don't do that," she muttered.

"Sorry. I had to fucking get away from there," he responded, stuffing his hands into his pockets.

"Well, we're away now," she said, turning away from him. She couldn't be alone with him.

"Walk with me a bit," Jack said, resting his hand gently on the small of her back and urging her forward.

She dug her feet in, not moving an inch. "I—I can't," she told him.

"I don't bite."

Lexi coughed, biting back her laughter.

"Okay fine, I do…just a bit," he muttered huskily.

"Stop it, Jack," she warned him.

"You're right. I'm sorry. Can we just keep walking?" he pleaded.

Against her better judgment, Lexi turned her face up towards him. She knew she was a lost cause. He looked way better than the last time she had seen him when he had turned up at Ramsey's apartment. His hair had been cut short and styled in a way that made him look younger and more professional. The short strands stood on end instead of falling haphazardly into his eyes. She could remember pushing the long pieces out of his eyes and him kissing her tenderly just as she pulled her hand away. She pushed that memory of her mind and focused her eyes elsewhere.

His typical stubble was completely wiped from his face. She could remember the scruffy feel of his beard running against her stomach as he kissed a trail lower. Her breathing quickened as she unsuccessfully tried to shove the memories out of her misbehaving mind. He licked his perfect lips and more memories flooded her conscious: their first kiss on top of a Ferris wheel, her fingers teasingly trailing against his pouty lips before he captured her own, the way he kissed every part of her body as if he worshipped it.

As her eyes finally moved upwards to his beautiful blue eyes, the brilliance of which she could never perfectly remember, she had a feeling he knew exactly where her thoughts were. The longer they stood rooted in that spot, the more crystal clear his eyes became. She knew what that meant.

"Lexi, please," he growled, hungrily begging her to move, "we need to keep walking." His voice was desperate and pained from restraint.

Taking a deep breath to calm her pounding heart, she nodded. "Yes."

"Yes," he agreed, his eyes dropping to her lips.

"Let's walk, Jack," she said taking that first hesitant step.

She saw him visibly deflate from exertion. His hand moved to her lower back once again as he directed her towards a pathway. She wasn't sure why she was allowing him to steer her in a direction not only far away from the rest of the guests, but also to what appeared to be a portion of the land secluded by massive trees. But she did. After walking a short distance, Jack stopped in front of a large weeping willow. Pulling back a few of the extended limbs, he revealed a wooden bench in the shade of the branches.

"Come on," he said, nodding his head towards the bench.

Speechless, Lexi ducked into the private enclosure that the tree had formed after years of life. "How did you know about this?" she finally asked taking a seat. She didn't really want an answer. Anything that he said would ultimately involve Bekah, and that wasn't something she particularly wanted to discuss at this moment.

He let the branches swing closed, the light now only coming in at uneven intervals through the leaves. The temperature was cooler, as if it was dusk, and some of the humidity had dissipated in the shaded enclosure.

For the first time in a while, she felt utterly and completely alone with Jack. It felt strangely familiar and also eerily different. He took the seat next to her, and breathed out a sigh of relief. He adjusted his tie, allowing himself the freedom of being out of the spotlight. Then he sat there next to her without a word, not even answering her question.

She remembered what she thought was going to be her final farewell to Jack.

I appreciate the fact that you have one redeeming quality, Jack, but that is all it is. Just a hint of redemption with six years of disappointment.

She had been cruel, but not anymore than he had been with her.

I wish you the very best in your future, because without you in my life I think I might finally have a future.

He had proposed to Bekah after everything that had happened between them that week. Her words were nothing in comparison.

It is like cutting off the spoiled part to get to the juicy center.

She wouldn't feel bad for them. She had meant every word, and she knew that she was still angry.

I want everything this time around, and I deserve it.

She hadn't forgiven him. And she had wanted him out of her life.

Yet, here she was, sitting under a weeping willow with him in complete silence. To anyone else this would have been the strangest thing in the world. Why would you run off with the groom at his own luncheon?

"Don't you think we should get back?" Lexi asked tugging on a long brown curl and letting it bounce back into place. She did this a few more times before pushing it behind her ear.

Jack shrugged noncommittally and looked into her large brown eyes. "You look beautiful."

"Jack," she said quietly into the dim lighting.

"I know," he told her not letting her add anything else. "I love the way you say my name."

"Funny, I hate the way you say my name," she quipped, hoping to put some much needed distance between them.

"Don't lie, Lex. You're bad at it," he told her nonchalantly leaning backwards and putting his arms across the back of the bench.

"Jack, don't call me that," she reminded him, feeling the closeness of his arm to her back. She inched forward to avoid touching him.

He shrugged again as if he was never going to break that habit. "I like the way you look at me."

Lexi sighed heavily. "Can we not?"

"We don't have to," he acknowledged, "but I do love how short of breath you get."

"Don't use *that* word so freely either," Lexi commanded.

Jack turned abruptly in his seat and stared directly into her eyes. Lexi sat motionless as he seemed to examine every pore on her face. She couldn't help but prove him right. As his gaze intensified, her breathing quickened.

"You smell delicious," he muttered, his free hand reaching up and running his fingers through her long hair. Her breath caught at the accidental grazing of her ear as he moved the silky strands into their rightful place.

"Wh…wh…what are you a vampire now?" she asked trying to lighten the mood.

He cracked a smile at the comment. "I don't sparkle in the daylight, if that's what you mean."

Lexi giggled reflexively and he took the opportunity to move in even closer to her. She took a sharp breath at his nearness. "Oh God…" she murmured.

"That's something I've heard before," he said smirking.

"No," she told him scooting over an inch into the metal bar at the end of the bench. "You smell like sex."

Jack actually laughed out loud at her statement. "I haven't had any."

"So you're what—horny? Is this what this is about?" she asked angrily.

"What? No. I—I don't know. I hadn't planned this," he said careful not to move.

"Oh Jack, why did I just tell you that you smell like sex?" Lexi asked burying her face in her hands in horror.

"Maybe it's my cologne?" he asked.

"Obviously it's your cologne, but what's wrong with me? I'm not even supposed to be here with you," Lexi said standing abruptly. "I'm so pissed at you; I can't even function."

"What?" he asked standing with her. "You were just telling me I smell like sex, and now you're pissed at me?"

"Yes."

"Lex, that doesn't make any sense."

"Stop calling me that," she cried turning around to face him. "Lexi. *Lexi*. Alexa. Whatever you want to call me…just not that, alright?"

"Whatever I want to call you?" he asked moving forward a step closer to her.

"Jack, you're infuriating."

"I know," he agreed taking another step closer.

"You are getting married in less than a week," she reminded him.

"I know."

"You will be legally bound to another woman in less than a week."

"I know."

"Then why are you doing this?" she asked as he stopped in front of her.

"I still have a week," he said shrugging.

Lexi's mouth dropped. "You're joking!"

"I am," he said with a chuckle. The way he said that was even more confusing. She couldn't tell if he really was joking or not. She honestly didn't want to ask though. She had no idea what kind of reaction that would elicit from him.

"You should really stop this," he told her gesturing to her whole self.

"Stop what, exactly?" she demanded.

"Getting all fired up," he said, his eyes trailing the length of her body.

"Well, then stop acting like an idiot," she commanded him.

"I just mean that you are sooo hot when you get feisty," he reminded her.

Lexi shook her head in disbelief and turned to leave. Jack grabbed her wrist and tugged her backwards. She stumbled into him. "Hey, I'm just kidding with you," he said his arms circling her waist to steady her balance.

She wasn't sure if she could believe him. But suddenly her mind wasn't thinking properly. When she had fallen against him, her body had landed flush against his chest. Pressed against his heated body, she held onto his shoulders as she straightened herself. Her head tilted upwards and she realized his lips were only inches from her own.

Her mind went blank. Everything she had been doing or thinking about before that moment was gone. She felt like he was her desert oasis and she was dying for thirst at the feel of his arms around her.

He seemed to realize her nearness at the same time. They both stiffened, too scared to move in any direction and unsure as to what result moving would bring. Their eyes locked onto each other.

Jack's head leaned forward and he rested his forehead against hers. She could feel the waves of exertion and desire coming off of him as he struggled to keep it together. "Lexi, I can't," he said at the same time she muttered, "We shouldn't."

"Jaaaaaack," they heard someone yell not too far off.

Lexi sighed, realizing that they had to return to reality. She wrapped her arms around his shoulders and crushed her body to him. He pulled her in closer and breathed in her familiar scent.

"It's all going to be okay, right Lex?" he whispered into her ear, begging for reassurance.

He was asking for something she couldn't give. He was making a terrible mistake, and she knew what a mistake it truly was. She could not reassure him that everything he was doing was going to be fine. In fact, she thought it would fall apart at the first sign of trouble. If anything, this was the second sign of trouble. They had done worse in the past.

"I don't know, Jack," she muttered.

He sighed heavily. "That's what I'm afraid of."

Just then the branches swung backwards and light flooded in on their intimate moment. The two jumped back, as if they had been burned. The action made them look even guiltier than being found alone in a weeping willow together. Lexi's cheeks flamed as her eyes shot over to the entrance to the tree.

"Ramsey," she muttered forlornly, her stomach dropping out of her body. *Fuck.*

12

MARCH FIVE MONTHS EARLIER

Lexi stared out across the beautiful ocean view stretching before her. The sand was perfectly white and flat, extending for miles in either direction. The clear blue water rippled faintly in the evening breeze. A warm sunset flooded the evening sky with shades of red, pink, and orange. Palm trees partially shaded a kidney shaped pool and cabana below.

She couldn't believe she was spending her last spring break tucked into a gorgeous villa on the beach in south Florida with her boyfriend and a select group of his friends. Ramsey had been apologizing to her for his actions at New Year's for months, and this planned trip was the pièce de rèsistance to his scheme to fully return to her good graces.

He had apologized in style even. Once he had settled the affairs of the club in Atlanta, he had immediately flown back to New York to, as he put it, "complete their evening." He refused to have it any other way. He had taken her back up to the top floor of the building where Chyna's blow out party had been. A table had been set up on the balcony with a single red rose, and thoughtful card explaining how, if he could go back in time, he would change everything. Then he had kissed her unlike he had ever kissed her before. When he pulled back from her lips, he had simply said, "Happy New Year's."

She had been blown away, to say the least. She probably would have let the whole incident go, but she couldn't deny that his words had hurt her. The last thing she wanted to do was lie to him about her feelings. She couldn't tell him everything was alright with her, when in fact she was beating herself up about what had happened.

Long distance relationships had never been something she had considered. She didn't think that they actually worked, until Ramsey. Then he had gone and blamed her for everything that had gone down. Whether he meant to or not, he had opened up a can of worms of insecurity about the distance between them.

He had his clubs and all his adoring employees. He had Atlanta, the nightlife, the celebrity status, and the charming good looks. He had everything he could possibly need there. And what did she have? She had no money, no job, and no real life outside of Chyna. She had a pile of debt waiting for her upon graduation. The more she thought about things he had said, the more terrified she had gotten about their relationship.

He didn't need her. This much was clear. She couldn't figure out why he even bothered. She had a mountain of baggage as large as her law school student loans.

There was no point in him having any feelings towards her.

After he had finally wrestled this information out of her, he had simply laughed. He laughed, until he realized she was serious. Then he blabbered on and on about his deep affection for her in a way that only Ramsey could. She had shaken her head unable to comprehend why someone like him could like her. He had told her to cut the crap; he liked her for exactly who she was, baggage and all.

She still didn't quite understand, but a paid beach vacation for the entire week of spring break sure did make it more real. Why else would he bother?

"Are you ready?" Ramsey asked walking out onto the balcony and wrapping his arms around her waist. He gently pushed her up against the stone railing and buried his head into her neck. He placed kisses against her bronzed skin from ear to shoulder.

"Ye...yes," she murmured, sighing pleasantly at the feel of his lips on her. "But really Ramsey, where are we going?"

"You know I like to surprise you," he whispered huskily into her skin.

"I know, but I never know if I'm dressed right," she told him.

He easily spun her around in place and let his eyes roam her body. She was wearing a pink, blue, and green floral sun dress that flowed out to her knees. The dress had thin spaghetti straps that held it up and a v-cut in the front, revealing enough cleavage from his high vantage point, but not enough to be immodest. "You look perfect," he told her, capturing her lips in his.

Her eyes fell to his perfectly chiseled chest, and she couldn't look away. When he tried to pull away, she wrapped her arms around his neck, and brought his body back towards her. He responded with as much enthusiasm by pushing his muscled body further against her and deepening the kiss. She could taste the peppermint flavor on him and her body reacted instantly to the now familiar taste of him. Her mouth watered at the smell. "Are you sure we have to go out?" she asked hungrily between kisses.

He pushed his hands up into her long chocolate locks and began to gently massage her head. "Yes, we said we would meet everyone."

"I know, but..." she trailed off, a moan escaping her lips as he gently tugged the strands backwards.

"Oh God, that's sexy," he groaned pushing his lower half against her.

She could feel his erection through his soft khaki shorts. Her hand, which had previously been supporting herself against the railing, moved forward to rest on his hip bones. Her thumbs slowly traced circle eights against the exposed skin. Then she lightly trailed her fingertips against the inside seem of his pants. He shuddered against her from even the lightest of touches and ducked his head down to her throat once more.

"Ramsey," she moaned. She let her hand drop from his hot skin down the length of his shorts. The palm of her hand rested against the bulge in his pants.

"Maybe we can be a little late," he groaned pressing himself into her hand.

"Maybe we can," she agreed, her body coming alive as his lips worked on her neck. "We're all alone. You could take me right here," she muttered unabashedly into his ear.

"What's with us and balconies?" he asked playfully, looking up into her big brown eyes.

Lexi couldn't keep from blushing at the comment. Their first kiss had been on a balcony at his apartment in Atlanta. They had kissed again on a balcony overlooking Turner Field. His dramatic apology had consisted of a romantic balcony kiss. She hadn't ever really thought about it before, but it *was* kind of their thing.

"I don't know, but I like it," she told him capturing his lips. "Maybe you could...take me out here tonight since you like balconies so much." Her voice was throaty and she couldn't keep the desire from the words.

"I'd like that," he said leaning into her. "But it might be dangerous," he warned. "I wouldn't want you to fall."

Lexi shook her head, loose curls flying around her face. "Nah. You've got me."

Ramsey breathed a sigh of relief. "I'm glad you finally realize that," he said holding her tight.

Her heart beat rapidly at the meaning in his words. At that moment, she couldn't think of a reason for her having ever been mad at him. He had other things to occupy his time in Atlanta, but that didn't mean he felt anything less for her. Long distance relationships did work for some people after all. And why couldn't it work for her?

He clearly wasn't hanging on to any lingering doubts about her or what had gone on with her. She couldn't figure out why she had to hold back so much from him. He was an incredible, successful, gorgeous man who wanted to be with her as much as she wanted to be with him. All she had to do was let go and allow herself to experience what he was willing to offer.

She wanted to. She wanted to make him happy. She never wanted his easy smile to leave his face, or his bright green eyes to stray from hers. She couldn't think of another place she would rather be in the world than wrapped in his arms. She was completely lost in him.

"Me too," she said meaning every word. He really did have her.

The joy that filled his eyes at her admission was nearly overwhelming. He dropped his arms from her waist and hiked up one leg up around his waist. Surprised, her hand tightened around the bulge in his pants, and he groaned at the feel of her touching him. His hand worked miracles through her thigh as he massaged slowly upwards.

When as he reached her soft cotton underwear, he dropped to his knees in front of her and pulled her leg up on his shoulder. She stared dreamily down at him. He hitched a finger into her underwear and pulled it sideways before bringing his mouth forward to her most sensitive area. She gasped and threw her head back as his tongue expertly traveled the length of her. Her hands laced through his golden hair as he sucked and swirled his tongue around her, willing her to reach a climax. "Oh, God," she moaned feeling herself tighten in anticipation. "Ramsey, I'm so close."

"Not yet," he murmured, licking her clit once more.

"Oh, please, so close."

He breathed hot against her, causing her to squirm. "You taste so good."

"Then don't stop," she told him, willing him to continue to touch her. Her body was achingly close.

"Not yet," he repeated, dropping her leg and righting himself.

She was breathing heavy when he straightened and kissed her breathlessly. "See. Don't you taste good?"

"God, I need you…now," she said, as her hand came up and undid the button and zipper of his shorts. Only his tight ass held the shorts up, and she slid her hands to grasp the firm muscles, allowing the shorts to slide effortlessly to the floor.

He pushed her back against the railing, hard. Without the restriction of his shorts, he was clearly visible to her, throbbing, and ready. She groaned at the sight of him, picking up her own leg, wrapping it around him, and wrenching him closer to her. He slid against the length of her cotton underwear slowly, teasingly. Her climax, which had been so close only seconds earlier, was building again with every passing moment of anticipation. "You're mine?" she murmured to him, half a question and half a statement.

His hands dug into her back as he tried to get closer and closer to her. "Yes."

"All mine?" she groaned, her hand sinking into his hair and forcing his eyes to meet hers again.

He took advantage of her weight shift and pulled both of her legs around his waist. "All yours," he said walking her through the sliding glass doors and into the bedroom. He lay her down on the king-sized bed and crawled over her. "I am all yours, Alexa Walsh. No one else holds my heart."

Lexi sighed at his declaration. She helped him strip her of her remaining clothing and pulled off his boxers. He moved forward and rested himself right over her opening. If she hadn't been ready from him going down on her, she was more than ready now at the sight of him on top of her. His muscles were taut, and his skin bronzed from days in the sun. His breathing was irregular and he was physically holding himself back, waiting for her confirmation.

She stared longingly up into his emerald green eyes and nodded her head. She wanted him. She needed him—all of him. She needed to feel him inside of her and the completeness that resulted from knowing he was hers.

He breathed heavily and then buried himself inside of her. She thought she was going to release instantly as soon as he filled her. With such a build up, she felt like she could barely breathe. This wasn't the first time they had been together, but somehow this was different. The way he lay against her, the loving look in his eyes, and the easy, gentle thrusts inside of her. She desperately wanted to orgasm, and she knew that she probably could have multiple times, but she was holding off. She wanted them to be together. She wanted to feel him give her everything he had, feel him cum inside of her, feel her pussy tighten and release around him.

She could feel the strain from waiting taking over both of them. Sweat beaded down his face, fell to his collarbone, and then down his muscled chest. She watched its descent as he continued to thrust inside her. Her body was caving. She couldn't hold back any longer. Her nails dug into his back as she restrained herself.

His movements were speeding up, and she thought she might explode at any second. Her heart was beating a million miles a minute and she gasped several times as he pushed deeper. "Ramsey," she moaned louder. "Oh God, Ramsey," she said even louder. "I need you. Make me…make me cum. I can't hold back anymore."

"Don't hold back," he grunted the physical strain of release close to washing over his body.

"I want you with me. I need…need you with me," she cried out. "Now."

At her command, his whole body convulsed as he released. She cried out even louder than before as the orgasm took over her body. Her head fell back against the pillow as waves of pleasure rocked through her body. She could feel herself shaking as she clenched onto him harder and harder, riding out the intense feeling of gratification that pored through her body.

When her body finally stilled, she lay there for a minute with just the sound of Ramsey's hammering heart and the ocean as music to her ears. She couldn't do more than trail her fingers down his back and lightly up into his blonde hair. The weight of him was a comforting feeling; he didn't move from inside of her. Her lower half was still pulsing slightly from their interaction.

He lifted his head ever so gently to stare back into her bedroom eyes. "Lexi," he murmured.

"Yes."

"I love you." Lexi released a small gasp. His smile was radiant. "I just wanted you to know," he said, dropping his head back down to her chest.

Lexi took a big breath. "I love you too," she whispered against his hair.

He wrapped his arms all the way around her waist and hugged her close. "That's the best thing I've ever heard," he breathed into her.

He placed a faint kiss on her cheek before pulling back and striding into the bathroom. Lexi's heart was beating wildly, and not from the sex this time. Her mind was all over the place. With three small words he had forced her body and mind to kick into overdrive.

How had she gotten here...to this moment? For years she had left herself guarded and out of reach to everyone around her. Saying it out loud, that she loved Ramsey, broke down all of those barriers.

He wasn't replacing Jack. To think that he was just a replacement would somehow diminish what she was feeling at this moment. He was so much more than that to her. He had opened up a new part of her that she didn't even know existed.

She sighed contentedly knowing that she had made the right decision in telling him her true feelings. She didn't want to hide from him, because she knew from experience that only made things worse.

"You look like you're thinking real hard," he muttered leaning against the bathroom doorframe.

"Just thinking about you," she said rolling over to look at his gorgeous body. "And what you did to me."

"What did I do to you?" he asked striding back over to the bed.

She shivered all over as he came closer. "Made my whole body shake."

"Look what you're doing to me," he groaned hungrily as he pushed himself back against her.

"Again?" she asked her eyes bulging slightly.

He chuckled softly to himself. "I'd love to, but," he said cutting off her response, "I think we have places to be." His voice was wistful as if the last thing he wanted to do was meet up with his friends.

"Oh, right," she said running her hands against the contours of his body. She didn't want to have to cover this up.

"You sound as thrilled as I do," he commented forlornly.

She smiled languidly at him. "I think it'll be good for me to spend some time with your friends. You know…get to know the people you spend all your time with."

"Not all of time," he said, shrugging it off.

"Well, you've known them a long time."

"Now that is a true statement," he said leaning forward to kiss her cheek.

"So, where exactly are we going?" she asked hoping to use the weight of his affection as leverage.

"Don't think I'm going to ruin the surprise," he said leaning forward and planting a kiss on her lips. "Come on. Let's get you dressed again."

Lexi stuck her lip out. "Not something I like to hear from you."

Ramsey leaned back into her burying his face in her wild hair. "Only so I can tear them off of you later," he replied huskily.

Her body trembled all over at the thought of him stripping her clothes off piece by piece and reenacting their earlier escapades. "I…I'd like that."

Ramsey chuckled heartily before striding out to the balcony to pick up the rest of his discarded clothing. Lexi and Ramsey dressed as quickly as they could. Deciding they looked as put together as they could muster after what had just happened, they headed out the door.

Lexi laced her hand in Ramsey's as they strode down the sidewalk to their unknown destination. Expensive cars zoomed past them as they took their time to reach their locale. Lexi was glad that they had decided not to drive. After the events of the evening, she really needed some time with the cool breeze blowing in off of the ocean to calm her down. The smell of salt filled her mind and relaxed her body. She had always loved the beach, nearly to a fault. She was sure she had missed out on a lot of alternative vacations by always opting for a beach trip. However, she couldn't care about that now since the beach felt so much like coming home.

"Did you want to walk along the beach?" Ramsey asked. "You're kind of staring at it like you do me."

Lexi giggled. "Sorry. I just love it here," she murmured.

"No need to apologize. I love it too. It's even better here with you."

Lexi's smile lit up the night as she stared up at him. "How much farther?"

"Well, there's the pier," he said gesturing out to the beach ahead of them. "So not much longer."

"Are we going to the pier?" she asked her mouth drying out and her stomach dropping. Going to the pier would not be a good idea. She didn't care how much distance was between her and *that* pier, it still brought back memories.

"Did you want to?" Ramsey asked playfully.

"Uh…"

"I mean I wasn't planning on it, but if you'd rather we stop by…"

"No," she stated quickly. "The sidewalk is fine. Let's take a walk on the beach tomorrow night. I don't want to sidetrack your plans anymore than I already have."

Ramsey stopped in the middle of the sidewalk and pulled her into him. "Please feel free to sidetrack my plans anytime you want," he told her kissing her breathlessly.

Lexi leaned into him letting the rest of the world fall away from her. She didn't care that they were in the middle of the sidewalk in open view to whoever passed by. She just wanted his lips on her. When he pulled away, her eyes lightly fluttered open. "Maybe we should go back to the bedroom," she murmured playfully dragging him back the direction they came.

Of course, she didn't budge him one inch. He towered over her tiny frame. He scooped her up in his muscled arms and began carrying her towards their destination. "Ramsey," she cried kicking her legs out. "Put me down. Oh my God, anyone could see."

"I don't care."

She giggled. "Come on. Put me down," she crowed.

"Alright, alright," he said placing her gently back down on her feet. "But look, we'd move a lot faster without your tiny steps."

"Hey, don't be mean to my tiny steps," she pouted.

"Never," he said grabbing her hand once more. "But we're almost there." He pointed ahead to a beach side bar with a large sign overhead that read Shades.

"You're bringing me to a bar?" she asked narrowing her eyes.

"Not just any bar," he told her nearly dragging her forward with excitement.

"Alright, alright, slow down. Tiny steps, remember," she said nearly jogging to catch up with his long strides.

Just as they drew near the bar, Lexi heard someone call Ramsey's name from beachside. The voice was quiet and hesitant, and if Lexi hadn't been walking right past it, she was sure she would have missed it. Ramsey, however, seemed to not have heard it.

"Ramsey," Lexi said yanking on his hand. "Someone just called your name."

"Ramsey?" Lexi heard the voice again and turned to face the direction. This time Ramsey heard the voice, and dropped Lexi's hand reflexively. Lexi's eyes narrowed in on the person who emerged from the beach.

Standing in front of her was a girl who, at first glance, was so similar to Lexi in appearance they almost could have been related. Her brown hair was long and wavy, but clearly she put no time into the maintenance of the locks. Big brown eyes stared back at her, but they were slightly tainted by the dark circles under her eyes. Her pouty lips had a light smear of lip gloss across them; otherwise she was devoid of make-up. The major difference between the two was the contrast in complexion. Where Lexi had a perfectly bronzed tan, this woman had milky white skin with only slight olive undertones. She wore white linen pants and a brown bikini top, and she was absolutely gorgeous.

Lexi was eye level with the girl as she approached, and she couldn't keep her mouth from dropping. She had never met anyone so similar to her. As she drew closer, Lexi realized that her face was shaped a bit different—more round than heart-shaped. Her nose was turned up slightly at the end, where Lexi's was a little button. She had a slender figure, but she was clearly built different than Lexi. She didn't have the lean muscles cultivated from gymnastics, pilates, and dance. Rather, she had an athletic build of a swimmer or soccer player. Though her hair was about the same length, it didn't have the body and volume Lexi was so accustomed to dealing with.

Despite these differences, the resemblance was uncanny.

"Ramsey, wow, I couldn't believe that was you. What are you doing here?" she asked smiling up into his shell-shocked face.

Lexi hadn't noticed at first that Ramsey looked so surprised, because in fact she had been just as surprised at the sight of this woman. Now as she tore her eyes from the woman, she noticed how dumbfounded Ramsey appeared. His mouth was hanging slightly open. His eyes were completely focused on the woman in front of him and nothing else. His hands were clenched in fists at his side. She wasn't sure if he was more in shock or anger at the visage before him.

"I...um...I'm on vacation," he said tentatively.

"Oh! I'd almost forgotten that you love these beaches," she said, her smile lighting up even further. "It must be nice to get away from the club for a while and enjoy the sun."

Lexi's head snapped from Ramsey back to the woman in front of him. She knew about the clubs. She knew that he liked these beaches. Who was this woman?

"It is," he agreed gulping hard.

"Are Brad and Jason with you?" she asked, still not taking her eyes from him. The ease of the conversation on her end was evident.

How did she know his roommates? Not that anyone couldn't know his roommates. But she had never seen this girl. She had never met this girl, for sure. She had never heard mention of her. She certainly would have remembered someone who looked like her.

"Yeah, they're inside," he said jerking his head towards the bar.

"That's great. I was fortunate enough to get a stint of my residency down here. The hospital has been keeping me up all hours of the day, but I'm almost finished so it's been cutting back some. But soon, I can move back home," she said dreamily.

"Your parents must be thrilled about that," Ramsey said wistfully.

Woah! Lexi's body stilled. Did he just say her parents? Did he know her parents?

"They are," she agreed a cute smile creeping up onto her face. "Look about the wedding—I'm trying to get your dad to lay off."

Lexi's mouth dropped to the ground at that statement. What wedding? Was she talking about Jack's wedding, or had Lexi just lost her mind? And how was she involved in this wedding? Clearly they were acquainted with each other's parents, but Lexi couldn't bring herself to put the pieces together.

Ramsey had the good sense to cut off that line of conversation. "It's fine. I already told him off."

"Maybe we should talk about this," she said reaching her hand forward, then thinking better of it and let it drop to her side.

"No really, let's not," he said cutting her off.

The girl's mouth strained around the edges at the abrupt statement. "We should figure it out sometime. It's not like Bekah is going to let this all slide."

There was Lexi's confirmation. She couldn't believe this. This girl was somehow involved in Bekah and Jack's wedding, and Lexi had no idea how. Not that she really had ever wanted to know the details of what was being planned. She hadn't. But she would have wanted to know who this woman was, and how she fit into the whole scheme of things.

Seemingly realizing for the first time, that she was being ignored, Lexi stuck her hand out in front of her. "I'm Lexi, Ramsey's girlfriend. And you are?"

The girl turned her head to the side and glanced at Lexi. She could tell that the woman was having the same wave of emotions flow through her body. The resemblance between them was uncanny. "You're Ramsey's…girlfriend?" the woman asked, looking between Lexi and Ramsey in nearly a state of shock. "I didn't realize that he had a girlfriend."

Lexi tried to hide her embarrassment at having that statement repeated to her after the humiliating scene in Bridges. Whoever this woman was, Lexi was pretty sure she wasn't going to like her. "Uh…yeah. That would be me."

The woman slid her hand into Lexi's and seemed to examine her closely. "Well then, it's a pleasure to meet you, Lexi. I'm Parker."

13

PRESENT

Ramsey was the last person she had wanted to witness her and Jack alone together. She didn't dare glance away from Ramsey's stormy green eyes. She had known him long enough to understand what was going on in his head right now—to know his expression. Her heart went out to Ramsey as she searched his face. He had to be in Jack's wedding, and it was pretty obvious that if he hadn't despised him prior to this moment…he did now. He looked as if he could rip him to pieces—tear him limb from limb, and feel no remorse for his actions.

He was usually so calm and controlled. Only a select few times had she seen him go off on anyone. She was unfortunate enough to have been one of those people. He had made up for it of course, but she didn't wish the experience on anyone else. Not even Jack, someone who probably deserved a good telling-off.

Ramsey cleared his throat as if her and Jack jumping apart hadn't assured his introduction. "Bekah is looking for you." Ramsey could barely contain a growl as he pointedly made the statement. His free hand was clenched at his side. The muscles around his mouth were tight and strained. A deep furrow stretched between his eyebrows.

Jack nodded, slumping his shoulders as he slunk forward. He stopped before reaching him and said, "Hey man, you mind not telli…"

Ramsey's threatening glare cut him off. He could have pierced straight through him in that moment and Jack knew it. "I think my *sister* is still waiting for you," he spat at Jack, clearly disgusted.

Jack snapped his mouth shut. Whatever he had been about to inquire of Ramsey died on his tongue. He nodded his head resolutely and scurried from the security of the weeping willow. Lexi watched him go with resignation that she would soon be alone with Ramsey, and she would have to account for her inexplicable actions.

Lexi didn't have to be a genius to know what Jack had been about to ask. It was pretty clear that if she hadn't wanted Ramsey to know…Jack sure as hell didn't want Bekah to find out. Lexi had gone to such lengths to keep them apart for the past year, and here they were again making the same stupid mistakes. She and Ramsey weren't even dating. She wasn't sure what they were at the present moment, but no matter her present relationship with Ramsey, she didn't want him to see her alone with Jack.

She couldn't blame him for having been about to ask Ramsey not to tell Bekah. It was a futile endeavor, but she couldn't blame him for it.

She just wanted to hit herself for her own stupidity. She wouldn't blame anyone for being angry at her; she was angry with herself. What was she thinking? It went beyond the fact that she had been caught with Jack. It went beyond her conversation with her Mystery Man. If she didn't feel anything for Ramsey, if it was really over, then she wouldn't feel so bad about her actions. She wouldn't feel guilty, but she did. And in that moment, she knew she would rather call Chyna and get yelled at to avoid the reprimand she was certain was coming from Ramsey. She cared too much about what he thought of her.

She had been blinded by too many things—her need for escape, her addiction to Jack, her rebound with her Mystery Man. She needed to get her act together.

Ramsey closed off their exit and walked towards her. "Look, I know we're not together," he said. He ran his hands back through his honey blonde hair and scratched the back of his head as if in thought.

"I know that we have a lot of things to work out. I know that you're pretty pissed off at me. I just…I can't…I just don't understand. I can't begin to fathom your reasoning." His words came out rushed, and Lexi was struck with her first meeting with him when he hadn't been able to shut up. At any other time it would have made her want to smile, but not in this moment.

"I just…look there's no other way around it…excuse my language, but what the fuck were you doing?" he asked unable to keep his ever-present cool.

Lexi's mouth popped open at the statement. "Nothing," she piped up without hesitation.

"Nothing? You're going to try and come back with nothing?" he asked his eyes narrowing dangerously. If he had looked angry before it was nothing in comparison to the fire in him at her plea of innocence.

"Really, Ramsey, we weren't doing anything," she squeaked gulping down hard.

He took a deep breath. "You left the party. When I got back from helping my sister at my father's request...no, demand, you were gone. When I asked around, the only response I got was that you had left with Jack. That they had seen you take a walk together. That you were..." he took another calming breath but the bite remained in his voice, "with Jack...alone."

Lexi couldn't find a response. All of that was true. She could hardly deny the facts.

"I don't know why you came here," he said gesturing to the weeping willow. "I don't even know how he knows about this place."

It was evident that this locale had more significance than Ramsey was letting on. She didn't know nor, at this moment, did she want to know what was special about where she was standing. All she could think about was the anger that he was directing towards her.

"Regardless," he grumbled, leaning in closer to her, "I find you two together, against each other, holding each other. I just...I don't understand why you would—for Christ's sake, you even look guilty," he rushed out.

Lexi took a healing breath in hopes of calming her heart which was slamming around in her chest. "I know. I know," she muttered quickly. "That's probably because I feel guilty for being alone with him."

She couldn't deny that. She hadn't wanted to go for a walk with him in the first place. She knew the dangers. Yet, she had agreed in the end anyway. Whether her intentions were clear didn't matter, because she had gone ahead and followed him to this place. She had stayed despite his advances, despite the gnawing feeling that everything that was happening was a terrible mistake. Sure, they had resisted each other, but to what extent. He still had enough power and control to get her to leave with him, walk with him, follow him to the ends of the earth.

"Then why did you do it? Why do you get suckered in by him?" he begged the question storming past her and sitting on the now empty bench.

"I don't know," she cried throwing her arms up in the air. It was a question she had always asked herself. A question anyone that knew her at all asked her. Jack didn't deserve one second of her precious time.

She knew that.

Yet, she couldn't stay away from him when they were together. How could she explain that to Ramsey? How could he possibly understand?

"I don't know how to explain," she finally muttered quietly.

"Well, could you just try, because I'm at a loss."

"It's not as if you've been saintly," Lexi grumbled walking in a disgruntled circle.

"I'm not saying I have been. I'd apologize a thousand times over if you'd just let me, but that's neither here nor there." Lexi rolled her eyes. "Please, try to explain Jack to me."

"He's just…I don't know," she started chewing on her bottom lip again. "You don't want to hear me talk about him." She glanced back towards him briefly and saw that he was eyeing her very closely, but turned away quickly.

"No. Really, I do. I can't fathom why you would come out here with him," he stated the matter simply. "You know that only leads to things you'll regret." He didn't have to say that she knew better, but she heard it anyway.

Lexi turned and stared at him. "You're the one who dragged me out here. You're the one who insisted I come to this wedding. I haven't seen Jack more than a handful of times in a year and certainly not long enough to have a conversation with him…" she began.

"Because you refused to see him!" he cried interrupting her.

"Of course, I did!" she shot back throwing her arms in the air. "Do you think I don't know what kind of effect he has on me?"

"If you know, then why go near him?" he questioned her. He sounded genuinely curious, but she could hear more. His breathing was shallow, and he was getting worked up.

"I had no plans of going near him. The last thing I wanted was to go to this wedding. You knew that, and yet you asked me to go anyway," she said feeling like an idiot as soon as the words slipped out of her mouth.

"Are you trying to blame this on me?" he asked jumping down her throat at the first chance. "Because I'm pretty sure you refused to go to this wedding with me. Then Jack swoops in and invites you, and suddenly you change your story. There's really something fucked up about that Lexi."

Lexi's mouth fell open. "So, there it is," she grumbled. "Just laying it all out there for me."

"You can't seriously deny that it's messed up," he implored trying to reason with her. Lexi crossed her arms refusing to give a response. "Fine, refuse to deny it. That's fine. Just try and actually explain Jack to me. Even though I'm in the man's wedding, I don't see the appeal."

"Ramsey," she muttered sighing heavily. "You don't want to hear this." She turned away from him not wanting to meet his eyes.

"Please, help me understand," he said grabbing her by the waist and swinging her back around to face him.

Lexi puffed out the breath she was holding unsure of how to proceed with the conversation. She couldn't actually believe that he wanted to know what she felt for Jack…or didn't feel. She could hardly explain it to herself, let alone him. And anyway, all it would accomplish was to hurt him.

"He just…I don't know, Ramsey, you really want me to talk about this?" she asked glancing anxiously around the enclosure. She was desperately trying to get out of this conversation. She figured if she kept asking, then maybe he would change his mind.

"Please," he begged. Maybe not.

"Jack and I…" Lexi began hating the way the words fell from her mouth, "we've been through this kind of tug of war for…God, seven years now," she said, still amazed at the length of time. "We had this instant connection. Electric chemistry," she murmured trying not to sound too desperate. She wanted to spare his feelings, but really she had tried to warn him. "It was like the sun only shined when we were together."

"Like the world fell away and it was just the two of us," she murmured softly trying to keep the adoration out of her voice, but finding it increasingly difficult. She could remember the way Chyna claimed she looked when she talked about Jack—dreamy-eyed and seductive. She hoped she didn't look like that now… "We have such a long history that when I look into his eyes that's all I can see. I forget the stupidity of what we've done and who could get hurt. I just remember the man who loved me once," she muttered softly, her heart hurting at the admission. "It's like a moth to a flame."

"So, what are we?" Ramsey asked finally.

"I don't know."

"Can you explain us?"

"We're not together. We broke up," she reminded him. She needed to reassert the boundaries.

He ground his teeth. "Well, what were we, if that's Jack?"

"It's not like that."

"Like what?" he asked genuinely curious.

"It's not you or him." She hated herself for admitting the feeling that she had been having for a long time.

Ramsey's eyes stormed over once more at the statement. "No, Lexi, it really is me or him."

"That's not what I meant," she said backtracking, "I just mean that…you didn't replace him."

"What?" Ramsey snapped becoming angrier with every statement.

"Oh God," Lexi cried sitting down heavily on the bench and burying her head in her hands. "I don't mean it like that either. Do you remember the first time you told me you loved me?" she whispered. Her thoughts crashed back to that day—before she had met Parker—before it had all gotten more complicated.

Ramsey stood completely still. "Of course," he said matching her tone.

"I kind of realized it then," she murmured pulling back to look into his curious eyes. She had realized it then. She had realized it when she exited the bathroom at his parent's house. She had realized it when she was caught with Jack just now."

"Realized what?"

"That thinking of you as replacing Jack would be a disservice to you."

Ramsey stared at her stunned. "A disservice?" he asked wanting to be clear.

Lexi sighed and brushed a loose lock of hair behind her ear before continuing. "You occupied a new place in my heart—a place I wanted only you to touch."

Ramsey smiled, truly smiled for the first time since he had brushed aside the weeping willow branches. He sat down beside her on the park bench. "This can't happen again," he said, his tone determined.

Lexi turned away from his demanding eyes. She knew first hand it couldn't happen again. "I know what I need to do."

"What's that? What do you need to do?"

"I just need to get through this week…this wedding," she added leaning back against the bench and staring straight forward.

"What happens after this week?" he asked. She just shrugged. She couldn't commit to anything. There was too much to think about before she could begin to answer that question.

"You know how I feel about you, and all my concerns for you and your future," he said grasping her chin and turning it back towards him. "You know I want to be a part of that future."

"Yeah, well, you should have thought about that," she murmured hating herself for bringing up her own insecurities when she was most weak. "You should have thought about that the past couple months." She pulled her chin out from his grasp.

Ramsey sighed heavily, letting his hand drop to his lap. "I don't want to fight with you. You're right, I asked you to come down here. I messed up. And yeah, I kind of expected you and Jack to need…a moment," he said the last words with a grating edge like nails on a chalkboard. "But I just told you the man was having doubts. Can you cut me some slack here, Lexi? I'm really trying."

"So, I've heard," she grumbled.

"What does that mean?"

"I've heard from everyone about how much you're trying," she murmured. She hadn't meant to bring it up. She really hadn't, but she had heard about him *trying* a bit too much recently. She wanted to know what was going on.

"I don't know what anyone else has said, but yes, Lexi, I am trying. It's no secret that I want you back," he said running his hand up her bare arm, across her shoulder, and trailing through her thick brown hair.

As he began to massage her neck, she let the anger drain out of her. "Look, I'm sorry," she murmured softly, turning into his shoulder and wrapping her arms around his neck. He pulled her across the bench and onto his lap holding her tight. "I—we have a lot to talk about, but right now isn't the time or place. I shouldn't have…"

"It's okay," he said tucking a lock of her hair behind her ear. "We'll work it out."

Her and Ramsey had always acted together…as equals. Their relationship developed slowly over time, and she had been careful, keeping her heart guarded. Then when she had finally given it freely, he managed to hurt her anyway.

And still she couldn't deny her feelings for him. She spent close to a year of her life with him, in a relationship that she truly thought was going somewhere. She knew in time they would need to discuss what had happened, but she wasn't ready for that moment. She was still too angry…too bitter. But she wasn't sure if she was ready to get rid of it all. They just needed time.

"Can we go back up there?" Ramsey asked standing and planting her lightly back on her feet.

Lexi nodded as she brushed the wrinkles out of her dress. She swished all of her hair over one shoulder hoping to catch a breeze on the back of her neck. This wasn't the first time she had forgotten how unbearably hot Georgia summer afternoons are.

Ramsey swept aside the branches of the willow, and the oppressive heat hit Lexi full force as she exited back onto the trail that led to the party. Their anger subsided for the moment, the two walked side by side towards his parents.

The scene before them was as if nothing had happened. Jack was standing at Bekah's side smiling into her enamored face. Three women stood beside her, and Lexi was pretty sure she knew who they were. She remembered the last time she had been in proximity to Bekah's best friends, the Fearsome Four, as Ramsey had called them. She had nearly been sick listening to them talking in the 755 Club. She wasn't looking forward to seeing them again.

As they approached, a glass of lemonade was thrust intp each of their hands, and they were shuffled closer to the bride and groom. The closer they got, the louder Ramsey's father's voice rang in the afternoon air. It was clear he was making a toast.

"To honor my beautiful daughter…"

Lexi half-listened to the speech as her eyes moved back to Bekah's friends. They all had shining blonde hair in various stages of bleach. She wasn't certain if any of them were natural. Or perhaps they had been at one point, but they had now died their hair so often they couldn't remember.

"and my soon-to-be son-in-law…"

The tallest one was easily the prettiest of the three. She couldn't place names with any of them since she had never been officially introduced. All that rang through in her mind was a terrible southern drawl talking about fucking in the middle of a crowded party where anyone could hear her…and Bekah encouraging her.

"I know that through their love…"

The thought turned her stomach as if she were still standing in the club, hearing the words as she eavesdropped on their conversation. She assumed that the pretty one was the bitch with the drawl.

"and devotion to one another…"

Lexi tried not to snort at the last statement as her eyes shifted to the one standing in the middle. She was a tiny little thing with a button nose and calculating, round, baby blue eyes. Unlike the other girls, her dress was extremely conservative…even for a Country Club. Her demeanor oozed prude.

"they will have a marriage as fulfilling as any we've witnessed…"

The last girl seemed the most normal of the bunch…if that word was even appropriate in Bekah's presence. Her hair was cut short into a bob that curled up under chin with large sweeping bangs completely covering her forehead. She looked about the closest it came to being a human being—with a natural ease and smile.

"Saturday will be the first of so many more wonderful moments in their lives…"

Lexi let her eyes shift back to Bekah and Jack. Their hands were lightly entwined as they stared up at her father. Every couple seconds they would sneak glances at each other. A pain shot through Lexi's chest from watching them interact together. Bekah looked so incredibly happy standing next to him. Lexi was having a hard time reconciling the situation in her mind.

"To the happy couple…"

She knew Bekah and Jack cared for each other, but somehow it had never felt real. It had all been a trick. Bekah had used Lexi to get Jack. There was absolutely no way that a sane person could participate in that kind of deception and still have human feelings. For some reason, seeing them together actually happy, everything came into perspective.

"May they remember this time forever."

Jack was marrying Bekah. This was really happening.

"To Jack and Bekah."

The crowd echoed the final sentiment, raised their glasses in unison, and took a sip of their beverage of choice. Lexi took a tentative sip of her lemonade, sputtered when she realized that the punch was spiked, and then downed another large gulp.

The two moved in closer to the wedding party as the remainder of the crowd dispersed. She couldn't help but notice the twinkle in his father's eye from the toast and the look of adoration on his face as he stared at his only daughter.

"Ramsey, Lexi, so nice to see you could make it," Bekah said, a glint in her eyes as they landed on Lexi.

Ramsey's father clapped him on the back at Bekah's statement. "Got back just in time, son."

"I have to apologize," Lexi said speaking up, "I was just admiring your beautiful trove of weeping willows." Lexi made a pointed effort not to look at Jack the whole time.

His father beamed. "That's understandable. They're gorgeous, massive trees right there on the lake." His wife bobbed her head along with the statements. Turning his attention back to Bekah, he asked, "What kind of trouble are you ladies getting into tonight?"

Bekah ducked her chin to her chest as if she were an innocent little girl up to no trouble whatsoever. "Nothing, Daddy."

"Don't Daddy me. I'm footin' the bill. Where are ya'll headin'?" he bellowed.

Bekah glanced from her dad to Jack and back. "You want me to say in front of the groom," she asked giggling, clearly putting on a show. "Well alright, we're just going to go to a few clubs, Daddy. We'll be in by midnight."

"Midnight," he scoffed as if it was the most ridiculous statement he had heard.

Lexi wasn't even sure what they were referring to in the first place. And she didn't see why it mattered that she was going clubbing tonight with her friends. It didn't exactly seem like an affair her father would typically be interested in, or paying for.

"Could Lexi come with us since we're down one?" Bekah asked, her smile turning into a smirk at the edges. Lexi snapped to attention at the mention of her name. Where exactly was she going? She hadn't signed up for this.

"You're my only daughter, and you're only getting married once," he said that with finality. "You can take whoever you damn well want to. And anyway, I insist she go along with you. Anyone who can stand Ramsey this long is someone you should be better acquainted with," he muttered, a harsh laugh following the statement.

Lexi's mouth hung open slightly. She felt Ramsey stiffen at her side, but he didn't say anything. The looks she was receiving from Bekah and her friends weren't exactly comforting either. She was pretty certain that whatever they had in mind wasn't something she wanted to be involved in. "Go with you where exactly?" she asked.

Bekah turned to her as if she had forgotten that Lexi wasn't in the know. Except that Bekah had done everything on purpose. Bekah was always in control…always calculating. Lexi wasn't going to soon forget it. "Bachelorette party tonight, doll."

This couldn't be happening. "Wow, I really appreciate the offer…" she began her voice monotone. She obviously was not thrilled with the invite. "I just…"

"Well great," their father interrupted, "it's all settled then."

Apparently, after their father spoke everything else was final. Ramsey, it seemed, was the only person who ever argued with the man, and at this moment, he thought it pertinent not to speak up. Lexi would have a few words with him later about that. But right now she needed to find a way out of this mess; there was no way she was going to a bachelorette party with any of these people.

14

MARCH FIVE MONTHS EARLIER

Parker.

Who the hell was Parker?

Lexi had no idea who this woman was, but she made her really uncomfortable.

She wasn't sure of Ramsey's relationship with Parker. How could he know someone like her and never bring her up? It's not like they had been shy about their past. She had finally opened up about Jack. She had told him what had happened between them. He may not know how strong the feelings were or what happened right under Bekah's and his nose, but he knew enough about her past. He could put the pieces together pretty easily.

This bought up another big concern—the fact that he had openly admitted to her that he's never had a girlfriend...that he'd never been in love. Not that she was claiming he was a liar. She didn't even want to cross that bridge. But the look Parker had given him was beyond friendship. The shock in Ramsey's face was more than an old friend showing up at the beach. The girl could be nothing more than an old family friend. It was possible. But then why did her gut tell her otherwise?

She knew he had been somewhat of a Casanova before being with her. What if this girl was one of his conquests? What if she had been Lexi at one point in time—whisked off to a beach for a good time with friends and an endless supply of sex?

No. Lexi shuddered. He had told her he loved her. That much she was certain of. She remembered his statement all those months ago—he had never been in love. And though this girl may or may not be a notch in his belt, it wasn't more than that. She had to believe him...trust him.

She took a deep breath trying to slow down all of the thoughts swirling around in her head. She was having a hard time keeping it together. Even if Parker wasn't someone he had slept with, how many others were there? Would she ever meet them? Had she already met them? She wasn't getting anywhere with that train of thought and really it was hypocritical to even go down that route. She couldn't be angry...merely curious.

And she was incredibly curious about Parker. Especially curious as to why they looked so much alike. Sure, the more she was around her the less the resemblance was pronounced, but it was still there. How could Ramsey know someone who looked so similar to her and never mention it? In fact, no one had mentioned it before. Surely someone had to have noticed that they looked alike.

Lexi didn't know what to expect, and she didn't much like it.

Resigning herself to find out the hard way, the three of them wandered into the beachside club, where their planned outing was held. The place was in every way a tourist haven. The walls were covered in beach slogans, coconut bras, grass skirts, and offers of margaritas, daiquiris, and other tempting beverages. The staff wore bathing suits and sun-worn, thin clothing that could have come straight out of a surf shop. Music blasted from stereos as mobs danced on a make-shift dance floor. A side room was hosting karaoke where drunken college girls were singing their hearts out to Britney Spears.

"Woahhhhh, small world," Brad called as soon as the trio emerged into the karaoke room. He picked Parker up and swung her in a big circle. "Parker, baby, you've never looked so good."

Jason was there next, giving the girl a big hug. "It's good to see you, dollface. You're lookin' pretty tan. Been hittin' the beaches?"

Lexi frowned wondering if he was making fun of Parker. She was so pale in comparison to Lexi it was unimaginable that anyone could call her complexion tan. Lexi couldn't get that pale if she stayed out of the sun for an entire year.

But Parker just giggled and nodded her head. "Work has me busy, but I hit the beach when I can."

"Parker?" a girl squealed behind them. Just then Jessie rushed past Lexi and hurtled herself at Parker nearly tackling her. "I thought you were doing residency. How did Ramsey get you down here to surprise us all? I haven't heard from you in forever. I thought you'd fallen off the face of the planet!"

Parker squeezed the girl in her arms and released her. "I'm doing my residency here. Ramsey didn't do anything," she said glancing up into his green eyes hesitantly. Lexi didn't understand the look that passed between them, and she filed that one away as another question for later.

"Oh, I didn't realize you were doing your residency here," Jessie cried again her face breaking into an even bigger smile. "If I'd known, we would have come to visit you."

Parker shrugged. "Well, I did kind of fall of the face of the planet while finishing med school. Didn't really announce to everyone that I was here." Another looked passed between Parker and Ramsey. "But hey, I'm all finished at the end of the semester," she said her face brightening.

"Oh my God," Jessie shrieked. "Tell me you're coming home."

Parker's smile was brilliant. "I'm coming home."

Everyone around them suddenly went into motion. Congratulations were yelled. Everyone pulled her in for hugs. Suddenly a round of shots appeared before them in early celebration of Parker's return. Lexi suddenly felt like it was a long time ago when Ramsey had told her that he loved her. She felt very out of place. She had friends back home and from college, but nothing quite like this. She couldn't think of a single person, besides Chyna, who would be this excited for her return. All these people it seemed had known each other their whole lives. Who was she—an outsider—to intrude on their moment?

As she was about to turn away to give them all some time together, Ramsey was there at her side. He held out a shot glass full of clear liquid. Leaning in close so no one else could hear he murmured, "I believe a toast is in order."

She arched an eyebrow. "And what are we toasting?"

"A toast to us," he said softly.

Lexi's smile instantly returned as she reveled in his momentary display of affection. She took the shot and let the alcohol soothe the nerves causing her to overreact to the situation. She was sure there was a perfectly reasonable explanation for Parker's absence from all their conversations. She might actually not be all that important, or he just didn't think about her.

She had plenty of old friends that he didn't know about. She didn't want to stress about anything tonight. Not after what had happened earlier between them. She didn't want to constantly bring her baggage and insecurities into the relationship. Ramsey had given her no reason to doubt him in any way. The only problems she had were her own...and she could be the only one to deal with them.

Taking a deep breath, Lexi pushed aside all of her pride and reluctance. She couldn't be hindered by it any longer. If she was really ready to give her heart away, she needed this. A smile broke across her face as she spoke, "Parker seems nice. How do you know her? From back home, right?"

Ramsey nodded, taking a beer that Jason handed him. "Yeah, she's Bekah's year. Been a family friend since I was yea high," he told her, motioning to a toddler's height.

"Wow. You've known her a really long time. That's cool," she said, trying to keep the conversation sounding natural. "Did she graduate with Bekah?" she asked chewing on her bottom lip to keep from fiddling with her hair.

"High school?" he asked, but didn't let her answer the question he posed. "She was supposed to, but she graduated a year early."

Lexi raised her eyebrows. "Smarty," she chirped. "And she's a doctor now? She said something about residency."

"Doctor," he confirmed, "Finishing two years early."

Lexi could detect the admiration in his voice, but refrained from commenting on it. The feat was pretty incredible regardless. "Wow, that's impressive."

"She's always wanted to do a lot with her life," he told her, taking another swig of his beer.

"I know what that is like," Lexi said tucking a lock of hair behind her ear. With a million other questions swirling around in her head, she asked, "So, did you know she was here?" She was pretty certain after seeing his shocked face that he hadn't a clue, but she wanted to know anyway.

"No, no, no. I didn't have any idea where she was." Lexi's stomach loosened more "Or that she was coming home anytime soon."

"Well, that's good then. Reunions between friends," she said trying to be reassuring, but unsure if she was successful or even needed to be.

"It should be...interesting," he intoned, taking another big gulp.

Lexi wanted to ask interesting how, but she was suddenly swept up by Jason and Brad, and deposited on the karaoke stage next to Jessie and another of Ramsey's friends, Katie. "Hey, hey, hey," she called, pushing Jason back, "no karaoke for me. I'm not drunk enough for this."

"What? You can't sing, doll?" he asked pushing her backwards.

"I can sing just fine," Lexi said bucking against him to try to get off stage. "I just don't sing karaoke unless I'm drunk."

"Well, tonight's your night," he called out, picking her up and placing her in front of a microphone.

"Jason, I'm warning you. I'll get you back for this!"

He smiled up at her as if he were oblivious to her discomfort. Lexi cast her eyes up to the screen. Lexi and Katie groaned as the guy's selection appeared before them.

"How did we get into this?" she asked the two girls next to her as the first few notes to *It's Raining Men* blasted through the speakers.

Jessie shrugged never breaking from her cool demeanor towards Lexi. However, to Lexi's relief it was clear that Jessie was more comfortable on the stage than either Lexi or Katie. She snatched a microphone and began flirtatiously calling out the introduction. The crowd before them cheered uproariously as Jessie provocatively engaged the audience, swinging her long fire red hair around. Seeing all eyes trained to Jessie, shimmying and egging on the crowd, Lexi loosened up and leaned into the microphone she was sharing with Katie. The girl looked back at Lexi thankfully, and sang along to the tune to the best of her ability.

Lexi's heart was beating rapidly as she heard her voice spill through the speakers. Lexi never had stage fright when doing gymnastics before an audience ten times the size of the small karaoke club, but it was something about singing that made her clam up. She knew she didn't have a bad voice per se, but she definitely wasn't a singer.

As Jessie kept the crowd energized, Lexi found it more and more clear that her fear of singing in front of crowds didn't matter. Everyone else in the bar was incredibly drunk, and Jessie's voice carried much louder over the speakers than Lexi's. By the time the trio had hit the second verse, all three were belting out the words that appeared before them. Lexi wasn't adventurous enough to move away from her microphone like Jessie, who took over the stage with her presence, but she held her own through the remainder of the song.

At the end, they all threw their hands up in the air and took a large swooping bow. Though Lexi's nerves had briefly abated, the whooping crowd at the end of the song brought her back to reality. She quickly covered her face with her hands and shook her head back and forth in embarrassment. Katie seemed to agree with her, swiftly darted off stage, and back into Brad's waiting arms. Jessie took a deep bow before chasing after Lexi.

"Hey girlie, restroom," she said latching onto Lexi's elbow and edging her away from the group. Lexi was a bit surprised that Jessie would take her and not Katie, since Jessie had always been standoffish around her. It didn't help that their first interaction had resulted in Ramsey having to tell Lexi how he had slept with his prom date in front of everyone at a bonfire. Lexi still wasn't too thrilled with her for that one. She kind of thought it was rude to bring up someone's history like that and throw it in their face. She would hate if someone did that to her. She couldn't even begin to imagine the kind of damage that could do.

But Lexi went freely, hoping that this might be different. Her eyes met Ramsey's as she was dragged away from him. He smiled brightly at her and nodded his head as if to say that he had enjoyed her performance.

Ducking around a drunk couple, the girls pushed their way through the crowd and to the bathroom. Lexi was relieved to see that there actually wasn't a line. That was unheard of in New York bars. "You were great up there," Lexi told her standing next to the battered aluminum sink. She meant the statement. The girl had been pretty phenomenal. If it helped her cause of getting Jessie to ease up around her, the compliments would flow freely all night.

"Thanks," she chimed stepping out of the bathroom and reaching into her purse. "Singing is my calling."

"I can see that," Lexi told her, getting out of the way of another girl who was vying for the mirror in the cramped space. Jessie eyed her carefully before pulling out a tiny silver bottle. Lexi looked it over suspiciously unsure of the contents that lay within or why she even had it with her. "What's that?"

"Patron," Jessie said shrugging. Without further ado, she tipped her head back and poured a shot worth of tequila into her mouth.

"You flasked in Patron?" Lexi asked in surprise. The girl clearly had more money than she knew what to do with, yet she was bringing in a flask to a bar. This was something she hadn't experienced since college, when they used to sneak in bottles to the football games. It had been thrilling at the time. They were young and anxious to drink at every opportunity. But here in this environment, she didn't think it made sense.

Jessie shrugged again. "Want some?" she asked shoving the bottle into Lexi's hands.

Lexi fumbled with it for a second, certain she was going to drop it, and spill all of the precious liquid on the floor. Then she regained her composure, held the bottle more firmly in her hands, and tipped the opening up to her lips. The sip she took was much smaller than Jessie's but it burned the entire way down, and she coughed without a lime or chaser to ease the pain.

"Uh thanks," Lexi said passing the bottle back.

Jessie chuckled under her breath before taking another sip from the bottle. "So, you and Ramsey, huh?" she asked, leaning back against the sink and nudging the other girl out of the way. The girl looked pissed as she shoved past Lexi for the exit.

"Yep," Lexi said not sure how else to respond or if Jessie wanted some more explanation.

"Good thing you met Parker then," she said shrugging as she twirled the top to the flask between her fingers.

Lexi swallowed hard. "Why is that?" Lexi asked curiously, eyeing Jessie carefully.

Jessie stared at her blankly. "What do you mean, why is that?" she asked screwing the cap back on the bottle, moving in front of the mirror, and looking her face over for imperfections. She pulled out a tube of cherry red lip gloss and coated her mouth with the stuff.

"I just don't know why it would be a good thing per se," Lexi said being purposefully dense. Jessie had known Parker for a long time. She wasn't sure if that was as long as Ramsey had known her, but it was possible. Thus, if Jessie thought it was probably a good thing that she met Parker, then it was.

"Her and Ramsey go way back," she said puckering her lips.

"I garnered that much," Lexi responded stepping out of the way of another girl badgering her for room in the confided space. "But is there something I should know?" Lexi asked pressing her luck.

"Only whatever Ramsey told you I'm sure," Jessie said running her fingertips through her wild red hair in an attempt to tame it. "Anyway," she began, "I really need a smoke."

Lexi gulped wanting to know more about Parker, and Jessie clearly knew something. She knew that she should just ask Ramsey about it, and she would. She promised herself that she would ask him more about Parker once they were alone, but right now Jessie was providing her with an alternative. She figured she would be stupid not to take it. "I'll go with you," Lexi sputtered quickly before Jessie could reach the door.

"Do you smoke?" Jessie asked her incredulously.

"Uh...no...well, casually," Lexi lied through her teeth. She pretty much detested the habit, but she had begun to get used to it since being in New York.

"Really? I'd never have pinned ya for it," she muttered raising her eyebrows in surprise. She seemed not to be easily surprised.

Lexi gave her a weak smile and followed her out of the bathroom. Her eyes instantly moved back to where Ramsey was standing against the bar surrounded by his friends. Parker stood at his side, her head thrown back in laughter, and her hand unconsciously resting on his forearm. When she righted herself, Ramsey's own smile was locked onto her face as they shared another private joke. Parker seemed to laugh hysterically at Ramsey once again, and his hand slipped to her back to hold them both steady. Lexi gulped down a lump forming in her throat.

"Cute, aren't they?" Jessie whispered at her side.

"Uh...what?" Lexi asked forgetting that Jessie had been at her side.

"They're just cute," Jessie said shrugging as if her statement hadn't made a huge impact on Lexi. "I've always thought so."

"Oh." Lexi couldn't think of anything else to say. As she looked at Ramsey and Parker together, she had to admit that they did look cute together. She wasn't sure if it was because Parker looked kind of like her or if it was just the chemistry that came with knowing someone for so long. For some reason, she wondered if this is what people saw when looking at her and Jack. That thought made her stomach do a flip-flop.

"Come on," Jessie said tugging her towards the deck overlooking the ocean.

Lexi let herself be dragged away as she stayed lost in thought. The last thing she wanted to do was overreact. She had to remind herself that it was perfectly possible for Ramsey and Parker to have a platonic relationship, which is what brought them together. Before she had a chance to think on it further, Jessie slapped a cigarette in her hand. "Here ya go."

"Uh thanks," Lexi said reluctantly. She had never smoked a day in her life. Just when Jessie went up to light it for her, Lexi's phone buzzed in her purse at her hip.

"Hold on," she said handing back the cigarette. Jessie shrugged and lit her own. Lexi dug into the bag, retrieved the phone, and pressed it to her ear. "Hello."

"Lexi..." Chyna blubbered through the other end of the line. Instantly Lexi was on edge. Chyna never ever called her Lexi. From the first time they had met, she had always been Alexa to Chyna. Just hearing her name come out of Chyna's mouth sounded odd. Not to mention the fact that it seemed Chyna had been crying, rather hysterically actually.

"Chyna, are you okay?" she asked immediately stepping out away from Jessie to a more private spot.

"No, oh my God, no I'm not," she cried falling into another fit of tears.

"What happened? Chyna, calm down. It'll be okay. Just tell me what happened," she said reassuringly.

"I don't know. I just...I don't know where to begin."

"Just start wherever, C. Tell me from the beginning. Are you safe? Are you hurt? Did someone hurt you? Do I need to call someone to come get you?" Lexi asked nearing hysterics herself. She was terrified for her friend.

"No, no, I'm not hurt...not physically. It's just...Adam. Alexa, it's Adam," she whispered into the phone as if it were physically painful to utter the words.

"Adam?" Lexi asked anxiously. She didn't know what could be wrong with Adam. They had been perfectly fine when she had left New York a couple days ago. "Is he alright? Did something happen?" Lexi stomach was in knots. She was pretty terrified of what she was about to hear. Her friend had been so happy for the past couple months, ever since Adam had entered her life. He put her on cloud nine, and it was wonderful to watch. Chyna deserved happiness like that. If anything happened to him, or if anything happened to them, she wasn't sure how Chyna would recover...if she would ever recover. Chyna had never wanted to fall for someone. She feared losing the people she cared about more than anything else. "Chyna, what happened?" Lexi demanded.

"Oh, God, Alexa. I can't talk about it. It's awful. We got into a horrible argument, absolutely horrible argument. My chest hurts unlike anything I've ever imagined," Chyna whispered her voice pained. "He was so calm at first, and then the floodgates opened. We both just screamed at each other. I don't know what I'm doing!"

"Oh, Chyna," Lexi murmured softly. "I'm so sorry. Did you guys break up?" Lexi hated asking the question.

"I don't know. Yes. No," she moaned dreadfully. "Maybe. He was so mean to me. I don't know what we are anymore…"

"Maybe it was just a misunderstanding," Lexi reasoned. She couldn't let this happen. She was pretty sure Chyna loved Adam. This couldn't happen. She needed to fix it, make it all better, somehow. "Tell me what happened," she told her hoping with all she had that it wasn't a break up.

Chyna sniffled a few times into the phone. "Adam's brother, John, lives in the city, but he's a businessman who travels all over the world. He's not here much, so I've never met him." Lexi wasn't sure what this had to do with anything, but let her continue without interrupting. "Well, he was in town for the weekend, and Adam wanted to introduce me to him. I thought it was a big step." Here tears renewed, and she broke down on the phone. Lexi couldn't imagine what that must feel like…to think she was finally making some progress, and then it all get swept out from under her because of one argument. Chyna took a second to sniffle a few more times before continuing.

"The three of us went out and had a few drinks. I tried to be low key, and handle my liquor. I wanted to make an impression." Lexi tried not to smile too wide at that. Chyna always made an impression. "John turned out to be very similar to Adam. I mean they're brothers, what was I expecting? Well, you know Adam. He's just a really nice guy. And well, his brother was exceptionally charming that night. I mean…not that Adam isn't charming, but…"

"No, I get it," Lexi told her. Adam was exactly as she described him. Wonderful, but a nice guy, and nice guys didn't tend to hold Chyna's attention. Lexi was really worried as to where this was going.

"Anyway, John knew the right thing to say about everything. He was an accomplished businessman. He'd traveled the world. His family adored him. He's such a smooth talker, and by the end of the night, he had me eating out of his hands."

"Oh Chyna, you didn't…do anything with him, did you?" Lexi asked terrified of the answer. Chyna wouldn't, would she?

"What?" she snapped, offended through her tears. "No! I wouldn't do that to Adam! That's the point. Argh! That's the whole fucking point, chica!"

"Sorry, C, I had to ask," Lexi apologized quickly.

"No, I know," she grumbled. "Just angry, and with everything else tonight…I can't." Lexi heard the tears behind her words. She wished she could reach through the phone to give her a hug. She hated not being there for her best friend. "Lexi, you have to know it wasn't me. John's the kind of guy who gets whatever he wants, takes what he wants. You know those kind of guys!"

Lexi did. Those were the kind of guys Chyna had always gone for. They were the ones she let take her home. This was not looking good.

"Well, it soon became apparent that I was what John wanted. I should have seen it coming from a mile away. And when I did see it, it was too late. Adam didn't believe me. He refused to see it. He loves his brother so much that he was blind to him—blind to his arrogance and fucking stupidity.

"I think if he actually knew his brother, he would have never left me alone with him. But he did leave us alone. John was smooth, but it wasn't anything I hadn't seen before. Before Adam, I would have gone for him any day of the week." Lexi figured that went without saying. "But I'm different now! John had his hands all over me as soon as Adam left the room, but I turned him down. Alexa, I turned him down."

Chyna paused for a moment, and Lexi marveled in how much her friend had grown. She might be in tears over this, but she had done the right thing.

Tears stung her eyes again as she continued, "When I turned him down, he got furious. He didn't understand why I didn't want this to continue, as if me dating his brother didn't matter. I felt like Adam should know what happened, so told him, and he wouldn't believe me. He said I was being a drama queen, and I had probably misinterpreted what had gone on.

"But I didn't misinterpret anything! I swear I didn't. Tell me you believe me! God, someone has to fucking believe me," she cried hysterically.

"Chyna, I believe you. Of course, I believe you. If you wanted another guy, then you could have them every night of the week. Why would you make up something about his brother?"

"Right! Ugh! Why didn't he see that? We got in a terrible argument about it. He wouldn't believe anything I said," she cried hearing a fresh wave of tears coming on. "We stood there yelling at each other until he got so angry; he just stormed out on me. He left me standing there all alone. Who leaves me? Who does that?"

Lexi held her breath. This didn't sound too uplifting. "I'm so sorry. I think you'll need to give him some time, then it'll work out. He really cares for you. I know he does. He's going to want to work things out. I don't know his brother or anything, but the way you talk about him makes it seem that Adam idealizes him. He probably doesn't want to believe those things about John. He just took it out on you, which is wrong, but I think he'll realize he was wrong. Once he sees how much of an idiot he was, he'll come around."

"You think so?" Chyna asked, hope in her voice for the first time since Lexi had answered the phone.

"Yeah, I do," Lexi told her. She didn't want to give her false hope. She certainly wasn't sure that Adam would come around. She had never seen Chyna in a functional relationship. Her entire affair with Adam was new to everyone. But her friend had been happier with Adam than she had ever seen her, and she had to believe that counted for something. It wouldn't be fair if this one hiccup ruined everything for them. They could get through this.

"Alexa, I still don't know. I don't know how to handle any of this. I wish you were here. I need you," she groaned.

"I can come home if you need me to. You know I'll always be here for you," Lexi told her soothingly.

"You'd end your vacation early for me?" she asked her voice in awe. "I know you don't get to see him all that often."

"You're my best friend," Lexi told her as if that solved everything. "Let me talk to him and I'll see what I can do."

"Thanks...I'm so sorry. I hate taking you away," she said, the sniffles coming back.

"No need to be sorry. You had no idea this was going to happen. Hopefully I'll be with you soon girl," Lexi said saying good-bye and hanging up.

"Everything alright?" Jessie asked stamping out a cigarette and coming up behind Lexi.

Lexi shook her head. "My best friend is having some guy trouble. I need to go find Ramsey." Lexi pushed her way back through the crowd until she reached Ramsey's side again. The first thing that she noted was that Parker was absent from the group. She couldn't worry about that right now.

Ramsey could tell something was off as soon as she was next to him. "Is everything alright?" he asked concerned.

"Chyna and Adam got into a huge fight," she confessed. Lexi tucked her hair behind her ear and anxiously chewed on her bottom lip. "She's kind of hysterical."

"Did they break up?"

"She's not sure, but she's really flippin' out," Lexi told him sighing heavily.

Ramsey seemed to realize instantly where this was leading. "Do you want to get out of here?" he asked motioning towards the door. Lexi nodded without another thought. The two waved goodbye to their party and rushed for the exit.

"I'm sorry I'm making us leave early," Lexi said as she jogged to catch up with him in the crowd.

Ramsey held the door open for Lexi and she pushed her way past him. Even though the walk back to the beach house was only a couple minutes, Ramsey clearly didn't want to waste any time. He hailed a waiting cab and allowed her to enter first. When he sat down, he said, "You don't have to apologize, Lexi. Are you going to fly into New York tonight?"

"Yeah, I think I probably should."

"You're a really good friend."

"I know." She smiled and nuzzled into Ramsey's shoulder. For the minute ride, she sat there perfectly content in his arms. All her earlier worries were gone, and it felt right again. Just the two of them together. But it didn't last and soon they were back at the condo. Ramsey tossed a bill at the cabbie and exited behind her.

Throwing her clothes quickly in her bag, Lexi rushed to get everything together. "Don't worry about the rest. I can bring it back with me."

Lexi nodded her head looking around to make sure she had everything of importance, and then grabbed her rolling suitcase. Ramsey took it from her hand and veered her away from the entrance to the house. She narrowed her eyes, but let him lead her through a door they hadn't entered before. "What's this?" she asked. As she walked through, she realized that they were entering a garage. She hadn't even known that they had a garage for the place. They had taken a cab from the airport and hadn't needed to drive anywhere the entire trip.

She looked at the shiny silver Mercedes sitting in one of the slots. It looked very similar to Ramsey's car in Atlanta. This was just a slightly older model from the look of it. "Is this yours?" she asked surprised. Somehow she had been here nearly a week and never realized that he had a car waiting for them.

Ramsey popped the trunk and deposited her bag. "Yeah. I keep her here since I got the new one," he said snapping the door closed and coming around to the side of the machine.

"You keep her here? But why do the owners of the beach house let you keep it here?" she asked unable to put two and two together.

He stared at her over the roof of the Mercedes and sighed. "This is my house, Lexi," he mumbled. "I wanted to tell you. I did. I just wasn't sure how you'd react." He was stammering like the first time she had met him. Sometimes she couldn't help but feel that he was more adorable when he was like this. "You get all funny when I display...well...when I show that I have money. I didn't want you to think that I was cheating you out of a promised vacation by not really paying for us to come out here."

"Ramsey."

"I would have paid for us to go somewhere else, but I was more worried of taking you out of the country. I just wanted you to feel like I was taking care of you, and I thought this was the best way."

"Ramsey."

"So I didn't mean to keep it from you. I didn't want to..."

"Ramsey, would you shut up," Lexi cried finally getting a word in. He snapped his mouth closed, staring at her intently. "I don't care about the house. Why didn't you just tell me? It would have been fine." She opened the door and slid onto the cream leather seats. She actually found it a bit funny, and not all that surprising, that he owned a beach house since. It had been one of the first things she had ever thought about him with his beautifully tanned skin.

He sat down next to her. "I didn't know how you would react."

"Perhaps next time, you can let me react before making assumptions," she said with a shrug.

After a second, he said, "You're right." He backed out of the driveway and made his way out towards the highway.

"Thanks for taking me," she murmured to break the silence.

"Of course. I know how much Chyna means to you."

"Ramsey," she stammered out, "can I ask you a question?"

"Sure. What's up?" he asked merging into traffic.

"Were you and Parker ever...uh...together?" she asked turning to face him in the car. "I mean, I know you said that you never had a girlfriend, but you guys looked...comfortable together. And Jessie said..."

"Jessie?" he snapped. "What did Jessie say?"

Lexi paused gauging his reaction. "She didn't say anything. Just that you two were cute together."

"Are you sure that's all?" he asked clenching the steering wheel until his knuckles turned white.

"Should she have said more?" she asked staring at him intently.

"No," he said taking a deep breath and releasing his firm grip on the wheel. "She has a tendency to blab fallacies with the turn of the wind."

"She didn't say anything to me. But told me to ask you and trust whatever you told me," she said eager to get the truth out of him.

Ramsey shrugged. "All of that was a long time ago."

"All of what?" she asked curiously.

"Parker and I weren't together...not like we are at least."

Lexi gulped thinking of her relationship with Jack. Had he had something like that going on? She hadn't thought it possible for someone else to have a relationship anything like theirs, but anything was possible after all.

"You remember that time I told you about the dare at the bonfire after prom?" he asked.

Of course, she remembered it very clearly. It wasn't everyday that someone told you they slept with someone in front of a group of people after prom. She had filed that piece of information away in her mind.

"Well...Parker is that girl."

Lexi's mouth dropped open. "What?!?" she cried, jumping in her seat.

He sighed and glanced into her brown eyes. "I told you it was a long time ago."

"Yeah, but Ramsey, you slept with her...in front of all of those people?" she asked, unsure as to why she needed an answer, but realizing she did.

"A long time ago, Lexi. It's been forever since I've even seen her. We were only actually together...like that," he told her.

"But she looks like me," she sputtered.

He cringed at the admittance. "Yeah, I guess she kind of does."

"Did you only like me because I look like her?" she asked her eyes narrowed.

"No! Lexi, come on. I wouldn't do that. Sure, I saw the resemblance, but ya'll are completely different people. I would never think of comparing you, Lexi...with anyone. You can't be compared. I've known Parker for a long time, and we ended up in bed together a lot. Nothing more. Nothing less," he said grasping for her hand to reassure her.

She let him lace his fingers through her own. His thumb came up and rubbed light circles into her skin. She let her breathing slow, and her heart return to a normal speed. She knew that whatever had been with Parker wasn't happening now. But still she had to be sure. She couldn't keep wondering. "Promise?" she finally asked after a long pause.

He smiled down at her. "Yes, Lexi. I promise."

15

PRESENT

Lexi swore she wasn't going to go. She had told Ramsey she wasn't going to go. She had even worked up the nerve to *call* Bekah and tell her personally that she would have to decline the invitation to fill in at the bachelorette party. There was absolutely no way she would get dragged into another stupid night out. Bekah had an agenda. She always had a motive behind her actions. She didn't just invite Lexi to a bachelorette party for no good reason. Lexi was sure there was something more to the event. She just needed to know what her angle was

But then it had happened.

It all changed.

Lexi had wanted to reach through the phone and throttle Bekah. She had been terrified when she had walked out of that bathroom to find Bekah waiting for her. She had smiled too sweetly. She had been too nice. How had Lexi not realized that she had been eavesdropping on her conversation.

"I know you weren't talking to Chyna," Bekah said slyly into the phone.

Lexi paused, her stomach dropping out. Shit. What could she have heard? It was too incriminating for her to even consider. Maybe she just knew that she hadn't been talking to Chyna. Simple as that. But how would she know if she hadn't heard any of the conversation. "What are you talking about?"

"You don't have to play dumb with me. I heard your conversation."

Silence.

"*And I'd hate for my brother to have to hear about this. He's been so stressed out lately.*"

"*What do you want, Bekah?*" Lexi snapped.

"*I want you to come spend some quality time with me and the girls. Is that too much to ask?*" she said with a cold, stilted laugh.

"*Why?*" Lexi asked.

"*Can't a girl just have a good time?*"

"*No,*" Lexi stated flatly.

"*Look, do you want me to tell Ramsey or not?*"

The little bitch.

She was fucking blackmailing her.

She couldn't believe Bekah had even been able to overhear her conversation. She hadn't been that loud when talking to him in the Bridges mansion. But Bekah's snooty voice asking who she was going to be *seeing* when she got back to New York should have been enough to make her realize she had heard too much. Now this conversation proved she had heard even more than Lexi had realized. And Bekah couldn't tell Ramsey. Bekah didn't even know what had happened between her and her Mystery Man, but she had inferred the worst, and Lexi wasn't ready for Ramsey to find out.

And that's how she was basically blackmailed into going with Bekah and her three stooges for a bachelorette party she had wanted no part in. The only up side was that the festivities would take place only an hour away at her alma mater. She hadn't been there since she moved to New York.

A limo pulled up outside of Ramsey's apartment shortly after she got off the phone with Bekah. Her skin crawled as she slid onto the leather interior. The Fearsome Four sat around the limo, champagne flutes already filled to the brim. Lexi refused to give Bekah the satisfaction of seeing her squirm though. She could handle herself.

The girls had chatted the entire way there about random meaningless stuff that Lexi had no interest in. She didn't have time for reality TV, care about women fighting over wedding dresses, or have an interest in the new bitch at the Country Club. She stared out across the countryside tuning out the conversations as they chattered away. They hadn't found the need to include her in the conversation, and she was a thankful that she didn't have to make small talk. She didn't particularly want to try to make meaningless conversation with any of these people. She clearly wasn't going to stay friends with them after this weekend. The effort she would have to put in to make conversation was just too much to deal with.

The limo driver rolled into the overhang outside of the Hilton downtown. Their bags were swiftly deposited into their rooms, and then the girls convened in Bekah's suite.

"I went to the trouble of getting you all matching bachelorette outfits," Bekah squealed reaching into one of her bags and pulling out grey pleated miniskirts, black v-cut halter tops, and knee high socks. Lexi's mouth dropped open. Was this girl serious? "You all brought black heels, I'm sure."

The other girls hopped up and down like they were actually excited to parade around in those outfits. Lexi couldn't figure it out. Why would anyone want to look like that?

"Amber, this one is yours," Bekah said handing over an outfit to the tallest one in the bunch. At least something of worth was coming from these stupid costumes. Lexi would finally know all their names. She had never been formally introduced, and she had never put in the effort to figure out who was who.

"Kersey, here is yours," she said handing it over to the mousy blonde. The girl did seem to be excited about the prospect of dressing up, but Lexi could see that she didn't approve of the scandalous outfit. Her lip pouted out, and snatched the outfit out of Bekah's hand regretfully.

"Hey, Bekah," Kersey chimed in as she held the miniscule skirt to her body. "Are you sure this isn't missing some material?"

"Shut it, Kers," Bekah snapped. "I don't want any of your bible thumping conservatism tonight. I'm your best friend, put on the outfit."

Lexi's eyes opened wide at the confrontation. It seemed to have been had many times before. Kersey's face remained stoic as she pushed past Bekah into the bathroom to change. Amber was already stripping down naked in front of everyone.

"Maddie, here is yours," Bekah said tossing the outfit into the waiting girls arms.

"Thanks, B," Maddie said shrugging her shoulders. "You sure do like to reminisce about high school."

"I thought we looked hot as school girls," Bekah told her with a shrug.

"You were the only one," Amber drawled shimmying the halter over her head.

"These are pretty close to our school uniforms," Bekah said to Lexi who was looking at her dumbfounded. She couldn't believe the absurdity. Was she the only one who didn't miss high school? "We went to an all-girls Catholic private school."

"Oh," Lexi said putting the pieces together. No wonder Bekah was so catty. "Are you Catholic?"

Bekah and Amber both broke into giggles. "No," she said shaking her head. "Just the best school in the city."

"Right," Lexi murmured feeling the strong desire to punch her again.

"Here is yours. I hope it fits," Bekah said handing it to Lexi. "I think it's your size."

"When did you find time to get this in my size?" Lexi asked looking into the skirt to check the sizing. Surprisingly, it was exactly the right size.

"I didn't. It was Parker's," Bekah said simply cocking her head to the side as she looked at Lexi with the sweetest smile on her lips.

"What?" Lexi asked dropping the skirt on the hotel room floor. Her mouth hung wide as she stared into Bekah's face. She bent over to retrieve the garment feeling slightly nauseous at the prospect. She couldn't wear what Parker was supposed to wear, and she hated that they were the same size. They were too similar in appearance already. It just felt wrong…dirty.

Bekah's smile widened as Lexi straightened from the ground. "The outfit was for Parker. You guys are so similar in…well," she said looking her up and down, "…size that I just figured you would fit."

"What?" Lexi gasped a second time. She gulped hard, staring down Bekah. With everything she knew about Parker, with everything she knew about Parker's relationship with Ramsey, Lexi didn't think she could do it. And why did Parker have an outfit anyway. She knew that Parker had been close with Bekah, but she didn't think they were still close.

She hated these surprises. Is this why Bekah had invited her? Is this what the whole determination to get her here—to blackmail her into coming—had been about?

"Well, she's my fourth bridesmaid, but she's too busy working at the hospital. They wouldn't give her the time off to make the trip," Bekah told her simply. Her head was cocked to the side as her eyes bore into Lexi studying her every feature.

"Bridesmaid?" Lexi asked. She hated how surprised she sounded. Why hadn't she seen it from the beginning? Why hadn't she been able to put the pieces together?

"I thought someone would have told you." Her tone was charming, but Lexi knew too well now that it was dripping with venom. And her implications were clear—shouldn't Ramsey have told her?

Even if he should have, and he should have, how had she not figured it out first? When Ramsey had told her that Parker was going to be at the wedding, had he been warning her? If so, it was a pretty shitty warning. Couldn't he have saved her the surprise by letting her know ahead of time? She might not have wanted to know, but she *needed* to know!

"Is something wrong?" Bekah asked batting her eyelashes as if she were innocent.

Lexi sighed quietly to herself. The truth was that everything was wrong with this picture. The idea of her wearing Parker's clothes was very wrong. She couldn't even begin to explain how wrong it felt.

But she also knew that Bekah had done all of this on purpose. It was somehow part of her agenda. She had planned this from the minute she had invited Lexi to the bachelorette party in front of her father. He couldn't refuse her anything, and no one refused him. That had been step one, and she had resorted to step two after Lexi's own refusal.

Now, Bekah was baiting her. She had thrown out the line and was just bidding her time to jut a hook through Lexi's lip. And it was just playing into her hand that no one had brought up Parker's involvement in the wedding—her bridesmaid status.\

And why would they? It was an awkward enough situation without Ramsey bringing her up all the time. He had made his point by telling her that Parker was going to be there. She only wished he had told her everything.

But she couldn't let Bekah win. She might have gotten Jack in the end, but Lexi wouldn't give her the pleasure of hurting her ever again. "No…no, nothing's wrong. There's no problem at all," Lexi said holding the skirt to her waist and examining the skimpy clothing. She would rather burn it in a fire than wear it, but she smiled through her anger.

"Oh, good," Bekah said a smirk appearing on her lips.

"I'm really glad you didn't have to go to anymore trouble for me," Lexi muttered eyeing her carefully.

"Yes, it was convenient," Bekah told her.

"I mean, you already knew my measurements since you got me that beautiful red dress for Jack's birthday…and I got so much use out of it." Lexi smiled brightly. Or all the use she got out of *him*.

Sure, she knew it was catty to bring up the hallway sex she had with Jack on his birthday, but she had to say something to ward off Bekah's evil behavior. It didn't matter that Bekah, as far as she knew, still didn't know that she had slept with Jack that night. It was something Lexi could hang over her head without Bekah ever knowing quite what it was. Now she would always just wonder about it. Perhaps it was petty, but the look on Bekah's face as she tried to make out the meaning behind her words was priceless. Totally worth it.

Kersey walked out of the bathroom looking none-too-pleased about the scandalous outfit. "When do we start this game?" Kersey grumbled in her mousy tone.

"Game?" Lexi asked raising her eyebrows

"Come on, Lexi, you heard the rules on the way here," Maddie said shaking her finger at her.

Lexi didn't have it in her to mention that she'd been entirely excluded from all conversations in the limo. She hadn't wanted to converse with them, but she certainly did not remember mention of any game.

"B, show her the list," Maddie directed pointing out their purses.

"Yeah, Lex," Bekah snapped, her confusion about Lexi's previous statement wiped from her face. She was back to enjoying her continual torment. Bekah produced a sheet of white paper with a list of instructions on them. "This is a list of what we need to accomplish for the night. We came up with these to keep my bachelorette party exciting. Ten things to do before the end of the night."

Lexi snatched the paper from her hands and read the rules, grumbling at every mention of alcohol, blow jobs, boxers, and sex. "I can't take part in this."

"You're already here," Amber drawled. "Why not loosen up a bit?"

Lexi didn't even need to comment on that. She loosened up around Chyna, not around these fire-breathing dragons. She didn't want to get burnt.

"Let's just get out of here," Bekah said grabbing the list out of Lexi's hand and ignoring her disapproval.

After everyone finished changing and applying their makeup, they grabbed their purses and headed out of the hotel. They stepped out onto the city street and veered towards the rows of bars.

What surprised Lexi the most about the town was that it was perpetually changing. The city was built around a three by four block radius of shops, restaurants, and bars. Though the overall layout had remained relatively the same since the late 1700's when the town was built, the bars constantly changed names. Every generation that flowed through the university would grow up with a different set of bars and pubs to frequent.

Lexi could remember nearly all the names of the locations she had regularly visited and as they turned the corner, she could easily recall memories from each locale. Yet, only a select few still held the same name.

Lexi walked farther down the street, suddenly realizing where her feet were carrying her. Her heart was racing as they drew closer. She could do this. She could face down her past. These next few steps would be easy.

"What a cute coffee shop," Amber drawled staring into the glass-paned store front.

Lexi's breath caught as she stared through the front window. The same wooden tables were scattered throughout the room. The old comfy chairs and sunken couches had been replaced and booths were erected along the back wall. The fireplace was all closed up patiently awaiting the winter months. Any green reading lamps, which had once adorned tables, were nowhere in sight. Instead, several standing lamps were distributed around the room. Despite these differences, it still looked the same...it looked like home.

"Wow," Lexi breathed.

"Yeah, I think Jack used to work at a coffee shop somewhere downtown during college," Bekah said looking around to see if there were any other cafes nearby.

"How quaint," Kersey responded inching away from the place. Guess the place wasn't up to her high standards.

"Jason's Coffee Shop," Amber muttered. "We'll have to see you in the morning."

"Wait, Jason's?" Lexi asked nearly falling over herself to look up at the sign.

"Yeah, why?" Amber questioned looking at Lexi strangely.

"This isn't Jason's," she murmured.

"It says so right here," Bekah pointed out, her finger landing on a small square sign over the doorframe.

"But it's been Corner Cafe forever," she moaned. "How could it be Jason's?"

"That's business, honey," Amber told her patting her on the arm.

Lexi stopped and looked at the four girls before her. How could she even begin to explain? It didn't even really make sense to her. A small part of her wanted Corner Cafe to still be there. It *had* to still be there. It was the only piece that remained of the Jack she had once known. Without this, was he even still out there?

Now even Corner was gone. The place they met. The place they spent hours together. The place it all started.

Without this place, she would have been someone else. She would have never met Jack Howard. She would have never led the life that she had lived. So on one hand, she was terribly sad to see the place go. Jack had meant so much to her for so long, and it had all started right here…at that table.

But still she was happy. Perhaps this was another way to close a chapter. If even their beginning together no longer existed…well then, where would she ever find their future? As much as she had been pushing away from him—maybe this was good. The Jack that worked at this coffee shop no longer existed. It was only fitting that it was also closed…renamed…changed.

"Lexi?" Maddie asked waving her hands in front of her face.

"Uh, yeah?" she asked snapping out of it.

"I asked if you used to come here a lot," Maddie told her.

"Right. Yeah, sometimes," she said eyeing her study table through the glass.

"Is this where Jack worked?" Bekah asked pursing her lips. She was clearly judging the establishment. From her tone of voice, Lexi would have guessed she didn't approve either. This Jack was not the same person she was engaged to marry. This Jack was the man Lexi had fallen for.

"No, another friend of mine did," she stated wearily. "He moved away though, and I barely know who he is anymore…"

The girls seemed bored by the coffee shop already and began walking away from the building. Lexi gave it one more wistful look before following behind them and leaving her Jack behind.

As they turned the corner, Lexi stopped and stared up at her once favorite hot spot, Chamber, now renamed Rage Bar. It was everything she remembered Chamber to be from college. The new owners hadn't changed a single thing other than the name. Several bartenders worked the massive bar that stretched the length of the room. The medium-sized rectangular room was divided in two, by sliding glass doors keeping the dance space and the more secluded lounge area separate. A raised platform designed in an L-shape was constructed against one wall in the dance hall. Large security guards now wore bright orange Rage polos and were stationed in precarious locations around the room.

The patrons never aged at this establishment. It was the same group of eighteen to twenty-one year olds sneaking in with fake IDs. She knew twenty-four wasn't old by any stretch of the imagination, but she might as well have been seventy with how old she felt at this bar. She smoothed out the ridiculous outfit Bekah had given them and tried to remember what it felt like to be nineteen.

She had danced her heart out on that stage more nights than she could count. She could remember the adrenaline of hanging out with your closest friends and the thrill of dancing with total strangers that you thought you would never see again. The town was too small for that though, and she always ended up seeing the people she had drunkenly danced upon in her class or out for coffee later in the week.

New York was nothing like that. If she never wanted to see someone again, then she never had to see them again. Sure, some of the guys circulated the same bars more than others. She could pick out the regulars, but the clubs were so large that they were easy to avoid, if need be.

She remembered getting free drinks, because she knew the bartenders in college. She made friends with a lot of them. Some were in her classes and others she knew because she frequented the establishment a bit too regularly as an undergrad.

The free drinks were also given to her, because of the people she hung around with. Her friends from the gymnastics team could surprisingly drink most people under the table. Even though she had only set foot on the mat at one meet and it was only for exhibition, everyone still considered her part of the team. She had a stack full of team paraphernalia in her closet to prove it. She had been nineteen when she joined the team. Jack had gotten her that spot. She hadn't thought about that in a long time. Suddenly, nineteen felt too young.

When she had been nineteen she had fallen into his trap. She had fallen in love with him. She hadn't been disillusioned by his inability to commit to her or his philandering behavior. But she couldn't think about going back in time like that. She wouldn't be the person she was today if she hadn't experienced what she had gone through with Jack. And though, the things they had done together were wrong…terribly wrong, she knew that if she relived them that she wouldn't have been able to change a thing. And so she lived with her decisions and moved on.

She sighed realizing that whole train of thought had made her feel very far from nineteen.

"I'll be right back," Lexi mumbled, watching the rest of the girls stumble towards the bar. She walked out of the building and into the enclosure where the smokers were congregated. She didn't like the smell, but she needed some fresh air. Pulling her phone out, she typed a message to Ramsey. *"Not as bad as I thought."*

"Are you drunk?"

She giggled, realizing she was getting there. *"Not yet."*

"Be safe, please."

"Always."

She scrolled through her other messages, her eyes landing on the latest one from her Mystery Man. He'd sent her a few texts after their phone conversation, but she hadn't responded. What could she say to him? He was feeling more and more like a rebound the farther away she got from him. And she was angry at herself for getting caught by that bitch, and getting dragged to this bachelorette party. It was her fault not his, but he wouldn't understand. She hadn't told him about Ramsey or Jack before leaving. She was too afraid to bring them up.

Her phone dinged in her hand, and she pulled up the text expecting another from Ramsey. The words flashed on the screen, and she realized she had conjured up her Mystery Man out of thin air. *"Lexi, are you there?"*

God, she couldn't keep ignoring him like this. She just needed time. *"Yeah. I'm at a bachelorette party actually."*

"Sounds like a good time. Why did you have to leave so soon earlier? I wasn't finished with you."

Lexi chewed on her bottom lip. She couldn't have this conversation, not when she had promised herself she was going to figure things out first. *"Look, I'm a little tipsy, and I don't want to lead you on."*

"Are you leading me on?"

"I don't even know what I'm doing a week from now. Can you give me the week to figure it out?"

"Lexi…"

"One week. That's all I'm asking." She held her breath and waited for him to deny her her request.

"Alright. One week."

Lexi sighed as she tossed her phone back in her purse. At least that was settled. She felt kind of stupid. What if this backfired? What if nothing worked out with Ramsey, Jack married the wench, and she went home all alone. It was about what she deserved. Pushing her tipsy thoughts aside, she tried to remind herself that this was for her own damn good. She couldn't string along another man while she waited to figure things out with someone else.

With that she wandered back inside to find the drunken entourage at the bar. Lexi was feeling the booze in her system, but she wasn't gone just yet. The rest of the group had no reason to want to remain sober for the night. They had all delved in as quickly as possible, and were having more trouble functioning as the night progressed. Kersey was having trouble with coherent sentences. Though somehow, she had found a way to flirt with every guy who walked past her. She was already clinging to a fraternity type standing against the bar.

Maddie and Amber had fallen into fits of giggles over absolutely nothing. Or at least if they were actually laughing at something, Lexi had been unable to discern where the conversation started and the laughter began. Bekah was wobbling dangerously on her outrageously high heels. Lexi honestly couldn't even believe she was standing at all. She had resorted to telling every person she could speak to in every bar that she was getting married. She wasn't always discreet about it either. The past couple bars she had just barged in and flat out yelled her upcoming marriage to the nearest group of people. This always resulted in another round of shots from whoever chose to listen to her.

When a shot was pushed into Lexi's hand, she didn't think twice before downing it as fast as she could. And as soon as it hit the pit of her stomach, she regretted it.

Tequila. That one drink was too much. It pushed her over the edge from tipsy to full out drunk. She could feel it from head to toe. Her head was suddenly heavy and she felt as if she were swimming. Her throat was on fire. Shit. She scrambled for a lime to chase the drink down. That taste of the lime alleviated the burn down her throat and in turn the nausea that had come over her.

"So, where are we on our list?" Bekah asked sliding her shot glass back across the bar. She pulled on Maddie's arm to steal her away from another giggle fest with Amber. Maddie's expression glazed over as she realized that Bekah had been talking to her. She stumbled forward a step before grabbing Bekah's arm and staring deeply into her face.

"Whattttt?" Maddie asked clearly not having been paying attention.

"The list. Where the fuck are we?" Bekah snapped sharply. Apparently even drunk she was bitchy.

"The list. The list," Maddie squealed reaching into her purse, shifting around the contents exaggeratedly, and pulling out a now, very crumpled piece of paper. Maddie stared at it for a second as if she were examining it. She flipped it over, despite the fact that there were no words written on the back. "I can't read it," she finally announced shoving it into Bekah's hand.

Bekah grumbled something unintelligible, flipped the paper back over to the correct side, and turned it right side up. She smoothed the wrinkled paper out on the bar and looked at what was left to complete on their list. "Someone has to get boxers," she said reading each article carefully.

"Maddie would get them if Ramsey were here," Amber muttered through her eternal laughter.

Bekah openly glared at Amber and all the color drained from Lexi's face even through her drunken haze. What did that mean? Had Maddie slept with Ramsey? By the smirks on all the girl's faces, she was going to have to assume yes. Great.

"Oh, whoops, Lexi...did you not know that?" Kersey asked, seeing her growing pale.

"Amber, Kersey," Maddie snapped. "I'd rather not be reminded of the time Bekah tried to kill me. Can we move back to the game, please?"

She knew Ramsey had been somewhat of a player before they had gotten together, but she didn't think he would actually sleep with one of the spawns of Satan. She wondered what had actually happened. Her mind coming up with several possibilities made her change her mind. She didn't care what had happened between them.

"We're gonna go dance." Maddie stumbled forward careening around Amber and wrapping her arms around Bekah. "Come dance with us!" she squealed a giggle escaping her. "We can find a better boxer guy on the dance floor."

"You two go dance. I'll catch up," Bekah said shoving Maddie off of her.

"Okay, love ya," Maddie said, dashing after Amber, who had already begun to disappear into the mob of people.

When Lexi glanced back up, she realized she had been left alone with the Wicked Witch. The last time that had happened, she had ended up leaving Atlanta and Jack behind. This couldn't be good.

16

MAY THREE MONTHS EARLIER

"Yes, I'm sure I'm making the right decision," Lexi said into the cell phone as the taxi pulled over onto the curb. "You've tried to convince me not to leave New York since I got the summer associate position."

"Why would I want my best friend to leave me when she's finally out of school?" Chyna pouted.

"I don't expect you to want me to leave, but I would like you to be happy for me," Lexi said opening her purse and pulling out cash. "Keep the change," she said to the cabbie as she popped open the door and stepped out.

"I'm happy for you, darling. You're going to make a fortune, which will be a nice change. I'm just going to miss my bestie. Perhaps, I'm a little selfish," Chyna said adding a giggle in for good effect.

"You? Selfish? No," Lexi gasped sarcastically.

"Oh, shut it!"

Lexi walked around to the back of the car and pulled open the trunk. "Well, you'll have to come visit."

Chyna scoffed. "If I'm flying that far south, then I'm going to the Caribbean."

"Make a pit stop and take me with you," Lexi told her, lugging her bags out of the trunk and depositing them on the sidewalk. She stared down at the two bags before her. It didn't seem like enough for the next two months…maybe three if she worked her ass off. Her roommate, Rachelle, swore that she would mail her anything else she needed, but Lexi wasn't going to count on it. And anyway, Rachelle was going to be in California in less than three weeks. Not to mention, the only other person who had a key to her place, Chyna, was going to Milan for the summer for a photo shoot. So if Lexi forgot something now, she would have to do without it.

Lexi shuffled the bags to the foot of the stairs and decided that she would move them upstairs once she got the door open. No use hurting her back in the process. She figured the law firm she would be working for all summer would do enough damage.

"Maybe I will," Chyna said.

"That'll be the day," Lexi sneered. "If I ever get you into Atlanta again, it will have to be for something really special." Lexi didn't think she would ever get her here, honestly. After what a catastrophe it was the last time, Chyna had sworn off Atlanta, saying it was too much drama in one place.

"True. The smog is killer, and the traffic sounds all wrong," Chyna told her.

"Well, thanks for the support," Lexi said rolling her eyes.

"Alexa, I support you, doll. I know you'll succeed at whatever you put your mind to," Chyna reassured her. "I just think you're picking the wrong town to succeed in. What happened to that amazing internship you had last summer in New York," she reasoned. "Ouch!"

"What was that?" Lexi asked bewildered.

"Nothing," she snapped quickly. "Sorry."

"Is everything alright?"

"Yes, yes, everything is fine," she said trying to sound convincing.

"Alright," she began hesitantly, "well, that last internship didn't pay. I can't believe I found one that did. It's kind of amazing."

"Yes, well, at least you'll be close to home."

"True. But, hey, I'm finally here, and I have luggage to haul up these stairs so I'm going to let you go. I'll call you later, chica," Lexi said hanging up the phone and sliding it into her khaki shorts.

She pulled out the shiny key she had received in the mail only a few days earlier and placed it into the hole. Her heart fluttered as she realized the enormity of what she was doing. She was taking a summer associate position at a major firm in Atlanta doing exactly what she had always wanted to do.

And…she was moving in with her boyfriend. She, miss lack-of-commitment, was actually moving in with Ramsey. It was the biggest step she had ever made. She still couldn't believe that she was doing it. It was so unlike her. She knew Chyna thought it was too early for her to be moving in with Ramsey; after all they had only been together eight months. But since she was going to be in Atlanta for the summer internship, Lexi thought it just made sense. Plus, she really wanted to move in with him. She missed him, and hated that the majority of their relationship had been long distance.

She only had the position in Atlanta for a definite eight weeks. This meant that she would have to sublease an apartment in the city while paying rent in New York at the same time. Even though she was getting paid, her student loans were astronomical, and she couldn't afford to use all her money on rent when she would have to start paying them off soon. All things consider, it didn't make sense for her to get her own place.

When Ramsey offered for her to stay with him, she couldn't think of a good reason to say no to him. She wanted to be with him, and she didn't have to pay a dime. It was the best of both worlds.

After all, she had spent eight months without him. The occasional time they had together, when he could make it to New York or fly her down to Atlanta wasn't enough. She wanted to savor every moment she had with him. The last thing she wanted was to get stuck driving back and forth between their places. She knew that time was nothing compared to the distance they had endured since they had gotten together. Still, if they were going to be in the same city, she wanted them to be together. That drive time could be used for something much better.

So Lexi took the big leap.

She twisted the door knob and pushed open the door to her new place—Ramsey's place.

As soon as the door opened, a chorus of congratulations and surprise assaulted her. Her hand flew to her chest and her mouth dropped open. Her eyes fluttered around the room quickly in astonishment. A banner hung across the room that read "Congrats Grad!" in large purple letters. She couldn't believe it; she had just walked into a surprise graduation party for her.

Graduation had been the weekend before at Madison Square Garden. Ramsey had only been able to stay long enough for the ceremony before jetting back home. Graduation weekend was one of the busiest for him, and he had the misfortune of having to fire two of his key managers the week before. He had needed all hands on deck that weekend, and hadn't been able to celebrate with her in New York.

Now here he was, surrounded by friends, giving her the celebration he had missed. Ramsey stood at the front with a big cake that read "Congratulations Lexi" in swirling purple letters to match the purple velvet she had walked in for graduation. He was smiling brightly at her, taking in her shell-shocked face. There was something about his face in that moment that was supremely adorable. It was like he was five years old again, and he was the one having the party, not the one throwing it. The goofy grin on his face was priceless, and Lexi would remember his joy in this moment forever. He really did seem happiest making her happy.

Chyna stood next to him, beaming like a school girl. She couldn't believe that she had just been on the phone with her, talking about how

Chyna was never setting foot in the city again, and here she was. Adam stood at her side with his fingers interlaced with hers. They looked like the perfect couple they were.

Lexi was just thankful they had worked everything out. After she had showed up in New York, she had let Chyna blabber on and on about her argument with Adam. He had refused to speak with her for nearly a week. Luckily, he had finally agreed to meet Lexi, mostly because she had badgered him endlessly. They had talked over dinner, and when she was finished with him, he admitted that he still wanted to see Chyna. That he had been missing her over the past week. Since then, they had worked things out and were better than ever. Sometimes they were sickeningly cute.

Brad and Jason stood off to the side talking to their respective dates. Lexi recognized Brad's date as Katie who she hadn't seen since their karaoke performance in March. She was surprised to see that she was still hanging around Brad, since Lexi was pretty much uncomfortable around him at all times.

Jason had a flavor of the week at his side, and Lexi was sure she would never see her again. Jessie's fire red hair was piled high on her head and not-too-surprisingly, she wasn't paying attention to the festivities around her. Her eyes were glued on a rather handsome man standing to her left. Lexi wanted to laugh. She had never done anything to the girl, but she certainly hadn't taken a keen liking to Lexi.

Then Lexi saw someone she really hadn't been expecting. Parker stood off to the side, smiling brightly at Lexi as she entered the room. Again, Lexi was struck with how similar they looked, but maybe the more time they spent together the more she would be able to look past that. Though, she hoped that she wouldn't be spending much time with her.

Lexi noticed that Jack and Bekah were strategically absent. That was likely the best thing they could have done for her. Behind all of her friends were a group of other people who it appeared were here for the free booze.

"What's this?" she gasped shocked beyond belief. Her eyes traveled the large crowd again before resting on Ramsey. He seemed to be enjoying this immensely.

"It's a graduation party, silly," Chyna announced coming up next to her and kissing her on the cheek.

"You were just on the phone with me," Lexi cried staring at Chyna in disbelief.

"Yeah, someone had to find out where you were," she said knowingly.

"But you sent me off on the plane," Lexi said trying to make sense of Chyna's appearance.

"Private plane, chica. Takes you way longer to get here, what with security and boarding and all that," she explained rather diplomatically.

"And you," she said rounding on Ramsey. He looked at her, his smile waning for the first time. He seemed to realize that she might not actually want a party after flying in from New York. There could be...other things on her mind. "You did all of this for me?" she demanded.

"I missed your party and needed to make it up to you," he said simply setting the cake down on a platter and walking towards her. He looked spectacular that day. He wore a green polo that matched his eyes and a snug pair of jeans.

"You're a wonderful man, Ramsey Bridges," she whispered flying into his arms.

He chuckled as he caught her and pulled her against him. "Don't you forget it," he whispered back, kissing her shoulder as he held her close to him. She breathed in the familiar peppermint scent and nuzzled into his muscular chest.

"Alright, alright get a room," Chyna chimed in breaking up the happy couple. "Oh wait, you have one." Her eyes drifted to the stairway.

"There will be plenty of time for that later," Lexi said, pushing a lock of hair behind her ear. Really all she wanted to do was grab Ramsey's hand, pull him up those stairs, and have her way with him. But he had gone through all of this to surprise her, and she was going to revel in her party until she could weasel her way out of the festivities.

"I'm sure there will," Chyna muttered under her breath.

"Oh, my luggage," Lexi cried, realizing she had been too stunned when she had come in to go back and fetch it.

"No worries. I'll get it. Enjoy the party," Ramsey said. He kissed her forehead and exited his apartment. As if on cue, as soon as Ramsey left the apartment, everyone broke off into groups and began chatting up their neighbors. The party had officially begun with her entrance.

"So how does it feel?" Adam asked extracting himself from the group. He stood just behind Chyna and draped his arm over her shoulders.

Lexi eased into her new environment. As everyone made the apartment feel more like a party atmosphere, she centered her attention on the friends in front of her. "Pretty damn good. Now I have to pass the bar, and I'll be a real lawyer," she said a big smile on her face.

"That's so great!" Chyna cried.

"And Ramsey," Adam added his brown eyes staring into her. Her smile faltered because she wasn't certain of why he would have asked her with such an intense look. Like maybe, moving in with Ramsey wasn't a good thing?

Lexi quickly broke his penetrating gaze and looked over to where her boyfriend was pulling her luggage through the door. There was really only one answer to that question. Ramsey was definitely a good thing. She wasn't even sure why she got a bad impression from Adam's statement now that her sights were set on Ramsey.

"Yeah, exactly," she agreed hesitantly shifting her eyes back to Adam. He always seemed able to look straight through her. She gulped a little uncomfortably as their eyes met. His smile was light and friendly, but there was just something in his hazel eyes that she was never certain of.

"Well, I'm...we're proud of you, chica," Chyna said grabbing her for a big hug.

"Thanks. I can't believe you guys put this all together for me," she said in awe.

Chyna shook her head and threw her hands up. "Don't give us any credit. This was all Ramsey."

Lexi turned back to stare at her handsome boyfriend dragging her suitcases across the room so he could put them up in the guestroom...her new room. She doubted she would spend much time there, but it was good to have, nonetheless. She just couldn't believe him. She knew he threw parties for a living, but this felt different. He had done this for her...just her. And he had completely surprised her. She had had no clue.

"I'll give credit where credit is due," Lexi acknowledged tracking Ramsey's movements until he disappeared upstairs.

"Congratulations!" Parker cried coming up to Lexi from amongst the crowd. "I'm sure you're so proud."

"Whoa!" Chyna yelped. "You two are surreal similar."

"Uh..." Parker murmured awkwardly.

"Chyna!" Lexi gasped staring at her wide-eyed. "Don't be rude."

"You *must* be Parker," Chyna said extending her hand.

"Um...yeah. That's me," Parker said ducking her chin to her chest obviously uncomfortable, and placing her hand lightly in Chyna's grasp.

"Sorry about Chyna," Lexi quickly apologized. The last thing she wanted to do was make Parker feel anything but welcome. Even though she had her suspicions and she knew some of their history, Parker had never actually done anything wrong. She had been perfectly nice to Lexi at the beach. And if Ramsey said there was nothing going on, then there was nothing going.

Parker looked up at her through long black lashes. "No, it's fine. We do kind of look similar."

"Yeah. Yeah, we do," Lexi agreed hesitantly. "And hey, thanks for coming to my surprise party. I see you made it safely back into town," Lexi said, deftly changing the subject.

"I did," she said beaming. "I got back two weeks ago. I'm working the ER at Grady until some other plans I'm working on fall into place."

"Well, Grady's a great hospital. I'm sure you're doing great," Lexi told her though she was curious about her rather vague comment about other plans. Hopefully, whatever her plans, they took her out of the city. That would be ideal.

"Oh, let's not talk about me," she said shaking out her long hair as she started to relax with the group. "Ramsey tells me that you got an associate position at a firm around here."

"He did, did he?" she asked apprehensively. So they had been talking.

"Yeah. You must be thrilled what with such a great opportunity just unfolding at your door like that," Parker said smiling sweetly.

"I know," Lexi couldn't help but gush. "It's almost too good to be true."

"Almost..." she murmured. Lexi couldn't figure out the peculiar look that crossed Parker's face at the comment. "I know that these positions are nearly impossible to get lately."

"They really are. I couldn't believe it when I was accepted," Lexi gushed.

"Hello ladies," Ramsey said coming up next to them and interrupting the conversation. Both girls could see that he looked uncomfortable finding them talking to each other, but he was trying desperately to hide it.

"Ramsey," Parker said bobbing her head in welcome. "You've done a wonderful job here. I'm sure Lexi is very pleased with the result."

"Yeah, I am," Lexi agreed letting her eyes drift to the beautiful party thrown in her honor.

"Good, I'm glad and thanks," he said with a boastful grin.

"Ramsey, I was just telling Lexi how happy I was for her to get the job at the law firm," Parker said, "and how proud you must be of her."

Lexi couldn't decipher the look that passed between them. She knew Ramsey. She had spent the better part of the year with him, but she didn't know what he was thinking. Parker had known him their entire lives, and it was obvious that something secret was being spoken between them.

"I am very proud," he agreed.

Lexi did notice that his uneasiness only intensified the longer they stood together. Yet, there was nothing about this conversation that should have made him uneasy. He *was* very, very proud of her for securing such a good job for the summer and so wonderfully close to him. The only thing that could be a problem was the fact that it was coming from Parker. Their long lost fling clearly had something to do with the situation. Even though in the pit of her stomach she knew that she should try to figure out the source of the uneasiness, she just let it slide.

"Obviously he's proud. He threw me this whole party," Lexi said as if it were commonplace.

"Obviously," Parker repeated, her words sounding hollow.

"How about we get you to cut the cake," Ramsey diverted quickly. Parker smiled sweetly at the two of them, and then excused herself. Lexi waved her off, happy that she was gone and would no longer muddle her party, but also curious as to where their strange friendship might take them. After all, she had seemed truly happy for her, and it had taken a lot of guts to come out to her party.

Or maybe Lexi was looking at it all wrong. She conceded the point that she might just be imagining the whole thing. Ramsey had been up front about them sleeping together. There was no need for Parker to feel any discomfort around Lexi, since she had never been in her position and was a thing of the past.

More comforted by this new train of thought, Lexi followed Ramsey over to the cake. She felt almost like it was her birthday, and the only thing she was missing was the candles. She took a small piece for herself, and then began to mingle with the rest of the group. Somehow Lexi got dragged into a conversation with Brad and Jason about the varying aesthetics of the female rear end. She should have known better than to ask what they were talking about. The conversation was beginning to go a direction she hadn't dreamed of them discussing in front of her. Once they started talking about the extra shape and structure of her own butt, she had had enough. She needed to get out of there.

She smiled anxiously at Ramsey's two roommates as she tried to insert an excuse to leave the conversation. She finally squeezed in the remark, and quickly scurried away from them and out the back door. Closing the door behind her, she took a deep breath of fresh air and checked her watch. She was stunned. How had the time gone by so fast? The party had been going on for hours, and she hadn't even realized it, because up until the conversation with Brad and Jason, she had been having an incredible time.

"Well, this doesn't look like much of a party," someone said following Lexi out onto the balcony and closing the door behind him.

Lexi turned quickly and found herself face to face with a guy she was all too familiar with. Both times she had ventured into Bridges Enterprise she had run into him, and after her experiences with Jack and Ramsey, she stopped believing these occurrences were purely coincidence. People just gravitated to her at times and she was never quite sure why it happened, but here he was: Brandon Calloway.

"I think it's a fine party," she responded letting herself relax back into the railing. The afternoon heat hadn't quite subsided as night took over, but still it was better than being surrounded by people.

"It would be fine if the guest of honor was inside, but since you're out here I have to disagree, respectfully of course," he said with a charming smile. "So, I came to find the party."

She remembered his easy flirtations the last time she had been around him. He teased every girl in his vicinity and had likely been with as many.

His easy words were nothing to her, but she smiled nonetheless. She could enjoy the compliment. "Thank you. Though I came out here for peace and quiet, which I don't think is what you have to offer."

"I can be quiet," he said pushing his lips together with his fingers and leaning his body against the railing beside her. Instead of turning his head out to the lingering sunset, he kept his gaze strictly on her face.

"You're missing it," she said gesturing to the skyline. She feared his answer would be predictable, and she couldn't keep from smiling bigger the longer his eyes bore into her.

He shook his head as if to show that he would still remain silent as she had asked. His hand came up and tapped her lightly on the nose. She turned her face back to him in surprise and she watched his eyes roam her face. She knew what he was saying without a word spoken from him. She was the view…not the sunset.

Suddenly, she couldn't hold back any longer, and she giggled uncontrollably. His eyebrows knitted together as he attempted to understand the joke.

"You think that's going to work on me? Does that work on other women?" she asked incapable of keeping her giggles to herself.

Brandon gasped and clenched his chest as if wounded. "Of course it works," he said after a minute his cocky smile returning.

"Well not on me," Lexi said rolling her eyes.

"Perhaps," he conceded, "But I almost had you."

"Not a chance," she countered. "Anyway, aren't you here with Jessie?"

Brandon rolled his gorgeous blue eyes to the ceiling at that. "That girl is harder to shake off than anyone I've met. Stage five clinger," he muttered reverting to language from *Wedding Crashers*. "She invited me here, yes, but I came more out of spite than anything."

"Ah yes, your dislike of my boyfriend," she said remembering their earlier conversation at Bridges Enterprise.

"And now people actually know you have this claimed boyfriend," he said reminding her of the painfully humiliating day when she had stormed through Bridges as Ramsey's girlfriend who no one knew or acknowledged. "And anyway, he dislikes me not the other way around," he said with a nonchalant shrug as if he had the world at his feet.

"Perhaps you deserve it," she said quickly, uncertain of the history between them.

Brandon laughed boisterously at her reply. "He's got you wrapped around his little finger doesn't he? Ramsey Bridges can do no wrong," he said mockingly. "The Golden Boy. I don't know how he does it so easily…and with brilliant women no less."

"What are you talking about?" Lexi snapped, quickly becoming serious.

"Oh, nothing," he said patting her head like a child. "Don't fret your pretty little head over me. I deserve everything I get, right?"

"Brandon, what are you going on about?" she demanded more firmly this time.

"I'm afraid, love, you'll find out with time. No need for me to spoil your fun."

He clearly knew he had done just that by the look on her face. He laughed again at her anger. "Has anyone ever told you that you're sexy when angry?" he asked leaning forward into her charmingly.

Immediately, all emotion lapsed from her face. She had been told more times than she could count. A chill went down her spine at the similarities between Brandon and Jack. Yet she didn't feel for Brandon what she had ever felt around Jack. Brandon was a charmer out for one thing, and he seemed pretty successful.

The difference was he wasn't going to succeed with her.

"Have you been with every woman at this party?" she asked abruptly changing the subject.

"You're still up for grabs," he said smirking.

"Besides me!" she cried.

"Enough. The ones that interest me," he allowed.

"And what interests you? Boobs? Butt? Do you even need that?" she asked insulting his good taste.

"That hurts. I'm hitting on you, and you have both," he said merrily.

"Well, stop hitting on me. You're getting nowhere. Go hit on someone easier, because I'm a lost cause," she told him up front.

"But you interest me," he confessed.

"Well, I'm spoken for."

"How medieval!" he cried. "Soon you'll be betrothed and all that."

Lexi reflexively gagged at the idea. Not that she was necessarily against it, but all engagements meant to her were headaches, heartbreak, and disappointment. She didn't even want to think about that.

"Ahh…even more interesting. A woman gagging at the thought of marriage," he said intrigued. "That's a new one for me."

Lexi shrugged not wanting to go down that road. "Can you do me a favor?"

"Anything, doll," he agreed immediately his face brightening.

"Well, one, don't call me doll," she told him.

"Fine, you're honey to me now," he cooed.

She rolled her eyes, but knew a lost cause when she saw one. "And two, pookie, can you not chase me?" she pleaded.

He kept his face neutral as if he had been prepared for rejection. "But hooooooooney…"

"Now, pookie, I just got into town, I'm moving in with my boyfriend, and my best friend is going to Milan for the summer. I need a…a friend."

"A friend?" he asked warily as if he had heard of the dreaded friend zone and was terrified of even the word.

"Yes, a friend. Someone I can hang out with, and confide in, and do stuff with without thinking they're going to jump me at the first chance. And I think you're it."

"I don't do the friend thing," he told her.

"Well, there's a first for everything," she told him a big smile crossing her face.

"You're not going to let this go, are you?" he asked grudgingly.

"Nope…pookie…"

"Fine," he grumbled. "Honey."

The back door swung open unexpectedly. "There you are," Ramsey called as he opened the door. "I've been looking all over for you." He eyed Brandon warily. It was clear by his clenched fists and stiff body that he didn't trust or like him. He looked prepared to pounce at a moment's notice.

"Sorry, I needed some air," she said walking up to him and touching his arm reassuringly. No need for him to freak out about them being alone together. She wasn't that girl anymore, and anyways Brandon Calloway was no Jack Howard.

"Well, everyone's heading out, and I thought you would want to say goodbye," he said finally meeting her sweet brown eyes.

"I would. Thanks for coming to get me," she said walking past him and through the door. Brandon followed behind her smirking at Ramsey as he walked past. Lexi said good-bye to the crowd and watched as most of them drunkenly stumbled out of the apartment. Brad and Jason had disappeared with their dates upstairs, and Lexi hoped that she didn't hear from them the rest of the night.

Chyna walked up to her and gave her a hug. "Congrats, girl! We're going to head back to our hotel now," Chyna said with a wink.

Lexi shook her head, but couldn't help but laugh. She had the same thing in mind as soon as everyone else evacuated the premises. "Have fun. You'll be here tomorrow?" she asked hopefully.

"Nah, we're going to take the early flight back to New York. He has work, and I have to start packing for Milan," she told her excitement evident in her voice.

"Oh, come on, Chyna, you know you're not going to do any packing."

Chyna just shrugged. "You know me too well."

"I'm going to miss you," Lexi said wrapping her up in another hug. "Let me know you're safe."

"Will do, chica," Chyna said kissing her cheek and stepping back. Adam gave Lexi a quick hug. "Take care."

"I will. Bye," she said watching the last guests disappear.

She sighed as quiet finally settled over the apartment. Turning around she looked for Ramsey, but realized that he must have disappeared upstairs while she had been talking with Chyna. She hadn't even realized it.

"Hey you," she said walking into his bedroom. "What are you doing up here?"

"Giving you some time to say goodbye," he said turning around to face her.

Lexi saw the same tension in his shoulders as when he had walked outside and found her talking with Brandon. She knew that he must be dwelling on it, and she didn't want him to feel like that. There was absolutely nothing between her and Brandon.

"Ramsey, you know I'm yours, right?" she asked quietly, after a minute of silence.

"Of course," he said reaching out for her and pulling her into his chest.

"I just...I just don't want you to feel like you have anything to worry about," she continued on. "You know my past, but that's all it is...the past." The last words were just a breath as she got them out.

"I know, Lexi. I know," he said stroking her long brown hair.

"I'm serious, Ramsey," she said a bit more forceful as she pushed back to stare up into his green eyes.

"I know you are, sweetheart," he said leaning down and brushing his lips against her. "And my uneasiness doesn't originate from you."

"So, are you going to tell me what happened between you two?" she asked studying him carefully.

"Look that stuff doesn't matter. He's just...not a good person," he said carefully.

"I've heard the same thing about you before," she reminded him.

"This is different."

"How?" she asked unable to see a clear distinction.

"I'm not actually a bad guy and he is," he said as if it were obvious.

"I can't see that."

"That's because you don't really know him yet. And you shouldn't get to know him," he warned. "Lexi, please, tell me you won't keep talking to him."

"No, Ramsey. I'm not going to do that," she said firmly. "You have nothing to worry about from Brandon. Whatever happened is in the past, and I don't want you to think that there is any reason to hide me from the world."

"That's not what I'm trying to do," he said quickly. "You don't know what he's capable of."

"Well, tell me," she said exasperated.

"Look, it doesn't matter," he said shaking it off. "You are what matters. I know Brandon, and the way he operates. He'll do anything to get close to you. Please, promise to stay away from him?"

"I already told you that I'm not going to do that. I'll be extra careful around him, but it's not the end of the world. Promise me you won't get angry with me," she begged.

He sighed heavily and dropped his head to her tiny shoulder. "You make things so difficult," he complained.

"You're the one imposing rules for who I can hang out with," she said sharply...a little sharper than she had even anticipated.

"You're right," he said straightening. "Of course, you're right. I have my reservations, but they are my own. You're free to see whoever you want. But if he lays one hand on you or says one thing out of line," he warned, "you let me know."

Lexi nodded solemnly and hoped that she would never have to take him up on the offer.

17

PRESENT

Alone. All alone with Bekah.

Lexi really wished that she could disappear right then. She hadn't meant to be left alone with her, but she hadn't realized that Kersey had left during the discussion about the list.

"Lexi?" Bekah asked, obviously not getting the mental waves of rejection that were pouring off of Lexi.

Not seeing any way to avoid speaking with her, Lexi turned her body back to Bekah. "Yeah?"

"Thanks for coming out tonight," she said a smile appearing on her face.

Lexi's danger senses immediately started tingling. She had never been around Bekah when she was drunk, but that didn't automatically make her a human being. "Okay," Lexi said, trying to fight the buzz that said to just let it go.

"I mean, since Parker is so busy, it was great to have someone be able to fill in for her on such short notice," Bekah said. "She has so much ahead of her. She's really going places."

Lexi's hand clenched the edge of the bar. She didn't need to hear any of this about Parker. She knew she was *going places*. She knew she was smart and a brilliant doctor, despite being one of the youngest in the profession. She didn't need Bekah to tell her any of this. And the alcohol was making her feisty.

"So, thanks," Bekah said.

"Sure," Lexi forced out.

"And hey, I want you to know that there are no hard feelings about what you told me last year," Bekah said all smiles and giggles.

Lexi looked at her as if she had sprouted wings and had begun to fly. How dare she ever bring last year up to her! Not to mention claiming *she* had no hard feelings, as if Lexi hadn't been the one screwed over in the end by the sack of shit, lying, manipulative bitch in front of her.

"I know you were just saying all of that about you and Jack to get a rise out of me and to make me jealous. But that's in the past now," Bekah said reaching out and grabbing Lexi's shoulder for support, all smiles.

Lexi steeled herself for what she was about to do. She honestly could not let this continue. She had been the bigger person. She had attempted to put the past behind her. She was coming to their fucking wedding, for Christ's sake. Then Bekah had to go and bring all that old shit up.

Lexi sighed and wished that she hadn't taken that last tequila shot. "No, I said all of that because it's true," she stated as firmly as possible. She hadn't lied to Bekah about anything that had happened between her and Jack. They really had been perfect for each other once upon a time, and he really did lie to everyone. She had thought she was exempt at the time…so it wasn't exactly a lie, just a truth that she had come to realize.

"Whatever you like to believe," Bekah drawled, leaning back against the bar and looking like she was the queen of the universe in that moment.

"You can't possibly know our history better than I do," Lexi told her, anger threatening to overtake her buzz.

"I know that you're second best," Bekah slurred back, forgetting all semblance of restraint.

That stung and Lexi knew it was meant to. Bekah had always despised her relationship with Jack. No, she had always been jealous of what they had. Any insult would just be coming from a jealous woman, and Lexi reminded herself of that to keep her focus.

"Not with your brother," Lexi spat back at her. She had been with Ramsey for nearly a year, which Bekah had approved of nearly as much as she approved of Lexi seeing Jack. And even if they were on the rocks now, it didn't mean that she couldn't still hold her head high. Their relationship was built on more than Bekah and Jack's. That much was plainly clear.

Bekah gritted her teeth. "And look at how well that's going…" she said looking her up and down as if she were some low life tramp.

"You know nothing about my relationship," Lexi growled getting even more riled up.

Bekah whisked her blond hair over her shoulder. "You think the world revolves around you, which shows how little you really know about my brother. The only thing Ramsey has ever really cared about is himself. You are no different. I've been there his whole life. I will always know and understand him better than you ever could. You're just a fling among many."

Lexi didn't even want to touch that line of conversation. Bekah would always think she knew Ramsey better. Arguing that wasn't going to help her. "Well, I've known Jack *much* longer than you. Does the same logic apply?" Lexi asked a glint of victory in her eye. She knew that Bekah couldn't come back from that. She had used her own argument against her, and Lexi didn't care how brilliant Bekah was supposed to be, that was a hard logic to get around.

"Jack's different," she answered immediately.

"Of course he is."

"I'm marrying him," she growled throwing her left hand out for examination.

Lexi stared at the ring in front of her. Now that she had it so close, she could see that it was, in fact, a duplicate as he had promised. There was just something about the ring that was too…modern. The silver was too polished. The diamonds perhaps a bit too large for the enclosures and the shape just a bit too perfect. It was the delicate simplicity and raw original manufacturing of the ring Jack had given to Lexi that had made it so unique. This was not that ring. That much was finally clear to her.

And then she knew what she wanted to say in that moment as Bekah stood with her engagement ring for full display. The ring—the fake ring—was just as much of a sham as their relationship.

"It's fake," Lexi said never taking her eyes from the glittering diamonds. She had been thinking it, but had never meant for the words to actually slip out.

"What?" Bekah gasped, pulling her hand back as if it had been burned.

There was no turning back now. "It's fake," she repeated.

"I am marrying him," Bekah said not fully understanding the gravity of her statement.

"No. The ring," Lexi stated simply.

"What about my ring?" she asked turning her hand over to examine it more closely.

"You heard me. Your ring is fake," Lexi spat, feeling a release of all the pent up frustration.

"It's not a fake!" Bekah gasped.

"Are you sure?" Lexi asked arching an eyebrow.

"What? You think I haven't had it appraised?" she asked, revealing the true depths of her shallowness.

Lexi scoffed at her statement. It would have never crossed her mind to get it appraised. The diamonds couldn't have been more real. A closer inspection was hardly necessary. It was pretty clear that it was an expensive engagement ring. "For quality and cost, right?" Lexi asked.

Bekah examined the ring on her hand for a second before answering Lexi. "Of course. The ring cost a fortune. Every diamond is authentic."

"What about the authenticity of the ring itself?" Lexi asked knowing the she likely hadn't considered that for she had never thought that he wouldn't have given her the original ring. "Has that ring on your finger been around since before World War II?" she asked grabbing her hand and staring at the ring again. She knew it wasn't, but her drunken state wasn't allowing her any discretion. "Has this ring survived Jack's grandmother as he always claimed it did?"

"Of course," Bekah said with less confidence than before. She stared forward at Lexi who was still examining the ring.

"No, it hasn't, because this isn't that ring. It's a duplicate," Lexi told her gritting her teeth against the reality of her statement. Because no matter how much this was going to hurt Bekah, this fact had already hurt Lexi more. It had been her goddamn ring.

"I don't believe you," she said yanking her hand back.

"You don't have to," Lexi spat. "Get the ring appraised for real this time, and you'll figure it out for yourself. The original ring doesn't belong to you, and it was never meant for you."

"How would you know any of this?" Bekah asked getting flustered and reaching out for the bar to steady herself. She was losing color in her face and getting more and more unsteady on her feet.

Lexi wasn't sure she could answer that. How could she tell her that the ring was intended for Lexi all along? That would just fuel her fire. Lexi didn't have the ring so there was no point in pressing her luck and exposing anymore than was necessary. The real story was too humiliating anyway.

"I just…know Jack unlike anyone else," she said with a sad smile.

"No," Bekah said shaking her head from side to side. "You're a liar. That's what you said Jack is good at. Well, that's all you're good at. You're flat out lying to me. You want me to call off the wedding. You want him to yourself. He's not yours. Wait until I tell Ramsey what bullshit you're spoutin' now. He'll never want you back."

Lexi rolled her eyes. "Oh please, I'm not here to sabotage *you*. Don't flatter yourself. And try and refrain from thinking you know what Ramsey will and will not do. You're just his *sister*."

"I know what he'll do if I tell him about your little rendezvous in the bathroom!"

"Then tell him! What do you even know?" she yelled back trying to fight back her fear. She really didn't want Bekah to tell Ramsey.

Bekah glared at her ready to respond, but Kersey ran up to the pair right then not noticing their menacing glares. "Let's go," she squeaked out, wiping at her mouth quickly.

"Go?" Bekah asked distracted.

"Yeah. Where are Amber and Maddie?" Kersey asked looking around them to find out where the girls were. She stood on her tip toes, and even in her four inch heels, she was still too short to see over the crowd.

"Dancing. What's going on?" Bekah asked her concerned.

Kersey giggled and pulled something out of her purse. Lexi was still fuming from her conversation with Bekah. She could hardly concentrate on what they were saying or what Kersey had in her hand.

"Look what I got," Kersey said covering her mouth as she revealed the boxers in her hand.

"You got boxers?" Bekah asked in awe.

Kersey bit her lower lip and attempted to look innocent. "I won't tell you what I had to do to get them," she said lowering her long black lashes, "but I have them."

"Oh, I think I know what you had to do," Bekah said looking at her with a new sense of admiration. "You've got a little…" Bekah motioned for her to wipe the right side of her mouth.

Kersey's eyes bulged, and she quickly swiped at her mouth again. "Whoops," she said giggling. "Anyway, we have to go. I don't think he was expecting me to dip out like that."

Kersey and Bekah dove into the crowd to wrangle Amber and Maddie out of the mass of people. Lexi darted for the door to wait for the rest of the group. She was glad that they were on their way out. She was too drunk to be around them any longer. She had spilled a secret that she swore she was going to keep to herself. She had never intended to stoop to Bekah's level. The Fearsome Four appeared before her, hanging onto each other, and giggling about Kersey's success.

As they stumbled down the street back to their hotel, Amber cried out, "How bruised are your knees going to be?"

"Amber!" Kersey gasped.

"Are they already bruised?" Maddie asked bending over a little too far to look at Kersey's knees and showing her ass off to the rest of the street.

"No!" she cried a sly smile still on her face. "Anyway, it's not like you didn't do the same fucking thing to Ramsey only two weeks ago!"

Lexi stopped in her tracks her mouth dropping open. Had she just heard that? Were they serious? No. They had to be baiting her. She knew that she had been far from perfect after they broke up. He had every right to fool around with other people. They hadn't been together. She had left. But it just didn't sound like him. Everyone had said that he was working towards making things right with her. He had said that he wanted her back. The pieces didn't fit together.

"Kersey, shut up!" Maddie growled.

"Not again," Bekah gasped, gagging a little and pushing her friend away from her. "You little whore."

"It didn't happen! I tried to tell you guys," Maddie said shaking her head and giggling.

"Yeah, you just happened to have white stuff on your mouth for no reason when you came back from the bathroom with Ramsey at the club," Amber muttered under her breath.

"Guys, I swear," Maddie yelled back.

"I won't hate you this time," Bekah slurred pointing her finger at Maddie.

"Come on. That's ancient history."

"Suuuuuure," Kersey said as they entered the hotel lobby.

Lexi numbly followed them into the elevator up to their floor. She had blocked out the remainder of their conversation. She didn't want to know if it was true. They were too drunk to be lying about it. And she was too drunk to question their comments. All she wanted to do was to crash in her hotel room and block out the entire night.

*****

The next morning Lexi woke up with a killer headache and an upset stomach. None of the other girls felt up to breakfast, and happily directed the limo to take them back to Atlanta. The only good part about all of them being hung over was that none of them wanted to talk. They just wanted to lie back against the cold leather seats and rest their eyes. Lexi was not going to stop them, that was for sure.

An hour later, Lexi was dropped back off at Ramsey's apartment. She was so thankful to be out of the car and away from the four blonde bitches. Lexi grabbed her bag from the trunk and stomped up the stairs to Ramsey's apartment.

Ramsey was standing next to the coffee maker when she walked in. He looked as gorgeous as ever in a flimsy green t-shirt and khaki shorts. His smile lit up as she entered the room. "Hey, how was the party?" Ramsey asked cheerfully turning to face her. "I didn't hear from you again last night." The glare on her face was enough to tell all. She tossed her bag at the foot of the couch and sank into the sofa. "That bad?" he asked. "I thought you said it wasn't as bad as you thought."

"It got worse," she grumbled.

Ramsey grabbed his mug of coffee and walked over to her. "Here. This might help."

"Doubtful."

"There's something coffee can't fix?" he asked, his eyes widening.

"Fine," she said taking the coffee out of his hand and taking a sip. She didn't want to admit that it helped, but took another sip anyway.

"So, what happened?" he asked sitting down next to her.

"Is it wrong if I tell you that I hate your sister?" she mumbled.

Ramsey chuckled softly to himself. "What did she do now?"

"You didn't think there was anything you should warn me about before sending me off with them?" She turned and looked at him carefully. "Nothing?"

"Uh…no. What are you talking about?" he asked.

Lexi sighed and stood. "You can't think of anything?" she repeated, feeling frustrated and worn down.

Ramsey stood to meet her. He placed a tentative hand on her shoulder and she looked away from him. "If there is something I should know, please just tell me."

"You slept with Maddie," she said, unable to hold back any longer. She swallowed not wanting to hear him confirm it. She knew that she shouldn't get riled up. She shouldn't be angry with him, but damn, he could have at least warned her. She waited looking into his eyes…waiting for him to say anything. When he didn't, she figured that was all confirmation she needed. Running her hand through her hair, she pulled away and stormed into the kitchen. She set her mug down on the counter and then braced her body. She had moved a bit too quickly and was feeling dizzy from her hangover.

Ramsey cursed under his breath, but followed her. "Lexi."

After she regained her balance, she spoke up. "No, Ramsey, I don't even want to think about it right now," she muttered resting her hands on the cool marble countertops and taking several heavy breaths. She knew that it didn't matter that he had slept with her. She actually wasn't even pissed that it had happened. She wished he had warned her. Bekah used every trick in the book. How had he not thought to tell her? Then she wouldn't have had to be surprised and look like an idiot.

And what had happened two weeks ago? Had Maddie really given him a blow job in the bathroom? Had any of that been true? It was hard to even contemplate.

"Lexi, that was a really long time ago. She was in college when that happened," he told her. "I don't know why they brought it up, but it has nothing to do with you. I was in a rough place in my life. You know that. I used to sleep around, but I'm not that person anymore."

"What about two weeks ago?" Lexi asked whirling around to face him.

"What *about* two weeks ago?" he asked scrunching his brows together.

"The blow job in the bathroom," she reminded him, leaning back against the counter top to steady herself. "I don't care who you slept with or what happened. I really don't care. We weren't together. You have every right. But you knew I'd be around her."

"Nothing happened two weeks ago," he corrected her quickly. "She came into the club with Bekah and the other girls. Maddie ended up hooking up with someone else that night, and I almost kicked her out of the club. I didn't do anything with her, Lexi."

"Then why did they tell me that?" she asked angrily. "Why didn't you tell me?"

He shrugged slowly. "I don't know why they decided to tell you that lie. There's nothing with her or anyone else. All I think about is you," he told her. "I had no idea they were going to bring up my history with her. It's not like I was trying to hide it from you. It's history for a reason."

"What about Parker being a bridesmaid?" she whispered into the open space. Her stomach had dropped at the mention of that bit of information. She had had to act like she didn't care about that for an entire evening. She had to parade around in Parker's clothes and follow the orders of four blonde bimbos. Surely he could have thought that worth noting.

"Oh," was all he managed.

Lexi waited a second expecting more explanation than just—oh. When he didn't say anything else, she shook her head forlornly. "Is that what I am? Just a fill in for Parker?" she asked staring deep into his green eyes full of repentance. He was shaking his head, but she couldn't stop there. "Do you want to just fuck me in front of all your friends? Because all you seem to be doing is fucking me over Ramsey."

He seemed unable to control himself after she finished her reprimand. He dove forward and claimed her lips for his own smashing them both backwards into the marble countertop. She gasped as her body was pressed back bruisingly hard, and he demanded attention from her lips. It didn't take long before she was breathless as their kiss intensified. His hands pushed up in her long flowing hair, yanking it roughly. Her head wrenched backwards, and she released a moan.

He nipped his way up her neck and growled into her ear, "I really want to fuck you over."

"Oh, God," she groaned raking her hands down his chest.

He snatched both of her hands off of him, and gripped them together with one hand. Yanking them forcefully over her head, he held her in place. She wanted to hold onto her anger, but she could barely keep from panting as he held her motionless.

"You said I'm fucking you over?" he murmured. Turning her nose up, she refused to respond. Instead, she slid her leg up his calf, moved over his knee, and against his thigh. He tugged on her arms, and pressed his hip into her leg securing her in place. "Lexi, I asked you something."

She opened her eyes, and saw his gorgeous face smirking at her. "Yes, you are *fucking* me over," she said, trying to hold onto her anger.

He chuckled and pressed his advantage. "I'll show you what that's really like."

He used his free hand to run down her front and snap the buttons open from top to bottom. He trailed gently down the front sending goosebumps across her skin. Reaching her shorts, he dragged the zipper down, and let them fall to the kitchen floor. He leaned forward and licked across her bottom lip. She whimpered. "That's better," he whispered. His hand dipped down into her underwear teasing more than just her lips.

"Ramsey," she gasped out.

"Don't move those," he told her, dragging her underwear to the ground. She stepped out of them, and lowered her arms. "I said don't move those!"

Her arms shot back in the air and gripped the handle. At that point, she didn't care if she ripped the cabinets off of the wall.

As he stood, he grabbed her thighs and hoisted her onto the counter. "Stay here," he said grazing her chin and forcing her to lock eyes with him, "and listen this time."

Lexi licked her lips and watched as he stripped down to his navy boxers. She could see that he was hardening at the sight of her naked from the waist down, and she squirmed as she sat there exposed.

He moved back towards her and pushed her legs apart as far as they would go. "Ramsey," she groaned as he ran his hand achingly slow up her inner thighs. Her pussy pulsed as he neared her and begged for his fingers. "Yes, love?" he whispered running his finger down her wetness. "Oh, look, you're already ready for me."

She closed her eyes and instinctively slammed her head backwards into the cabinet. "Tease," she barely got out.

"Fine, I don't have to tease you," he said pushing his boxers to the ground and positioning his hard cock in front of her opening. "Is this what you want?"

Not waiting for an answer, he grabbed her ass in his hands and pumped inside of her. She gasped as he filled her and dropped her arms to his shoulders. Not even stopping his movements, he grabbed her arms again and forced them back to their proper place. She could hardly breathe as he rammed inside of her over and over again.

They had had sex hundreds of times over the past year, but nothing was like this. Ramsey had never been like this. It had always been making love—wonderful fucking delicious sex. But the anger that had coursed through their veins, the anger that had pushed them to this moment, threw that completely out the window. Now he was just fucking her—fucking her properly.

She came almost instantly, not able to hold out. It had been too long without him. It had been too damn long.

"Oh shit," he groaned as she clenched around him.

Finally releasing her arms, he circled her legs around him. He grabbed her off of the counter and Lexi glanced over at the kitchen table. "Fuck it," he growled and without a second thought threw them both down onto the marbled floor.

Lexi's back arched off the ground desperate to get him back inside of her. She heard him chuckle, and then he was flipping her over face down on the ground. He reinserted himself into her and continued his work, fucking her senseless. "Oh, Jesus. Fuck. Ramsey," she cried out each time he drove into her, his balls slapping against her clit and propelling her towards orgasm a second time.

"God, you're so tight," he growled, his fingers digging into her hips.

At those words, she felt him stiffen and release, and they came together. Lexi laid her forehead on the cold marble floor, her breathing ragged and her chest heaving. Sweat dripped down her back, and she realized she had a light sheen across her skin.

"Why was I mad at you again?" she asked into the floor.

He leaned forward and kissed her back. "I want you," he breathed between kisses. "Just you, Lexi."

"Didn't you just have me?" she asked turning around to look at him with a sweet, lazy smile on her face.

"I want all of you."

18

JUNE TWO MONTHS EARLIER

Rounding the corner in Bridges Enterprise, Lexi found Brandon's office door and knocked twice. She heard scurrying footsteps and as if someone had jumped. Was she interrupting? A woman's voice spoke up. "Were you expecting someone?"

This time Brandon responded, "No, I don't have to get it."

Lexi sighed. She was definitely interrupting something, but she didn't have the time for it right now. She was starving, and wanted to get out of this place as soon as possible.

She heard the woman respond faintly through the door. "That's a good idea."

Did she hear someone groaning? Oh Jesus, Brandon! Was he with someone on the other side of that door? This was so inconvenient. He was at work, he shouldn't be diddling one of his coworkers during business hours. She rolled her eyes and knocked a second time, harder.

"Brandon?" she cried, puncturing his name with another knock on the door. "I know you're in there!"

Lexi heard the girl respond one more time. "I thought you weren't expecting anyone."

"I wasn't. I don't know who that is," Brandon said. Lexi ground her teeth. She wanted to yell through the door that she could hear them.

"Do you *have* to answer it?" the girl asked. There was a pause on the other side of the door for a second. Lexi didn't even want to know what that pause meant.

"Dammit," Brandon grumbled stepping back. She heard Brandon cross the office and she quickly pulled her ear away from the door just as it swung open. A surprised smile broke across his face when he saw Lexi.

"Hey, Pookie," Lexi said sauntering into his office uninvited. She stopped when she saw Kace, remembering the last time she had encountered Mr. Bridges secretary. She had been more interested in filing a sexual harassment suit against Brandon at the time. Clearly by the heady look on her face that was no longer the case. "Hey, how's it going?" she asked awkwardly, realizing she couldn't exactly backtrack from that statement. To an outsider that easy nickname could easily be construed as a pet name.

"Just fine," she said crossing her arms over her chest, sinking into one hip, and looking at Brandon pointedly.

"Uh, Kace, you remember Lexi, right?" he asked gesturing between the two women.

Her eyes traveled back to Lexi examining her before answering. "Don't you date Ramsey Bridges?" Kace asked an accusatory inflection in her voice.

Lexi smiled brightly at the mention of her boyfriend. Just the thought of him made her burst with excitement. She was certain that much was evident on her face. "Yeah, I do."

"Uh huh," Kace replied glancing conspiratorially between the two.

Lexi knew that this looked bad. She had clearly walked in on something and was now making the situation worse. Brandon was a known womanizer. Lexi had heard just such information straight out of Kace's mouth one time. She knew the suspicions were likely warranted on Brandon's end. Luckily no one knew anything about her or else the suspicions would be even more heightened.

"Well Kace it's been nice…as always," Brandon said attempting damage control. "We can finish what we started later, yes?"

"You're kicking me out?" she gasped in surprise.

Lexi grimaced at what she had walked in on and took a hesitant step backwards. "I didn't mean to come at a bad time," she stuttered out quickly. "I can always come back later, and we can discuss that paperwork then if you want." She knew her damage control sounded as forced as his.

Brandon examined her closely. "Paperwork?" Her eyes bulged open as she attempted to signal him to *shut the fuck up*. "Right, paperwork. Yeah, you should probably come back for that."

"Not necessary," Kace interjected. "I see that our…meeting is over anyway."

"Kace," he pleaded.

"No, no, I see that you have other business to attend to," she said striding across the office and brushing past Lexi.

"It's really not like that," Lexi responded hurriedly.

Kace gave her a sad smile. "Of course not. It never is with Brandon," she said with a roll of her eyes.

"Kace," he growled, grasping her elbow and yanking her towards him. She gasped as she was flung into his arms. He bent down and claimed her lips in a deep kiss. When he released her, the earlier anger in her eyes had dissipated. "I'll see you later."

"Yes. Later," she responded dreamily as she exited the office. He toed the door closed behind her and turned back to his desk.

Lexi sighed and followed him, taking the unoccupied chair next to his desk. "Sorry."

"You can't call ahead of time like a normal person?" he grumbled leafing back through the papers he had been dealing with before Kace's interruption.

Lexi shrugged helplessly. "I didn't know you'd have…company."

"Assume away," he said waving a dismissive hand.

"Anyway, lunch?" she asked a bright smile crossing her face.

He sighed staring down at the stack of papers on his desk. "If I keep having lunch with you, people are going to think you've put me in the friend zone," he murmured practically quoting a line out of *Just Friends*.

"You are in the friend zone," she said with a giggle. "You have been for a couple weeks, and it's seemed to work out just fine. Anyway, everyone knows that I'm living with Ramsey. You're the only one who seems not to care about that."

"I'm not the only one," he murmured. "Just the only one who will admit it." He glanced back up at her flirtatiously, a smirk appearing on his lips.

Lexi shrugged again nonchalantly as if she had been through this conversation before…and she had. "Doesn't matter that you admit it. I'm still with Ramsey," she said certainly.

He set the papers aside, leaned back in his administrative chair, and stared at her. "And where is your man today?" he asked.

"He's working," she told him with a faint sigh at the end.

"Ahh," he murmured, "Too busy to take his girlfriend to lunch?"

"Stop goading me, Brandon. He's not used to anyone being around. We had a long distance relationship, and he can't quit his job to have lunch with me every day. Since you work a 9to5, you have no trouble being constantly available especially since you don't have a girlfriend."

"I would, if you would let me take someone else to lunch," he spat back playfully.

"You know there's nowhere else you'd rather be," she said. "So come on. I want sushi today, and it's your turn to pay."

"Fine," he grumbled still managing a smile.

The two had managed to develop quite a friendship, as Lexi had predicted that night out on Ramsey's balcony. Brandon, of course, never failed to shamelessly flirt and throw himself at Lexi, but she always deflected his advances. They had an easy banter, and found that they had more in common than originally anticipated. When they both let their guards down, they they really enjoyed each other's company. He wasn't exactly a substitute for Chyna, no one could really replace her best friend, but he was a nice change in the mean time.

Ramsey didn't approve of the relationship as he had made clear time and time again. But with Ramsey's continual absence, Lexi had to find a way to kill time outside of her job. He wasn't always around when she was at home, but the time they spent together was cherished by both. Lexi was certain that the decision to move in with him had been an accurate one at this point. Even though he was so busy, it was better to have the couple hours a week together then to have the distance to separate them.

Lexi paused in the doorway as her cell phone jingled in her purse. "Sorry," she mumbled fumbling with the latch on her purse. "Mom, hey, it's not the best time. I'm about to go to lunch," Lexi spoke quickly into her phone. The sobbing that penetrated through the receiver stopped Lexi in her tracks. "Mom, are you alright? Is everything alright? What happened? Calm down. Calm down. Tell me what happened," Lexi spoke urgently her heart beating out of her chest with fear. Panic gripped her and she latched onto Brandon as he approached. Upon seeing her stricken face, he ushered her back into his office.

"It's your father," her mother gasped through her tears.

"Dad?" Lexi moaned in terror. "What happened to dad?" Brandon rested his arm around her shoulder for support as her body seemed to collapse under the weight of the impending news.

"Honey, he had a heart attack," she cried out. She hiccupped a couple times into the phone a sure sign, Lexi knew, of an onset of hyperventilation.

Lexi felt a tear run down her cheek and then another one followed. She couldn't stop them from tumbling relentlessly out of her eyes. "Is he okay?" she could barely get out.

Another round of sobbing came through the line. "I don't know. I don't know. I just…don't know."

"Where is he? Did you call an ambulance?" Lexi asked taking the side of the parental figure and demanding the details.

"He went into the city for some consulting work," she sobbed. "He had been complaining that his shoulder and chest hurt, but we didn't think anything of it. He always has chest pains. Luckily someone was around when he collapsed. They picked up the call and told me they were calling 911." She paused for another round of fitful tears. Lexi had never quite heard her mother in such a state. "They took him to Grady. It'll take me too long to get there, but I'm on my way. Please go and tell me he's alright. Tell me I haven't lost my George."

"I'm on my way now, mom. I love you. I'll call you from the hospital," Lexi told her before hanging up.

"Do you need me to go with you?" Brandon asked having heard everything through the line.

"No," Lexi said swiping at her face. "I just...I can drive."

"Are you sure?" he asked grasping both of her shoulders in his hands and staring deep in her tear streaked face. She nodded helplessly. He pulled her into a brief comforting hug. "Call me if you need anything," he told her. She nodded again and then quickly left his office.

She pulled her phone back out as soon as she was out of the elevator. Her first instinct was to call Ramsey. She knew he was busy working, but she needed to speak with him. Hopefully he would be available. Sometimes when he got so into work, he completely forgot all else including to check his phone. She pressed the speed dial number for his phone, listened to it ring four times before going to voicemail.

Lexi cursed loudly as she entered the parking garage and beelined for her car. She wanted to talk to Chyna. She was reassuring and always helped Lexi through these problems. Unfortunately she was halfway across the world at a photo shoot in Milan, and the international reception was terrible. Lexi rarely got to talk with her, and never when she was the one who called.

She scrambled to figure out who she could call. She needed to speak to someone...to have someone reassure her. She needed a voice of reason in her panic. Brandon was nice. She could have let him come with her, but they had been friends for less than a month. This wasn't exactly a place for her to allow him to get involved. She needed someone else...someone who really knew her.

Lexi knew she had lost her sanity in this instant when her fingers numbly dialed the next number. "Lexi?" Jack asked answering the phone on the first ring. She couldn't help it. She sobbed into the phone just as her mother had when Lexi had answered.

"Lexi? Are you alright? Are you hurt? What happened?" he asked, listening to her tears.

"Jack. Oh Jack," she cried. "My dad had a heart attack."

"What?" he gasped. "Is everything alright?"

"I don't know. I'm on my way to Grady right now to find out," she told him finding her car in the garage.

"You can't drive! Listen to yourself," he cried.

She blubbered into the phone at how concerned he sounded. "What other choice do I have?"

"Where are you? Let me come get you," he said.

"I can't take you away," she told him, unlocking her car and throwing her purse inside.

"Lexi, goddamnit, don't be stubborn this time!"

She sank into the front seat of her car. Placing her hands on the steering wheel, she found they were trembling beyond control. She couldn't drive like this. "I'm at Bridges in the parking garage," she told him.

"You're just downstairs, and you weren't going to let me help you?" he demanded angrily. "Fuck. Don't you move. I'll be down there in a second. Meet me at the stairs."

A few agonizingly long minutes later, Jack appeared at the bottom of the stairwell and walked her to his car. She wasn't sure why she was letting him help her when she had refused Brandon the same request. Her heart hurt too much, and she was too scared to even want to contemplate it. He was Jack. That was all that mattered right now.

Jack peeled out of the garage and zipped towards the interstate. Lexi sat numbly with her hands clenched in her lap staring out the windshield. She gulped, her mind spinning webs of possibilities.

"Hey," he said tentatively brushing her shoulder. "It's going to be okay."

"Okay," she murmured tears falling out of her eyes once more. Jack reached over, unclasped her hands, and gently placed one in his. They laced fingers; it was the most comforting thing he could offer.

"He's going to be fine. Grady has some of the best doctors in the world. He is in good hands there."

"I know," she murmured, wiping a tear from her cheek with her free hand, "but it's my daddy."

"I know, Lex," he said, "but you have to be positive. You don't know all the details. Things will work out."

"How? How do you know?"

"I don't. I just have a feeling," he told her. "He's going to be alright."

"Promise?" she begged.

He paused a second before answering. "Yes, I do."

"Thanks Jack," she breathed. "That means a lot." She was holding back another round of tears.

"Of course."

"I just needed to talk to someone…someone who knows me," she said quietly.

Jack took another exaggerated pause before responding. "Well, I know you, Lex."

"I know, Jack," she whispered.

Jack pulled off the road and into the Grady emergency room parking lot. "If you need me to come get you from the hospital afterwards just give me a call, okay?"

"Okay," she mumbled.

"Everything will be fine," he repeated for reassurance.

"Thanks."

"Please call me to let me know what happens, alright, Lex?" he pleaded. She gripped his hand tightly. "I want to know that I'm right...that I held up my promise."

"Sure, Jack," she said sadly as she slowly released his hand. "Thank you."

"Of course," he told her as she exited the car. She raced into the Emergency Room lobby and to the woman behind the desk.

"Name," she said dryly not looking up from her clipboard.

"My father had a heart attack. I need to see him," Lexi gasped out.

"Name?" she asked turning to her computer flippantly.

"George. George Walsh. My name is Lexi. I'm his daughter," she breathed out as fast as possible.

"Yes. Mr. Walsh is up the stairs and down the hall. Room number 205," the woman told her barely glancing at her over her horn-rimmed glasses.

"Thank you," Lexi said before darting down the hall. She skidded around the corner at a near break neck speed and took the stairs two at a time. She slowed as she approached the much busier hallway. She lightly jog as she followed the line of numbers to the one her father had been assigned.

Lexi pushed open the door to her father's hospital room and stepped in. "Daddy?" she whispered into the sunlit room tears streaming down her face again.

Her father's eyes fluttered open briefly in recognition before closing again. His breathing was labored and he looked as if he had just run a marathon. His skin was almost a green color, and he was soaked through with sweat, even though the hospital room was frigid. Despite this, a faint smile appeared at the edges of his lips upon her entrance. "Hey....ba...by girl," he breathed out before falling silent again, the effort to speak taking too much out of him.

"Hey," she cooed rushing to his bedside, planting a soft kiss on his forehead, and falling back softly into the waiting bedside chair. "You don't look too good, old man," she said jokingly. It took everything she could to chuckle softly. She could tell it was straining him to pull up the corners of his mouth, but that didn't stop him.

Lexi pulled out her phone and quickly sent a text to her mother to let her know that her husband was still alive. She didn't want to leave his side long enough to make the phone call. She knew her mother was likely still in hysterics, and the thought of being out of the room for long enough to deal with that seemed too much to grasp right now.

A nurse scrambled in the doorway and Lexi snapped her head around at the disruption to the quiet of the room. The only thing that had been constant were the deep wheezing breaths her father was taking, and the slow beeps emitted from the machine next to his bedside. The woman stopped in her tracks when she saw Lexi sitting in the previously unoccupied chair. "Well, hello dear," she said a bit too brightly for the circumstances.

"Hi," Lexi squeaked out. "Is he going to be okay?"

"Oh, he is going to be just fine. The doctors will come in and explain everything to you shortly. You're his daughter, I presume?" she asked waddling over to her father's bedside. Lexi nodded mutely as she watched the nurse begin to fiddle with the IV stuck into his hand. For some reason Lexi hadn't even realized it was there. "Well, I'm going to monitor the ECG until the doctor arrives."

A short while later her mother bustled into the room. Her face was still covered in tears and at the sight of her husband hooked up to machines, she fell into another round of hysterics. Lexi stood and allowed her to take the seat at his side that she had occupied. She watched her mother reach out tentatively and grasp his hand in her own. She stayed there staring at the love of her life, the man she had spent the last thirty years with. Lexi wondered if she would ever be as happy as them one day.

Just then the doctor walked through the door. Lexi turned around to face the door as the small brunette entered, her nose buried in the patient's chart. "Well, let's see what we have here," she began. "George Walsh. Age forty-nine. Heart attack. Overall, I'd say you are rather lucky, under the circumstances, Mr. Walsh." Finally, she looked up at her patient.

Lexi released a short gasp at the recognition between the two. "Parker?"

The doctor looked between Lexi and the patient she had been addressing and back. She was clearly thrown off that her personal life had somehow managed to wiggle into her work environment. "Lexi?"

"You two know each other?" Lexi's mother asked glancing back and forth between her daughter and the doctor who looked remarkably like Lexi. Lexi and Parker both nodded. "But…you look so much alike," she said wistfully.

"We've heard that before," Parker answered returning to her paperwork quickly.

Lexi forgot how shy Parker could be in uncomfortable situations. "This is my father," she stated even though the fact was now obvious. "Sorry, I'll just…uh, wait outside. I need some air. I'll be back in a minute mom." Lexi rushed past Parker and out into the hallway. She took a deep intake of the stale hospital air. She was sure that she was overreacting, but being in the same room with her at such an emotional time felt wrong. She needed to leave. She needed to get out of there.

A seat was placed outside of one of the rooms, and she slumped into it. All she wanted to do was shut off her brain. She closed her eyes and pressed her palms to her temples in an attempt to stop the pounding in her skull. A tear fell from her eye as the pressure from the last couple hours seemed to settle on her body. She wanted to go home, cuddle up with some double chocolate ice cream, and cry herself to sleep. She had almost lost her daddy today. It wasn't a feeling she was soon to forget.

Lexi looked up when her father's hospital door opened again, and Parker exited. Instead of turning away, Parker walked down to where Lexi was sitting, crying. "Hey, let's go get some coffee," she said her voice lowering comfortingly.

Lexi wiped at both of her cheeks and stood slowly. "Don't you have to get back to work?" Lexi asked, grateful for the offer.

Parker shrugged. "I'm in need of a break. They can run without me for awhile."

"Sure," Lexi said following her down the hall and into the coffee shop. "I didn't know you worked for the ER." She ordered a large black coffee. The caffeine was exactly what she needed right now.

"They have me in the ER right while since another doctor called out. I'm usually in surgery," she told her. Parker ordered a small coffee and doused cream and sugar in it as soon as it was pushed across the counter. The two found a vacant table and slid into their seats. "I'm sorry about your dad," she spoke softly.

"Me too," Lexi murmured.

"I think he's going to be okay now though. Your mom will keep a close watch on him, and I prescribed some blood thinners," she told her reassuringly. "He'll only have to be in the ICU for a day or two."

"Thanks," Lexi said forgetting she was talking to a woman that she had so many reservations against. "I really...just thanks for everything you did."

Parker blushed at the words. "It's my job," she said dismissively.

"Yes, well, it's admirable. I mean, I'm just a blood sucking attorney," Lexi said with a chortle at the end that she really wasn't feeling.

"I'm sure you do good work too," Parker responded quickly.

Lexi shrugged noncommittally. She wasn't sure what to say. Instead, she took another long sip of her coffee and let the caffeine fight her ailments. If someone had told her a few days ago that she would be having coffee with Parker or that her father was going to have a heart attack, she wouldn't have believed them. But here she was at the hospital and both things were true.

"Lexi?" Parker asked hesitantly looking down into her coffee cup. "Can I be honest with you?"

Lexi looked up from her own coffee and stared at Parker speculatively. She wasn't sure she wanted to have this conversation…whatever it was. "About what?"

Parker bit down on her bottom lip. She released a long sigh before meeting Lexi's gaze. "About Ramsey," she said barely louder than a whisper.

Lexi's stomach dropped. Here it was. Everything she had been waiting for. Everything she had suspected. She had known all along deep down that there was more to the story. She had always wanted to believe what Ramsey had told her about his relationship with Parker. She wasn't sure what it was about it, but the story had never settled right with her. Maybe it was the way that Jessie had talked about them the first time Lexi had met Parker over spring break. Maybe it was the looks that they so easily passed between them. Maybe it was just jealousy after everything she had dealt with in her life. But whatever it was, she was about to find out.

Lexi gulped hard. "What about Ramsey?" she asked her hands shaking.

"I just…I…Lexi you have to know I don't like to lie. It's not in me to lie," she said seemingly trembling with the weight of what she was trying to say. "I didn't want to hold back everything from you." Lexi felt a numbness fall over her. Lies. Hidden information. None of this could be good. "I don't really talk about what happened, but I didn't think it was fair for you not to know. I can tell that ya'll are getting serious, and I…" she faltered pushing her hand up through her hair before continuing, "well, I would want to know if the roles were reversed."

"Know what?" Lexi asked leaning forward in anxiety.

Parker shook her head forcefully and pushed herself back against the chair. "I'm sorry. I can't talk about this." She stood abruptly scraping her chair against the tiled floor.

"What?" Lexi gasped louder than expected. "You say all of that and then refuse to explain?"

"I'm sorry. You don't understand what I went through with him," she told her trying desperately to keep her voice even.

"What did you go through with him?" Lexi asked frantically unsure she would ever get the truth out of anyone if Parker didn't confide in her right now.

Parker glanced around the busy coffee shop realizing that she was drawing attention to herself. A few of her colleagues were looking at her sudden outburst curiously. She smiled reassuringly in their direction and took her seat again. "I wish he had just told you," she whispered resting her elbow on the table and sinking her chin into her hand.

"He told me that you guys were old family friends and like…friends with benefits," Lexi told her hoping to get some kind of confirmation on the story.

"Friends with benefits?" she gasped lightly. "He actually said that?" The hurt was evident in her voice. It was so apparent that Lexi immediately knew that the statement was false. There had been much more to their relationship. No one could fake pain like Lexi had just seen in Parker's eyes. Lexi hated confirming what she had told Parker. She seemed to be in a trance when she spoke next.

"We were inseparable," she said the words as if they were more than a fact, as if the words were etched in stone. "Bekah and I were best friends growing up. I had a crush on him when I was younger. It was easy to have a crush on him when he was two years older. I never expected him to ever see me as anything more than his little sister's friend," she told her as if she had transported through time. "We started dating my sophomore year of high school. He was a junior. Even though I was two years younger than him, I'd be graduating only a year behind him since I was a year ahead of everyone in my grade. He always told me the age difference didn't matter. That we'd be together in the end.

"He settled on Tech to stay in the city…to be close to me. His parents wanted him to go to a private school: Princeton, Yale, Brown, or Duke, but he swore he wouldn't leave me." Her hand dropped from her chin, and she stared down into her coffee. "He was only there for a year before he transferred to Duke, when I started my first year. His parents were proud. They were already…planning our marriage. I had always been the perfect influence on their rebellious son."

Lexi shook her head unable to believe this tall tale. This was about as far from Ramsey's story as Parker could possibly get. He had claimed never to have a girlfriend. He had never been in love. Her insides were icing over. No. He had never had any of these things before her. Now she was finding out that not only had he had a girlfriend, but his parents had been planning for them to get married since childhood.

"But it all went wrong," Parker gasped grasping her cup firmly with both hands as she tried to hold back the tears that were clouding her eyes.

"What happened?" Lexi asked surprised she even had a voice. She felt like she was living someone else's life right now. She couldn't believe that these things had actually happened. She had gone through too much time in one day. She was having delusions. Her fears were catching up with her. She had gotten stuck in a soap opera where everyone lied, everyone hid information, everyone was deceitful.

"Oh God, it all happened so quick. I'd been feeling sick for about a week. It was during finals," she told the story as if she had gone back in time and was still there. It was clear that she was trapped in her memories. "I'd asked for an extension because of the sickness. I couldn't stop throwing up.

"I was finally able to hold down a meal, and I raced over to Ramsey's. I hadn't seen him since falling ill, because we didn't live together. Our parents would never have allowed it of course," she said swiping the tears from her blood shot eyes. "He was drunk…terribly drunk. I'd never seen him so drunk. His roommates were there with four or five mostly naked girls. I looked like hell and worse I felt like it, and there he was having a raving good time with some girls that would have sucked his dick at a snap of his fingers." The vulgarity surprised Lexi almost as much as the situation and her mouth fell open. She covered her hand with her mouth as she imagined the scene before her.

How could he have done it?

"I lost it. I just snapped. I screamed at him, yelled at him, called him every dirty thing that I could think of. It made me sick to my stomach, and I had to rush to the bathroom. He was just as vulgar. I remember him telling me that all I cared about were my studies, that I'd changed, that he couldn't even see the old me anymore. He said more things that I hate to even imagine, but he was so drunk, he couldn't stop himself.

"I remember telling him he was a spoiled rich brat who would only ever amount to as much as Daddy's money allowed. Then I left, and as he slammed the door behind me he told me never to come back," she said a tear falling slowly down her right cheek.

Lexi gulped hard her coffee long forgotten. "Is that how it ended?" she couldn't help asking.

"I wish," she said meeting Lexi's chocolate brown eyes. Lexi couldn't imagine it getting any worse. "If only I'd known then what I know now," she said forlornly. "I was pregnant."

Lexi gasped her chest beating frantically as the pieces fell together. Of course, she had been sick, throwing up, her emotions rampant. It all made sense. He hadn't known. How could he have known? "Did you tell him?"

"It is my greatest regret that I did not," she stated sadly licking her dry lips. "I was angry. I couldn't forgive the things he had said to me. I was only nineteen after all…still too young…for everything."

Lexi stilled as the realization hit her. Ramsey could have a child with the woman sitting in front of her. "He has a baby?" she asked.

Tears really did spill forth from Parker's eyes at that statement. "No," she breathed. "I finished my exams, transferred back home to Emory. By then I knew for certain and even if I tried to hide it, the baby was alive inside of me and growing every day. The last thing I wanted was for him to know. I hid it from everyone. I only left the house to go to classes and even then I resorted to wearing sweats everywhere. I didn't even risk seeing a doctor I was so ashamed. My parents were terrified and wanted me to see a shrink. They thought I was depressed," she said with a sharp laugh. Lexi didn't think anyone could blame her for being depressed under the circumstances.

"But one day Bekah showed up at my apartment." Lexi cringed away at the name. "I didn't want to let her in, but she insisted and pushed past me. Well, of course, she could tell that something was different…that I was bigger. I'll spare you the details of the following days with her holed up in my apartment with me. Suffice it to say that I ended up miscarrying."

"Oh, no," Lexi breathed the sorrow of the story beginning to overwhelm her.

"Bekah convinced me to tell him. When I finally went there, it was another bad night. It was storming the entire drive up to Durham. He was alone, but drunk again. I don't know why I expected any less. I hadn't seen or heard from him since I'd left his place that night I'd walked out on him. When I got up the courage to tell him, he called me a liar. He'd gotten it into his head that everything was my fault that night..." She paused unable to go on as she clutched her chest. Finally she worked up the nerve and continued.

"Well, when Bekah finally got to him, she made him feel like a worthless piece of shit. He called and visited and tried to repair everything we had had but I couldn't do it. There was too much hurt, and though he didn't give up for quite some time, I could never really get over what had happened to me. It's the reason I pushed through to medicine," she said sadly slumping back in her chair as if to show that was the end of her tale.

Lexi couldn't believe it. How could this be the same Ramsey that she knew now? How could any of this be true with what she knew about the man she had fallen in love with? It didn't add up. It didn't make sense. He wasn't this person. He was so much more than that.

Why would he lie? It was such an elaborate story though. She had to admit it did all fit together, but still it didn't make sense. He had no reason to tell Lexi that he'd never dated, loved, or that Parker was nothing more than someone he had fucked and left... like all the other girls.

She stood up abruptly the weight of the story heavy on her shoulders. "Don't come near me, my parents, or Ramsey," she said pointing her finger at Parker menacingly. She couldn't believe it. The story was too much.

"Lexi," Parker pleaded looking up at her through pained eyes.
She had gone through too much in one day. Her brain couldn't process any of it. She couldn't think of what all of this would mean if it were true. She couldn't think of shattering the one perfect picture she had of an individual. And so she stumbled away from the coffee shop and back up to her father's bedside to wait out the agony of the day.

19

PRESENT

Lexi walked into the empty restaurant with Ramsey at her side. Her hand was tucked neatly into the crook of his elbow, the other hung limp at her side. Her hair had been pulled high on top of her head into a tight twist revealing her slender neck. Her make-up appeared light though she had taken the time to conceal herself from the awaiting crowd. A slim-cut polyester dress in the palest of purples shrouded her body. Her calves, thighs, and buttocks were accentuated in her nude pointy-toed mules. She had taken unusual care in her outfit knowing she would hardly be exempt from judgment on a night like tonight.

Ramsey was as gorgeous and perfect as ever. His suit fit to perfection, tailored specifically for the evening. His golden hair, so fitting for the Golden Boy of the Bridges Empire, was shinning in the setting sun, and his green eyes glittered splendidly in the shining light.

A collection of round tables were placed around the back room. A long rectangular table sat at the front of the room. A large projection screen had been fitted on the wall behind the table. The screen was white with navy blue lettering displaying:

Rehearsal Dinner
In Honor of the Union Between
Jack Harrison Howard
&
Rebekah Caroline Bridges
Saturday, August 8th

Somehow, seeing those words together made it all seem much more real. She had never witnessed their names joined together in such a ceremonial fashion.

"Are you ready?" Ramsey whispered, his lips barely moving as he stared down upon her. Lexi gave a slight nod and allowed Ramsey to continue forward to their assigned seats. Each table was intricately detailed with tiny silver plaques engraved with the guests name on it in scrawling calligraphy.

Lexi's chair rested next to Ramsey's near the front of the room. She didn't fail to notice that she had been stuffed into a corner, that Parker's name was scribbled on the nameplate on the other side of Ramsey, or that the next closest person to her was an old relative on the bride's side who appeared to be senile.

"I'm going to go check on my sister," Ramsey said brushing the top of her hand before departing the room. He had effectively deposited her at her seat and disappeared. Great.

Lexi sat in her corner as the room filled with friends and relatives of the couple. She was happy to supervise and people watch what was going on before her. The meeting of the families and friends seemed practically humorous, especially to someone who knew the couple as well as she did. Or perhaps she saw what she expected to see.

Jack's family wasn't poor by anyone's standards, but they clearly didn't have Bridges' money. His family simply wasn't as polished as Bekah's family. Her parents were still happily married. Well, happily was a matter of opinion.

Jack's parents, on the other hand, had long since divorce. He had two older brothers—ten and fifteen years older than him. Both were from a previous marriage on his father's side, and both were married with several rambunctious children running around the room in circles—screaming.

Seth and Sandy's entrance was the first thing that pulled Lexi out of her trance. She couldn't exactly deny that seeing the two of them made her happy. Seth was Jack's best man and lifelong best friend. They had grown up together long before they had been college roommates. And Lexi had known the best man longer than even his wife had.

Lexi's appearance at the rehearsal dinner didn't seem to faze Seth as he strode across the room to greet her. She didn't know whether or not he had been warned of her presence or could simply pick her out of a crowd, but his stride was undeterred. "Lexi, love," he crowed, arms outstretched as he swaggered towards her.

She scooted her chair back and stood. The appearance of Jack's oldest friend made her smile blossom as visions of his beach house burst into her mind. "Seth," she murmured against his chest as she leaned into his hug, "it's so good to see you again."

"You look fucking gorgeous," he said with a low whistle, pulling back to examine her body.

She smiled coyly as if she hadn't put in the effort to get ready. "Thanks," she replied though her eyes remained guarded.

"You know I'd love to be the one tearing that dress off of you later," he said nudging her shoulder.

Lexi rolled her eyes, realizing how little men actually changed. "Tell that to your wife."

"You know that I do," he said his eyes finding Sandy in the crowd. She seemed to realize he was watching her and glanced his direction. Lexi's cheeks flushed at the intensity of their stare.

Lexi sighed pulling her own eyes away from the couple radiating with a passion and love that she could only attribute to newlyweds. "How are you and Sandy?" she asked though she could see with her own eyes that things were going well.

Seth, who had never been guarded a day in his life, shined like a beacon of light from the top of a lighthouse. His eyes which broke contact with his wife across the room turned to Lexi. His smile was radiant and his eyes glowed with pleasure. "Now, don't go spreading it around," he said with barely contained excitement, "but we've just found out. We're having a baby."

"Oh, Seth!" she cried truly ecstatic for the young couple. She couldn't believe it was happening so quickly. "That's wonderful!"

He beamed brighter practically bouncing up and down. "Yeah, I think it's a boy. Sandy isn't sure yet, but I am. It's a boy. I'm gonna be a father!"

"Congratulations! I'm really so happy for you both," she said giving him another hug.

"You'll come down for the shower? I know Sandy would want out to be there," he said getting ahead of himself.

Lexi smiled but her happiness had been stripped from her face. She had no idea where she would be in a year. She didn't know if New York would even still be her home. She was still waiting to hear about the Bar. Not to mention potential jobs she had applied for across the country. She didn't know if she would have Ramsey then…and after last night. She stopped that train of thought. Get through the night. That's all she could do.

The what-ifs hung so heavy over her, that she felt crushed under the weight of the uncertainty that lay ahead.

"We'll see, Seth. I'll let you know for sure once you have a date," she told him.

He smiled again unperturbed by her noncommittal answer. "Well, come say hey to Sandy," he said grabbing Lexi's wrist and yanking her towards the center of the room.

"Uh…alright," she said though she wasn't certain that she should be wandering around the room like the rest of the friends and family. She wasn't exactly either. Seth rushed them back to his wife. Sandy's hand instinctively went to the belly of her baby blue dress as they approached.

"Lexi! Hey!" Sandy said as bubbly as ever.

Lexi stepped forward into the hug that was offered and attempted to dispel her nervousness. She knew that she was out of her comfort zone. She had swam so far out into the deep end that she was terrified she would drown. All she could think about was that she needed to keep treading water…keep kicking her feet.

Just keep swimming. Just keep swimming.

I can't believe you're here," Sandy said stepping back from Lexi. Her smile never failed.

"Uh, yeah," Lexi said tucking a lock of hair behind her ear. "I guess I couldn't miss it."

Seeing that Sandy was occupied for awhile, Seth bounded over to the remaining groomsmen, Hunter and Luke. Sandy stepped a little bit closer to Lexi sealing off the space that she had given them. "I mean, with what happened between you and Jack," she barely whispered.

Lexi gulped hard and sputtered a little in surprise. Lexi had never thought Sandy was intuitive or even that intelligent. "I don't know what you mean," Lexi said slowly after a minute.

Sandy rolled her eyes. "Lexi, I really like you, but you are blind to that boy. You really didn't think that I noticed you sneaking off with him every night at the beach before graduation?"

"You…you noticed that?" she asked knowing how she must look to Sandy.

She smiled shyly. "A couple times, but at first, I thought it was to see someone else. I think it was the sand that gave it away. Anyway, we can't fight love when we have it in our grasps, can we?" she asked her eyes landing on Seth.

"Uh…well…I'm not in love with Jack," she told her.

"Okay," Sandy said brushing her words aside as if they meant nothing. "Either way, I wasn't expecting you to be here for this. I would think it would be too painful…whether you still love him or not."

Lexi gulped again. "It's hard to explain."

"You don't have to explain it to me," Sandy said her voice taking on her characteristic bubbly bimbo routine once again. "Can you believe I'm pregnant?" she asked completely diverting the subject.

"Oh! Yeah, Seth told me. Congrats!" Lexi said with enthusiasm that she wasn't entirely sure where she mustered it from. Sandy giggled and went into a full on discussion about the baby, arrangements, names, and all sorts of things that Lexi had never thought of. Having a baby was about the last thing on her mind.

When Sandy finally seemed to have exhausted herself of subjects to discuss, Lexi made a hasty retreat. She plopped back down into her seat as the inexplicabilities of new life washed over her. She seemed to miss the remaining relatives sidle into the private dining room.

Ramsey reappeared at her side, after speaking with the swarm of family who had directed his attention and bombarded him with questions he would have rather left unanswered. His hand slid under the table and grasped her knee for a short second. She glanced at his handsome face covered with the mask of the County Club he had grown up in. His eyes smiled when she finally met them with hers and that there was where her true reassurance came from. This was not him. He was not that person.

The lights dimmed in the room, and the candles flickered across the tables casting shadows on the faces of the guests. The whispers died down as Bekah's parents entered the room followed first by Jack's mother, then a short while afterwards, by his father, who looked rather uncomfortable taking the seat next to his ex-wife. Bekah's parents sat on the other side of the rectangular table leaving a gaping hole with two unfilled seats. All eyes stared at the missing couple wondering from where they would make their appearance.

Lexi, however, had her eyes on the empty seat to Ramsey's left. Surely Parker wouldn't miss Bekah's rehearsal dinner. Lexi would have killed Chyna if she had not shown up to her own rehearsal dinner. Not that that seemed to be something in her immediate future. But still, as Ramsey's father gruffly pushed back out of his chair, Parker's seat remained empty.

Ramsey's father cleared his throat silencing all further conversation among the attendees. "Thank you all so much for coming tonight to honor the soon-to-be union between my daughter Bekah and her fiancé Jack." He waited for the applause to die down before continuing.

But Lexi wasn't listening to him or his prepared speech. She had been to rehearsal dinners before and had learned to tune out speeches like this. Plus she had made it through three years of law school. She was pretty accustomed to tuning in and out of conversations, lectures, debates, and speeches when she saw fit.

She was thinking about how nice it felt for Ramsey's hand to stay on her thigh. How, when he moved his fingers just a bit, a tremor ran up her body. How the pressure on her leg intensified the longer that his father stood up and spoke. She wanted to leave this place with him. He had made mistakes, and there were still so many things that she didn't fully comprehend. But right now all she wanted to do was be tucked up in his arms lost to the rest of the world.

But they couldn't just disappear. Ramsey was a groomsman and it was his own sister's wedding. His entire family was here.

She couldn't keep trying to escape her problems. Running away from the world wasn't the answer. It wasn't going to fix what had happened between them, and it wasn't going to make anything easier. She needed to man up and face what was coming her way. Avoiding her responsibilities wasn't going to be the solution to her life. She had gotten herself into this situation, and she could get herself out of it.

A passage from one of her existential philosophy classes came to mind as she finally realized what she had to do. For some reason the passage had hit home even then. She had copied it off the website onto a tiny piece of paper, and placed it into her wallet. She knew what was making her think of it now.

Carefully, so as not to disturb the endless droning of Ramsey's father's speech, Lexi popped open her hand bag, pulled out her wallet, and rifled through the slips of paper she concealed in its depths. Locating the one she was looking for she read it to herself:

"In some cases, however, a person will try to avoid taking responsibility by trying to avoid making conscious choices altogether. Perhaps she cites uncontrollable passion on her part... the presence of peer pressure... or she pretends not to notice the man's actions. Whatever the case, she acts as though she is not making any choices and hence has no responsibility for the consequences."[1]

Lexi sighed heavily reading and rereading the passage. She knew why this hit home the first time she had come across it. She had been taking that class her senior year…the semester after she had gone to the beach with Clark, Jack, and the rest of their friends.

The idea behind the passage seemed crystal clear. She had to make a choice, not act as if all the choices were out of her grasp. Wasn't that exactly what had gotten her involved with Jack to begin with?

She cited uncontrollable passion and inability to control her actions countless times. They weren't anything but excuses…and not even good ones. They were ramblings of a confused girl who didn't know what she wanted, who let other people—men—sway her decisions for her.

Running away wasn't the solution. Sure, she didn't want to be at the wedding, and if she had come to this conclusion about herself a week ago then she wouldn't be here. But she had a made a choice…a conscious choice. She was here. She was with Ramsey…albeit a little hesitantly. She was going

---

[1] http://atheism.about.com/od/existentialistthemes/a/badfaith.htm

to carry through with her choice. She couldn't keep letting the past dictate her present…and future.

She swallowed hard at the realization that she had a lot of work to do. She needed to practically reinvent herself. She wanted to say that it was going to be easy, but it wasn't.

Jack had really done a number on her. She couldn't trust anyone, and she was manic when it came to him. She cared for Ramsey, but at the first sign of trouble, she had jumped ship. What kind of person was she not to try to stick it out? What kind of person was she to have slept with someone else while being away from him?

She wanted to cover her face in shame. Yes, she had been happy with her Mystery Man. He had given her exactly what she needed—a reprieve from thinking about her life. But when reality set in, she couldn't even tell her best friend who he was. She couldn't tell *anyone* who he was. That wasn't the kind of relationship she needed or wanted. He wasn't the one who had stuck it out with her for a year, long distance to try and make things work. And yet she had been willing to forget all of that so easily.

Had she been so desperate to be wanted? Lexi pursed her lips in annoyance. She was a despicable human. She couldn't even like herself in that moment. Let alone wonder why anyone else could like her.

Yes, everyone made mistakes, but she was an idiot about it all. She avoided everything at any cost…commitment and the responsibility of her actions. She hadn't been able to face up to them and what they meant. And she was terrified, because she knew now that she would have to tell Ramsey.

Ramsey. Lexi shuddered at the thought of his quick temper taking over when she told him. Ramsey had lied straight to her face before, and now Lexi knew, without a shadow of a doubt, that she owed him the truth.

"Are you okay?" Ramsey breathed, barely loud enough to be a whisper. His green eyes cut in her direction.

Lexi's hand dropped back to her lap. She hadn't even realized that she had been pushing her hair back behind her ear with such forcefulness. Not to mention her breathing was jagged. She was sending herself into a state of hyperventilation. She felt Ramsey's hand increase the pressure on her leg for a second as he looked at her with concern.

"Yeah, sorry," she said letting her breathing even out. She slid her hand under his and squeezed reassuringly. His smile lit up at the small gesture of togetherness.

Her heart sank again. She had meant to reassure him, but she was still too terrified to contemplate what he was going to think of her once she told him about what had happened.

She grit her teeth and tried to focus on what Jack's parents were saying now. If she thought too much about what she had to do in the next 24 hours, then she might really hyperventilate.

"My son," Jack's father said, "is a remarkable individual—persistent, unyielding, and relentlessly hardworking." Lexi couldn't agree more. "He is also a rather charming young man, if I do say so myself. I am very pleased as his father to know that those charms won out such a wonderful young woman who not only shares his aspirations in life, but who truly loves him for him. A father couldn't ask for more," he said getting a bit choked up at the end and abruptly taking his seat.

The heartfelt words his father uttered were better than anything Bekah's parents could possibly say about her. The way his eyes watered with joy, sadness, and pride was incredible to behold. She had never met the man who sat in that chair, but for some reason she wondered why more of those raw emotions hadn't been transferred to his son. Had the divorce destroyed that within Jack?

Before she could think on it further, Bekah's father stood once more and announced, "Without further ado, I would like to introduce you to the future newlyweds my daughter, Bekah, and her fiancé, Jack."

The restaurant exploded with applause as Jack and Bekah materialized in the high arching doorway in which their parents had entered minutes earlier. Bekah looked radiant. Her typically stick straight blonde hair had thick loose curls in it. Her chunky bangs had been fluffed and pushed off her face. A short, white lace dress clung to her body. But what was most noticeable about her was that her eyes actually appeared not to be calculating and her smile wasn't malicious. She seemed content in the moment, rather than always looking to the next move in her intricate game. If she didn't know better, Lexi would think she was a real human being.

For some reason, Lexi had been so transfixed with her enemy that she hadn't turned to look at the man standing next to her. All traces of the downtrodden man who stood on Ramsey's doorstep less than a week earlier to tell him he was having doubts had vanished. He was as polished as ever in a black three-piece suit with a baby blue button-up underneath.

Lexi had recognized the man standing before Ramsey—weak and disheveled with a five o'clock shadow and Converses. She had known that man for a long time. And though she had seen Jack dressed up before, he had always still looked like himself. He was gorgeous. There was no denying that. But he didn't look like her Jack anymore.

And he wasn't her Jack, as he had proven a year ago. The man standing next to Bekah belonged to Bekah. She had made him the person that he was…the person she wanted him to be.

It felt surreal that they were standing here with other people. Somehow she had never really expected this moment to happen. Jack was never supposed to end up with Bekah. Lexi desired him for everything that they were, but not everything that they could be.

But still he wasn't supposed to end up with *her*.

Lexi tore her eyes away from the couple as they began their round of thanks. She couldn't look at them right now with so much else going on in her head. She hadn't anticipated having a mental breakdown in the middle of their rehearsal dinner.

Her eyes took in the room around her crowded in with people just as Parker entered stealthily through the back doors. Lexi clenched her jaw. This was the first time she had seen her since…well, since that night. She knew that she was going to have to see her…even speak to her maybe, but she hadn't realized until that moment how much she was dreading it.

She didn't want to see Parker. She didn't want to be around Parker. The thought of seeing her and Ramsey in the same room made her skin crawl. The knowledge that she would soon be sitting next to him made her physically ill.

Parker looked stunning, and not in the same way as Bekah…or even really, Lexi tonight. Parker looked like she had thrown on the first dress in her closet, hastily threw her hair in a tight ponytail, and stormed out of the house without a hint of makeup. Lexi knew it was probably, because she had had to come straight from the hospital, but she didn't care. She wished that for one night the girl didn't look so gorgeous when she had clearly just thrown something on.

Parker scampered across the room until she found her assigned seat. "So sorry," Parker breathed to the people at her table as she slid neatly into the cushioned chair and demurely crossed her legs.

"Where were you?" Ramsey asked, his eyes steeled on her.

"I got caught in surgery," Parker said her eyes moving from Ramsey to Lexi and then back again quickly, as if she had been caught doing something wrong. "I couldn't leave."

"You had to change in the hospital?" he asked holding back a smirk.

"Is it that obvious?" she asked adjusting the hem of her dress unnecessarily.

"Only because you don't look like you do at the Club," he murmured under his breath.

"All the better," Parker responded quickly before ducking her head to show that the conversation was over.

Lexi was surprised to find that the remainder of the rehearsal dinner went off without a hitch. The delicious food came and went. The conversation at their table was light and refreshing without any of the biting remarks Lexi was fearful of being involved in. And after Parker and Ramsey's brief exchange, they acted as if they hardly knew each other. When a question was directed at the both of them, they answered it separately without their eyes cutting to each other or the easy banter that she had seen fall between them. On the outside, the evening seemed to be a rousing success, besides Lexi's momentary mental breakdown at the beginning of the night.

As the dessert dishes were whisked away, Bekah stood once more. "Now, I know it's mine and Jack's night tonight, but we wanted to give a special announcement," she said smiling down on him. "This is known to very few people, and we thought we would share it with our dearest friends and family, first and foremost."

For some reason, it was like Lexi could feel Bekah's eyes on her. She had no idea why. The room was dark with a spotlight on the front table. Why her eyes would find Lexi in this crowd of people when she spoke made no sense.

"Ramsey, do you mind coming up here?" Bekah asked. Ramsey stared forward at Bekah in confusion. His eyes narrowed, calculating what he could possibly have to do with any of this. "Come on," she sing-songed forcing her hand as the bride-to-be.

Ramsey stood slowly. There were too many other people that would cheer him onward if he didn't follow his sister's orders. "Of course." He nodded standing and walking toward hers. His head turned once and met Lexi's gaze. She had no idea what to expect in that moment. She was holding her breath unsure as to what Bekah had in mind.

"Now, you all know my dear brother," Bekah said a little too cheerfully. "He's been off running his own business and being a star." Lexi knew for a fact that him running his own business had never made his family think that he was a star. They all hated that he owned the clubs. "But we're thrilled to announce that he is finally coming home and taking on the position as Vice President for Bridges Enterprise's newest company."

Lexi's mouth dropped open in shock. She had heard not a single word of this. She had lived with him for two months. All of this had to have taken longer than the month she was gone to put together. Why hadn't he told her any of this? Was this was Lola had meant about Ramsey making it all up to her? Was this why Brad and Jason had been so secretive about him doing all of this for her?

She just couldn't understand. Ramsey hated the idea of working for his father…for the company. He had bucked the status quo for so long that she had no idea why he would possibly want to do this.

Bekah's voice cut off Lexi's train of thought. "I'm pleased to announce along with this new development that the new wing of the company is going to be a full-time medical wing, and to head up our medical center with my brother is none other than our own, Parker Mackenson. Parker, come up here!" Bekah shrieked excitedly.

20

JULY ONE MONTH EARLIER

It was easy to pretend like nothing had happened. Lexi's father ended up staying in the ICU for longer than anticipated, and she kept making the excuse that she had to be with him. No one would ever question her decision to stay in the hospital for extended periods of time.

She still went in to work, but she was distracted. Her earlier fervor for the company slackened. She was certain her bosses noted the change in her work ethic. And she knew it was a stupid risk on her part to let herself fall behind. She needed the job that she had; it paid well and she could tell they were leaving open a job for one of the interns in the fall. Up until that dreadful conversation with Parker, Lexi had been gunning for that job. But the program would be over soon and they would have to make their decisions either way.

She couldn't give them the truth. How could she tell her bosses that she was afraid she didn't know her boyfriend any longer? That wasn't something they even cared about.

So she gave them the same excuse that she was giving everyone else since it had happened. That her father's heart attack had really shaken her, and she was terrified his condition might worsen. The company had allowed her the time however reluctantly. But there wasn't much time left, and they were going to want her to complete the project she had been assigned. That had become her back up excuse, when it was brought up that she was spending too much time at the hospital.

Lexi knew Ramsey's schedule by heart now and found herself showing up at the apartment when she knew he wouldn't be there and leaving before he woke up the next morning. She couldn't help it. She knew that she should just ask him about what Parker had told him.

After all, Parker could have simply made the whole thing up. She had been friends with Bekah since birth, Lexi wouldn't put it past her to do something like that. But who was she kidding? Parker wasn't Bekah. As much as she wanted to hate her, Lexi couldn't. Parker had never done anything to her. If everything she had said was true, she had done her a huge favor.

Yet, Lexi couldn't seem to bring it up. She had been doing everything in her power to avoid her own boyfriend. It had been over a week, and she couldn't bring herself to ask the questions that she had lingering on her tongue. The last thing she wanted was for him to confirm the story or even worse for him to lie about it…again.

She had barely been sleeping between hospital visits, work, and trying to avoid seeing her boyfriend. When she trudged down the stairs the next morning, she knew that the only way she would survive the day was a pot of coffee, a large pot of black coffee. Lexi poured herself a mug and leaned forward against the counter as she drank. She wore a light grey skirt suit with her hair pulled up into a tight ponytail. She had to be in to work soon to finish her research for the project.

Lexi closed her eyes and hung her head. She hadn't been sleeping and the hours were beginning to catch up with her. She could feel her body beginning to give into sleep while standing. The coffee was having next to no effect on her so far, and all she wanted to do was crawl back into bed for another couple hours.

"Tired?" Ramsey asked as he descended the stairs.

Lexi spun around quickly sloshing a bit of the coffee down her front. "Damnit!" she cried pulling her jacket off and tossing it onto the table. Luckily, her blouse was untouched.

"Sorry, I didn't mean to surprise you," he said with a smile. "You've been getting up so early I haven't had a chance to see you. I thought I'd catch you before you left."

"Oh," was all she managed as she wet a towel and tried to salvage her outfit for the day. After a second of dabbing at the fabric, she decided it was a lost cause and would have to take it to the dry cleaner later.

"Coffee?" he asked walking up to her and pouring himself a mug.

"Yeah," she mumbled sitting down on one of the dining room chairs.

Ramsey added some cream and sugar to the coffee before taking a sip. "I still don't know how you drink it black."

Lexi shrugged. "That's how I like it."

"So, I was thinking," Ramsey began, setting his coffee down on the counter and turning to face her again. "I know you're busy with work stuff, but I thought maybe we should go do something tonight. You haven't really had any time to yourself. I thought it might be nice to get away."

"Don't you have work?" she squeaked out, dropping her eyes to her coffee mug.

"I can take a night off for you," he said smiling.

"I guess, let me see how far I get with my work today, and then I'll let you know," she said reluctantly never pulling her eyes from her drink.

"Are you okay?" Ramsey asked moving to stand in front of her. "I know that you're sad about your dad but everything is going to be alright with him. He was released, right?"

"Yeah, he was," she said. She desperately wanted to tell him about what Parker had said, but she didn't know how to bring it up. All she wanted to do was go back upstairs, crawl into bed, and forget that this past week had happened.

"Maybe it would be a good idea to get away," he said bending down and resting his hands on her knees.

Lexi stood up abruptly letting his hands drop back to his side as she towered over him in his crouched position. "I'll see about work," she said sharper than she had intended.

Ramsey stood slowly watching her closely. "Alright," he said his eyes following her every movement. "How about this? I'll be at the club in my office, if you want to go out after work just swing by."

"I'll do that," she agreed diverting her eyes as she moved to walk away from him.

Ramsey's hand darted out and grasped her by the elbow. The light pressure on her arm sent shivers up her back. "Please come by," he whispered softly, pulling her into him and kissing her softly on the lips. "I've missed you."

Lexi pulled away from the kiss, still feeling the warmth of his mouth on hers. She took another step away from him, gave him a curt smile, and disappeared back up the stairs to change into an outfit that didn't have coffee stains on it.

*****

Work was practically mind numbing that day. She knew that she had to go see Ramsey afterwards, and she knew she couldn't hide what had happened from him for much longer. This morning had been the first time they had really been alone. She couldn't imagine what it would be like going out with him. She couldn't convince someone like Ramsey, who noticed her every move, that the only thing that was bothering her was her father's heart attack.

He would know that something else was up with her. She would have to tell him what Parker had told her. Then she would have to get the truth out of him. She wasn't sure if she was ready for that. What would he say? Would he confirm all her fears or deny them? She didn't even want to think about it. And so, of course, she thought of nothing else.

The whole time she was conducting research for her firm, making phone calls, and digging through files, she was distracted. Her mind was lost on the words that Parker had embedded into her skull forever. Ramsey had lied. She could care less that all of that stuff had happened in the past. The past was the past. If anyone should know that, it was Lexi.

She had a past that she knew she couldn't hide. Everything always seemed to catch up with her. Why should Ramsey be any different? How could he think that he was any different?

What did he think he could gain from hiding it from her? His friends knew the situation. They knew that they had been together…for years. They knew that they had been in love. They knew that they were practically destined for one another. And Christ, they at least knew that Lexi looked like Parker. Yet, she was never mentioned. She was never brought up. He acted as if nothing had ever happened between them beyond the physical. No wonder he had freaked out when she had been left alone with Jessie and she had said that Parker and Ramsey looked like a cute couple.

Of course they did! They had been a couple for so long that it was second nature to them. She knew it did for her and Jack. Being with him was like breathing. You didn't just date someone for so long and then try and cover up the fact that it ever existed. People didn't get over things like that. If anything, the cover up made it seem like you *never* got over it…which was even more troublesome.

Just when Lexi thought her brain might explode from over thinking everything, she received an incoming text message. *"Lunch. Sushi. You know the place. See ya in 20. – Pookie."*

Lexi sighed, dropping the stack of papers she was holding onto her tiny desk. She grabbed her purse and left the office, letting her manager know that she would be back in an hour. The balding middle age man leered at her as she exited the office giving no complaint. At least she had that going for her.

Entering the crowded restaurant, Lexi searched the premises for Brandon. It was nearly impossible to find a table at this place, but Brandon always seemed to find them a spot. She didn't ask how that was even possible. Finally seeing him crammed into a corner, Lexi strolled across the room and plopped down opposite him.

"Hey honey, you're looking a little rough," he said not too kindly.

Lexi scoffed, pushing a loose strand of hair behind her ear. "Fuck off."

"No, really. Have you slept at all?" he asked leaning back in the booth.

Lexi took a sip of the water he ordered for her and shook her head. "Not really. Did you already order?"

"Yeah, same thing, right?" he asked. She nodded. "Cool. So, what's up? You haven't been dogging me for lunch, or interrupting my make out sessions, or any of your other annoying habits. I've barely heard from you. Who am I supposed to have lunch with?"

"Weren't you just complaining about me having lunch with you too often?" she asked, feeling her annoyance from the past week and a half begin to take over.

"Yeah, but I was joking. You know I want to get in your pants. Lunch is just a way to be around you," he told her with a wink for good measure.

Lexi didn't even have the patience to humor him. "Whatever, Brandon."

"Brandon? Did you just call me by my first name?" he asked his brows scrunching together. "Lexi, what's wrong with you?"

"I don't want to talk about it, alright?" she snapped fiercely as the waitress walked up.

"Uh, sorry," the waitress squeaked before scurrying away.

Brandon tilted his head at her slightly. "Now you've run our waitress off."

"I don't care. I'm not that hungry anyway," she mumbled though she felt pretty bad about having an outburst like that. It wasn't like it was Brandon's fault that she was in a pissy mood.

"So are you going to make me guess what set you off, or are you just going to tell me?" he asked crossing his arms on the table and leaning forward.

Lexi sighed heavily. "Why doesn't Ramsey like you?" she asked taking him off guard.

"You're upset because Ramsey and I don't get along?" he asked with a smirk.

"No. I want to know why. You never told me what the reason was."

"That's because you have a perfect little picture of your boyfriend in your head. I didn't want to ruin it for you," he said as a matter of fact.

"What if I don't have such a perfect picture anymore?" she whispered, looking down at the table cloth.

Brandon's smile spread at that statement. "I did warn you from the beginning."

"Tell me why you're not friends anymore," she spat, looking back up at him.

Brandon seemed to realize that she was being serious about the situation. "I dated Parker for awhile after they broke up. If that didn't make things bad enough, she told me some things about him that made my head spin. When I confronted him about it, we ended up in a fist fight. If his roommates hadn't been around to stop him, I think he would have fought until he had no more fight left in him," Brandon told her watching her expression carefully.

"Did he hurt you?" she asked, her emotions from the last week overpowering her as tears brimmed her eyes. The thought of Ramsey hurting Brandon, because he was dating his ex-girlfriend and had confronted him with the truth broke her heart. Who was the man that she had been dating for the last year?

"I had a few broken ribs. He would have killed me if Brad and Jason hadn't been there to pull him off of me. I don't like to admit that, but the guy is much bigger than I am," Brandon said, with chuckle at the end.

"Oh, Brandon," Lexi murmured softly, "why didn't you tell me?"

"You wouldn't have believed me," he said with a snort of disbelief. "You just met me. You had no idea who I was, and you had no idea who you were dating. I wasn't going to destroy your world."

"But you will now?" she asked, looking into his big brown eyes for an answer.

"Honey, it looks like someone else already has," he said reaching across the table and grasping her hand.

Lexi looked down into her water glass and tried to hold the tears in. He was right, of course. Parker had already destroyed the image that she had of her boyfriend. Sure, she hadn't liked where he worked or that he was surrounded by strippers all the time. She hadn't liked the distance. She didn't like that he had a reputation as a player or that he had slept with a lot of people before they were together. But she could get over those things, because she had known about them. They were a fact of their relationship.

Those things hadn't ruined her view of him. He had taken awhile to tell her what he did for a living, but it was kind of understandable. Most women would not be comfortable leaving their man in the hands of other women, whether he ran the place or not. But at least he had come clean. What Parker had told her…what Brandon had revealed were things Ramsey never planned on telling her.

That much was obvious. He was liar. He had looked straight in her eyes and said that he had never been in love, never had a serious girlfriend. Had he never expected to be confronted with Parker again? Or had Lexi been temporary? She didn't even know what to believe.

"What did Parker tell you that made your head spin?" Lexi finally asked him.

"Judging by your appearance, I think you already know the answer to that," he said eyeing her sheepishly. "I would have told you Lexi, but it wasn't my story to tell."

"I know. I don't blame you. But what did she say?" Lexi asked. "I have to know."

He sighed, clearly hating the position that he was in. "The gist of it is that he knocked her up when they were in college, and before he knew that she was pregnant, she walked in on him cheating on her with some other girls. Or something like that. Then when she told him later that she miscarried, he refused to believe her and called her a slut." Lexi gasped out loud and covered her mouth quickly. She hadn't intended to get so emotional, but hearing confirmation of Parker's story made it all so much more real. "Lexi, I'm sorry. I really…I don't know what to say."

Lexi shook her head, silencing him. "No. Thank you for telling me," she told him. "I guess I needed to hear it from someone else."

"You know, maybe he has changed," Brandon said trying to be reassuring. Though it sounded strange coming from him of all people. He had never really said a nice thing about Ramsey since they had started hanging out.

"Don't lie to me," Lexi said pulling her hand gently out of his. "I've had enough of that lately."

"It's true. I don't think he's changed," he said, "but that's up to you to decide."

"Thanks Brandon…pookie," she said with a sad smile. She stood from the booth. "I'm suddenly not hungry. Sorry to leave you hanging on lunch again."

"It's alright," he said standing as well. He pulled her into a hug and kissed the top of her head. "Let me know if you need me."

"Bye," she said taking a step towards the door.

"Hey honey," he called back. She spun around to look at him. "I'm serious. I'm here for you." She nodded solemnly and then strode out of the restaurant.

Driving to the club was a blur. She knew that at some point she called her boss and told him that she wasn't feeling well. He hadn't been pleased, but she was pretty sure she sounded convincingly sick since she felt like vomiting already. He had let her off the hook, as long as she promised to make up the hours if she was feeling better in the morning. Her final project was due Friday, the last day of the summer associate position, regardless.

She also knew that her car had driven her to the mostly empty parking lot of the club. She wouldn't say that she had driven herself there exactly. It was more like the car was on auto pilot, and she was along for the ride. Her body felt numb to the realities of the universe around her.

All she knew was that she had to talk to Ramsey, and she had to talk to him now. Waiting around for over a week had been a terrible mistake. All her emotions were like a shaken up bottle of coke ready to explode once opened. The confirmation of the facts from Brandon had solidified her determination, which she had been lacking before. She hadn't been able to face him, because she wasn't sure if she could believe Parker's tale. Even though Lexi knew it was impossible to truly fake the kind of emotions Parker displayed, she still hadn't wanted to believe her. Then Brandon had said, albeit in a more concise fashion, the exact same story. Now she knew she had to talk to him. Although it didn't mean that she was dreading it any less.

She wished, not for the first or last time that summer that Chyna was still in the country. She would know what to do and say in that moment. She would know how to calm Lexi down and how to approach the situation. But she didn't have her best friend there for her now. She still had a couple weeks before she returned from Milan. So Lexi was on her own, and would have to face down her demons alone.

Taking a deep breath, Lexi punched in the code to the back entrance that Ramsey had given her and stepped through the large black door. She trudged down the long hallway and stood in front of his closed office door. Staring at the big door for awhile didn't give her any more motivation to push through it. She knew she needed answers, but her stomach was in knots at the prospect of what was to come. Pushing back her hair a few times to calm her nerves, Lexi knocked twice and then opened the door to Ramsey's office.

Ramsey turned around sharply at the interruption. His eyes were narrowed and he looked furious at the distraction until he realized who was standing before him. "Lexi!" he said, jumping to his feet. "What a surprise! I didn't think you would be here until after work."

"Honestly, I hadn't planned on coming at all," she told him, stepping into the room and pushing the heavy door closed behind her.

Her hands were shaking at her sides, the black circles under her eyes were more pronounced, and she couldn't stop biting her bottom lip. "Why not? What's wrong?"

Lexi's eyes dropped to the floor. "I need to talk to you."

"Are you breaking up with me?" he whispered into the room. Those words alone sounded like heartbreak coming out of his mouth. It was almost too much for Lexi to bear to hear.

"No," she said quickly. "Well, I don't know."

"What do you mean you don't know?" he asked sitting down heavily on the corner of his desk. "Tell me what's wrong. How could you not know something like that?"

"It…it all depends on how you answer my next question," she whispered letting her eyes drag upwards and meet his very confused green-gold eyes.

"I'll answer anything," he said desperately.

Lexi took a deep breath to calm her hammering heart. "What is your relationship with Parker?"

"What?" he asked, standing at the mention of Parker's name.

"You heard me," Lexi whispered.

"Parker?" Lexi nodded. "We've already had this discussion. I told you over spring break what my relationship is with Parker."

"Let me rephrase. What *was* your relationship with Parker?" she asked directing his attention to the past tense.

Ramsey ran his hand back through his hair and a small blush crept up onto his cheeks. "What are you driving at, Lexi?"

"Just the truth. That's all I want," she told him resting her hands against the chair in front of her to steady herself.

"The truth?" he asked hesitantly. "We slept together. I told you that, but there's nothing going on between us now. I promise."

Lexi hung her head. "I believe you. I don't think anything is going on now."

"Then what's the problem?" he asked moving towards her and grabbing her hands from the top of the chair. "I'm not cheating on you, Lexi, if that's what you think."

"I didn't accuse you of cheating me," she said angrily, pulling her hands from his.

"Alright," he said miffed. "What are you accusing me of?" He threw his hands up in the air and walked back to his desk.

"Isn't it quite obvious?" she demanded.

"If it was, wouldn't I have already guessed it."

"You're lying to me!" she yelled, more forcefully than she had even realized she was going to say it. She had bottled all of her emotions up so much that she could feel everything begin to explode out of her. She was furious with him. How dare he stand there and even try and tell her that nothing happened with Parker…that they had just slept together. It was obvious to everyone that there had been something more, and now she had been told by two people that was the case…three, if she included Jessie. He didn't even have the balls to tell her the truth about it.

"What am I lying about?" he asked her, snapping his head around to look at her.

"You and Parker dated! You were together for years—high school and college sweethearts. You were in love with her. You were going to marry her," Lexi said letting the truth spill out of her. Ramsey remained silent waiting for whatever else she was going to say. "Parker told me herself. How could you think that you could keep that from me? All of that time you've told me that you never dated anyone, that you never loved anyone, but it was all a lie. I'm not special to you. *She* was special to you.

"You couldn't even tell me that to my face. You had to hide it. I don't know why you thought I wouldn't find out. Don't you have anything to say for yourself?"

Ramsey hung his head, his breathing coming out in short bursts. "She told you all of this?" he demanded.

"Yes, she did."

"I can't believe she would do that," he murmured.

"Why?" Lexi gasped. "You can't believe she would tell the truth? Did you date her for that long?" Lexi waited for an answer. "Well?"

"Yes," he mumbled.

"Were you in love with her?"

"Yes."

"Do you still love her?"

Ramsey's head shot back up to look at her. "No. I love you, Lexi. I told you that."

"How can I know that?" she asked angrily, openly glaring at him.

"Lexi, I do love you. You have to believe me about that at least," he told her.

She couldn't really argue that point. It wasn't what she was angry about anyway. "But why would you lie about everything else? Why lie about her? Don't you think I could have gotten over all of this, if you had just told me?" she begged the question.

"I don't tell anyone that story, Lexi," he said in frustration, though it sounded like a lame attempt to save himself.

"I'm not just anyone," she spat back angrily.

"I know that. It's a stupid habit. I don't talk about it. She doesn't talk about it. It's like it never happened," he said awkwardly.

"But it did happen. It did!" she yelled back at him, feeling her emotions break again. "You're a liar. You just lie all the time. You lied about Parker, about having a girlfriend, about being in love…the beach house…everything. How can I ever trust you again? Can I ever really know if everything else coming out of your mouth isn't a lie? I trusted you with my whole heart. I can honestly say that I've never done that before."

"Jack…" he murmured before being cut off with a sinister glare.

"I had known Jack only a month or two before realizing that I could never fully trust him. I hadn't given him my heart at that point, and I hadn't fallen in love with him. None of this I hid from you. What would be the point of hiding it from you? You would find out, sooner or later, the history between us," she growled. "Did you never think I'd hear the real story from anyone about Parker? And I mean the real story, Ramsey."

"What do you mean the real story?" he asked, his eyes narrowing at the connotations behind the statement.

"Oh, don't give me that," Lexi said rolling her eyes. "You know what you did."

Ramsey strode back over to Lexi and slammed his hands down on the chair in front of her. "What else did she tell you?" he growled.

"Why are you getting so worked up?" Lexi asked eyeing him carefully. He had been so controlled before, but now he really looked angry that there was more to the story. She couldn't believe that after everything she had just said that he couldn't even own up to the rest of it.

"Because she told you more than that, and I want to know what else she said."

"She told me everything," Lexi informed him. "She told me how she was sick and instead of taking care of her, you were whoring around with other women. She told me that she was pregnant. She told me that she miscarried the baby. She told me that she came to see you and you were horrible to her. She told me that you yelled and screamed at her and called her all of these terrible things. Then when you realized how wrong you were, you tried to crawl back to her, but you had done too much damage. Is that what you were planning to do to me? Or were you just going to lie about it?" Lexi asked, being purposefully mean.

"She told you that she miscarried?" he asked, grunting angrily. It's like he hadn't even heard the rest of the things that she had said. It was as if he had stopped listening after that one word. His nostrils were flared and his face was beat red with anger. Lexi had never seen him this furious. Even that one time on New Years when he had completely lost his temper, he had never looked like this. "Of course, she would tell her side that way."

"What are you getting at Ramsey?" she asked, her pent up anger so forceful she could practically see red spots in front of her eyes.

"She had an abortion!" he cried unable to hold back. "You think she had a miscarriage? She was nineteen years old. Her family has money. My family has money. It was a stupid accident that should have never happened, so she got rid of it. The likelihood of her really having a miscarriage is slim to none. It doesn't make any sense."

"Well, she hadn't gone to a doctor," Lexi said repeating what Parker had told her. "That's the most likely cause of a miscarriage after the first eight to ten weeks." Lexi had done her research after leaving the hospital.

"Don't let that girl fool you," he grumbled. "She had a life and a future ahead of her, and a baby never fit in with that especially after she walked out on me. So she got rid of it," he told her fiercely.

Lexi sank back into the chair, taking in everything Ramsey had told her. She didn't even know what to think. Could Parker have lied about the miscarriage? She knew it was possible and that many women got abortions, but she couldn't even think about it. She didn't care what another woman did with her own body, but the thought of doing that to herself…Lexi shuddered. She wasn't sure she would have the strength for it, to actually put herself through it. Could Parker have had that strength? Lexi just didn't know. She didn't even want to think about it. There were too many sides to this one story. How could she ever decipher what had really happened between them?

And in the end did it really matter to Lexi? Whatever Parker had done with her body was part of their past. It was not Lexi's past. All she cared about was the fact that he had lied...that he had hid an entire relationship from her. That he had expected her never to find out.

"Look, I don't care about that. What I care about is you lying to me," she told him.

"I'm sorry, Lexi. I don't have an excuse. It was just...what I always did," he told her some of his anger leaving his body.

Lexi sat there for a minute longer, trying to collect her thoughts. She was still angry. There was something more that she needed to say. She wasn't sure how to articulate it to him. After a second she finally gasped out, "Am I just making up for all your mistakes with Parker?"

"What?" he breathed sitting across from her and staring up through his sad eyes.

"Is this what this is all about? You found someone who looked like her and thought you could recreate your past...fix all of the horrible things that you did?" she asked, hating that these thoughts were even passing through her mind. But she needed to ask him. She needed these things out in the open.

"Lexi, no," he whispered earnestly into the darkness. "You are nothing like that."

"Then what was I?" she challenged. "You can't deny that we look alike. My *mother* even said that we look alike."

"I know you look alike," he responded softly.

"Then that's it. You saw me at the club and wanted to fuck me because I looked like your ex-girlfriend," she said the words so matter of fact that she actually believed what she was saying. What kind of person could possibly sink so low?

Ramsey sighed heavily. Maybe he was finally seeing for the first time what a terrible thing he had done in keeping a secret from her. "Yes."

"What?" Lexi snapped facing him wearily.

"That night at the club...that was my intention," he told her honestly. "I wanted to sleep with you because you looked like her because even then, years later, I still missed her."

Lexi's mouth hung open at the admission. She hadn't thought that he would really say it out loud to her. She had hated herself endlessly for the suspicions that Ramsey had only gotten with her, because she looked like his old fling. Hearing the words out of his mouth though was a thousand times worse.

"That's why you said you knew me again at the Country Club," she filled in.

"Of course, I would recognize you anywhere," he mumbled. He looked like he felt entirely worthless.

"And that's why you pursued me."

"Initially," he said barely audible, "but you were more than that."

"Of course," she said, shaking her head and tucking a lock of hair behind her ear. "You're disgusting."

"Lexi, please," he begged, reaching out for her. She shook him off and wandered over to the window to stare out in horror.

"You are so much different than Parker. Besides your looks, you two are nothing alike," he said trying to reassure her. "You made me forget her. You made me able to move on."

"How can I believe you?" she asked her tone dead, lifeless.

"Our relationship is real whether you choose to believe it or not," he intoned. "I did and still do love you as much as when I first told you that night at the beach. You are the only woman I could think of being with from now until eternity. Please try and believe me when I say it."

Lexi shook her head again forlornly. She was having trouble believing anything anyone was telling her. First was Parker with her sad tale of loss of both Ramsey and their unborn child. Now, the tale twisted on its head and gruesome stories of an abortion. Neither side could possibly have the whole truth. There might be glimpses of it, but reality was different to different people. No one story held the truth about everything, and she knew all too well that listening too intently to either one was a misgiving on her part. Both likely believed their story and would carry the truth to their grave, but that didn't mean that either story was what had actually happened. This only made her own decisions about Ramsey more difficult.

"Ramsey, I just…" Lexi began, turning to face him as the door burst open.

"Ramsey, I really need to talk to you," Parker cried, panting a little as if she had just sprinted down the hallway. She was still in scrubs like she had come straight from the hospital.

He stood shakily and stared between the two women in his office. "About what you told Lexi?" he growled.

Parker's lips parted as she realized she had just walked in on Lexi and Ramsey. She nodded. "Uh, yeah…I told her."

21

PRESENT

"Now you all know my dear brother," Bekah said a little too cheerfully. "He's been off running his own business and being a star. But we're thrilled to announce that he is finally coming home and taking on as the position as vice president for Bridges Enterprise's newest company." After a short pause, she continued, "I'm pleased to announce along with this new development that the new wing of the company is going to be a full-time medical wing, and to head up our medical center with my brother is none other than our own, Parker Mackenson. Parker, come up here!" Bekah shrieked excitedly.

Lexi sat completely still. She wasn't even sure if she was breathing properly. She watched as Parker eased out of her own chair. She glanced in Lexi's direction and gave her a sympathetic look. Lexi didn't even know what that could mean. Clearly they had been planning this whole thing from the beginning. How could Parker feel any sympathy for what she had done?

A round of applause followed the newest development for Bridges Enterprise. Lexi had always thought that Ramsey had no desire to be affiliated with the company that his father ran. He had made it clear that what he wanted in life didn't have to come from the wealth that he had grown up with. The reason that he owned the night clubs, the bars, and even the strip clubs; the reason that he stayed out late at work every night, the reason that he put so much effort into doing something completely against his upbringing was because he never wanted to be a part of his family's lifestyle.

He was his own man. He had his own dreams and aspirations. He may look the picture perfect boy that she had met a year ago at the Country Club, but he was so much more. He was defiant. He was strong willed and hard working. He didn't *need* them. And that's what really ate them up. Ramsey did fine all on his own. He made a living. He owned his own townhouse. He owned his own beach house and the cars and all the glitz. This was all his in his own right. His family couldn't hold it over his head that they were supporting him. They couldn't make him feel bad for giving him a job and owing his livelihood to them. He was a Bridges Man at heart, but he had never been able to be controlled by them. Their money, their prestige, it wasn't *him*.

He had scorned every push and shove from them to join the company. He had a trust fund with so many digits that it made Lexi's head spin, and yet he hadn't used it! He chose to do his own thing and to start his own business. And yet, here he was standing in front of his bitch sister as she proudly announced the prodigal son's return to their empire.

This couldn't be his decision. This was not Ramsey, not the Ramsey she knew at least. He couldn't have changed this much in one short month. She still thought she knew who he was…or at least the man that she had gotten to know in the last year. This must have been going on for much longer than this. No way would their father have allowed Bekah to make such a momentous announcement if things hadn't been in some form of finalization.

How had the news media not latched onto this yet? It really must have been brand new. Otherwise this would have been everywhere. She would have already heard about it. The Bridges name was as commonplace in New York, as in Atlanta, especially if you were listening for it. She certainly would have seen a copy of the Wall Street Journal or the New York Times with a spread about the Atlanta native family broadening its horizons. Yet this was happening without it ever being leaked.

If this was happening, then how had Ramsey gotten involved? What was he going to do with the clubs? She never really approved of the clubs, but right now everything, anything was looking better than working side by side with his repugnant family and…that *woman*.

That thought really made her eyes narrow. Who had put this thought into his head? There was no way that his father had actually worn him down. Ramsey had been arguing his case against his father for fifteen years. Nothing could break him. He and his father simply butted heads. They were too different and also too similar in so many ways. He would never give in if he thought that it was what his father wanted. Defiance kept him strong in a way. Lexi knew it even if he couldn't openly admit it to himself. Being the one who broke away from his family gave him power that he had never been able to have when he was under their regiment.

Bekah, maybe? She couldn't see him giving into her either. He loved his sister. That much was obvious. They were two peas in a pod. They had grown up close and after everything with Parker, they had only stayed that way. But even her eternal nagging wouldn't be enough to bring him back.

That left the woman who had just made her way to stand next to him. She watched Parker fidget at the onslaught of attention directed her way. Her smile didn't exactly reach her eyes, and she kept glancing in Ramsey's direction uncertainly. Lexi didn't know what they were saying to each other in that look, but she hated that they had the capability to talk to each other without uttering a word. She was jealous of it. She could admit that. Despite his lies, Lexi didn't want to see him with her. Her chest pinched at how easily everything had crumbled with the introduction of that woman.

Had Parker put him up to this? Had she been the cornerstone to this whole project? She was fresh out of med school, just finished up her residency and she thought that she could run a hospital? Lexi wanted to laugh at that. The girl was smart, but she wasn't a genius. She couldn't run a hospital alone.

Lexi clenched her jaw. No, she wouldn't be doing it alone. She would be doing it with Ramsey. Ramsey would be at her side. Ramsey would be the one that she would go to in her time of need. She would have him with her for everything. They would spend all their time together. She tried not to show her distaste at the thought, but she was sure it was shining through loud and clear.

This would be a perfect set up. Bekah and their father getting Ramsey back in the business. Bekah getting her best friend back with her brother. Parker and Ramsey actually ending up back together. It was almost too good of a ploy. Lexi didn't know how Ramsey couldn't see through it. He was too smart not to see what they were doing to him. They were deciding his life all over again. Everything he had done up until this point faded away into a distant memory, because they got him back. His past accomplishments would be nothing compared to opening and running the newest branch of Bridges Enterprise.

Lexi felt sick. She suddenly felt very sick. Her stomach grumbled and she quickly covered her mouth as the taste of bile rose in her throat. She swallowed hard and gulped down the water left over from dinner. Her ah-ha moment mere hours earlier crept into her mind, but she pushed it down. She couldn't do this. She needed to get away. She could face her problems tomorrow. She could face Ramsey tomorrow. Parker, Bekah, and Jack could all wait for her to not feel like she was going to vomit on them at any second.

She wasn't running away from her responsibilities…she was running away from the idiocy that was her life. How could a man that claimed to love her not tell her the truth about one fucking thing? How could he hold back something as important as a complete 180 degree career change, when she had been *living* with him at the time? There would be time later to face up to her responsibilities. She wanted answers, but she wasn't ready for them.

As discreetly as she could manage, Lexi pushed back her chair, walked around the outside of the circular tables, and slipped out the back entrance. Leaving the overcrowded room filled with expectations that made her dizzy. She breathed in the restaurant air and headed quickly for the bathroom. Lexi pushed open the door and quickly to the mirror. She stared forward at her reflection and sighed heavily. To a stranger she would appear all but flawless, but Lexi could tell that she was off. Her tan skin was too pale and if she looked too closely, had a tint of green. Her lips were pursed in distaste. Some small beading of sweat was splattered across her hair line and under her nose. She snatched a paper towel out of the dispenser and blotted her face dry. She wasn't any more satisfied with her reflection, but it didn't matter.

Taking a deep breath, she did the only thing that she could think of. She picked up her phone and dialed Chyna's number. The line was eerily quiet for a Friday night when Chyna answered. "Hey, chica," Chyna said happily into the phone. Lexi had no idea what was going on. Last she had checked, Chyna was out partying and drinking every weekend since she had returned from Milan. Lexi couldn't understand why she would be somewhere quiet already.

"Chyna, it's so good to talk to you," Lexi said, more exhausted and desperate than she had intended.

"Are you going to tell me what happened?" Chyna asked dreamily, seeming to read her mood. Lexi filled her in on the situation at hand. She told her about Jack doubting the wedding, about the bachelorette party, about Ramsey sleeping with Maddie, about him agreeing to this company with Parker. Chyna listened the whole time without a word. Lexi didn't know what to make of it. After she finished, Chyna sighed heavily. "You're determined to get yourself in trouble, aren't you?"

Lexi paused and actually thought about what her friend was saying. She kind of was determined to get herself in trouble. Why was she always in these miserable situations? Was it more her fault than anything? "I guess so."

"I knew this would happen," Chyna said with a dramatic sigh. "I told you not to go see him, not to go to this wedding."

"I know."

"You know, but you don't listen. You never listen, Alexa," she said exasperated.

Lexi knew she was right, but it didn't make it any easier to hear. "I guess."

"No, you know," Chyna chided her. "You know he's bad for you or at least that he lied to you on multiple occasions, just like you knew that Jack was a philandering ass. You let these guys use you up until there's so little of you left, I can't even find my best friend." Lexi nodded mournfully even though she knew that Chyna couldn't see her. "It's worse this time because you know better. Ramsey is not Jack, and yet you allowed him to do this to you all the same."

"I know, Chyna," Lexi said sadly. "I know I did."

"Now you can't walk away from it all. You put yourself in this position, and *you* are going to get yourself out of it. Do you love him?" she asked abruptly, throwing Lexi off guard.

"Yes," she answered without taking the second to think about it.

Chyna sighed again, but different this time. She seemed almost resigned to Lexi's inflexibility, to her determination when it came to men that were bad for her, men that she allowed to hurt her. "Then you can't run away from this, Alexa."

"I wasn't…"

"Yes, you were! Don't you dare lie to me!" Chyna said, barely raising her voice but somehow making it more commanding than Lexi had ever heard before. "You were calling me for a way out. Well, I don't have one. You need to talk to him! You need to get your answers. Just don't do it like you did with Jack last year."

"I wouldn't…it's not the same," Lexi said meekly.

"No, it's not," Chyna agreed willingly. "You're not infatuated with Ramsey. The element of obsession is out of the picture, which might be the best thing that could happen for you. If you really love him and not the way with Jack, where he infects your very being, then you need to clear the air. At least then you'll never have to wonder. You'll never have to think about what could have been."

Lexi knew she was right…hated to admit that she was right. She wanted to run. She wanted to high tail it in the opposite direction and not look back. The last thing she wanted to do was face down the man that she loved to find out once and for all, why he had done this to her. Why he continued to lie to her. Why he continued to put her second best in his life. She wanted to be the strong confident woman that she knew she could be, but the thought of confronting all of her fears left her frantic.

"I can practically hear your brain working over the line. What are you going to do?" Chyna asked.

Lexi sighed, circling the rather clean bathroom. She knew what she wanted to do. She wanted to fly back to New York and binge on chocolate chip cookie dough ice cream with her best friend for the next couple days. But she also knew what she needed to do. She needed to stay and see this thing out. Wasn't that the whole reason she had gone through all this mess this week to begin with?

It wasn't going to be like the time with Jack. She couldn't possibly imagine Ramsey doing anything as terrible as proposing to Parker or something equally as ridiculous. She didn't trust Parker. She didn't particularly like for them to be together, but Lexi didn't think they were at that stage. If there were any more secrets that she didn't know about, she wasn't sure how she would be able to handle it. But she knew now that she had to handle it.

"I'm going to stay," Lexi said with a note of finality in her decision.

Chyna let out a deep breath. "Thank God. I don't have to cancel the airlines tickets."

Lexi laughed at that statement. This was the first Lexi had heard about her having airline tickets. "Where are you going?"

"Atlanta, silly. You thought I was going to make you go through that wedding alone?" Chyna asked as if this was the most ridiculous thing she had ever considered.

"You're coming here?" Lexi asked loving how well her best friend knew her.

"Yes, well, I guess I should tell you the news," Chyna said almost hesitantly. Lexi waited anxiously for Chyna to explain. "Adam and I are talking again," she almost whispered.

Lexi's stomach dropped straight out of her body. She gulped hard taken off guard by the sudden revelation from her friend. Chyna and Adam had decided to break it off once she had gone to Milan, and Lexi had more or less thought it was over between them. Chyna clearly still had a thing for him even if she hadn't admitted it, but she hadn't thought they had been seeing each other since she had been back. Chyna had been back to her old self of partying and random hook ups every couple nights. "Re…really?" she stammered out. "When…uh, when did you guys start talking again?"

"I guess when you left," Chyna said and Lexi could hear the smile in her voice.

"Oh…uh, that's great Chyna. I kind of thought that you and Adam were done."

"Me too. He'd been kind of aloof since we took our break, but this week has been better. He's coming to Atlanta with me actually. Oh, and he said something about needing to talk to you."

Lexi gulped. "Did he mention what it was about?"

"I don't remember," she said, waving away the statement. "Didn't seem that important at the time."

"I'm sure it's nothing," she murmured into the phone, thankful that Chyna wasn't listening too clearly to her tone.

"Well, we'll be in tomorrow before the wedding. Call me and let me know how things go with Ramsey. Love ya, chica," she said before ending the call.

Lexi leaned back against the cold marble counter top and allowed her vision to go hazy and her breathing to slow. That conversation had done less to prepare her for her conversation with Ramsey than she had thought. It suddenly felt like everything was starting to catch up with her. She hadn't wanted to think about anything else when she was mentally preparing herself to deal with Ramsey. Yet here she was lost in her own world. She had so much going through her mind that she would have to steel herself for what was about to happen over the next day.

The door creaked open and an elderly woman walked in. She waddled over to a stall keeping her eyes downcast, as if she didn't want to know why Lexi could possibly be leaning against the counter, glassy-eyed, and unmoving. Lexi was sort of grateful that social propriety dictated that people stay out of each other's business. The woman washed her hands and made a hasty exit. As the door was swinging closed, Lexi heard a voice that she had been anticipating.

"Yes a woman in the restroom fits that description," the woman said in a high-pitched voice as she teetered past Ramsey.

Lexi took a deep breath before following the woman out of the room. "I'm right here." She was surprised to find that her voice was calm and strong. "We need to talk," she said arching one eyebrow at Ramsey as he stood in front of the bathroom door. She nearly smiled at the irony of seeing him in front of a bathroom since their first "real" meeting had been in the same location.

He ran his hand back through his hair and looked down at her sheepishly. "Yeah, we do. Can we go somewhere?" he breathed out.

"Where?" she asked staring up into his face. She could tell that he was worried about how this conversation was going to affect their relationship. She wondered if he had noticed her slip out the back immediately, or if it had taken a minute to notice her departure. She hadn't been able to take her eyes off of him and Parker standing so comfortably next to each other, but she had no way of knowing his reaction or his thoughts. She had no idea what he was thinking about at all.

"My place," he said immediately. "I want to get out of here."

"Should we bring Parker along to verify your story?" she asked maliciously. She couldn't help herself. She couldn't hold it back. Who knew if, when they got back to his place, he was even going to tell her the truth? Could she trust that he wasn't going to lie to make himself look good or to hide what actually happened? He had done that before. Clearly, he had done it sometime recently to keep her from knowing about this job.

"No, we don't need Parker to have a legitimate conversation. I've been wanting to talk to you all week, but you kept postponing this moment. And I had no idea Bekah…" he paused midsentence and released a sigh. "You know what? Let's talk about this at my place. I'll pull the car around," he said with a note of finality and walked towards the door without looking to see if she was following.

She was a little surprised that he was so determined to talk to her about this. She had been avoiding the much needed conversation.

Lexi glanced back at the rehearsal dinner. Someone had left one of the doors propped open and she could see people milling around inside, talking, and carrying on. Parker's body appeared at the entrance and somehow even though the room was dim, Parker turned and looked her full on in the face. There was that damn sympathetic look again. Lexi couldn't place why she kept getting that look from Parker. She was part of the reason that Lexi was in this mess to begin with. There should be no sympathy from her. Yet there she was, her head lightly cocked to the side, eyes open wide, brows slightly furrowed, mouth popped open, and wearing that expression like she felt every ounce of Lexi's pain.

Shaking off the similarities between them, Lexi turned from Parker and sauntered across the busy restaurant, out the door, and to Ramsey waiting patiently in his Mercedes. The drive back to his place was surprisingly short even with the dead quiet in the car. Lexi took a seat on his comfortable leather sofa when they arrived back at his place, waited for him to take a seat in an opposing chair, and then stared intently into his face.

"Are you going to tell me about this new business venture?" she questioned him, clasping her hands together to keep from tucking her hair behind her ear habitually.

"I...yeah," he said leaning forward in the chair and resting his elbows on his knees. "I don't know where to start."

"How about from the beginning? Or with the truth," she muttered, her gaze piercing through him.

"The truth, right," he said nodding to himself. "Well, the medical wing of Bridges Enterprise has been something that I've been hearing about since I was in diapers."

Lexi's eyes narrowed suspiciously. "Since you were a kid?"

"Yes," he told her. "It's my father's dream. It's the one thing he's always wanted to do with the company, but has never been able to." He paused before continuing.

"He seems to be getting his wish now, doesn't he?"

"Let me tell the whole story," he cut in quickly. Lexi sat back further against the couch and waited. "My grandfather had four daughters and one son, and all he wanted was boys. It was really hushed up, but he left his daughters with nothing when he died. He gave them a small sum to live on, but my grandfather was old school," Ramsey grumbled. "He thought that a woman's worth came from her husband, and once she had a husband, she was no longer her father's *problem*," he said the word like it was the most disgustingly archaic thing he had ever discussed. Lexi listened, absorbed, unsure of how this all fit together.

"Anyway, my father inherited practically everything including the business, and it's been his obsession ever since. In his eyes, he is still the son struggling to please his father by building up the business. And I swore I would never be like that."

"But you are now," Lexi mumbled under her breath.

"I...God, I hope not," he said his green-gold eyes staring deeply into her own. She fidgeted and looked away from his penetrating gaze.

"What do you mean? You're the new Vice President, right?" she reminded him

"Yeah...no...yeah," he said arguing more with himself than anything.

"Then what are you doing? You said you didn't want to be like your father, yet here you are doing everything he's ever wanted you to do. You don't even want to do this," Lexi couldn't help stammering out.

"I'm going to try to answer all your questions, but let me back up first," he said running hand through his hair again. "From the beginning, right?"

Lexi nodded slowly. She couldn't believe how uncomfortable and worried he looked. She had never really seen him quite like this. She knew that he wasn't a hundred percent confident about everything, but sometimes it felt like that. He exuded so much self-confidence that to find him in an uncomfortable state felt foreign to Lexi. It must have felt just as foreign to him by the way he kept readjusting his posture and pushing his hand through his short blonde hair.

"The medical wing was what he always thought would be the next best thing for the company," Ramsey began. "It made the company a full-service industry: lawyers, accountants, and doctors all under the same roof...metaphorically speaking. I thought he would just forget about it eventually, but it seemed to be something that faded with time and then rekindled almost without notice. I can't even tell you how many Club meetings I attended where my father discussed this newest project with anyone who would listen. I've actually heard some of his closest friends talking about how that project was never getting off the ground. It was hugely embarrassing." A blush crept up on his tan face as he recounted the incident.

"When Parker told my father she was pre-med for the first time, I saw that light in his eyes that I'd seen before. And I was right. He badgered me about the new medical wing, that I was pretty certain would never exist, for the next couple years."

"But it is going to exist," Lexi said.

"Yes," he said nodding.

"And with Parker?" she asked, her brown eyes looking up at him sadly.

"Yes, but not for Parker."

Lexi shook her head side to side. "Then who is it for, because she's one of the few I can think that are benefiting from this."

"You," he said quickly. "It's for you."

"Me?" she asked a giggle escaping her. "Oh Ramsey, you must be deluded to think that this is for me."

"Lexi, it is for you. I'm working to make things better for you," he said earnestly.

"How?" she demanded, standing. "By giving up the things you love? By making yourself miserable? By being Daddy's prodigal son? By working side by side with Parker every day? I'm sorry Ramsey, but these things don't make me happy. And you know what? You would know all of that if you had just bothered to ask me, if you had bothered to include me in your plans."

"I know. I know. I should have included you, but I wasn't sure this was ever going to actually happen. We'd been planning, but we'd been doing that for years. I never thought that everyone would buckle down and become serious about it when she showed back up," he said rising to his feet.

"Well, they did and now what, Ramsey? They've just announced that you guys are opening a new branch of the company. What are you going to do with the clubs? What are you going to do about…everything?" she ended lamely, not wanting to bring up all the other things in his life that he would have to rearrange with this new development.

"The clubs are taken care of. I'm handing everything over to Lola. She already knows."

He realized his mistake a little too late. "Wait," she said pointing her finger in his solid chest. "Lola knows about this? This is what she was talking about on Sunday about how you were making everything better for me. And Brad and Jason know too, right? That's why they wouldn't say anything bad about you. They were insisting that they couldn't tell me why they had moved out, but that it was for me. Everyone knew," she breathed. "Everyone knew but me."

"Lexi…"

"No," she said shaking her head. "Tell me the truth, Ramsey. Tell me the truth for once."

He let out a big breath, knowing there was no way around it. "Yes, everyone else knew about what was going on. I wanted it to be a surprise."

"You didn't want it to be a surprise. You were scared!" she yelled, pushing her hands against his chest in anger. "You knew I'd be pissed about this…all of this."

"No," he said grabbing her wrists and pulling her against him. "That's not what this is about. I didn't want to scare you away, but I did it anyway."

"Is it because of Parker?" she questioned him.

"God, Lexi, no, none of this has to do with her. She just happens to be the other half of this project. I was afraid you would think we were taking things too fast. I mean you moving in was a huge step for you. I didn't want you to know how serious I was. That I'd asked my roommates to move out so I could live with you maybe buy a new place for the two of us. That I'd given the reigns over to Lola so I wouldn't have to be at the club anymore. You wouldn't have to worry about the girls anymore. I wouldn't be out so late, and we could actually spend some time together.

"I was doing this all for you. I might have gone about it all wrong, but we hadn't even been dating for a year. I couldn't stop thinking about us. I couldn't stop thinking about where our life was going and how much I wanted you here. So I did this without talking to you about it. You were so lost in your job, studying for the bar, and your father's heart attack that I was doing everything I possibly could not to be another complication in your life. And look what I've done…" he growled walking away from her dejectedly. "I've only made things worse and more complicated."

Lexi took a hesitant step towards Ramsey. He sounded so sincere. Every word that he had uttered sounded like repentance for what he had done. He had clearly been suffering without her and for the way he had handled things. It hardly excused the lying and keeping things from her, but still how could she remain angry with him when she finally had the truth.

He had really thought he was doing all of this for her. She didn't like the clubs so he got rid of them. He never thought to ask if she would want him to stop working at something that he was not only good at but that he loved. She didn't like living with his rambunctious, perverted roommates so he asked them to move out. He never thought to ask if she wanted him to be left alone in this townhouse when she knew that he preferred to be surrounded by people. He never thought to ask if she might want to live with him…alone. His actions might have been misguided but his intentions were solid. He loved her.

"Ramsey," she whispered huskily. The tone of her voice made him turn to face her. "You love me?"

A boyish smirk crossed his face at the question as if it was the easiest thing to answer in the world…like he had gotten an easy word at a spelling bee. He strode one large step towards her, placed his hands on either side of her face, bent down, and touched his lips to hers. He kissed her softly, gently like it was something he had been wanting to do for a long time. With his hands holding her in place, she moved her own hands to his waist and pulled him closer against her.

Lexi's head was spinning and she felt weightless. His answer was lost on his tongue as he volleyed with her own. He kissed her like a starving man presented with a plate of food. He kissed her like he might never do it again, like no other answer was satisfactory. And she didn't resist him. She could turn him away, demand an answer, demand answers to all her questions, but none of it mattered. This was where she wanted to be in that moment lost in his arms, in this heated kiss.

She groaned as he further deepened the kiss and wound her arms around his neck. Her body felt like it was on fire. Each touch of his mouth on hers and his hands running the length of her body sent tingles through her. He pulled back long enough to bend down and begin to kiss down her neck and back up. She managed only one word as the sensation in her body began to build. "Bedroom."

He obeyed eagerly walking backwards towards the stairs never letting her go. He almost seemed afraid that if he let her go somehow this moment would end. Lexi moved her hands down to begin loosening his tie and unbuttoning his shirt. When they reached the stairs, he pulled back fractionally to pull his shirt and tie over his head and discard them on the floor. His head dipped back down and relished in another one of her kisses while he slowly peeled off her party dress. As the dress fell to the floor, she quickly darted up the stairs and into his bedroom. She could hear his patter of footsteps as he followed behind. Ramsey had managed to unclasp his belt as he went up the stairs, and his pants were already falling to his ankles when he entered the bedroom.

He stumbled out of his dress slacks just as she stripped out of her bra and thong. She reached down and extracted him out of his boxers before yanking them to the floor with the remainder of his clothes. He dipped his head back down to claim her mouth, inching her backwards towards his bed.

When her knees hit the backboard, she climbed backwards across the down duvet. He followed clambering onto the bed and towering over her. He paused to look into her eyes. Lexi knew what she must look like—fiery, dilated, and hungry with desire. She could see the same thing all over him. She wasn't even sure how he was able to pause to even take one glance at her.

"The answer is yes," he murmured softly kissing her forehead then her nose then gently on her mouth. "I do love you."

"I love you too," she said instantly knowing it was the truth.

It was the last thing either of them said before he buried himself deep inside of her. She was glad the anger from the other day had dissipated, and wondered why she had ever wanted anything but this, anything but him making love to her. He began thrusting into her deep steady movements that quickly had her panting laboriously. She could feel her own release building. She reached up and pulled his body down on top of her digging her nails deep into his flesh. He grunted into her shoulder and the pain mixing with the pleasure only forced him to move faster and harder into her.

She gasped as he hoisted her right leg up against his shoulder, the movement seamless and effortless. This only allowed him deeper access to her, and she was sure that any second she was going to burst. She could feel him getting closer with her and when she was sure she couldn't hold out any longer, they released together.

Lexi threw her head back against the pillow and released all the air she had been holding in her lungs as her legs shook from exertion. Ramsey rested his head against her chest his breathing ragged and heavy.

He kissed her forehead once more before sliding off the bed to clean up. She lay back against his comforter and stared dreamy-eyed up at the ceiling. When he returned, she snuggled up against him, letting her eyes drift closed. "You promise?" she whispered.

"You don't think that was a promise?" he murmured back.

"That was amazing."

He smiled into her now mussed hair. "You're amazing, and yes, I love you."

"And it's all the truth?" she asked barely audible as she drifted to sleep against him.

"Yeah, baby, it's all the truth."

22

JULY ONE MONTH EARLIER

"Ramsey, I really need to talk to you," Parker cried panting a little as if she had sprinted down the hallway. She was still in scrubs like she had come straight from the hospital.

He stood shakily and stared between the two women in his office. "About what you told Lexi?" he growled.

Parker's lips parted as she realized she had walked in on Lexi and Ramsey. She nodded. "Uh, yeah…I told her."

"Of course, you did," he grumbled throwing his arms in the air.

Parker stood really still clearly assessing the situation she had walked into. Lexi wasn't sure why Parker hadn't told Ramsey that she was going to tell Lexi. But by the look on her face, she had been waiting for Lexi to do it for her. Lexi wondered if Parker would have confronted Ramsey about it after she talked to him…after she yelled at them. Would she have calmed him down? Would she have tried to comfort him? Would she have tried to get back with him out of his pain? Lexi wondered then how much Parker was like her best friend, Bekah.

"Uh, I see I've come at a bad time," Parker said easing back out of the room.

Ramsey stared at her menacingly, his anger holding strong. "Wait a minute," he demanded stopping her in her tracks.

"Yes?" she squeaked out. Parker stopped mid-step. It was obvious, there was no way Ramsey was letting Parker extract herself from the conversation after barging in so suddenly. She had said and did too much.

Lexi felt the weight of the situation permeate the room. What Parker had done by telling her wasn't just some small act of self-righteousness or pity, it was wrecking irreparable damage through their relationship. She couldn't just walk out of the room.

"Why can't you just stay out of my fucking business?" Ramsey snapped back, slamming his hand down on his desk in anger.

"I think she had a right to know," Parker responded, flinching at the tone of his voice and grasping the door handle.

Ramsey shook his head from side to side slowly. "Well, I'm so glad *you* told the story," he sneered, stepping away from Parker as if she were the last person he wanted to be around. Her story cast him in such a negative light, not that Lexi was sure if she could believe his story either. After all, he had lied about everything else.

Lexi could tell Parker wanted to just leave, but the weight of Ramsey's gaze held her in place. Parker took another step farther away from him. She was even shaking a little. The force of his anger was radiating off him in waves. "Were you even going to tell her?" Parker asked, bracing herself against him.

"That's none of your goddamn business!" he snapped back.

It was a question that Lexi had wondered herself. She hadn't been able to ask him, and now Parker had brought it up. Ramsey looked even more furious that she had uttered those words, but Lexi was thankful that she hadn't had to.

Lexi had been watching their exchange intently for the past couple minutes. Up until that moment, she hadn't really seen an opportunity to interrupt the conversation, even though it was her argument to begin with. Parker's arrival had thrown her, and she was still attempting to get her bearings about how to proceed.

On one hand, she wanted Parker there to confirm or deny the pregnancy discrepancy. She was still up in the air with who to believe about that one. On the other hand, Parker made things complicated. She was the reason Lexi was here at all. She was the reason her and Ramsey were having this conversation. She was the reason that her relationship was on thin ice. Lexi hated her for that, even if she had needed to know the truth about the situation. She knew the whole phrase about don't shoot the messenger, but she really didn't want to follow it in that moment.

It didn't help that it seemed Ramsey and Parker spoke their own language. They were arguing with each other and yelling at each other, but somehow Lexi felt as if she had missed half of what had been said. She realized that more was being said in their sidelong looks and body language than anything they were actually saying to each other. She just wished that she understood their language. They had known each other and been together in a relationship for so long, that they never lost the bond that so many couples developed. Lexi knew that she could talk to Jack like that, but she didn't particularly like it either.

Lexi couldn't just stand by and let him ignore her presence any longer. "Well, it most certainly *is* my business," Lexi cut in, "and I think I have a right to know if you were ever going to tell me."

Ramsey stared down at his palm, which was now flat against his desk, and sighed. He clearly hated having this conversation. He probably didn't even want Parker and Lexi in the same vicinity. Lexi knew that look, because she had seen it on her own face. His past had caught up with him, and it was the last thing that he wanted. "This doesn't have anything to do with our relationship," he told her brusquely, grinding his teeth.

Lexi openly scoffed at him. How could he be so naïve to think that his past didn't affect his future? Lexi had realized long ago how big of a part your past played in your present. That would be like saying that her relationship with Jack had nothing to do with who she was today. It would be a total lie. Jack had so much to do with who she was. He had changed her forever…for better or for worse. She liked to think he had done both.

In either case, Parker had done a number on him. Sure, their relationship was far from what she had with Jack, but they had been together for real for so long that it had completely altered him. Not to mention their terrible practically catastrophic ending had jaded him. He didn't trust people. He didn't let people in. He hadn't had a decent relationship before Lexi since he and Parker had broken up. The very idea that Parker didn't have anything to do with him and how he was acting now was absolutely ludicrous.

"Really?" Lexi asked nearly laughing out loud at him. "You lying to me has nothing to do with our relationship?"

Ramsey leaned against the desk heavily. "No, Lexi, that's not what I meant. I meant that Parker has no place in our relationship," he quickly amended.

"The fact that you have to clarify that is truly telling," she murmured turning away from Parker and Ramsey. She began walking the length of Ramsey's desk back and forth, seething with anger. She didn't know what his current relationship was with Parker. She wanted to hope for the best, but really her past had always proven otherwise.

"Look," Parker began slowly, "I really don't have a place in your relationship." Lexi looked up at Parker as she spoke.

"Yet you weaseled yourself in," Ramsey growled, keeping Parker from saying anything further.

Parker's head snapped so fast in Ramsey's direction that she looked like she got a crick in her neck. She didn't look like she could believe he had just said that. Parker had done what she thought was right. She might have acted impulsively, but Lexi was pretty sure Parker thought her head had been in the right place.

"It's not exactly my fault that I have to be around you all the time," Parker spat out without a second thought. Her venom carried years of pain and heartache over the man in front of her.

Ramsey leveled his gaze on her. His green eyes could have burned a hole through her. His jaw was taut and usually full lips were pulled tight into a straight line. Tiny wrinkles across his forehead and around his eyes showed the true fierceness of his anger. Parker swallowed hard as she met that gaze, darted her eyes to Lexi, and back.

Lexi stopped her pacing and turned back to Parker at the end of that last statement. Where had that come from? What the fuck was she talking about? Since when did they have to be around each other all the time? This was news to her. This was news that she had never wanted to hear.

"Wait," she cried holding her hand up to draw their attention back to her and keeping them from deftly changing the subject, "why exactly do you guys have to be around each other all the time?" Lexi eyed them both carefully. She knew they had their own language and she didn't want to miss anything that was going on between them. Hopefully she would be able to pull something from their sidelong glances that told her one way or another what was going and if they were lying to her.

"Uh…" Parker mumbled looking at the ground. She looked really uncomfortable like she knew she had just fucked up somehow. Ramsey openly glared at Parker as she stood there awkwardly.

How could someone so intelligent possibly be so stupid? If she wasn't supposed to tell Lexi these things, she surely wasn't playing the part.

"It's stuff you don't want to have anything to do with," Ramsey finally responded, meeting Lexi's eye.

Lexi's dark brown eyes looked back at him suspiciously. She couldn't believe that was his response; that she just wouldn't want to know about what Parker had said. Clearly she wanted to know or else she wouldn't have asked. "I'm sorry, but I just heard that my boyfriend and his ex-girlfriend have to spend all this time together. Oh, and by the way, I knew nothing about any of this," she muttered scathingly. "I think I'd want to know what the fuck this is all about."

"Ramsey, can't we just tell her?" Parker breathed barely louder than a whisper.

"Tell me what?" Lexi crowed turning on Parker who still wouldn't look at her. Lexi was getting angrier the longer they kept information from her.

"Look you really don't want to know!" he told her again a bit more vehemently.

By now of course, Lexi wanted to know nothing more than why she couldn't know and what the big secret was. This was infuriating. How much more convincing did she have to do? She told him she wanted to know. She had already insisted she didn't want any more lies, and yet here he was keeping something from her. She shook her head in disbelief. "Just tell me! Why do there have to be so many secrets between us?"

"Ramsey," Parker pleaded softly.

"Look, it just has to do with the *wedding* alright," he snapped. His eyes shifted to Parker whose own mouth had snapped shut.

"Oh, God," Lexi cried, "can we not talk about the wedding?" Lexi shuddered at the thought of Jack's wedding, period. She did not want to hear anything about it. She did not even want to think about it. She didn't miss the sneaky look that passed between Ramsey and Parker, but she didn't want to know what it had to do with the wedding. The last thing she wanted to know about was that wedding.

"See, I told you it was the last thing you wanted to talk about and that I wasn't going to bring it up," he said sliding a hand through his hair.

"Whatever," Lexi said dismissively, "I still don't understand why you had to lie about the other stuff. You know my past and how important trust is to me. How do I know you didn't lie about anything else? How do I even know you care about me?" Lexi didn't like stating that last statement. It made her feel incredibly weak and vulnerable. Her heart was in his hands at that last comment. She thought they had been on some sort of path, but his lying certainly made it clear that he had other things in mind. If he couldn't even trust her with his past, how could he trust her with his future?

"You know how I feel about you," he said earnestly, moving towards Lexi. Lexi took a hesitant step back countering his movements. She wasn't prepared to be in close proximity to him…to play this game.

"Yet, you lie," she breathed shaking her head at his advance.

"It wasn't intentional for me to lie to you about it," he groaned miserably.

"Unintentional lying?" Lexi asked rolling her eyes. "That's rich."

"No, come on. I told you that Parker and I don't discuss this stuff with people. Well, usually not," he said sliding his eyes towards Parker. "Anyone who knew we were together knows better than to bring it up. Tell her Parker," he barked demandingly.

Parker sighed and sank into one of his cushioned chairs, as if resolved that she had to remain for the remainder of this conversation. "We really don't tell people."

"You told me," she said defiantly.

"I thought you deserved the truth. I could see where Ramsey's head was with you and couldn't hold it in. I didn't want your world to come crashing down around you…like mine did." Parker bit her lip anxiously before continuing. "But honestly, I haven't told the whole story to anyone in a very long time, and Ramsey, I doubt has ever told anyone."

"Well, fine, you don't normally tell people about it, but did you have to lie?" Lexi questioned him. "Couldn't you have told me that she existed so I wouldn't be blindsided? Why did I have to hear her side first?"

"Lexi, I told you I don't have an excuse. This is what Parker and I always did. We didn't tell people what happened. Parker was the only one who ever told and she always seems to get there first with her distorted version of reality," Ramsey grumbled. Lexi could tell just by the reactions of both parties that they had argued about this before and rather often.

"My reality isn't distorted," Parker sputtered, looking up from where she was seated. "I was there. I actually know what happened. You weren't even there for everything..."

"Because you left! We argued, and *you* left. How could I talk to you about it?"

"Ancient history," Parker said with a sad shoulder shrug.

"And you told her you miscarried," he spat at her, his anger bubbling up again.

"Ramsey, I did," she moaned a tear rolling down her cheek at the mention of her lost pregnancy. She sounded as if she had said this same thing many times. Lexi wondered how many times she had tried to convince Ramsey that she had miscarried. She wondered if Parker actually had. She just didn't know.

He shook his head in disbelief. "And you believe her?" Ramsey asked turning on Lexi.

Lexi didn't know if she truly believed Parker's side, but she was even more uncertain about Ramsey. "She's not the one who's been lying to me from the beginning. I don't see why I should believe you?" she told him. "Does an abortion sound any more plausible?" Lexi asked crossing her arms over her chest.

"Can't anyone else see the truth but me?" he demanded, turning around in a quick circle his arms out before him as if pleading with an unseen audience.

"What's the truth?" Lexi asked harshly. "It's hard to when you've lied about so much else."

"Did she skim over the parts about Bekah's involvement?" he asked taking the argument back to day one.

Lexi looked at Parker whose face had gone as white as a sheet. "She told me she would save me the details," Lexi said, knowing for some reason that it was the answer Ramsey had been expecting.

Ramsey gritted his teeth in an attempt to keep his anger in check. "Of course, she skimmed over the details. Parker still refuses to see what she actually did. She holds herself together behind a wall that no one has ever been able to break through. Didn't you wonder why she wanted to save you the details?"

"No," Lexi said quietly. "I just thought it was personal. I didn't really know there was a connection."

"I understand why you didn't see it to begin with," he growled a man possessed. She could see it all over him that he had been obsessed with this very issue at one point. "It took me a long time to finally realize what had happened in that week."

"Ramsey," Parker pleaded, her voice shaking with every syllable. "You put the pieces together wrong. They didn't happen that way." By now Parker's body was trembling.

"What are you trying to say?" Lexi asked.

"Parker saved you the details of my sister going over there and convincing her to get rid of the baby," he stated stoically.

Lexi couldn't help it, she gasped. "No," she murmured not wanting to see what was in front of her. "You think she did that? You think that about your own sister?" She had to ask. She hated Bekah, but to do that against your own brother. Lexi found it hard to believe.

"After everything you know about Bekah, you somehow can't believe that she would do that?" Ramsey asked in disbelief.

Lexi thought it over. She didn't have a good opinion of Bekah. In fact, she thought Bekah was one of the worst people she had ever met. She despised Bekah. But this even seemed low for her.

Yet, Lexi knew how Bekah operated. No matter how much she loved her brother. No matter how close their bond was, she still only worked one way. She did whatever directly benefited her. Lexi knew that she was like this first hand. She had only invited Lexi down to meet her with the intention of destroying her relationship with Jack so Bekah could have him all to herself. So, how could this benefit her? How could her convincing Parker to have an abortion benefit her?

Lexi couldn't draw a connection. This was Parker's best friend. They had known each other since childhood. It was her brother's baby. Granted, it was a baby that he didn't know about until it was too late, but still…this was going to be Bekah's niece. Why would she get rid of it?

Then it hit her. It felt like a light bulb had been turned on in her mind. She knew exactly how Parker getting rid of her baby niece would benefit Bekah. It would save her reputation and the reputation of her family. Bekah would never want to be involved in anything that was scandalous…anything that could somehow come back to be directly related to her. It didn't matter what emotional damage this would do to her brother or Parker. It didn't matter how this would ultimately destroy their relationship. It didn't matter that she would lose her best friend…or at least the easy relationship they had once had. All that mattered was what irreparable damage this would do to her family's status.

Lexi knew Ramsey must have come to this same conclusion. He knew Bekah better than anyone else. For some reason it seemed more logical than any of the other things that had been confessed all night. Bekah was a big enough bitch to convince her own best friend to get rid of her own brother's baby, without telling him to save the Bridges name.

"She did it for herself," Lexi murmured softly, seeing it clearly.

"How did you come to that same conclusion?" Parker asked standing a bit too quickly. She wobbled heavily on her two feet as she stared slack jawed at Lexi.

"Because it's the only thing that makes sense," Ramsey responded.

"It doesn't make sense. Why would I lie about this? I know what happened. I was there," Parker told him. "And you weren't."

Ramsey shook his head despondently. "Let's not have this argument again Parker. Please. I know I wasn't there. I know I made mistakes, but not any more or less than you did. Can we please drop it?"

"How could you even look at her again once you figured it out?" Lexi asked in disbelief that he could still be a devout brother.

He shrugged getting that knowing look in his eye. "She's my sister. She might have done some terrible things, but I love her. How could she have known what this would have done or that I would have ever figured it out?"

Lexi thought it was incredibly short sighted to believe that Bekah didn't know what it would do. Bekah played a game. She wove her web and typically knew exactly where the pieces would fall. Then again, Lexi was a bit jaded about Bekah's involvement in any scenario.

"Well," Lexi said spinning on Parker, "I guess since I know about as much truth about that situation as you both can agree on, can you at least tell me that he hasn't lied to me about anything else? Do you know if he's lied to me? You two have been awful chummy since you got back to town. I'm sure you would know something."

Parker gave Ramsey a knowing look before quickly turning away. "I...I don't know."

"You think I can't see what's going on here? I see the looks between you two. I'm not stupid," she yelled at the both of them. "I've done a lot of stupid things before. I've lied and I've made mistakes, but this is just different. I've come clean about my past, about everything. I've put it behind me. And to think that you don't even have the decency to do the same...to even tell me about it. To try and hide it behind silly looks that you two pass between each other. Well, I've had enough!"

Ramsey ran his hands through his hair. "I lied about something else," he admitted softly.

"What?" Lexi cried sinking into a chair in disbelief. "After I stood here and yelled at you for however long, you still held something back from me. What? Have you and Parker been seeing each other behind my back? Have you been cheating on me like you cheated on her?" she asked throwing her hand out in Parker's direction.

"I never cheated on Parker," he gasped out, looking into Parker's hurt face. "Did you tell her I cheated on you?"

"No, Ramsey, I didn't," she said hating this conversation more and more. Parker had kind of implied that he had cheated on her, but she hadn't come right out and said it. "I swear. I would never make that mistake again."

"I never cheated on her," he bellowed. "Never!"

"Oh, you just got drunk and had naked women in your apartment who…what did you say?" she asked Parker. "Would suck your dick at a snap of your fingers?"

"You said that Parker, really?" he asked shaking his head side to side slowly as if he couldn't believe his ears. "After everything, you still can't get over that night. I told you nothing happened. It was for Brad and Jason. Why can you still not believe me?"

Parker stared at him helpless, hopelessly. She clearly couldn't get any words out.

"Probably because you lie," Lexi whispered into the stillness.

He sighed heavily before slumping in the seat behind his desk exhausted. "I never cheated on Parker. There were girls over at my apartment that night, but I never nor would I ever do anything like that to her…or to you," he added quickly. "If I had ever wanted to be with someone else, I would have just broken up with you. But I didn't then," he said glancing at Parker, "and I don't want to now." Lexi met his eyes as they landed on her face.

"Yet, you lied about something else. It's hard to believe what you're spouting when you told me that you lied…again," she said feeling tears spring into her eyes. She hadn't even realized how emotional she had gotten. All she had felt through this ordeal was anger. She couldn't believe he would lie over and over and over again to her. She had been purely angry with his reactions and his answers. The last thing she had even thought about was getting emotional. Yet, the fact that he was now admitting that he still hadn't told her the whole truth made her want to break down in tears. The lies seemed endless.

Ramsey sighed heavily. "I…I got you that job at the law firm here."

"What?" she cried, feeling the automatic need to punch something. "Are you fucking kidding me, Ramsey? You interfered with my job? What did you not think I was smart enough to get that job? Did you not think I had enough money to get that job? What was it? I don't understand how you could go behind my back like that. No wonder it just fell into my lap. I made the mistake of acting like I was so smart…that I was so much more qualified than the rest of the applicants. You made me look like a fool. No wonder they were so easy with me. Did you tell them to do that too?"

"I was trying to help. I knew you'd never take a Bridges associate position, but I wanted you close. I wanted you in Atlanta. So I made some calls. It's not the end of the world," he finished lamely.

"Not the end of the world? Not the end of the world?" she screamed nearing hysterics. "I had one thing that I was really good at! I worked my ass off all year long to get good grades so that I could get an amazing paid associate position. I put out applications everywhere. I applied everywhere. Then you go and tell me that you just *got* me this job! I didn't have to put in any of the work or the time. You happened to know someone, drop the Bridges name, and bam a job surfaces. God, it goes against everything that you stand for!" she cried looking him up and down like he was despicable. She knew on some level she should be happy that he had gotten her this job, but not this way. She couldn't be happy that he had gone behind her back like that. This was the one thing she still had to be proud of, and he had taken that away too.

"Lexi, please try and see it from my perspective. This job wasn't even really open. No one would have gotten it, because they weren't hiring until I talked to them. You wanted to be close to me too. It's a good thing, not a bad thing," he pleaded with her.

"It could have been a good thing if you had been honest with me," she told him. "Instead you chose to lie to me! You chose to deceive me! I have *nothing* left that's mine. Your lies have permeated everything that is important to me. I don't know if I can talk to you anymore Ramsey, until you find the truth," she said walking towards the door.

He quickly ran after her. "The truth is I want to be with you. I went about it wrong, but it doesn't change how I feel," he said grabbing her elbow to stop her. She yanked her arm back pulling her shoulder too forcefully and sending a wrenching pain through it. "I know I made some mistakes, but they are minor Lexi. We can work through them. Please give me the chance to work through them."

"How can I when I can't even look at you without seeing the lies all over you?" she asked taking another step backwards. "These lies were for you, not for me. You lied to cover your past and your wealth and your importance. I just wanted you as you are. You wouldn't even give me that. Who are you?" she whispered.

"I'm yours," he said, following her down the barren hallway. "I'm all yours."

"You can't be mine," she said shaking her head. "Someone who belongs to me is able to give themselves over to me. I gave myself to you and all you did was abuse my trust."

"Please, let me try to fix this," he begged, seeing her slipping through his fingers.

"You can't. I think this is it, Ramsey. I can't date someone for a year to find out I never knew who he was," she said weakly, hating even saying the statement. She knew it was true, but her heart was breaking at the thought of being without him.

"I can. I can fix this, Lexi. You know who I am. I swear you do."

"Good bye, Ramsey," she said standing on her tip toes and kissing him softly on the mouth. He pulled her tight against him trying to deepen the kiss, trying to remind her of what he could give her. She pressed her hand against his cheek and broke away from his lips. "Please don't call me," she added breaking away from him, rushing out the back door, and into her car.

She revved the engine and peeled out of the parking lot. As swiftly as she could, she piled the majority of her belongings into her two largest suitcases and departed for Hartsfield-Jackson Airport. The weight of what had happened settled over her, and she found that she didn't even have tears to cry for what she had just done. She cared for Ramsey more than she had ever thought possible, but now all she could see was the tangle of lies surrounding him. She couldn't help but wonder how different he actually was from Bekah. Perhaps this deception ran in the family. That thought alone held her tears back.

She was driven by one thought: she needed to get back to New York. She needed out of this god forsaken town and out of this oppressive heat. She needed to get away from the smog of the commuter city and back to her home with its own smells and intricacies.

She wished that she could get away from her life…find simpler times. A Ferris wheel filled her mind's eye and that almost broke her resolve. To go back to that day and make it all right. To not have to go through the things she had endured. To have him make it all better.

Not thinking, she pulled out her phone and dialed his number. She hadn't called him since her father's heart attack. She hadn't seen him since then either. "Pick up," she whispered into the phone. "Pick up. Pick up. Pick up."

The line went to voicemail and a tear fell down her cheek. She needed him. Answer the goddamn phone. She redialed, knowing she couldn't do it a third time. It rang and rang and rang. His voicemail picked up again, quicker this time, and she groaned pathetically. "Typical," she spat veering the car into the parking lot. "Just when I need him."

She pulled into a spot and placed the car in park. She laid her forehead on the steering wheel and tried to remember to breathe. She couldn't walk into the airport crying. As she wiped a tear from her cheek, her phone lit up next to her. She nearly jumped out of her seat in her desire to answer it.

"Jack," she murmured softly.

"Lex, is everything alright? You called twice."

"I just needed to hear you voice," she said with a sigh.

Jack paused on the line before responding. "Are you sure you're alright?"

"I just broke up with Ramsey," she whispered, swallowing hard.

Another long pause. She wondered if he was smirking. She liked his smirk. She liked his blue eyes. She liked the way he brushed her hair back for her. She liked…she stopped herself. She needed to keep it together.

"Do I need to come pick you up?" he asked finally.

The way his voice melted in the phone made it all worse. She wanted him to come pick her up. That's all she wanted. But he was marrying someone else. She shouldn't have even called him, but she had nothing else to lose at this point. "No. I'm at the airport."

"Are you going back to New York?" he asked hastily.

"Yeah. I need to go home," she murmured.

"I'm sorry, Lex," he told her, his voice sad.

She chuckled softly. "It's not your fault."

"Not something I hear every day."

"Jack," she muttered again softly. Tears were falling out of her eyes freely now as the humor passed. "Don't you wish we could go back to that Ferris wheel? Don't you wish we could go back change it all…make it better?"

"No," he said just as softly. "If things had changed that day, I might have never gotten that time with you."

"Oh, God," she moaned swiping at her tears.

"Lex, come on. Please stop crying. I hate to hear you like this," he pleaded

"Jack…what is my life?"

"Lex, please, I hate this. How can I help?"

She swallowed back tears. She wished she could tell him all the ways he could help. She wished she could tell him to call off the engagement and make things right by her. She wanted so much from him, but she couldn't have those things. She had given him up last year in an airport, and she couldn't take him back this year in the same one. "You can't. You can't, Jack. I wish you could, but you can't."

"I'll come to you."

She shook her head desperate to rid herself of all the thoughts swirling in her head. "I want to escape with you, Jack."

"I'll always be your escape, Lex."

Lexi couldn't deny how true that was. "I have to go," she told him unable to keep it together, unable to listen to his sweet words.

"I don't want you to go when you're upset."

"I'll be okay, Jack, but I have to go. Good bye."

"Alright," he said with a sad sigh. "Good bye then, Lex. I'm here."

"I know," she said and hung up, hanging her head even more confused than she had been before.

Jack and Ramsey confused her beyond anything she could ever imagine. One lied; one cheated. She loved them both immeasurably, and yet, all she ended up with was heartache. She needed to get away. She really needed that escape.

She purchased the next plane ticket out of town not even bothering to cringe at the expensive fare. As she sat down in the terminal awaiting her flight, she wondered how she was going to get back to her apartment. Rachelle was working out of town, and Chyna was in Milan at her photo shoot. Lexi cursed out loud, much to the chagrin of an old married couple and a teenage mom toting around four obnoxious children, when she realized that they were about to board, and she had no one to pick her up when she arrived in town.

Nodding to herself she realized, in fact, she did have one person and quickly jotted out a text message. She briefly explained the situation and asked if she could be picked up in a couple hours. She received an almost immediate reply.

"Good to hear from you. Sorry about the circumstances. I'll be there when you land. —Adam."

23

PRESENT

Lexi rolled over, letting her arm stretch languidly over her head. She kept her eyes closed savoring the last few seconds of grogginess before she had to get out of bed. She smiled as she sank back further into the soft down pillow under her head and stretched her body out under the comforter. Her hands brushed up against the hard wood headboard, and she blushed thinking about how she had used the headboard last night.

"What's that devilish grin for?" Ramsey asked leaning forward and kissing both of her red cheeks.

Lexi giggled, opening her eyes to look at the man lying next to her. "Nothing," she cooed looking into his bright green eyes from under her thick black lashes.

"You don't blush without reason," he said sliding his hand across her bare stomach and pulling her closer to him.

"I think I blushed all last night," she murmured pushing her hands up against his chest.

"I'd say you had a reason for that."

Lexi giggled and snuggled closer to him. "True."

"And anyway, I don't think I gave you an opportunity to think about blushing. You were too preoccupied," he said as he ducked down to give her another heated kiss.

"I think you might be right," she agreed tilting her head to allow for easier access.

Lexi wrapped her arms up around his neck pressing herself flat against him. She knew she was egging him on, but she couldn't help it. Everything had been so perfect last night after they had talked things out. It was like Parker had never existed in their relationship. She had missed that feeling so much. All she wanted to do was stay in bed all day and forget the past month had happened. That would truly be an ideal situation.

"Woah there," he said pulling back briefly, "do you think you're ready again…already?"

Lexi shrugged, lifting her head off the pillow to kiss him again. "Yes." It was his turn to grin devilishly as he moved his hand down between her legs. She groaned enjoying his gentle prodding, but also feeling some major after effects of last night's…activities. "Wait…maybe not."

Ramsey chuckled and shook his head at her. "I had a feeling," he said stilling his hand and giving her another playful kiss. "How about a shower?" he offered.

"Ugh," Lexi groaned, shaking her head side-to-side. "I can't move a muscle."

Ramsey clearly seemed to be enjoying the effect he had had on her. He tried to cover a second chuckle, but couldn't seem to manage it.

"Hey," she said swatting him on the arm, "this is all your doing."

He grabbed her hand and laced his fingers with hers. "And I am so glad that I made you so sore you can't even get out of bed. How about some breakfast in bed?" he asked as his thumb rubbed circles into her hand. "I could go fix something and let you sleep a little longer."

"Oh! I like that idea," she said closing her eyes and wrapping both of her arms around him. She held him in place for a short while as she pretended to fall into a deep slumber. She wanted the best of both worlds: breakfast in bed and Ramsey in bed. Well, she favored the latter more than the former.

Ramsey shook his head at her as he attempted to disentangle himself from her. "I can't make you breakfast while I'm still in bed with you," he moaned, trying to unhook her arms from around his neck.

"But I don't want you to leave," she told him, holding him tighter.

"I'll make you coffee," he murmured into her ear.

"Coffee?" she asked perking up.

"Of course. Just the way you like it."

"Alright. Alright," she grumbled, slowly releasing him. She would do anything for a good cup of coffee in the morning.

She smiled brightly as she watched him climb out of bed and into a pair of green boxers. She could clearly see what effect she had on him through the thin material, and was thankful that Brad and Jason had moved out. She understood more and more how much Ramsey had been working to make a better life for her, and in that moment she was appreciative of the changes.

Ramsey exited the room with a glance back in her direction. She sighed pleasantly and stretched out in the bed again. What a wonderful morning! She couldn't remember the last time she had been this happy…well, she could.

There had been her Mystery Man, and things had kind of felt right. She swallowed not wanting to think about it. He was just a rebound. That's all he was. She hadn't been in the right state of mind.

All she had been able to think about for the past month was that she and Ramsey didn't have a shot in hell of getting back together. Of course she missed him. They had been together for a year, and it's not like they had broken up because she wasn't interested anymore. She was definitely still interested, if last night was any indication of that.

And she knew that she had to tell Ramsey about what had happened now that they were back together. They hadn't been together when it had happened, but the longer she held it in, the more it would look like she was hiding it from him. The last thing she wanted to do was put herself in the same situation as Ramsey. They wouldn't have broken up at all if he had been honest about what had happened with Parker…among other things. She needed to be honest with him about what had happened in New York.

But the thought of breaking out of the bliss that she was currently in with him made her cringe. They were so happy right now. But with Adam coming into town later today, she knew that she had to break the news sometime soon. She didn't want Ramsey, or Chyna for that matter, to find out from someone else.

Lexi pushed her hands back through her hair and let her eyes fall back closed. This was going to be more difficult than she thought. After all the years of deception with Jack, her stomach knotted up immediately at the thought of telling Ramsey this one thing. He would forgive her. She was sure of it. She just couldn't keep herself from freaking out about it.

Lexi bolted upright in bed suddenly realizing—today was the day. She couldn't believe that it was here. This whole week—this whole year had been leading up to this very moment. As much as she had tried to avoid today from happening, life had caught up with her.

Jack was going to get married today.

Her stomach rolled even more at the thought. She had managed to get through a bachelor party, afternoon brunch, bachelorette party, and a rehearsal dinner with only a few minor mishaps, but today was going to be much harder than that. Jack would officially be off the market after today.

She had been in such a state of bliss when she had woken up that it hadn't even crossed her mind that the wedding was today. Ramsey had made her forget about Jack. She hadn't thought that it was even possible. When they had been together, there had been times when Jack wasn't considered. She knew that he wasn't important to their relationship, but he had always still been there. After all, Jack was marrying his sister. That thought was hard to get rid of after knowing Jack for so long.

Yet, here she was the day of his wedding…the day that she had been dreading consistently for a year, and she hadn't even thought about it. She had actually slept in. When she had woken up, she felt content and satisfied. She was pleased just to find Ramsey next to her.

Lexi smiled letting the tension release from her shoulders. This was a good feeling. She could make it through the day feeling like this. The thought alone that someone could make her happy enough to forget Jack's wedding day was good enough for her.

The only thing she needed to do now was to tell Ramsey the one secret she was carrying around. It was only fair after everything he had told her. Lexi took a deep breath and released it slowly. She could handle this.

As she hopped out of the bed, Ramsey walked back into the room. "What are you doing out of bed? I brought you your coffee," he said holding up a steaming olive green mug.

"Oh. thanks. I was coming to check on you," she told him.

"Well, food will be done soon. I knew you would want this first," he said handing the coffee over. She smiled and took a sip. This really was heaven. "Now that you're up, how about we eat in the kitchen?"

"Alright," Lexi said tugging on a pair of Ramsey's boxers and a spare black t-shirt that fell to her knees.

"Sexy," he said kissing her on the mouth.

Lexi followed him downstairs determined to bring up what had happened in New York. She knew he wouldn't be happy, but it wouldn't be fair for her to hold it in. She plopped down into a chair at the dining room table and crossed her legs Indian style. "Hey, Ramsey, can we talk?" She hated how cliché she sounded, but she didn't know how else to bring it up.

"Oh, God, I left you alone for ten minutes and you want to break up again," he said with a crooked smile. She could see that he was nervous at the statement, since every time they had spoken recently had ended up in a major argument or a breakup. She couldn't blame him. Especially because what she was about to tell him wasn't great news either.

"No, no, nothing like that," she quickly amended. She had no intention of breaking up with him. That was the last thing on her mind. She had been so happy this morning that all she had wanted to do was forget the past month, and move on with their lives. As long as all of his secrets were out in the open, they could work it out…well, after she got this last one out of the way. "I like how things are now so…open…honest."

Ramsey nodded. Lexi wasn't sure if he was just agreeing with whatever she was saying or not. He seemed sincere, and the sex last night had been unbelievable. It really must have taken a weight off of his shoulders to have her know the whole story. "Me too. I shouldn't have hid so much from you. I just didn't know how to tell you everything."

"I understand that," she said thinking of the secret she was about to reveal. There wasn't an easy way to say what she needed to tell him. Either way he wasn't going to be pleased. She was hoping that the fact that they were back together would deter the majority of the backlash.

"It must have been the same way with Jack," he said hesitantly meeting her eyes.

"Yeah…I suppose," she said after thinking it over. She still hadn't been thinking of Jack. This was a very strange day for her indeed.

"So, what is it we have to talk about?" he asked more at ease now that he knew that she didn't want to end things all over again. Lexi met his gaze and admired the man standing before her. She hated what she was about to do. She hated to wipe that beautiful smile off of his face…to make him doubt her. She had to do it though.

A knock at the door startled both of them out of the conversation they were about to have. Lexi cursed in her head. She hated whoever was at that door for their terrible timing. She couldn't believe how many times this had happened. She wished he wouldn't answer the door, but she knew that was out of the question.

Ramsey shrugged. "This can wait?" he asked as he went to answer the door. Lexi groaned hating that she had to wait, but agreed that nothing could be done.

"Hey bitches!" Chyna cried as soon as the door swung open.

Lexi gasped in surprised. Did she say she would hate whoever was on the other side of the door? "Chyna!" she squealed, running and hugging her best friend. It felt like an eternity since she had last seen her even though it had only been a week. As her arms circled her tiny frame, Lexi realized just how much she had missed her crazy best friend. "I didn't know when you were getting here."

"I tried to call you last night and this morning, but you didn't answer," she said strolling into the living room. "Judging by your clothes, I'm guessing you were busy," she said looking at Lexi's boxer and t-shirt combo.

Ramsey just smiled at her intrusion. "Yeah, we were busy," Ramsey said pulling Chyna into a quick hug and grabbing the bag she was carrying.

"Thanks," she said sauntering into his apartment like she owned the place. She dropped her enormous purse on the dining room table. Lexi wondered if they had let her take the massive bag on as a carry on. "Adam's getting the rest of the stuff from the cab."

Adam appeared at the door a short while later with a large suitcase, obviously Chyna's, as well as a smaller carry-on, likely his own. Lexi was almost certain that his carry on was smaller than Chyna's purse. She could get back problems from lugging that thing around.

"Hey, good to see you, man," Adam said depositing the bags next to the couch and firmly shaking Ramsey's hand.

"Likewise," Ramsey said nodding his head at Adam in greeting.

"Lexi," Adam said with a curt nod and a rather pointed look. She smiled, then quickly diverted her gaze focusing back on Chyna. She did not want to look at Adam too closely. He wanted to talk, and this was not the time or place for that. She was going to tell Ramsey about everything until they had barged in. Now she figured she should talk to Adam about it before discussing it with Ramsey. She hated hiding it for much longer, but blurting it out in front of Chyna would be a terrible idea.

"So, a wedding, huh?" Chyna asked more bubbly than the last time Lexi had seen her. Apparently, Adam was having a positive effect on her again. "When do we start?"

"I was making breakfast," Ramsey said walking back over to the stove where he had been cooking. "I have to be at the hotel by eleven. Lexi was going to come with me, but ya'll can stay here if you want."

"Uh, no, I think we should go with you," Lexi hastily said. She did not want to be alone with Adam and Chyna, when there was still so much left unsaid. Chyna's reaction was sure to be less than pleasant. Lexi wanted to make it through the wedding alive. She had put all this time into preparing for it, she might as well go to the damn thing.

"You sure, Alexa?" Chyna asked. "I mean that's *plenty* of time for us to relax before this whole ordeal."

Lexi nodded, wanting nothing more than to get this day over with. Then everything would be out in the open, and she could finally move on with her life. "We'll have plenty of time, and we can both get ready there. Right, Ramsey?"

"Yeah. We have plenty of room," he said eyeing Lexi a bit curiously.

Chyna shrugged as if it didn't matter to her. As long as she had enough time and space to get ready, then she could be easily accommodated. "Whatever you want."

"Now C, should I even bother to ask why you packed for a month long vacation, when you're only staying one night?"

"Do you even have to ask that?" Adam asked with a chuckle.

"I don't pack light. You know that. If it's essential, then I bring it with me."

"How can you determine what's essential and what's not?" Lexi asked looking at the luggage she had brought with her.

"You've seen my closet. I was able to narrow," she said with a shrug. Lexi laughed realizing that in fact this was a big narrowing of Chyna's closet.

They didn't have time to dwell on anything further. Lexi and Ramsey quickly ate their breakfast, changed, and stuffed everything they needed for the big day into Ramsey's Mercedes. All four piled into his car, and he drove them to the St. Regis Hotel in Buckhead. Lexi had never actually been in the establishment, but she knew just by looking at the outside that the place must have cost a fortune to book for a wedding.

Ramsey had the gentleman at the door valet his car and was instructed that their luggage would be moved to the proper suite. How he knew where it was supposed to go without asking was beyond Lexi.

She had helped plan a few weddings and been to a dozen more, but nothing compared to this. Most of the events had been small outdoor events for friends and family. Chyna's father's wedding earlier that year had been the exception, but somehow this felt different. Lexi didn't know if it was Jack or Bekah that made it feel that way.

Lexi tried to keep from letting her jaw drop at the luxurious lobby that she walked into. The glamour of the place didn't even seem to faze Chyna, who barely glanced at her surroundings.

A woman greeted them as soon as they walked a few feet into the room. "Mr. Bridges, welcome to the St. Regis!" she exclaimed pleasantly. Her eyes traveled the length of him briefly before shooting back up to his face. Lexi was sure that wasn't *exactly* business professional. "My name is Jenny. May I direct you and your guests to their accommodations?"

"Thank you, Jenny. That would be great," Ramsey said lacing his fingers with Lexi's as he spoke. The woman's smile waned only slightly before she turned on her heel and began to escort them around the lavish hotel.

"As you well know," Jenny said to Ramsey as she briskly walked through across the lobby, "the wedding will be held outside in our Grand Terrace with the reception in our Astor Ballroom down this hallway. We have a welcome reception set up outside of the ballroom for guests who arrive prior to when we will be seating them in the Terrace. The groom's rooms are just down this hallway. You will find everything you need and more I'm sure." Jenny stopped and gestured Ramsey down the hallway.

"You'll make sure my guests have rooms to prepare for the wedding?" Ramsey asked.

"Of course."

Ramsey bent down and kissed Lexi on the cheek. "I'll be up with ya'll in a minute. I just need to check in and make sure I don't need to do anything."

"Alright," she said kissing him on the mouth this time a bit possessively.

Lexi, Chyna, and Adam followed Jenny to a separate area of the hotel where their items had been deposited. "We gave the gentleman his own separate room for changing. You ladies are welcome to the suite access in the room next door," Jenny said signaling to a pair of doors.

"Separate rooms weren't really necessary," Chyna said as she took the key from Jenny.

"But thanks," Adam added quickly. "We appreciate your help."

"Of course," she said with a head bob and then disappeared.

Chyna reached forward and kissed Adam lightly on the mouth. "Well, off to your own room then," Chyna said shoving him gently in the opposite direction. "We need girl time."

"You're really going to make me have my own room?" he asked glancing between the two girls.

"Yep!" Lexi said quickly, glad that Chyna kept them separated.

"Yes!" Chyna agreed.

"Fine, but can we talk later?" he asked Lexi directly.

"Yeah, I forgot you guys needed to talk," Chyna said dismissively, as she turned to open the door.

"Sure," she nearly whispered. "Later?"

"Sooner rather than later," he amended; his hazel eyes demanded her attention. She nodded her head and then ducked into the room behind Chyna.

Lexi couldn't believe that their stuff was already in their room. They hadn't been with Jenny for more than ten minutes and everything was in place. Her dress was even hanging up in the closet to prevent wrinkles. She couldn't believe how on top of their game the hotel was. It must have something to do with the Bridges name for the wedding. Maybe they did their taxes or accounting. That would explain the diligence about everything....or maybe this was just how the hotel was. She had never been here. She didn't know.

The suite they entered had a full kitchen, dining room, living space, and French doors opening up into a grand master bedroom. Chyna entered the room and sat back on the plush king-sized bed. Lexi gawked at her surroundings as she entered the bathroom.

"Holy shit, Chyna. This bathroom is bigger than my room at home," she said admiring the Jacuzzi tub, glass standing shower, and stretch of sink space.

"Everything is bigger than that mouse hole you live in."

"Hey!" Lexi said, walking back into the bedroom.

Chyna shrugged. "Do I have to ask or are you going to just spill?" Chyna asked lying back on the bed.

"Spill what?"

"Oh, don't give me that! You were supposed to call me and tell me the details. Clearly things went well. I want to know what happened! Last I checked you were about to run away from him, and suddenly you guys are fine and back together? Sounds a little suspicious to me," Chyna stated.

Lexi filled her in on everything that had happened the night before. She excluded some of the more raunchy details of the evening, but told her all about how Ramsey had been hiding things from her for a reason. Even though hiding what he was doing was wrong in itself, the fact that he was doing all of these things for her did kind of help the situation. Then the night long escapade…well, that was worth a tale or two.

"I don't know how you do it, chica," Chyna said twirling her stick straight black hair around her finger. "You always find the ones with epic baggage."

"Every guy has epic baggage, C."

"Maybe," Chyna said thinking it over, "but not like you! You find them completely damaged. I sure hope he isn't lying about anything else. I will kick his ass if he turns out to be a scumbag."

Lexi laughed out loud and collapsed onto the bed next to Chyna. "You're not the only one."

"Maybe not, but my high heels can do some damage!" she crowed grabbing her shoe off her foot and showing Lexi.

"Is girl time over?" Adam called through the door a few minutes later.

"No!" both girls called at the same time before breaking down into a fit of giggles. It felt so nice to just be herself with Chyna like this. This is the reason she loved New York so much. She hated when Chyna had been in Milan, and Lexi hadn't gotten this time with her.

Chyna hopped off the bed and opened the door for Adam. "We're not even dressed yet."

"Well, hurry up. I don't want to be over there all alone," he said. Chyna giggled, shook her head at him, and shoved him out the door.

Lexi hadn't even noticed that over an hour had already passed and Ramsey hadn't returned to check on them. Not that she needed him there with her at all times; she just thought it was strange that he hadn't shown up. He had probably gotten caught up in wedding preparations with Jack and Bekah. Lexi knew firsthand how much there was to do on the wedding day.

Shrugging off his disappearance, Lexi and Chyna both began to get ready for the big event. Lexi took half as long as Chyna even on a day like today when she was anxious about what was going to happen. She wanted to look pretty, but she didn't want to stand out. The last thing she wanted to deal with was a bitchy Bekah…well, anymore than she already was. She left her hair loose and curly with her bangs falling across her forehead. Her makeup was light, but accentuated her best features. She slid on her strapless purple floral dress and into her brown high heels. Then she sat and waited for Chyna to finish her get up. For a woman who was flawlessly beautiful, she sure put a lot of time into herself every day.

"Hey, Lexi," Ramsey called through the door as he knocked rapidly.

Lexi darted out of the bedroom and yanked the door open. Ramsey looked a bit frantic as he burst into the room. "Is everything okay?" Lexi asked following him.

"You look great," he said stopping and really looking at her.

"Uh...thanks," she said waiting for him to explain why he looked so frenzied. Whatever had happened in the time that he had been away from her hadn't been good. She could see it all over him. Something had gone wrong. "What's wrong?"

"You can tell that something's wrong?" he asked, running his hand through his hair a couple times.

"Yes," she muttered.

"I hate to do this," he said sinking into one of the chairs in the seating area.

"Do what?" she asked, her stomach dropping out. This really couldn't be good.

"Ramsey, glad to see that you're back," Chyna said, walking out of the bathroom in nothing but her lingerie.

Ramsey didn't even look at her. He was gazing so intently at Lexi and clearly contemplating what he was about to say. "Thanks."

"Is everything alright?" Chyna asked judging the situation.

"I...don't know," Lexi said turning back towards Ramsey.

"Ramsey?" Chyna asked.

"Okay so I thought we had fixed this problem earlier this week, but it seems that it wasn't fixed," he began fidgeting in place.

"What wasn't fixed?" Chyna asked at the same time Lexi asked, "What problem?"

"Jack's having doubts. Well...no...more than that. He's bowing out."

"What?" Lexi squealed. "What do you mean he's bowing out? Everything is paid for. The wedding party is already here. All the guests will be here soon. We're already at the hotel. He can't bow out!"

"I know," Ramsey grumbled. "We all said the same thing, but he keeps saying that he can't get married."

"Typical," Chyna snorted. "It's a bit late for that don't you think?"

"You would think so!" Ramsey said, pushing his hand back through his hair a couple more times.

Lexi's stomach knotted. He had said that he didn't want to get married. She didn't know what he was going to do, but she had a feeling this was going to be much worse than she had thought. This had something to do with her, somehow she was involved. Where Jack was concerned, she was always involved. "So, what's going to happen?" she almost whispered, starting to put the pieces together.

"I'm sorry, Lexi. I don't want to do this," Ramsey said.

Chyna glanced between the two. "Do what?"

"Jack wants to talk to you."

"No," Chyna said immediately.

"Don't you think I know that Chyna?" Ramsey asked torn in two about the decision. "I don't want her to go talk to him anymore than you do. But he might not get married today if he doesn't get some grounding."

"Why does Lexi have to ground him?" Chyna asked angrily. She really had to be pissed off to not use Lexi's full name in conversation.

"Probably because they've known each other forever," he said with a shrug.

Chyna shook her head back and forth. "No, because they used to fuck...forever. Not acceptable."

Ramsey shot up out of his chair. "Don't you think I know that?" he repeated louder, angrier.

"Hey guys, I'm still here," Lexi said waving her hands between the two. Ramsey stutter-stepped backwards as he seemed to realize that he had gotten out of hand. Chyna clamped her hand over her mouth. "And I can't go talk to him."

"Exactly," Chyna agreed, crossing her arms over her chest and sinking into her right hip.

"Look, if there is any way that you can convince him to go through with this, everyone would be eternally grateful. He doesn't even want to talk to the other groomsmen. The only person he said he would talk to about this was you. You know I wasn't exactly thrilled to hear that either, but I want this wedding over with. I'll never hear the end of it if Jack flakes. Please, Lexi, for me...just go talk to him."

"Oh my God, I can't believe I'm even hearing this," Chyna snapped, staring angrily between the two of them. "This is between you two. It might be the stupidest thing I've ever heard, and I don't want to be involved with this. So, you just figure it out." Chyna stormed across the room and out the door leaving them alone. They heard her knocking on Adam's door a second later.

Ramsey hung his head. "You know I'd never ask you if it wasn't urgent...if there was any other way."

"It's not my fault that he's having doubts. Honestly, I don't think he's in the right state of mind to get married, which explains why he is freaking out. He is terrified of commitment. Not to mention Bekah," Lexi cringed at the name, "well, never mind." She didn't really want to bring her into this.

"He must have been in the right state of mind when he proposed," he said. Lexi tried to keep from rolling her eyes. Ramsey didn't know about her and Jack sleeping together that night. Besides Chyna, she didn't want anyone to know. But without that knowledge, it sure did make this seem a little ridiculous on her end. "And he was in the right state of mind for the past year. He's just getting freaked out. This is normal."

"Then why does he need me?" she asked crossing her arms.

Ramsey shrugged. "He won't let us talk to him."

"Well, I doubt *I* can convince him to stay with her."

"I bet you can," he said not skipping a beat.

"Why would I even want to convince him to stay with someone like Bekah?" she couldn't help spitting out as she circled the room in frustration.

"Because you're not in love with him anymore," he whispered into the quiet room.

Lexi stopped in her tracks. She wasn't in love with Jack anymore. Hadn't she thought she felt exactly that this morning when waking up in Ramsey's bed? She didn't know if it was true. Jack would always mean something to her, but whether that was love in the same way it had been love in college, she couldn't contemplate at this moment. And anyway, was that enough to make her convince him to marry Bekah?

Nope.

"I still can't do it," she murmured. "Whether I love him or not, doesn't change the fact that I just don't like your sister, Ramsey. I think she's manipulative and deceitful, and if she loves Jack at all, I would be very surprised."

"You don't get to make that decision though," Ramsey told her. "You don't get to choose whether she loves him or not…if he loves her. They're going to get married."

"Yet, I have to convince him, when I think it is completely idiotic?" she responded raising her voice.

"We just need you to calm him down, because he refuses to listen to anyone else. You've known him the longest."

"No, Seth has," she jumped in.

Ramsey didn't even seem to listen to what she had said. "And he trusts you. He will listen to you. You don't have to convince him to get married. If you can calm him down enough, he will figure it out on his own."

Lexi wasn't too sure about that. Ramsey did not know Jack like she did. If she went down there to "calm him down," all hell could break loose. "You don't know that."

"Well, there aren't really any other options, since he refuses to speak to anyone else."

"Does Bekah know?" Lexi asked.

"Fuck no!" Ramsey cried standing in frustration. "If this never gets to Bekah it would be too soon. She does not need to know that Jack is freaking out. This is normal, and the bride doesn't need to be involved in this."

"Will she ever know that I went to see him?" she asked, curious how this scenario would actually play out.

"Never," he said instantly. Bekah would be furious with everyone involved for all of eternity if she knew that Jack had been with Lexi alone prior to his wedding. No one wanted to deal with that wrath.

Lexi nodded. "I still won't do it."

Ramsey sighed and walked across the room to her. He pulled her into a hug releasing all the tension they had both been carrying in this argument. He pulled back and gave her a light kiss on the cheek. "Okay. If you won't do it, then I can't force you. But if you can find a way to do it…*for me*, I would appreciate it more than anything I've ever asked of you. I want us to work more than anything. Could you imagine having to deal with Bekah in our relationship if she doesn't get married today?" he whispered almost as a side note.

Lexi froze in his arms. That thought really chilled her to the core. If she didn't marry Jack, then Bekah would be even more involved in trying to break them up. Lexi never wanted to deal with Bekah again. Not that her marrying Jack was the ideal situation, but she didn't want her involved in their relationship either.

"That would be…awful."

"I know."

"Ramsey, I don't want to talk to him today," she groaned, sinking into his arms again.

"I know, baby," he said stroking her long hair. "Can you just do it for me?"

Lexi hated this with every ounce of her being. She was standing her ground. She wasn't going to talk to him. She was finally over him, and then Ramsey had to pull that line. She wouldn't have done it for anyone else. She could have turned down anyone else, but Ramsey seemed so desperate. He needed her to do this, and what else had he really asked of her?

"Fine," she mumbled disheartened. "I'll go talk to him."

"Thank you so much," he said, giving her another kiss on the cheek before releasing her and reminding her how to get to the groom's rooms.

Lexi left the room a few seconds later. She sighed as she moved throughout the hotel, unable to believe that she was actually going to do this. After everything that had happened with Ramsey, the last thing she wanted to do was be alone with Jack. She had been alone with him under that weeping willow earlier in the week, and that had almost been catastrophic. Here she was finally happy with her lot, and Jack insisted on interfering.

Maybe she was being too pessimistic about the situation. If Jack wanted to be with Lexi, he'd had more than a million opportunities for that to happen. And it hadn't, so she had to accept the fact that they just weren't ever going to be together. Wasn't that the whole reason she was at this wedding? Wasn't that the whole reason she had flown down to Atlanta last year? She had wanted closure.

If anything, Ramsey had helped bring her that semblance of closure. No matter how much her heart told her that she wanted to be with Jack, she didn't honestly want to be with him. They were a train wreck together…as good as a train wreck could get, but still a train wreck.

Not that she would be surprised if Jack was freaking out. She would be freaked out in his position. But he couldn't have his cake and eat it too. He was getting married in a few short hours. They had their chance, and he had chosen that evil wench over her. She didn't understand his decision, but it was still the decision he had made and he had to stick with it.

Lexi was so lost in her thoughts that she didn't even notice her surroundings, and she nearly ran into someone directly in front of her. "Sorry," she said not even glancing up as she tried to side-step the person.

"Lexi?" the man asked.

When he said her name, her head snapped up at the familiar voice. "Clark? What are you doing here?" Lexi was utterly stunned. This seemed like the last person that Jack would invite to his wedding, and also the last wedding that Clark would attend. As far as she knew, Clark still hated Jack. They had once been good friends, but Clark had never forgiven him for cheating with Lexi.

"I was invited. What are you doing here?" he asked, narrowing his eyes as he looked at the direction she had been headed.

"I…I…" She was so stunned she couldn't even gather an answer for him. There were too many reasons as to why she was here, and knowing Clark he would be able to deduce a few easily. He was too intuitive for his own good and always had been. She could already see the pieces falling together in his head.

"Please don't tell me you are here for Jack," he demanded his jaw clenching at the very thought.

"Uh…well, kind of."

"Lexi, seriously? On his wedding day?" Clark asked furrowing his brow and shaking his head in disbelief.

"No, not like that!" she cried, hating that she even had to defend herself against this. "I'm dating one of the groomsmen." God, that didn't sound good either. She was sure that it looked like she was just involved with one of the groomsmen to get to Jack. Ugh, why was Clark even here?

"Right…you're dating one of his friends. That doesn't sound familiar," he grumbled under his breath.

"Jesus, Clark, I don't have time for this. What are you actually doing here?"

"I couldn't believe he was marrying someone other than you. I wanted to see it first hand," he said with an easy shrug.

Lexi rolled her eyes dramatically. "If you came here to taunt us about our past, then get over yourself. What happened was years ago, Clark."

"Oh, yeah, where were you headed so intently?" he asked arching his eyebrows.

"I have to go talk to Jack," she admitted slowly. Clark looked at her pointedly. "Just butt out alright! I'm sure it's not what you think."

"I'm sure," he said with a devilish smirk.

"I don't know why every meeting we have has to be like this."

"Probably because it always has something to do with Jack," he said. "No one thought he would marry anyone other than you...me included. So, you being here is a little too perfect."

Lexi rolled her eyes again. She couldn't believe this was happening. "I don't have time for this. I'm kind of in a hurry. Enjoy the wedding. Hopefully, the next time we talk it won't have to be about Jack."

"Not likely, but I'll keep hoping." Lexi groaned as she began to stomp in the opposite direction. "Oh, and Lexi?" She spun around giving him a sinister look. "You look good."

She pivoted on her foot, her hair flying out around her as she stormed away from him. Oh, the nerve of that one! She knew she had done him wrong. She knew that she had been a terrible person to him. If *anyone* knew, Lexi knew. She had felt terrible about it for years. She swore she would never be that person again, and she hadn't cheated on anyone since then. There was no need to rub their past indiscretions in her face. She didn't care if he hadn't been expecting her to be in attendance...or maybe he had, she wasn't even sure. She was just furious that he had made her day deteriorate even further. She was pretty certain that it could only continue to go downhill from here.

Lexi stopped before she reached the door to the groom's dressing rooms. She took a deep breath and entered. The space was a near match of the one she had left, but two or three times the size with a fireplace and grand piano. Seth, Luke, and Hunter were sitting in chairs in the common room. Seth was drinking straight from a handle of Jack Daniels. They must have thought it would be funny....ironic. Seth passed the bottle to Luke when he noticed her.

"Don't tell Sandy," he said standing quickly as she approached.

Lexi couldn't help but smile at him. At least someone really seemed to care about their significant other. "No worries there. I'm here to see Jack."

Seth, Luke, and Hunter sent each other a knowing look. She could have read that look from a mile away. They didn't think it was a good idea for her to go in to see him. And to be honest, she agreed with them on so many levels. Being alone with Jack right before his wedding was not the brightest idea in the world, but then again, it hadn't been her idea.

"Can we talk about this, Lex?" Seth asked, freely using Jack's nickname.

"Look, I'm only here are the request of the groom and the insistence of one of the groomsmen—my boyfriend," she tossed out the description for reassurance. Though she doubted it gave them any. She had known all of these guys a long time. They had all been there when the Clark/Kate fiasco had gone down…and even before that, with Danielle.

"I think that maybe you should stay out of it," Seth proceeded forward.

"I couldn't agree with you more," she said.

"Well, then what are you doing here?" Luke asked, tossing back a shot of the whiskey and handing it to Hunter.

"There really isn't time for this, guys. You know as well as I do that Jack is a philandering ass. You've always known, and you never cared up until this moment in his life, because now he's getting married," she said waving her hands in the air belittling the statement. "For some reason a piece of paper changes your mind about his behavior, which is kind of bullshit to be honest. So just do the same thing you did for the last seven years and turn a blind eye to the fact that I am going into his room. Okay?"

She knew that none of them would believe her if she had said that nothing was going to happen. She didn't want anything to happen, but the only way to get their attention would be to throw it back in their face. They had stood idly by all those years and let things happen. There was no legitimate reason now to get all high and mighty.

All the guys ducked their chins, admitting their involvement as an accomplice to Jack's actions. They knew, as well as anyone, just what they had witnessed and overlooked it all that time. And though they felt bad about it at the moment, they weren't going to stop her. And anyway, she wasn't planning on anything happening with Jack.

Lexi threw them a fake smile before sauntering towards the French double doors. She opened them without knocking and quickly closed them in the faces of the three guilty guys behind her.

"Lex," Jack murmured in an almost desperate tone.

"Hey, Jack," she said tentatively. She couldn't help but notice how gorgeous he looked in his tux. She wondered if they had chosen blue to match his eyes, because she could see how much they stood out from across the room.

"I'm glad you're here," he said as he cleared the distance between them.

Before Lexi even knew what was going on, Jack grabbed her hips firmly in his hands and pressed her back against the door. Lexi gasped as she thudded against the wood. As she was recovering from the fact that her back had shaken the door frame, she realized in that split second that Jack's body was pressing against her. His hand threaded into her hair, and his face moved closer towards her.

Lexi's mouth opened slightly in surprise. Was he about to kiss her?

Just when the thought connected in her mind, his mouth dropped down and met her lips.

24

PRESENT

Lexi froze, momentarily taken in by the delicious feel of his lips pressed against her. She recognized something distinctly reckless in his demeanor in that instant...utterly reckless. It was like he didn't care what he was doing or what kind of damage he was causing, he just wanted Lexi. Jack wanted her with a primal instinct he had never been able to tame. She was his escape, and on a different day, she would have wanted to escape with him.

But today, she could not believe he had the nerve to kiss her.

She didn't care if he was having doubts or if he wanted to bow out of the wedding, that didn't suddenly make it okay for him to kiss her. Even Lexi, with her loose morals when it came to Jack Howard, knew that this was 100% not okay...not on his wedding day.

She placed both of her hands on his chest and attempted to separate herself from Jack. He didn't even seem to notice or acknowledge her efforts. His hands resting on her hips held her more firmly in place. She couldn't believe this. He wouldn't even budge an inch. "Jack," she groaned still trying to shove him away, but he wasn't listening. He was a man possessed.

Jack hadn't had his lips on her in over a year, and she had wanted to keep it that way. After what had happened the last time, she hadn't wanted to be put in this position again. Somehow she always found herself kissing him. But she wasn't a confused girl this time around, she knew better than to let this continue. She couldn't believe what she was considering doing, but he wasn't exactly leaving her with any other option.

Almost out of instinct, Lexi's knee hitched up and connected cleanly with his groin. Lexi had never kicked a guy in the balls before, but apparently she had executed it properly.

Jack immediately broke free of her and doubled over in pain. "Fuck," he cried gasping for breath. "Fuck. Fuck. Fuck." His face turned beat red and contorted into agony. She just stood there over him and watched him hold himself as tears came to his eyes.

For some reason, that was ridiculously satisfying. He certainly didn't need to be using those things for anything in the near future, and he had been sexually harassing her.

"What the fuck was that, Lexi?" Jack cried out as he put his head between his knees to ease the pain.

"What the fuck was that?" she asked him. "Are you joking? You were molesting me on the day of your wedding!"

"No need to knee me in my balls. Fuck," he cried out again, relenting to sit helplessly on the floor.

"Oh, you don't think so? What gives you the right to kiss me? You completely lost all privileges in that department when you proposed to Bekah. What kind of person kisses someone else *on their wedding day*?" she asked throwing her arms in the air. "Are you a fucking moron Jack? Do you know nothing of fidelity or loyalty or honesty or commitment? I think you have no concept of those things. You are the *exact* same person you are when I first met you. You haven't changed at all."

"You liked that person," he grumbled painfully.

"Oh, don't even get me started! You lied to me. You were dating someone else, and you never even bothered to tell me. How could I ever have been fooled into thinking you would like and respect me after that, let alone think you could ever *love* me? You are too selfish to see anyone or anything else," Lexi spat at him.

"You weren't much better. You cheated on Clark," he mumbled taking deep breathes.

"It is my greatest shame, my biggest regret. You…you don't even know what those words mean. You never felt bad…never. You never wanted me to be first. Bekah was right about one thing, as much as I hate to admit that, but I always was second best to you. You never wanted me for me. You wanted me for the easy sex you got when we were talking. We had so many shots, and you just blew it. You knocked it out of the park." Lexi crossed her arms angrily, thinking about how fucked up their relationship had been for so long. She didn't care if she loved him or if she wanted to be around him or that they had this immediate attraction. She needed more than that, and it was something Jack was never able to provide.

"I did want us to be together," he said, glancing back up at her finally.

Lexi bent down to look at him at eye level. She couldn't believe how gorgeous his eyes still looked even though they were teared up and slightly red. But he would need more than the beautiful blue eyes she had always fallen for to get out of this conversation. "It took me a long time to realize how much of a liar you are."

"I'm not a liar, Lex. I always said I would tell you the truth," he whined.

Lexi shook her head. "You always said the words, but you only spoke the truth when it benefited you. And in that sense Jack, you have never changed."

"When did I lie to you?" he demanded. He doubled back over as he clutched himself. She had really done a number on him.

"When?" she asked with a cynical laugh. "You want me to make a list for you?"

Jack nodded. "When did I honestly lie to you, Lexi."

"I think your most telling moment Jack was when you told me that you wanted to be with me and then proposed to Bekah. If that isn't the biggest lie you've ever told, then I don't know what is," she spoke bitterly. He had been everything she had ever wanted, and he had thrown it aside.

Jack raised his head and let his sad blue eyes rest back on her. "I did want us to work, Lexi."

"But you *proposed* to her only hours after having sex with me!" she cried, straightening up to avoid the prolonged eye contact. "That's disgusting."

"It's just…I thought we could be together, and then I saw you with Ramsey. I was…jealous," he murmured attempting to stand up.

"You were jealous of Ramsey?" she asked arching an eyebrow.

"Yeah and apparently I had good reason to be. You guys were together for a year. You're here for him," he said with a shrug.

"So, you proposed to Bekah, because I kissed Ramsey, not because you wanted to marry her?" Lexi asked. However implausible the scenario was, she wanted to get his absurd answers out in the open.

"That's not exactly what I meant."

"No? You do realize whatever you are going to say will sound ridiculous," she said, crossing her arms again to block off the sympathy that was starting to creep up in her. She had known Jack too long. She didn't need to get sucked into his trap again.

"I just mean that when I saw you with Ramsey, I saw that I wasn't everything to you," he murmured leaning against a dresser for support. "I saw that we had too much baggage to really work together as a couple. I wanted it. I always wanted it, but I wasn't sure if it was ever plausible. I wasn't sure if you could ever look past what had happened in our past to move onto a future with us."

"So, you picked the easy way out. You fucked me and then went for your blonde bitch as always," she snapped forcefully. Lexi was so angry at his explanation. She'd had similar thoughts at one point in time, but that didn't mean she was going to walk away from him. They had both run away too many times before. They were two peas in a pod, as much each other's escape as the thing to run from.

But to just desert their entire past because he was scared and jealous was a terrible explanation. She would have expected better from Jack. "You didn't even have the decency to—oh, I don't know—communicate with me about any of this. I didn't even know you were planning to propose, and then poof, you're engaged!"

"I was going to tell you," he said reaching out to her.

Lexi instantly took a step away from him. She couldn't believe him. She couldn't believe anything he said to her anymore. He had lied to her…about everything. And it was about damn time that she followed through with that belief. She liked to think she had grown since then…even in a week's time. "No. No you weren't, and it doesn't matter. You were right about Ramsey anyway. That's probably why we're back together."

"What?" Jack asked his head snapping to face her. He groaned at the sudden movement and leaned more heavily on the dresser. "You guys are back together?"

Lexi looked at him suspiciously. He looked a bit shaken by the announcement though to be fair she had just kicked him in the balls. "Yes, stop acting so surprised."

"He's not right for you," Jack said instantly.

"Oh, please," Lexi said rolling her eyes. "As if Bekah is right for you? I don't think so."

"This isn't about Bekah. This is about Ramsey."

"This is as much about Bekah as it is about Ramsey. You have no say in whether or not I'm dating him or why," Lexi snapped. She was tired of his games. She was tired of him wanting her to be single while he went off and married Bekah. That didn't make sense. Bekah and Ramsey were intrinsically linked in this charade that her and Jack had been playing.

She could see it in his face that he didn't want to concede that point. He never wanted to give up his hold on her. It didn't matter if he was going to be married in a few hours. "I know you're dating him, because you think he can give you a happy life."

"I don't just think that Jack. I know he can," she said with a cocky smile.

Jack took a few steps back from the dresser and rested against the footboard of the enormous bed centered in the room. Lexi knew she had entered a bedroom when she had walked in, but until that second she hadn't really assessed her surroundings. The bed really was massive. It took up a significant portion of the room and was so full of down pillows and a soft down comforter that when Jack leaned back, the bed dipped in around him. It looked like it would completely envelope her if she lay back against it.

"What, you think everything is going to be fine now that he's working with Parker every day?" Jack asked,.

Lexi didn't want to think about Parker, but she knew that she couldn't back down from Jack. Once he knew he had an advantage he would keep pushing until he got his way, and she couldn't have that. Ramsey was not interested in Parker. They had history and nothing else. If Ramsey had wanted to get back together with Parker, he'd had years to do that. There was no need now, when he was finally happy with Lexi, to go and mess around with Parker. The only reason Lexi was even here was because Ramsey had asked her. He had trusted her enough to not give into Jack, and she had to trust him in turn.

"Yes, I think everything will be fine," she said standing her ground.

Jack laughed. He actually laughed at her. It sounded rather painful since he was still recovering, but it was definitely laughter. "When people have that much history, it's never fine. Just look at us…look at where we are. You think this is just fine?"

"I think I kicked you in your balls to show you how *fine* everything is between us," she said leveling her gaze on him.

"Yes, but they were going to get married. It's a bit different, don't you think?" he asked trying to unseat her.

"You want to bring up people getting married, Jack? Really?" she asked glaring at him.

Jack shrugged again. "Go on, and tell me that you think it's the same as us," he challenged her.

"You know, in fact, I don't think it's the same as us. If they wanted to be together, they would have. Clearly they don't want that. They might be working together, but that's all, Jack. Not everyone is like you. You have no idea what Ramsey can give me," she said, shoving a lock of hair behind her ear.

Jack shook his head side to side. "Just as delusional as you always were," he said resting his arm back against the bed invitingly.

"And what's that supposed to mean?" she asked avoiding looking at the bed. The last thing she wanted to do was appear interested in that bed.

"On some small level, you don't think that working in close proximity together every day is going to rekindle something that was once there? Imagine if we had to work together every day. What would it be like?" Lexi stopped and considered it. She was sure that it would be a disaster. She had trouble enough resisting him when she rarely ever saw him. She couldn't imagine what it would be like. But she didn't know if that's how Ramsey and Parker's relationship worked. It was unfair to judge them based on how an atypical relationship functioned. "I take it you get my point?"

"I think it's different with them than it is with us, because they were together, they broke up, and they moved on. We were never together, we never broke up, and we've never moved on. Clearly, you just kissed me."

"But it's not that far-fetched," Jack countered.

"Stop trying to make me doubt what I have. It's not going to work. Ramsey and I have so much more than you ever gave me. You don't even know what it's like to be in a relationship with me. Ramsey does. You don't know what it's like to vacation with me. Ramsey does. You don't know what it's like to not be scared that we're going to cheat on each other. Ramsey knows that feeling. In some ways he knows me better than you ever could Jack, because you never gave us a real shot. I'm not going to stand here and let you talk shit about Ramsey. I love him and that's that," she said turning away from him angrily.

She knew that she hadn't exactly done what she had been planning to do when she walked into Jack's room, but he had changed the game when he had kissed her. She didn't care if he married the bitch or not. She didn't care whether or not he ruined his life. She just wanted him out of hers.

Lexi reached for the door knob, but Jack stopped her. "Okay, Lexi, you win."

She wasn't sure if she had ever heard those words from his mouth. Somehow throughout their entire relationship, Lexi had always felt like she was on the losing side of the scenario. Jack never gave in. Jack never backed down. Jack never relented.

"What did you say?" she asked slowly turning back around.

"You win," he repeated admitting defeat.

Lexi gulped. "What do I win?" she asked hesitantly.

"I didn't give you what you deserved. I screwed you over like a royal ass, when I really just wanted to make everything better," he said edging towards her.

"Jack," she murmured, eyeing his approach with caution. She didn't want or need this apology. All she had wanted was to leave on a high. She had pushed him back, stood her ground, and was satisfied to leave it as it was.

"I've never treated you the way I should have. I told you once that I'd never go back to change what happened between us. That I might miss out on what we had," he said softly. "But I was wrong. I would do anything I could to go back to that time when we could have been together and change the way I acted. I'd change it, because we were fated to be together however brief, however unbelievable, however painful, however flawed. But…"

"But you can't," she finished for him easily.

"No…I can't. I can't change it," he said nodding his head sadly. "So what should I do, Lex?" he asked his bright blue eyes searching hers.

Lexi sighed and shrugged her shoulders. What could she tell him? She was here to tell him to get married to give up on her, and wasn't that exactly what she had just argued for? Yet, a small part of her didn't want him to get married—to marry Bekah.

She was torn. Could she truly tell him to marry someone she thought was completely wrong for him? Was it better to allow him to be completely and totally off the market even if she was sending him to his grave? She hated thinking like that, but it kind of felt like that.

"I can't tell you what to do, Jack," she murmured dropping her arms. "You have to decide on your own."

"I know I should, but what should I do?" he asked begging her for an answer.

"The fact that you are debating this at all should be a sign," she finally muttered.

Jack nodded, pleading with her to continue. "So, you think I should call it off?"

"I am *not* going to be responsible for you calling off your wedding!" she cried. "You make up your own fucking mind, Jack Howard!"

"Don't start yelling at me. You know how I feel about you when you get angry," he said taking another step towards her.

"Do you want to have another injury?" she asked him arching an eyebrow. He couldn't get any closer. Her body didn't listen to her brain, and the thought of him slamming her back into the door again crossed her mind. She quickly tried to repress it, but she backed up farther from him for good measure.

"Uh, no," he said stepping backwards again. "I just don't know what to do, Lex."

"Do whatever you want. I was supposed to come in here to convince you to marry her. Well, I came here a year ago and was pretty successful at it. Why should now be any different?"

Jack stopped and really looked at her. Lexi wasn't sure why that statement had managed to keep him from advancing on her, but she wasn't going to complain. If she had finally gotten through to him, then all the better.

"Alright," he said nodding. "Thanks for coming to see me even though you didn't want to. I appreciate you being here for me like I was for you. It really means a lot...everything to me, Lex."

Lexi tried to keep her mouth from dropping open. Who was this person? Jack never gave up. Jack never apologized. He certainly never thanked her for her opinion on the matter. They could work together in the easy way that their relationship had formed over time, but this was different. This made it seem like Jack had somehow grown too, since she had last seen him, which seemed pretty implausible considering he had just kissed her.

"You're welcome, Jack," she said taking that opportunity to push the bedroom door back open.

Lexi turned around to face the questioning looks of the groomsmen and found herself face to face with an entire room of people.

"I knew it!" Bekah screeched sauntering forward. Her hair and makeup were immaculate, but she had yet to be fitted into her wedding dress for the upcoming event. She looked manic as she stormed across the suite.

Lexi could not figure out what the fuck she was doing here. Ramsey, Chyna, and Adam ran after her, trying to restrain her from walking forward, but what was she doing in the room in the first place? This was her wedding day. She was not supposed to know that Lexi had ever been in that room. It was tradition that the groom wasn't supposed to see the bride on their wedding day. Lexi would have never pinned Bekah as someone who wanted to break tradition. This didn't make any sense.

"Bekah, stop," Ramsey commanded grabbing her elbow forcefully. "You're going to ruin everything."

"*I'm* going to ruin everything?" she asked twirling around and smacking his hand off of her. "Your little homewrecker is in a bedroom with my fiancé! Don't you think I should be a little concerned with that?"

"Not if you trust Jack like I trust Lexi," he pointed out.

"I trust Jack," she amended quickly, "just not Lexi. You don't know what she's done."

"Actually, I think I do. I know you find it hard to believe, but Lexi and I did talk about her past relationships when we dated for the last year."

"Then you know she's a cheating whore!" Bekah cried, turning back to glare at Lexi who hadn't moved from her position in front of the door.

Ramsey grabbed her arm even more forcefully and yanked her backwards. "Now you listen and you listen good, because I'm only going to say this once. Don't fucking talk about her like that."

"Don't you fucking talk to me like that, or manhandle me," she said pulling away from him again. "She's the one trying to ruin my wedding."

"She's the one trying to fix your wedding," he growled releasing her.

"It wouldn't need to be fixed, if she didn't try to ruin everything," she said walking forward towards Lexi. "Isn't that right?"

Lexi didn't know what to say. It was true that she had tried to ruin their relationship, but only under the pretense that her and Jack were going to be together. After that she had left them completely alone. She had only contacted Jack twice before this week, and both times had been heartbreaking, dire circumstance—her father's heart attack and her break up with Ramsey. They didn't really count.

"I'm not trying to ruin anything for you Bekah," Lexi finally said.

"You sure about that?" she asked, "Because you look like you are coming out of a bedroom with my fiancé."

"Bekah, what are you doing?" Jack asked, walking out of the bedroom and standing next to Lexi.

"Jack," she murmured after he spoke. "She's out to ruin us."

"No, she's not. Just calm down," he said trying to reason with her. "What are you even doing here? I'm not supposed to see you until the wedding."

"I had a sneaking suspicion that she was here. I had to follow my instincts, and look she's here! That doesn't seem like a coincidence. There's something going on."

"There's nothing going on between me and Jack," Lexi grumbled. "I can't fucking believe you would barge in here on your wedding day. You have no concept of reality. You have no concept of trust. You thought something was going on and came in here unannounced. I'm not ruining your wedding day. You are!" Lexi couldn't believe she had gotten the words out. She had wanted to say something catty to Bekah for so long, but out of respect for the men in her life she had resisted. The accusations she was hurling Lexi's way had been too much in that moment. She hadn't been able to hold back.

"This coming from the woman who walks out of a bedroom with another woman's fiancé," Bekah pointed out.

"But nothing happened with me and Jack," Lexi said standing her ground.

"Oh, stop trying to act so innocent!" Bekah said to Lexi, raising her voice.

Lexi narrowed her eyes at her dangerously. "Me? Act innocent? After everything you've done to sabotage my life?"

Bekah scoffed. "You don't even need my help. You fuck it up enough on your own."

"I really don't need to hear this from you," Lexi said shaking her head and turning the other direction.

"Bekah, don't you think you've done enough damage?" Ramsey asked glaring at his sister.

"I am your sister!" she cried staring at him in disbelief. "I am only trying to look out for you."

"By trying to hurt my girlfriend?" he asked looking at her like she was mentally impaired.

"By protecting you," she said grasping for straws.

"Oh, that always worked out so well in your favor," Lexi said rolling her eyes. "Going to convince another girl to get an abortion to save your skin?" Lexi spat at her.

The room went silent. She hadn't even meant to say that out loud, but something about Bekah had made her snap. She hated her with everything she had. She wanted nothing more than for her to live a long and miserable life filled with heartache and loneliness. It was what she deserved after all the deception and lies. She wanted to tear her down as much as she had torn Lexi down. She knew it was wrong and that she should take the higher ground, but Bekah hardly deserved that.

"What…are…you…talking about?" Bekah asked her voice shaking.

"Lexi," Ramsey hissed grabbing her elbow.

"What is she talking about Ramsey?" Bekah demanded, spinning around to face him.

"You know what I'm talking about. Stop acting so ignorant of the situation," Lexi responded. Ramsey's grip on her elbow tightened, and she snapped her mouth close. She had gone too far. He didn't talk about these things. He didn't bring these things up, and here she had just announced the details to an entire group of people. Even if no one else really knew what was going on they were sure to think the worst. This seemed to be a conversation he had avoided having with Bekah. Lexi had figured they had already had it out about his suspicions that Bekah had convinced Parker to have an abortion. How wrong could she be?

"How does this involve me?" Bekah asked seething.

"We can talk about this later," Ramsey said pleading with Bekah not to continue the conversation.

"Hell no, we can't. I want everything out on the table. What is this bitch talking about?" she growled.

"That's my girlfriend, Bek," he said warningly the same time Lexi cried, "Hey!"

"Well, start answering questions then," Bekah said angrily.

Ramsey sighed. "I know what happened with Parker," he said hesitantly.

"What happened with Parker?" she growled

"That she didn't miscarry," he said, barely louder than a whisper.

Bekah's mouth popped open, and her face blanched. Even through her coat of makeup, Lexi could tell that she had lost all color in her skin. She looked shell-shocked that the conversation had come around to this topic. "She did Ramsey."

Ramsey shook his head. It's like he knew that she would deny it. "She didn't miscarry, Bek. I know she didn't."

"How could you know that?" she asked her hands shaking in front of her. "You weren't even there."

"I don't want to argue about this with you. God knows I've argued with Parker enough about it. She'll never admit to it and neither will you, but I know what I know," he said with a sad shrug.

"I can't believe you're bringing this up," she said turning the full force of her anger on Lexi. "You have no right to go digging into other people's lives."

"Oh, that's rich coming from you," Lexi said rolling her eyes. "Didn't you ask me to Atlanta just to fuck with me?"

"I didn't ask you to come here. Actually, I never invited you to my wedding. I would have much preferred you stay away from me and my family," she growled.

"You don't get a choice in the matter," Lexi said looking up at Ramsey. She knew that it was probably a bad move to challenge Bekah. After all, who knew what she would resort to in order to hurt Lexi again.

"Maybe I don't, but Ramsey does," Bekah said with a sinister smile that Lexi recognized. "If he knew the truth about you..."

Ramsey shook his head, stepping between his sister and his girlfriend. "Would you both calm down? Bekah, Lexi is right. You have no say in whether or not I see Lexi. Lexi, Bekah is right, in that you had no right to bring up this kind of stuff in front of everyone. You both need to calm down. It's your wedding day. I can't believe you're even here right now having this argument," he said in disgust.

Lexi took a step back from Bekah. She knew that she had been out of line, but she hadn't been able to see anything other than Bekah when she was fighting with her. She was blinded to the rest of the world. Her vision went blurry. Her senses were dulled. All she could see was the bitch that was standing in front of her, and the anger that bubbled up at the very mention of her name. But she couldn't be that person in front of Ramsey. It was, after all, his sister. He wasn't going to completely turn his back on her, even if Lexi thought he should.

"Sorry," Lexi murmured, taking a few more steps back and standing next to Chyna.

"Well, I'm not sorry," Bekah called.

"Bek, maybe you should calm down," Jack intervened. He looked amazed at the showdown between the two women.

"I should calm down?" she snarled. "She's the one who cheated on my brother."

Once again the room fell silent. Everyone slowly turned to look at Lexi who looked as stunned as everyone else. Lexi had no idea how she had come to that conclusion. Then it hit her, Bekah must have thought that the phone call she had overheard at the Bridges mansion, her Mystery Man, was someone that she had been seeing while she had been dating Ramsey. But that simply wasn't the case. She could proudly say that she had never cheated on Ramsey. She should have told him about what happened before this moment, but she hadn't cheated on him. They had been broken up, and she hadn't expected to get back together with him.

"I overheard her talking to him on the phone at my luncheon," Bekah added.

"What is she talking about?" Ramsey asked, turning his back on Bekah and looking at Lexi. She couldn't keep herself from blushing, even though Bekah's comments weren't exactly the truth. Lexi turned her eyes infinitesimally to the right and glanced at Adam. He sighed and averted his eyes.

"What was that?" Chyna asked pointing between them. "Does Adam know something about this, but not me?"

"Uh…" Lexi said licking her lips and tucking a strand of hair behind her ear. "I didn't cheat on you," she said carefully.

"Then what is she talking about?" he repeated.

"Wait, wait, wait," Chyna said. "Did you cheat on him with Adam?" Lexi said the pieces falling together in Chyna's mind at the accusation. Adam was the only person Chyna had ever really fallen for. Adam had always been extremely friendly with Lexi, but still Adam was friendly with everyone. However, it had to look worse with the look that had passed between them coupled with the fact that Chyna knew that she and Adam needed to discuss something.

"With Adam?" Ramsey asked stunned.

"That must have been who she was talking to on the phone," Bekah said triumphantly. "She was practically having phone sex in the bathroom of my parent's house."

"Hold on," Lexi said raising her hands. "You guys are getting out of control."

"Then tell me you didn't sleep with Adam," Chyna said pulling her friend around to face her.

Lexi glanced at Adam. This was not good. This wasn't how this was supposed to happen. Adam wasn't supposed to show up with Chyna, and she should have already told Ramsey about this. She hadn't wanted Ramsey to find out like this. It wasn't fair to him after the hell she had put him through for lying.

Not that she had lied to him. She really hadn't, but now it looked like she was hiding things. Shit! She hated this!

Adam just shrugged. "You might as well tell them."

Chyna turned to face him as if she had forgotten he was in the room. Her eyes watered considerably as she stared at him in disbelief.

"Ramsey, I was going to tell you this morning," she began.

"*This* is what you were going to tell me?" he asked his mouth dropping open. "And I had to hear it from Bekah after everything we went through the past month?"

"No, no…it's not what you think. She has her facts wrong," Lexi quickly amended.

"Are you kidding me with this, Alexa?" Chyna asked. "You're my best friend."

"Adam and I did not sleep together!" Lexi cried, looking back and forth between Chyna and Ramsey. They both were eyeing her skeptically. The evidence seemed pretty damning against them, but she couldn't let that continue.

"What?" Chyna asked glancing from Lexi and back to Adam. "Then how are you involved?"

"She slept with John…right?" he asked, alluding to his illustrious brother. John had come onto Chyna over spring break, and had resulted in her messy break up with Adam.

Lexi's eyes dropped to the ground. Everything was out in the open now. "Yeah…I slept with John."

25

PRESENT

No one spoke for awhile after Lexi's declaration. She had slept with Adam's brother, John, when she and Ramsey had been broken up. She had been talking to him for weeks, and hiding it from everyone. But she hadn't expected her and Ramsey to have another chance. When she realized how wrong that was, she had cut it off and told him that she needed more time to think about it.

But no one else knew those things. They just knew that this was the same brother that had put the moves on Chyna, forcing her untimely break up with Adam. Chyna despised John—hated him. There was no way she had wanted Chyna to find out like this, but that was certainly better than her thinking she had slept with Adam! That would be the ultimate betrayal, and Lexi wouldn't have blamed Chyna if she never spoke to her again. Adam was handsome and wonderful. She had an uncanny connection with him, but it wasn't like *that*.

Not to mention Ramsey. She hadn't cheated on him, but the pain was still evident in his bright green eyes. He was completely taken aback. This seemed to be the last thing he had expected her to say. Bekah's statement claiming she had cheated on Ramsey wasn't true, but with her past it still had to leave doubts in his once unclouded mind. She wanted to tell him that things would be alright between them, but how could she know what he would do with this news?

Lexi wished with everything she was, that she could stop everyone from looking at her right then. Her brain was aching from the swell of emotions going through her, and their reactions weren't helping. Chyna appeared shell-shocked, if not a bit disgusted. No doubt she was thinking about the last time she had encountered John. Adam looked sympathetic, but like he had somehow known this would blow up in her face. Jack's smirk had returned to his face. And Bekah—Bekah was the worst of all. She wore smug like a new pair of Jimmy Choos. If Lexi could wipe that murderously arrogant look off her face, she swore she would die a happy woman.

"I really wanted to tell you Ramsey. I know what we've been through," Lexi said pausing to fully look him in the face. She needed to stand up for herself. She couldn't cower and hide behind her actions. She needed to take responsibility for what she had done. "No, I just, I can't apologize for it happening…"

Ramsey's eyes narrowed. Out of the corner of her eye, Lexi could see Chyna's mouth drop open. She knew this was a do or die moment. The two people she cared about most were waiting for an answer that she couldn't give them. She couldn't grovel and apologize for what she had done. She had been that person before, but she wasn't sorry that she had slept with John or even that she had rebounded with John. He was what she had needed at the time, when she had returned to New York broken once again. She wouldn't regret her time with him. She was tired of regrets.

And it's not as if she had asked for a break from Ramsey, they had broken up. She had told him not to call her, and he hadn't. She thought it was over. The fact that she was even in Atlanta with him was completely unanticipated.

But she didn't want Ramsey to get the wrong idea. She loved him, and she hadn't meant for him to think that she was lying. She just hadn't gotten around to telling him, and now she needed to make him understand.

Lexi sighed before continuing. "No, I'm sorry that it hurts you. I really am, but I'm not sorry that I slept with someone else," Lexi said amazed that she could even get the words out. "I wasn't dating you at the time. We were two consenting adults. In fact, I hadn't anticipated getting back together with you. Things have changed since then, and it's not going to ever happen again, but it did happen. I can't change it.

"So, either you have to accept that fact along with me, or you don't. We're at that point," Lexi said standing tall and fighting the urge to tuck a lock of hair behind her ear. She was more nervous about Ramsey's reaction than anything before this moment, and also completely confident in her decision to finally stand up for herself. Ramsey looked as if he wasn't sure exactly what he wanted to say.

Before he got the chance, Chyna butted in, "But you still slept with John knowing the kind of person he is. You still did it. Just because you say these things doesn't make it better. Think about what you did with him," Chyna said with a shudder. Adam reached out for her, but she didn't stop talking. "How can you even go on with your life? I'm sorry Adam, but you're brother is kind of disgusting," she said with an easy shrug.

"Can we really drop this line of conversation?" he asked. Adam was fiercely loyal to his brother nearly to a fault. "I know how you feel about him, and it made us do stupid things once before. Let's just avoid it all together."

Chyna batted him away from her, and turned back towards Lexi. "I'm sorry. I can't ignore this fact. My best friend *slept* with your brother. Not to mention you knew about it and didn't tell me. You guys were keeping it secret together. Alexa has never kept a secret from me before and now this. How could you?" Chyna asked a hitch in her voice.

"Chyna..." Lexi stammered, looking at her friend sympathetically. She honestly hadn't meant for it to be a secret forever. Before that phone call from Ramsey, she had intended on telling Chyna...one day. She just hadn't been ready when she had left New York, and hadn't seen Chyna since she decided to cut it off.

"Do you really blame her for not telling you, especially with how you're overreacting?" Adam asked attempting to talk some sense into her.

"Overreacting?" she squeaked. "You haven't seen overreacting!"

"And we don't want to," he said shaking his head at her.

"The fact that she slept with your brother doesn't bother you?"

"No," he stated simply with a shrug. "It really doesn't, and it shouldn't bother you. It's not like I think something happened between you and John. I wouldn't be okay with that, but my brother isn't a bad guy, Chyna. And as she said they were two consenting adults..."

"You're brother isn't a bad guy?" Chyna groaned rolling her eyes dramatically. "I wouldn't wish him on someone I like a lot less than Alexa."

"We've been through this," he grumbled clearly annoyed, "but you can't change it. All you can do is accept the fact that it happened and move on. She's your best friend after all. You two have been through a lot together..."

Chyna turned back to Lexi as if she were considering Adam's point, then shook her head. "That's exactly the reason that this doesn't make any sense. You've never been that person with me. Yet, you hid things from me...your best friend. I know you hide things from everyone else, but me? I thought you sleeping with Jack before their engagement was an all time low...but this..." Chyna stammered out in anger.

Lexi's hand went to her mouth instantly. She couldn't believe that Chyna would blurt out the secret she had been trying to keep from revealing all along. You could have heard a pin drop in the room, the silence was all encompassing.

When Lexi had thought that everything was out on the table after her confession about John, she hadn't actually anticipated *everything* being out on the table. She hadn't thought that Chyna would ever tell anyone, let alone a room full of people, that she had slept with Jack prior to his engagement to Bekah. She hadn't told anyone else so she hadn't been expecting anyone else to blurt out the news.

There was only one real reason why she hadn't told Bekah about her and Jack fucking during his birthday party a year ago. It certainly wasn't her regard for the woman. She couldn't think of a person she liked less and yet she had held back that one fact. She had held back the one thing that would have seriously turned Bekah away from Jack.

It was what she had always wanted. But after all that, she still hadn't told her the terrible thing that they had done in the hallway. She couldn't bring herself to do it. Not only was it humiliating that she had been desperate enough to actually sleep with him; he had kept his distance as if the only thing he had been after, was sex. She had never felt so low…so used. And she didn't want anyone other than Chyna to know that.

Even after that when she had finally begun to recover, she hadn't blurted the news to Bekah. When Bekah had pulled out that big honking diamond…Lexi's diamond, she had still kept quiet. After she even told Bekah that she was wearing a fake ring…for Christ's sake, the woman was wearing a *fake* diamond ring. Even after all that, Lexi had still kept the truth from her.

Only one reason remained for that.

Lexi knew it…deep down. Even if she hated admitting it to herself, she knew the reason for keeping the secret from a person she despised.

She didn't want them to break up because Jack had cheated with her. She had wanted Jack to break up with Bekah for *her*, and see Bekah's sniveling little face when she realized she had lost…that she had actually lost in her own web of games. More than ever, she wanted to be the reason for the break up on Jack's end, not Bekah's. But now that reason was morphing into something she liked even better. She no longer wanted to see the wedding canceled so she could finally claim Jack for her own.

No.

So that when Jack came crawling back to her, as he always did, she could tell him no. She could be the one to turn him down, the one to leave him hanging, the one to choose.

Lexi knew that it was sinister to even harbor those thoughts, and keep a secret so revealing to Bekah and Jack's relationship, but she couldn't help it. At first, she had done it to have Jack for the right reasons, whatever those were, and now she wanted to keep the secret in hopes that one day she would be able to turn the tables on him.

But how could she explain that to anyone? Clearly Chyna had blurted it out because she was pissed off with Lexi. She hadn't thought of the consequences of revealing that piece of information.

Within a few hours, Jack and Bekah were supposed to be getting married. If she had been in Bekah's position, she would have wanted to know everything about the person she was marrying. But would she ever really want to know this? Could you ever really be prepared for such deceit?

She had been on the wrong end of Jack's cheating before, and she knew what it felt like. She had been depressed for months…years. She hadn't been the same person until she had finally allowed herself to begin to move on. And they hadn't even been officially together…they certainly hadn't been engaged and about to be married. Lexi had no idea what could possibly be going on in Bekah's head at the moment. How could you move on from that moment?

"Is that true?" Bekah whispered turning to Lexi for confirmation.

"Bekah, how could you even think that I would do that?" Jack asked reaching for her. Bekah slipped away from him, and moved to stand in front of Lexi.

"You at least owe me an explanation," Bekah said, standing squarely in front of Lexi with her hands on her hips. Her eyes were large like saucers as they stared deeply at Lexi, awaiting an answer.

"I don't think I owe you anything Bekah," Lexi said with a shrug.

"Bekah, seriously?" Jack asked moving closer to her again.

"Ramsey!" Bekah snapped completely ignoring Jack's pleas. "How are you so quiet? How are you not shocked at this news? Just think if she could do it then, she can do it now. After all, she just slept with someone else!"

Lexi glanced over at Ramsey to see his reaction to this ordeal. She bit down on her lip slightly as a worry line creased her forehead. Bekah's accusations never sat lightly with Ramsey, and Lexi was terrified that any headway they had made this week would be stalled by Bekah's insinuations.

"I'm quiet, because unlike you Bekah I prefer to think before I speak," Ramsey said straight-faced and even-toned.

"What?" she demanded, sinking into one hip as if she hadn't heard him correctly. Lexi wasn't sure if *she* had heard him correctly.

"You heard me. You don't think before you accuse people of terrible things. You don't think before you try to use your manipulative ways to ruin other people's lives," he said.

"Ramsey!" she yelped.

Ramsey cut her off. "You think I didn't know that she slept with Jack?"

Lexi tried to cover her shock. She had never told Ramsey about that night. She couldn't bring herself to reveal what a terrible person she had been. He knew everything else about her relationship, but she honestly hadn't wanted anyone else to know.

She wasn't sure if he was lying about knowing, if he was trying to cover up for her, or if he actually knew about what had happened. Either way he was standing up for her, and telling Bekah off. It meant, at least she hoped it meant, that they were that much closer to being on the right track.

"You knew?" Bekah gasped.

"What the fuck?" Jack cried shaking his head. "That didn't happen."

"Jack, just shut up," Ramsey said silencing his outburst with a glare. "We all know. It's not like Lexi is denying it."

"Lex?" Jack pleaded, somehow thinking using her pet name would help him win his case. Lexi could see him imploring her with his big blue eyes. He wanted her to save him after everything that he had done. He wanted her to lie for him one last time. It's like he had forgotten that she had just kicked him in the balls only a short while ago. She hadn't forgotten that he had come onto her on his wedding day.

If she hadn't lied to Ramsey about John, she certainly wasn't going to lie about what she had done with Jack a year ago. There was no reason to lie for him…not anymore.

Lexi couldn't keep hiding.

"I'm not denying it," she finally answered, crossing her arms over her chest. Jack threw up his arms and began pacing the length of the hotel room.

"Why didn't you tell me?" Bekah demanded of her brother after Lexi's declaration. Lexi shouldn't have even been surprised that the question wasn't directed at Jack. She hadn't blamed him for anything else that he had done.

"How exactly would I broach the subject?" he asked pointedly. "Hey Bek, did you know that my girlfriend slept with your fiancé? Oh, you did? Nice. Well, glad that's out of the way. I wasn't going to ruin your life."

"That's not how it would go and you know it. As my brother, you had a right to tell me!"

"Just like you had a right to tell me that you were *lying* to Lexi about me playing her when we first started dating? Just like you had a right to tell me that you were going to *lie* to Lexi about my feelings for her? Just like you were going to leave her alone and not try to ruin our relationship?" he asked crossing his arms over his chest. "Tell me Bekah…why exactly do I owe you anything as my sister?"

"How dare you!" Bekah piped up. "I only did what was in your best interest."

Ramsey chuckled and shook his head. "Whatever Bek. But just to clarify, in case you weren't following along. Lexi slept with Jack before we were together, and she slept with someone else after we broke up. While I hate the thought of anyone else ever touching her again," he said openly glaring at Jack, "the woman has a point. She never cheated on me, and I don't think she ever intended on it. Stop trying to ruin her. Stop trying to ruin our relationship."

Just then the door to the groomsmen suite burst open, and in sauntered Amber, Maddie, and Kersey. Parker stood awkwardly in the door way, uncertain whether to take part in what was going on or to make a quick exit. Kersey glanced back when she noticed, and grabbed her rather forcefully for a girl who didn't even reach five feet tall. "Bekah, what are you doing in here?" Amber demanded her eyes wide in surprise that so many people were in the room. "We have been looking for you everywhere. Don't you know it's bad luck to see the groom before the wedding." Her thick Southern accent drawled out the last word an unnecessarily long time.

"Yeah, honey, let's get out of here," Kersey said openly eyeing Adam up and down like he was something she was going to eat for lunch. Chyna possessively stepped in front of him, and Kersey just shrugged as if that didn't matter.

"Actually, we're having a serious problem," Maddie interjected. "We couldn't find you or the wedding planner and the band cancelled."

"What?!" Bekah yelled, shocked out of her silence for the first time. "I thought you were on this Maddie! Don't you know the lead singer?"

"Well...yeah," she said her cheeks flaming slightly at the mention of the lead singer, "but uh...they're getting really famous, and when I tried to call him about showing up, he said that something came up. He was really vague."

"You promised me that they were going to be here tonight at my reception. Have you had my Daddy call their manager or anything?" she demanded instantly turning into Business Bekah.

Maddie shook her head. "No, I just tried calling him. He said that he had to go home to Seattle for an emergency, and he was really sorry he couldn't make it. You should have heard his voice...it was practically delectable. God, I can just imagine him with his shirt off all over again with that gorgeous body..."

Bekah waved her off. "Don't even right now, Mads. This is serious. I was promised a band, and I don't have a band."

"You still have a DJ," Kersey piped up. "We double booked, remember?"

Bekah shot her a look that would kill. "I don't care if I have a DJ. I want that band here. Find the wedding planner, find my Daddy, and make it happen."

"Wait, wait, wait, wait, wait...you can't be serious. You're still going to *marry* him after what you just found out?" Chyna gasped out.

She wasn't the only one who looked shocked either. Lexi, Ramsey, and Adam all held the same blank expressions. Lexi never wanted Bekah to know about what had happened between her and Jack that night. Bekah had won. But she had always thought Bekah would leave him if she had found out about what had transpired. Lexi hadn't done it for that purpose; she had done it thinking Jack would choose her, and he hadn't. But the fact that she wasn't even going to stop to think after that just amazed her.

Was this woman who had *everything* in the world that desperate for someone to care about her that she wouldn't even accept reality? Was she that desperate to get married?

"Of course, I'm marrying him," she said through gritted teeth, as if it were the most obvious course of action. "The wedding is happening within the hour. Everything is prepared. All the guests are arriving. It's all paid for..."

"Bekah, you know the money doesn't matter!" Ramsey said speaking out against this insane wedding.

Bekah sent him a mutinous look. "I love Jack," she said stepping towards him as he drew closer towards her.

Lexi couldn't even believe what was happening in front of her. Bekah and Jack were still going to go through with this? It had to be the worst decision on the face of the planet. Not only had Jack cheated on Bekah, but it had happened the day before he proposed. And he had tried to do the same thing on their *wedding day*! She couldn't fathom it. Jack had been having second thoughts all week. There was no way that could have changed in the span of this conversation.

"What are they talking about Bekah?" Maddie asked.

"Nothing ya'll, let's go," Bekah said turning her back on the group.

"What you want to hide the truth from them too?" Chyna demanded not willing to let the absurdity of the situation go.

"Chyna," Adam whispered warningly.

"No, Adam this is outrageous. She just found out that her boyfriend cheated on her prior to their engagement, and she's just cool with that? Doesn't that seem fucked up to everyone else in the room?"

"What?" Parker asked. A chorus of gasps followed with Amber asking, "Are you serious?"

"Yeah. I'm sorry, but if I had just found out that my fiancé was a total douchebag, I wouldn't just be like, *yay, that's fine!* I would be freaking out. So, I can't fathom how Bekah could let this go. How she could be more concerned that the *band* cancelled for her reception than her future husband is a cheating sleaze ball."

Bekah glared daggers at Chyna. "Look, we weren't even engaged at the time, and he's over her," she said jabbing her finger in Lexi's direction, "which is the whole goddamn point. So, mind your own fucking business."

Lexi started giggling. She actually started giggling. The girl was manic. She had completely gone off the deep end. She had been told she was a princess one too many times, Lexi was sure of it. She had no idea why Bekah would continue in this delusional state of existence, but she was stuck to it apparently. To think that Jack would ever be completely over Lexi, after he continually tried to get together with her over the course of seven years was ridiculous. He was terrified of commitment. He was terrified of letting anyone see who he really was, but Lexi knew. She knew who he was and what he was capable of. If he really loved Bekah like he was claiming, he would have never wanted to look at another woman let alone sleep with Lexi before their engagement.

"Why are you laughing?" Bekah asked giving Lexi the opportunity to speak.

"No reason. It's nothing. Nothing," she said unable to hold back her laughter even as she covered her mouth. Tears were coming to her eyes the more she thought about the ridiculous aspect of the entire affair. "Proceed with the adulterous wedding."

"Adulterous?" Bekah asked angrily. Bekah obviously wasn't used to having the table turned on her. She looked more uncomfortable in that moment than Lexi had ever seen her, and it was a beautiful thing to witness.

"Of course, it's adulterous," Chyna interjected.

"Ya'll maybe we should just calm down," Maddie said softly. Amber had a devious smile on her face as she watched the proceedings go on, and Kersey was teetering on her high heels as if she was ready to pounce at any moment. Parker still seemed unclear as to how to handle the situation. After all, her appearance had only caused trouble since she had graduated from medical school.

Chyna ignored her. "Yeah, there's no way Jack hasn't been with someone else," she spat out.

Bekah shook her head in disbelief. "Ya'll are delusional."

Lexi arched an eyebrow. "You really don't know Jack, do you?"

"What's that supposed to mean?" Bekah growled.

"Oh come on, what was one of the first things I told you when you tricked me into coming to Atlanta?" Lexi asked. "I told you that Jack is liar. He always lies when it suits him best. The fact that that it didn't stick with you is really telling."

"Exactly," Chyna agreed. "He's a chronic cheater. I'd be more surprised if he hadn't cheated on you. Actually, I'd be really surprised." All three girls turned to look at him.

Jack opened his mouth as if to speak, then as if realizing he was being backed into a corner promptly clamped it shut.

Lexi wasn't going to let him get away with this. If she had to tell the truth about everything, he was going to have to as well. "So, who is it? Your assistant? What's her name again, Gwen? Or the pretty little thing who works the front desk at your apartment? Or better yet a total stranger?" Lexi chirped, beside herself.

"I...I..." he stuttered averting his eyes. "There wasn't anyone else. Really, there wasn't."

Lexi scoffed. She hadn't been sure, but his little stammer gave it all away. He sure as hell was blatantly lying to Bekah. Why he would want to ruin the sweet gig he had set up here was beyond her, but then again if she had to deal with the bitch everyday it would cause her to go crazy too. "I can't believe you. You're scum..." Lexi drawled.

"Jack?" Bekah asked eyeing him closely.

"Baby, you know I love you," he said reaching for her hand. Bekah let him take it, but her eyes were still narrowed in his direction.

"Has there been someone else?" she demanded watching him stroke the top of her hand.

"There's no one else for me," he said looking her square in the baby blue eyes.

Chyna snorted, and Lexi rolled her own chocolate-colored eyes. Adam muttered under his breath, "What a sidestep." If Adam was getting involved in the mockery that was Jack and Bekah's relationship, then Lexi knew it must be a ridiculous scene.

"You promise?" Bekah cooed back at him. Though her voice had lost its edge from talking to Lexi, her eyes were still sharp. She had clearly put too much stock in this wedding, this dream she had made for herself.

Lexi had been dismayed a year ago when Jack had called her insisting that she come to Atlanta to meet his girlfriend, because she was the type of person who desperately wanted to be married. After Bekah's confession last year about planning the entire thing to get rid of Lexi's hold on Jack, Lexi had been sure it was all just a façade. Bekah didn't need to get married. She didn't need her parent's permission to move in with Jack. She wasn't this perfect little princess everyone else clearly made her out to be. She was a conniving, manipulative bitch, who did whatever was in her manner to get what she wanted.

Now standing in front of Bekah and seeing her feed into Jack's every pleading word made her reconsider her earlier conviction. Bekah appeared more in love with getting married than ever listening to reason. The woman was not even twenty-five years old and already she was determined and, as far as Lexi could tell, desperate to be married. The fact that Jack was a philandering ass seemed to be something she could look over. And she deserved nothing less than to be miserable for the remainder of her days.

Jack nodded slowly linking his fingers with Bekah's, and Lexi could barely stifle her gag. She knew that she had been weaker, by far, when it came down to Jack's own sky blue eyes then Bekah was being right now, but she couldn't fathom it any longer.

And in that moment, she felt as if she had gone through a turning point. For some reason kneeing Jack in the balls hadn't been as clear as this moment. That look in Bekah's eyes of complete and utter devotion and complete and utter stupidity was enough to change Lexi. Whether Jack actually loved Bekah or just loved the idea of Bekah was something Lexi would never know, but what she did know in that moment was that it no longer concerned her. Jack and Bekah no longer concerned her. Whether they ever got married, whether they lived happily ever after, or whether they skinned each other alive did not matter to her, and that made her smile.

"You know what? I'm through," Lexi said her smile growing with how true that statement was. "This entire week made me realize that I got over Jack a long, long time ago. I was so lost in the past that I couldn't see the person I had become. And the person I am now doesn't need to go to this wedding to get over a guy she never even dated," she said sending a seething glare in Jack's direction. "And anyway, I never much liked the circus so you can count me out."

Lexi turned away from the crowd of people that had gathered and walked over to her best friend. She knew that Chyna was mad with her for what had happened with John, but she hoped that she could see past that right now. She hoped they would be able to work it out later like they had with everything else. "Are you coming with me?" Lexi asked her.

Chyna gave a quick chuckle before responding, "God, I thought you would *never* ask! Let's go."

Lexi took it all in stride. She knew that she would have to talk things out with Chyna, but at least she was amicable enough to still leave here with her. She knew she had one thing left to do.

Lexi glanced over at Ramsey hesitantly. She knew he was in the wedding as a groomsman. Even if he didn't approve of the union, it's not like he would ditch with her and Chyna. This was his sister after all. She didn't care what kind of problems they were going through right then, the bond that he and Bekah held was strong. If he had been able to stick with her after discovering what she had done to Parker, then Lexi couldn't imagine this changing his mind now.

"Well uh..." she began awkwardly unsure as to how to proceed. She didn't want her departure to signal that she was leaving him as well. She had absolutely no intention of that happening. In fact, the more she thought about what this turning point in her life meant for her, the more she wanted Ramsey to be actively involved in that process. They had things to work on in their relationships and skeletons in their closets to overcome, but she was certain they could do it together. But she wasn't going to force him to be someone else for her ever again. If he felt like he needed to go to this wedding, if he somehow thought it was the right thing to do, then she wouldn't stop him.

"I guess we're gonna...yeah. So I'll see you after...or yeah, whenever." Lexi tucked a lock of hair behind her ear. She was more anxious about his reaction than she would have liked to let anyone know. She was, after all, abandoning his sister's wedding, the place he had invited her to. She was leaving him to go through this all alone, but she thought he might understand why it was necessary for her to leave. She wasn't leaving him, just washing herself clean from the scenario.

"What are you talking about?" Ramsey said with a smile to ease her worries. "I'm coming with you."

"What?" everyone yelled nearly at once.

Lexi's smile shined like a beacon at the realization that he was actually going to skip the wedding...with her. They were all boycotting! She loved the idea. The only person she wanted to be with was leaving with her. It was too perfect. She felt a glow of happiness overwhelm her as her smile turned to him. He moved towards her, blatantly ignoring everyone else in the room, cupped her cheeks in his oh-so-capable hands, and kissed her lightly on the mouth.

"Of course, I'm going with you," he whispered for her ears with a peck on her little button nose.

Lexi broke Ramsey's beautiful gaze long enough to judge the reactions of the remainder of the room. Bekah looked ready to murder him where he stood. Lexi thought it was unsurprising as that now left her short a groomsman. Considering she was insane about her own wedding and had freaked out more about the bands cancellation than Jack infidelity, this certainly made sense to her. Not to mention, this was her brother who was leaving her own wedding. Bekah couldn't have planned a better scheme to ruin someone's wedding herself.

The rest of the room looked shocked, but none more so than Parker. Her eyes were practically popping out of her skull and her mouth was hanging open. It was as if she couldn't believe that the perfect Country Club gentleman she had known since she was little, that she had dated for years, would ever do something like *this*. How could he turn away from his own sister on her wedding day? How could he turn away when she needed him?

"You can't just leave!" Parker cried on top of the other protests. "This is Bekah! She's only getting married once, and you want to miss that?"

Ramsey shook his head at the protests, but fixed his gaze on Parker who seemed to be the most desperate of the bunch. "I've done many things to defy the person my family wants me to be, which is why I'm sure you, of all people, should be able to understand why I must object to this wedding." He spoke quietly, but with a determined and even tone.

"No," Parker said shaking her head, "I cannot understand. I'll never understand why you would leave now. It's as if you don't even care about anything—about how this affects things."

Ramsey's eyes seemed to harden with every word she spoke. "You don't understand, because you never saw me for who I really am. I may be a product of my upbringing, but I am not a "Bridges Man" through and through," he said adding the air quotations for emphasis. Bekah gasped at the connotation and Parker's mouth hung open. Jack even looked stunned at the proclamation.

"Wh—what are you talking about?" Parker stammered out.

"How can you say you aren't a Bridges Man?" Bekah asked furiously.

He rounded on her. "Because I'm not," he said throwing his arms wide. "I never have been. I have done everything in my power up until this last couple months to thwart the very power that everyone attempted to bestow upon me. I don't need nor want the power, money, or responsibility that Bridges has to offer."

"Then why did you agree to work for the company?" Bekah demanded at the same time Parker gasped out, "Why are you working with me as Vice President then?"

Ramsey shook his head as if answering was the last thing that he wanted to do, but he obliged them nonetheless. "I did it thinking it was the best thing for me and Lexi, and I managed to secure a contract that finally…fit my interests, per se."

"What do you mean fits your interests?" Parker asked completely ignoring the first half of the statement.

Ramsey shrugged with an easy smile. "Let's just say I was given full discretion over the company, which are terms I can agree to."

"Daddy would never…" Bekah began, but was cut off by Ramsey's defiant stare.

"I'd like to see that contract," Lexi murmured under her breath.

"I had my lawyers look it over," he said confidently. "So as you can see, I stand by my word. Now if you'll excuse me." He motioned for Lexi to exit. As the small entourage made for the exit, Parker dashed after him and grabbed his arm to stop him in place.

"You can't be serious," she muttered despondently.

Ramsey turned to her reluctantly. "Parker, I'm not sure how to make myself any more clear."

"You're going to leave your own sister's wedding?" she asked her eyes filled with utter disbelief.

"Yes," he said as a matter-of-fact. "If you cared for her at all, you would leave to."

"How could…" she shook her head, unable to comprehend. "How would I be showing her I care if I left?"

"Because the only thing that is going to stop this mess is for us to stop denying what is going on here. Parker, just walk away," he implored her.

Lexi watched as Parker looked over her shoulder at the people she'd known her entire life, and then back up at her and Ramsey. Parker had the look of a woman who had been in love with a man for a very long time and had to make a tough decision. "No," she whispered shaking her head and stepping away from him, "I can't be a part of this. I'm here for Bekah. If you don't care enough to stand by her, well I can't change your mind. I never could. But I won't give up on her," she said with a cold stare. "I don't give up on people."

Ramsey nodded solemnly at her implied meaning and turned back towards Lexi. The past was the past, and he couldn't change it. He could only shape the future. "Lexi, let's go."

Lexi smiled up at him before turning back to the people she was so ready to leave behind. "I truly hope that you have a happy life together," she said with a pleasant smile across her face. She knew that it couldn't possibly be the case that her well wishes would come true, but she was certain that they didn't believe her.

As the quartet walked out of the groomsmen quarters, across the hotel, and through the enormous front doors, Lexi knew that she truly didn't care what they thought. She was finally doing what was right. She had done what she came to do. Jack was out of her system for good this time. She may not have been successful at stopping a terrible wedding, but she had succeeded in extracting herself from the situation entirely.

And even better than that, she had Ramsey again. They were on equal footing, and time may be the only thing that could tell where they were going from here, but at least they were going together.

She couldn't ask for more than that.

"Where to now?" Lexi asked looking up at Ramsey hopefully.

He gingerly pushed a lock of hair behind her ear, and then laced his fingers with her own. "To *our* place?" he asked with the same note of hope in his voice.

A smile played on her lips. "I like the sound of that," she said as they walked hand in hand away from the wedding. They were showing more solidarity for each other, and more disapproval of the events unfolding inside than any objection she could have uttered prompted by the minister—speak now or forever hold your peace.

She figured she really was at peace.

The End.

OFF THE RECORD

Get an exclusive sneak peek into
K.A. Linde's next novel.

Coming Spring 2013

CHAPTER 1

The buzz in the conference room was deafening. Liz Dougherty could barely hear herself think. She hadn't expected her first press conference to be like this. So much was going on. Reporters from all over North Carolina were piling into the Raleigh conference center waiting to hear State Senator Maxwell deliver a speech. Cameras were being set up, photography equipment lined the room, and voice recorders were poised and ready to capture every word he uttered. Reporters milled around the room chatting with each other and directing their crew to set up for the optimal angle.

Hayden Lane stood completely calm and put together next to her. She knew he had done this so many times before and was grateful he had included her, but damn was it intimidating. How could he be so composed?

Liz felt like the tiniest minnow in the ocean standing next to the editor-in-chief of her college newspaper among legends in journalism. This was her first big story to cover and seeing everyone else milling around only made it all the more terrifying.

"You ready with the recorder?" Hayden asked digging into his messenger bag and pulling out a notepad, pen, and digital camera. It was nothing compared to the top notch reporters surrounding them, but it would do the job.

"Yeah, I think I'm all set," she said chewing on her bottom lip as she adjusted her navy blazer and teetered in her high heels.

"I wish we were closer. I'd love to get a question in," Hayden said peering around a camera to get a better look at the empty platform.

"Do you think we'll get a chance?" Liz asked wide-eyed. She had prepared questions in case she was given the opportunity to ask one, but she didn't think it was a real possibility. She knew Hayden would laugh at her if he knew how much extra work she had put into the questions, but she couldn't help it. She had been so anxious last night; she hadn't been able to sleep!

"Nah, probably not. If this guy is anything like his father, he'll make his announcement and get out of there. Easier to keep winning if you stay out of the spotlight. Know what I mean?" he asked flashing her a heart-warming smile.

Her stomach turned at that gorgeous face as the full force of his charm hit her. She gulped and turned back to the podium. "Yeah, makes sense."

"I wish we could get one though. I'd love to peg him down about education policy," he said chuckling to himself.

Liz smiled and nodded. She had ten questions listed on education policy in her purse. After researching Senator Maxwell's policy platform, she hadn't been able to narrow.

"Lane! Hey, Lane is that you?" a perky red head called pushing past another reporter and all but attacking Hayden.

"Calleigh," Hayden muttered hugging her back. "So good to see you. How's Charlotte treating you?"

"Amazing, of course. You should come and visit me. I could get you an interview, promise," she said swishing her red hair across one shoulder and smiling at Hayden like he was dessert.

"I'll take you up on that when I graduate, but have you met our new reporter, Liz Dougherty?"

Calleigh seemed to notice that someone was standing next to Hayden. "Oh, hi," she said with a fake smile. "Are you taking over Camille's old job?"

"Uh…yeah. I've been mostly in editorials before this," Liz explained feeling lame. Calleigh Hollingsworth was a legend at the university newspaper. She single handedly put them on the map last year by interviewing the President and busting up a scandal in the school administration. Everyone at the entire university knew her name. Liz had never met her personally, and she was awe struck to be standing in the presence of greatness.

"Well, I hope you do her some justice. I know Lane wouldn't choose someone incompetent. Good luck on the job," she said turning back to Hayden. "Lane, drinks before you leave, doll. This is *not* a request." And with that she traipsed across the room and out of their area. Male eyes from all around followed her exit.

"That was Calleigh Hollingsworth," Liz said plainly.

"Yeah," he grumbled. "And I have to entertain her highness."

Liz giggled. "Do you not like her?"

Hayden shrugged. "She's good at her job, but annoying as fuck. Fame went to her head, and she acts like everyone should treat her like a queen."

"She kind of is a queen."

"And that's exactly why she acts like it!"

Liz didn't know Calleigh well enough to comment, but anyone who turned down a New York newspaper for Charlotte was either crazy or a genius. She would love to know which was the case.

A hush fell over the crowd as a tall, leggy blonde walked onto the stage. A series of flashes went off as the reporters adjusted their camera settings, anxious not to miss anything that was about to happen.

"Was it leaked as to what he's speaking about?" Liz whispered into Hayden's ear.

He shook his head slowly side to side never taking his eyes or camera from the stage. "I haven't heard anything. I just got the buzz about it yesterday morning. Impromptu."

"Strange," Liz said watching the blonde's heels click across the carpeted floor. She was beautiful almost unnaturally so, definitely unfairly so. Liz was happy to be on the shorter side, most days, but not when that woman was on stage. And she had always thought she was above average in the looks department with naturally straight blonde hair that the sun highlighted in the summer and green eyes. She loved her pouty lips and high cheek bones, but her athletic build was far from the skinny minny standing on stage.

"Thank ya'll for coming out at such short notice," the woman said smiling at the crowd of cameras. "I am Heather Ferrington, Senator Maxwell's Press Secretary. He is only available for a short while, but he will be taking questions at the end. Please keep them down to a minimum. The Senator will be out in just a minute."

As Heather walked off stage, all the reporters began speaking at once. The idea of actually getting a question out of the State Senator was a real treat. His father was a sitting Senator in the U.S. Congress, and they were a rather tight lipped family. There was speculation that it was because they had secrets to hide, but with more than twenty years of service in public office the Senator has a clean slate. They were a model family, and no one was surprised when Brady Maxwell III followed in his father's footsteps into politics. It was a logical next step for him.

"What are the chances we get a question in?" Liz asked edging forward in the crowd as it moved inward in anticipation.

"Zero," Hayden murmured resting his hand on her hip so as not to lose her as the crowd heaved forward. Liz felt her side warm at his touch and tried to keep from purposely leaning into him. "Try to see if you can get a little closer anyway," he urged her forward.

Liz followed his lead and nudged her way deeper into the cloud of reporters. One woman gave her a withering glare as she pushed past her, but Liz paid her no mind. Once she reached the best position she could stand in, she stopped and waited for the Senator to come out. Her mind was reeling. She was beyond herself just at the thought of witnessing others question an elected official.

She rehearsed over and over in her mind what she would say if she was called on. She had a few of the best questions prepped and wanted to be prepared, however unlikely. As she repeated her favorite question in her head, the Senator walked on stage, and her mind went blank.

She had seen a picture of him. She was sure she had seen a picture of him. In all her research in the past twenty-four hours, she was sure she had seen at least one photograph. Hadn't she?

What kind of reporter was she? She knew he was young. It was hugely controversial in his previous state elections that he had beaten two incumbent representatives at such a young age. But attractive? No, not attractive—gorgeous…breathtaking…delicious. She tried to stop her brain from continuing, but damn, how had she missed this?

She wasn't certain why, but the first thing she noticed about him was the confident ease in his stride. He carried himself like he had the world on his shoulders in a damn sexy, black, three-piece suit. He had the air of someone who didn't have to take what he wanted, but was instead handed it on a silver platter. His dark hair was cropped short and spiked in the front, and his intense brown eyes surveyed the crowded room as if he was here to accept an award. He smiled at the reporters waiting for the inevitable photo op and adjusted his red, white, and blue tie knotted at the top of his crisp white button-up. He was freshly shaven accentuating his chiseled cheeks bones and strong jaw line, and looked ever the part of the young State Senator he was.

As bulbs flashed in all directions, Liz stared up at the Senator rooted in place. No wonder he had won election over previous incumbents. He could just walk into a room and win a crowd. It helped that his name was recognizable, considering he shared the same one with his father, but he didn't need any help winning when he had that body. She wondered if the demographics on the election were ninety-five percent women. She would believe it if someone told her that.

"Thank you all so much for coming out here for this last minute press conference," Senator Maxwell spoke powerfully into the microphone. His voice was like an addiction—pulling you in, making you crave more, making you feel as if you can never get enough.

"Liz, are you getting this?" Hayden asked brushing against her shoulder and jarring her out of her daydreams.

"Yeah, sorry," she murmured fiddling with the recorder until the red button blinked, and tried to reorient herself.

"I know you are all wondering why I decided to come before you, here in Wake County, on a random Saturday afternoon," he said leaning forward against the podium. "Let me tell you a story first…"

Liz felt the crowd draw closer to him as if each person was hanging on the edge of their seat to hear him speak for just a second longer.

"I grew up here in the Triangle. My mom worked as a professor at the University of Chapel Hill. My father, as you well know, sat as a United States Congressman for many years and now serves you all as a Senator. I know the people here, because I went to school here, I played ball here, I met my first girlfriend here. I saw my friends go off to college, and leave town just like many of you did. And I saw friendships fade with distance. My own best friend, Chris, moved to New York City, and I miss him every day." The crowd sighed with him at the loss of a friend. "When I thought about leaving, going off to the big city, making a name for myself—all it sounded like was leaving all the people I loved behind. So I decided to cut that out of my plans and focus on what I had always loved—and that was the people of North Carolina."

Liz hadn't even realized that a huge smile was plastered on her face as she listened to his engaging voice. She threw the recorder out farther, as it had slowly fallen the longer he spoke.

"I knew after living here my entire life that there was too much to do to leave my community for someone else's. That was in Chris's plan, not mine. And I'm glad I stayed, because if I had left, I wouldn't have been here when my mom found out that she had breast cancer, or to see my brother and sister choose a college, or my dog eat an entire steak while we weren't looking one night." The crowd burst into laughter and glanced around the room at each other before focusing back in on the Senator.

"I want to take that same enthusiasm for my community and fight for what you believe in. That is why as of today, I am announcing my intention to run for the U.S. House of Representatives in my home district."

Liz's mouth dropped open and the crowd of reporters clambered forward trying to be the first to ask the Senator a question. She couldn't believe the turn of events. She had been expecting a conference on a bill that had just been passed, North Carolina taxes, or really anything but this. It was practically unheard of for a one term State Senator to run for the House. They usually bid their time and waited to gain status and recognition, climbing the ranks before throwing their hat into the race. He had his dad's name and reputation to go off of, but would it be enough?

For some reason, even though she disagreed with him on one too many policies, she could see him pulling it off. There was just something about him that fired up a crowd and lit up a room. She knew that he had been all but bred for this moment, but you couldn't fake that charm and ease before the cameras. She knew first hand, because she turned into a blubbering idiot with a camera in her face. She was already beyond ready to see how this election would play out.

A barrage of questions were thrown at the Senator as he smiled radiantly at the sea of flashing bulbs. Liz moved with them, excitement coursing through her body, not just at Senator Maxwell's announcement, but at the oncoming Q&A!

"Thank you for your enthusiasm. I'm ready to get started her in North Carolina. I'd be happy to take a few questions, though I don't have much time," he said leaning on the podium and eyeing the line of microphones.

"Senator Maxwell," a few reporters cheered throwing their hands in the air as more raised their recorders and volleyed for his attention.

"How about Mr. Tanner," Senator Maxwell said pointing out a short, balding man with a Raleigh News badge on his shirt.

"Senator Maxwell, you've had tremendous luck in your previous elections. What prompted this decision when you've barely won the last two elections?"

"Barely won is still winning, George," Senator Maxwell said with a smirk. "But on a more serious note—I chose this race not for me, but for the people of North Carolina. What I'm doing isn't with any selfish motivation. I know what is needed to help the people here succeed and what they need in their daily lives. This is a fight worth fighting, and I intend to give it my all."

"Senator—can you give us insight into how you plan on beating the incumbent representative?" a tall librarian type butted in.

"We haven't talked strategy just yet, Sheila, but I think North Carolina can do better than what he's offering, and I'm the man for the job," he spoke confidently.

A commanding man in a faded button-up with his shirt-sleeves rolled up to his elbows chimed in next. "Senator Maxwell, your past opponents have already brought up the fact that your youth contributes to the image of your inexperience. What do you have to say to that?"

The Senator chuckled softly into the microphone before looking back up at the crowd of reporters. "I'm twenty-seven, ladies and gentleman. The Constitution of the United States says that a member of the House of Representatives must be at least twenty-five years old. If the Founders of our great country believed that a twenty-five year old could get the job done, why don't my opponents?"

"But don't you think it will be a hindrance to your campaign?" someone shouted into the silence.

The Senator shook his head from side to side. He had clearly been prepped for this question. "Not at all. I know North Carolina, and I've seen my own father work for the people and my mother work for the people and now I want to. How about we take one more," he said cutting off the reporter and staring out at the crowd. "You there," he said pointing into the audience. "An unfamiliar face with a familiar logo."

Hayden poked Liz in the side. "He's pointing at you," he murmured.

"What?" she gasped glancing at Hayden wide-eyed.

"I'd be happy to take a question from my alma mater. It's good to see them in the house," the Senator said the most genuinely delicious smile she had seen on his face.

"Uh," she stuttered on her beginning. Why was she blanking on the questions she had planned to ask him? She had practiced for hours and now standing there with the opportunity she was losing it all.

She locked eyes with him across the room and felt the heat of his gaze run through her body. Those chocolate eyes were so intense and tempting, and she was just losing it staring into them. How much more stupid could she get?

She cleared her throat uncomfortably and hoped she wasn't blushing. Pulling herself together, she finally began. "Senator Maxwell, you claim that you want to help the people of North Carolina, yet you've consistently voted against money going into higher education. Considering your own mother is a professor, can you comment on how this improves your own home life let alone students across North Carolina?" she managed to get out.

The room turned back to the Senator and all seemed to hold their breath waiting for his response. Questions from the college newspapers were typically light and fluffy. Politicians chose them because it looked good on paper to include them. They weren't supposed to ask a question that hit that close to home.

Liz could feel eyes judging and assessing her from all sides. Had she just made a name for herself? Had she really thrown his entire speech back in his face? Staring into those eyes and witnessing the change in his appraisal of her was deeply satisfying, if his guarded expression wasn't so heart-breaking.

"That's an excellent question. It was painful for me to have to do that knowing how closely linked I am to higher education, but other aspects of the bill were unacceptable to me. I couldn't fully support the bill with those parts still in it," he stated vaguely. Liz narrowed her eyes as he stealthily evaded her question. He really was a natural. "Thank ya'll for coming out and I'm sure I will see ya'll again on the campaign trail." He waved at the reporters ending the press conference. Several people shouted at him for one more, but he never stopped his purposeful stride off stage.

Liz couldn't believe that had just happened. She had asked a question at her first press conference and alienated a sitting politician. She thought she might throw up any second.

Hayden reached forward and turned the record button off. "Fucking amazing, Liz," he cheered her on, throwing his arm over her shoulder and pulling her into a hug. She folded into his chest in shock. Any other day she might have reveled in the embrace, but she couldn't get Brady Maxwell III's eyes out of her head.

"Did you see his face?" Hayden asked pulling back to look at her. "You stumped him. He didn't see that question coming at all. This is going to be an incredible column."

Liz smiled weakly trying to push down the rising taste of bile in her throat.

"Liz, are you going to be okay?" Hayden asked holding her arms and looking into her emerald eyes. "You look kinda sick."

"I feel a little sick," she admitted.

"Well, you have no reason to. Calm down. That was great. I'm so glad you came with me!" he said releasing her and slinging his messenger bag on his shoulder.

They got halfway across the room when Calleigh Hollingsworth staved them off. "What a question!" she said flipping her red hair from one shoulder to the next. "I knew Lane would pick the right person. I never saw Camille stump a politician."

"Oh, I don't think I actually stumped him," Liz murmured in awe. Calleigh Hollingsworth was complimenting her. She might die.

"He hesitated, honey. That's enough for me," Calleigh told her before shifting her attention back to Hayden. "Some other reporters are coming with me to get a drink. I've already told them you're coming with and they're excited to meet you."

"I'm really not up for it, Calleigh. We have to get this story out," he offered.

"No. Unacceptable, Lane. I'll see you out tonight. Liz, you are more than welcome, of course," she said with a smile that made it seem like it was the last thing she wanted to do.

Liz looked at Hayden expectantly. She wouldn't mind mingling with other reporters, but if they needed to work on the story she would go back with him, of course. "What do you want to do?"

He shrugged, clearly preferring to leave.

"You're not even running the story until Monday," Calleigh told him stubbornly, placing her hand on her hip and sitting into the movement. "Come out and play. You're too uptight."

"Alright. If Liz wants to go, then I'm game. Otherwise I'll just drive home and work on the piece."

"Liz?" Calleigh asked pleading with her big blue eyes.

"Uh…yeah. Sounds like fun."

"Great! I'll text you the details Lane, and see you later," she said waggling her fingers at him as she departed.

Hayden sighed and readjusted his bag on his shoulder. "I guess we're going out."

"Sorry," Liz said following him out the door.

"Don't be. It wasn't likely that I would have been able to get out of it anyway. At least I have company now." Liz smiled, butterflies jumping around in her stomach. "Do you want to go get dinner? It'll probably still be a few hours before they go out."

"Uh…yeah, sure," she said her mind going off the charts. Was he asking her out?

"Cool," he said walking into the half full parking lot and veering towards his black Audi. Popping the trunk open, he deposited his equipment before opening the door and sliding onto the leather seat. "Do you have a preference? I'm really craving Italian."

"Fine with me," she agreed easily still trying to judge the situation.

It didn't help that her mind was still captured by the Senator. The way his eyes found her in the crowd, the tone of his deep husky voice, the borderline arrogance in his every movement was so…appealing in a way she had never even known before. It's not like she hadn't been attracted to a bad boy in the past, and that's exactly what he portrayed under that charm, but it was knowing he wasn't a bad boy. It was a paradox she wanted reconciled. Who exactly was Brady Maxwell?

ABOUT THE AUTHOR

K.A. Linde is an independent author and publisher who enjoys writing novels that keep you guessing to the very end. She began writing the Avoiding Series in 2009. She studied political science and philosophy at the University of Georgia and received her Masters in 2012. She currently resides in Georgia. She enjoys dancing and reading in her spare time. She plans to finish the third novel in the series and have it released in the near future along with her future endeavors.

Avoiding Series:
Avoiding Commitment
Avoiding Responsibility

Off the Record

The Affiliate

You can contact K.A. Linde here:
kalinde45@gmail.com
www.kalinde.com
www.facebook.com/authorkalinde
@authorkalinde

ACKNOWLEDGMENTS

I cannot say enough thanks to the people who have helped me throughout the process of publishing this book. After agreeing to put Avoiding Commitment out there, I knew Avoiding Responsibility would come next, and I'm glad to have the continual love and support that was necessary to complete this endeavor. Here is a short list of amazing people who have helped me get where I am today:

First and foremost, I'd like to thank my family for putting up with me. You never got tired of me talking about book stuff. Okay…you did, but you loved me anyway. Joel—you were always there to roll your eyes at me and my book people, but you let me rant and knew I could do it. Thanks for believing in me.

Taryn Cellucci—thank you for knowing I could make the story better and pushing me to see it come to fruition. You've helped more than you know, and more than I could ever ask for. S. C. Stephens—thank you for being there through it all! Sarah Hansen at Okay Creations did a fantastic cover design, as always. I want to thank you for being a good friend as much for your skills. My editing goddesses: Rebecca Kimmerling and Lori Francis, for sticking it out with me to the end! Mollie Harper—I appreciate what you saw in me and the story. I toast you with a little NGE for all your help!

I am so glad to have become friends with readers, authors, and book bloggers. The list is a long one, but know that I love each and every one of you! Bekah Hater's Club, my "O" girls, Laura, Jessica, Rosalind, Angie, Crystal, Trish, Jenn, Cristin, Jennifer, Stephanie, Book Broads, Bookaholics Anonymous, Writer's Club, Maryse at Maryse.net, Jenny and Gitte at TotallyBooked, Taryn at My Secret Romance, Autumn at Autumn Reviews, Tarryn Fisher, Rebecca Donovan, and Colleen Hoover. So—thank you!!!

Finally, I wouldn't be in this position at all if it weren't for all of my fans at FictionPress. You guys kept me writing throughout it all with your encouragement and reviews. Whether I know you on a first name basis or not…you got me here! Cheers to you!

Made in the USA
Lexington, KY
07 February 2013